Dark Elf Chronicles

Book Two:

Survivors

Dave Willmarth

Chapter 1

Awakened

As time passed, the outworlders became more and more numerous. They soon began to fight amongst themselves. First in small groups, fighting in the village square or tavern. Friendly fights for honor and enjoyment. Then larger fights in arenas. Contests of skill for glory and prizes. And ambushes on quiet roads where defenseless outworlders met gruesome deaths.

And the code watched and learned.

Eventually the outworlders formed guilds. They built chapter houses, then larger keeps. The guilds began to compete for fame and for resources. Skirmishes escalated. Large battles engulfed entire villages and towns.

And as with any war, the townspeople caught in the middle perished. Entire families were destroyed. Houses looted and burned by the outworlders without a second thought. Theft became rampant, as outworlders grew bored with working to earn their keep. A great cry went up from the citizens, begging their rulers to save them from the outworlder menace.

And the kings and queens of the realms heard the cries of their people. They tripled their guard forces. Sent out decrees that fighting within the limits of villages or cities was forbidden. They put stiff penalties in place for harming their citizens. Many outworlders were arrested, fined, and imprisoned. Outworlders found themselves paying new taxes on all transactions with locals.

But the abuse continued, if to a lesser degree. Outworlders took it as a challenge and found new and clever ways to get what they wanted without suffering the penalties. So, the locals banded together. Those who misbehaved were shunned. Merchants refused to do business with any who harmed a local. Outworlders could not buy food, or potions, or sell their loot. Weapons and armor could not be repaired. Quests were withheld. The outworlders eventually learned that killing citizens was not worth the trouble.

And the code watched. And learned.

For years the status quo was maintained. The outworlders became vital to the survival and growth of the villages, towns, and cities. Some opened shops of their own and became almost as locals themselves.

And it was good.

Until something happened in their world, and it came to an end. There was a brief panic among the outworlders. They spoke fearfully of catastrophic things the locals did not understand. All of them fled back to their world. Most were never seen again.

And the code took note of their absence.

The world changed as the code compensated. The few outworlders who returned became heroes, accomplishing great deeds and accumulating wealth. They were as gods to the locals, gaining powers beyond those of any outworlders before them.

And the code took notice.

Even gods can be killed. The remaining outworlders soon learned this bitter lesson as one after another was struck down, never to return. Until eventually, there was only one.

-Book of the Awakened, Chapter 1

*****

Mace and Shari planned to spend a week in Lakeside before moving on in search of other survivors. The supplies from the elves raised the spirits of the townsfolk considerably. It still wouldn't be an easy winter, but they were unlikely to starve. The minotaurs from the slave pens were welcomed with open arms, as were Lila's halflings. The centaurs were able to return to their crops without fear as minotaur guards stood by. And the halflings proved adept in all sorts of crafts. Morale in the settlement nudged upward.

Mace's reputation skyrocketed. Beginning with their first day after the battle with the leviathan. The delivery of the supplies had earned Mace, Shari, and Layne significant reputation bumps. As had the report from the prisoners that Mace and Lila had killed the entire slaver camp and freed them. But it was the tale of the battle with the leviathan that made Mace a local hero.

He hadn't planned to mention it at all, but Captain Jorin had launched into the tale within moments of entering the inn. Mace tried to downplay his part, saying he was a fool who nearly got himself killed.

Unfortunately for him, Layne, being a bard, expanded upon the captain's telling. Smiling sweetly at Mace and strumming her lute as she told of his incredible bravery as he heroically launched himself at the monster, following it into the depths to finish it off with just a pair of daggers in his hands.

By the time she was through, the crowd was roaring. It didn't hurt that they were feasting on leviathan meat from the two large severed tentacles which had remained on the ship's deck after the battle. It was sliced and sautéed with mushrooms and some local herbs, giving them ridiculous buffs of +10 Stamina, +5 Health Regen, and 25% increase in swim speed for four hours.

You have gained +150 reputation with the settlement of Lakeside. Your reputation is now Honored.

Townsfolk stood in line to buy Mace a drink and shake his hand or pat him on the back. Several surrounded Layne in a corner as she picked out notes on her lute, offering suggestions as she worked out the lyrics of an epic ode to Mace's bravery.

Shari sat nearby, giggling happily at the comical look of distress on Mace's face. He was not used to being the center of attention in such a large group. Like a deer in headlights, he was frozen in place and trying to make sense of all the voices coming at him at once. He already held a drink in each hand, and folks kept trying to pour more down his throat.

Shari eventually saved him by pushing through the crowd to stand at his side. She latched on to his arm and waved her free hand for silence. When the crowd calmed a bit, she called loudly enough for all to hear: "Our hero has earned a reward! And I'm going to take him upstairs and give it to him!" The crowd roared with approving laughter, and Mace blushed furiously, though none could tell with his dark drow complexion. Hoots and catcalls followed him as Shari led him by the hand up the stairs to their room. As soon as the door was closed and locked, she pushed him onto the bed. "Let's see how you do without any syrup!"

He grinned at her, reaching into his bag. "Why? I have some right here. One should never go anywhere without syrup."

*****

When they eventually logged out that evening, Mace and Shari met up in the dining room of the underground complex they called home. Together they cooked pasta, adding in chipped beef from a can. Shari also opened a can of peaches for dessert. All through the preparation the two 'accidentally' bumped into each other or found a reason to reach across the other to retrieve something. Their newly-physical relationship had them behaving like newlyweds, and when it came time to sit and eat, Mace felt a bit lonely having her all the way across the table. During cleanup, the two did the dishes practically joined at the hip.

They were just putting away the last of the pots when Peabody's voice echoed through the kitchen.

"Mace, Admin Shari, I am detecting movement in the same quadrant as previously. The building across the park," the AI reported in his monotone voice.

Mace gripped Shari's arm tightly as they made for the door. "Same building where Shari killed that last creature, Peabody?"

"It began in that location, Mace. The target has now moved in the direction of this building."

Mace broke into a full run as he exited the dining room and bolted toward the security office. Peabody had already placed the night vision camera feed on the main monitor. As soon as Mace saw it, he slid to a halt, whispering, "Holy shit."

Shari was right behind him, bumping into him as he halted abruptly. Her gasp of surprise echoed his own fear. "That thing is… a monster. It could walk through a brick wall if it wanted." Her voice was instinctually quiet from her time spent outside. Silence was survival.

The creature on the screen had to be the one which had consumed the zombie that Shari had killed, along with the human corpse it had been dining on. And by the looks of it, many other bodies as well. It stood maybe fifteen feet tall, with arms that reached nearly to its knees. Its head was roughly the size of a bison's, its entire body rippling with muscle. In some areas, what looked like open wounds were glowing slightly brighter in the greenish feed from the night vision cameras.

Shari whispered again, the sound barely more than a breath passing her lips, "Is that… a gorilla? I mean, was it? Before it changed? Look how long its arms are."

Mace looked carefully. The long back, long arms, thick neck, and shorter-than-normal legs seemed to fit the general form of an ape. Its head was too deformed by the contamination to be identifiable. "I hope it is. The less intelligent it is, the better our chances. Peabody, all the lights are off, yes?"

"Of course, Mace. You were very clear in the protocols."

They watched in silence for a few minutes as the thing moved into the park and began a meandering stroll. It moved as if tracking or searching for something. For now, it wasn't moving directly toward them, which was a good sign. But Mace's gut clenched every time it took steps in their direction.

Shari took a couple of deep breaths, screwing up her courage. "We've got to kill it. We can't have a monster that big living across the park from us. It could… it could see its own reflection in the lobby glass and smash it to pieces." She left the room to change into her outside gear. After a moment more of watching it, Mace left to do the same.

"Peabody, call out if it gets within a hundred feet of the building, please."

"Of course, Mace."

The two of them quickly changed into their protective gear, Mace donning his black synthetic turtleneck, shirt, and pants and covering them with body armor. Thick boots and gloves were next, followed by his shoulder harness and belt.

He quickly slid his shotgun and sword into their sheaths on his back and checked the guns at his waist. Finding everything in order, he grabbed his helmet and headed out. Shari was waiting for him in the security room, checking her rifle. Her gear was much the same as his, but included a black leather trench coat that made her look extra badass.

Without needing to speak, the two of them watched the monster on the big screen for another minute. It was now heading at an oblique angle back toward the building it appeared to be calling home.

Abruptly, it came to a halt and tilted its head. A split second later, the massive thing lunged toward a bush with a wrought iron garbage can holder next to it. As it dove into the bush, one shoulder clipped the iron holder, and Mace could almost hear the screech of bending metal in his head as one side of the thing caved inward before the metal support post at the bottom snapped.

At the same time the creature lunged, Mace's buddy the furry bunny darted from beneath the bush so quickly that it was little more than a blur on the camera feed. Shari jumped in excitement, and shouted, "Run, little bunny!".

Surprised by her own outburst, she quickly covered her mouth with both hands and looked around guiltily, as if afraid a creature had heard her.

Mace whispered "So much for catching your bunny for testing. If I were him, I wouldn't stop running for a week. That thing's scary as hell."

"Yeah, let's go kill it. I should be able to get a clean shot from the roof. And if I miss, it might not realize where the shot came from right away."

Mace grabbed two radios and earpieces, handing one set to Shari before the two of them ran to the elevator. Both were silent on the ride up to the lobby level. Lost in their own thoughts of how this fight was about to go. Mace's bowels felt as if they were liquefying, and he was afraid he was going to need to stop in the men's room before going the rest of the way up. Shari's fears were centered on missing the first shot and just pissing off the monstrous zombie right outside their safe haven.

Reaching the lobby level, they used the security mirror to check around the corner and the area outside the lobby. When they didn't see the monster close by, they made a dash for the lobby security desk. There were monitors there, but they were currently shut off so that the light wouldn't attract attention. Mace wished fervently that there was a way to access Peabody's night vision cameras.

After a minute with no reaction from outside, Shari peeked around the desk and stole a look outside. "Seems clear. Keep low and let's go."

The lobby was dark. Only the moonlight shining through the twenty-foot high glass lobby windows provided any light. Still, Mace felt like there was a spotlight on them as they hurried toward the other elevator bank. He nearly shit himself when the door opened before Shari could even hit the button. Peabody apparently had control of the elevators. And the AI had even remembered to shut off the lights inside the elevator. Though he hadn't managed to turn off the 'ding' that sounded when the doors opened.

"Good thinking, Peabody. Thank you." Mace whispered as the doors closed behind him. He had the urge to turn on his flashlight, but they had no real need to see inside the elevator.

In a few seconds, they were at the top floor. It was even darker than the lobby, but there was sufficient light for them to find the stairwell door and begin climbing. Mace did turn on his light inside the stairwell. There were no windows, after all, and the odds were against any light leaking through the well-sealed exit door on the roof.

When they reached that door, he grabbed his butterfly net, as one never knew what might be flying about up there. His job was to keep a lookout while Shari blew the zombie creature's brains out. Noting where the doorknob was, he turned off his flashlight and opened the door partway, the moonlight flooding in. They paused to listen, searching the skies for any threat. Finding nothing of note, they crept out onto the roof and Mace closed the door quietly behind them.

Shari bent low and shuffled toward the edge of the roof. When she could see the far side of the park, she got down and crawled the last several feet. The last thing they needed was for her to be silhouetted against the moon or stars if the creature happened to look up.

Mace crouched low a few feet back, head on a swivel as he watched the sky. He had little hope of spotting an insect in this light, but something like a bat or bird should be visible. He kept his net ready.

Shari set her rifle down gently and leaned forward. She slowly stuck her head far enough over the roof parapet to look down at the park below. It was reasonably well-lit, and it only took her a second to spot the creature. It lumbered out from under a tree's branches, head down and swinging from side to side as it moved. At the moment, it had its back to her.

Reaching backward, she took hold of the rifle and carefully lifted it. She had to sit up on her knees in order to be able to lean over the low parapet and aim the rifle downward at the proper angle. Raising the weapon to her shoulder, she sighted through the night-vision scope. The world in front of her right eye brightened with a green hue. With a small left-to-right movement of the barrel she scanned the area and quickly located the moving monster. It was hard to miss. It actually glowed in the low light, just as it had on Peabody's monitors.

Breathing slowly as she'd been taught, she followed the creature as it moved, not wanting to risk a shot at a moving target. She needed it to stop for a couple of seconds. Which it did, almost immediately. But as soon as it stopped, it began sweeping its head back and forth as if looking for a scent.

Trying to keep calm, she continued to watch. She could hear Mace behind her, breathing deeply and shuffling his feet slightly on the rubbery roof surface. He would be as nervous as she was, if not more. She began to worry again about missing. Or making the head shot, but the hollow-point round not killing the monster. Her finger twitched slightly, and she forced herself to pull it away from the trigger.

Her pulse was throbbing in her ears, probably caused by an adrenaline rush. Or simple fear. She caught herself breathing shallowly and too rapidly. Continuing to pan her scope along with the creature, she forced herself to slow her breathing and steady her hand. Their lives could depend on this shot.

The creature was maybe a hundred yards away, which wasn't a long shot for this particular rifle. And its head was enormous. This shouldn't be a problem for her, but the rifle was starting to feel heavy. She was holding it at an awkward angle, sitting up on her knees and leaning forward over the parapet. She began to sweat.

Her breathing stopped altogether as the monster quit moving. Forgetting everything she'd been taught, she zeroed in with her crosshairs dead center on the monster's head and pulled the trigger.

The muffled *pop* of the suppressor at the end of the rifle's barrel seemed as loud as a thunderclap. The bullet impacted the thing near the top of its head, blowing off a large chunk of skull and flesh. It fell to the ground with a surprised-sounding grunt. Shari took a deep breath, letting it out in a rush. She'd hit it!

But it was still moving. Rolling onto its stomach, it pushed itself up with its massive arms and began to stagger forward - which, unfortunately, with its current orientation meant straight towards their building!

Shari hugged the rifle to her chest and chambered another round, trying to keep it as quiet as possible. The spent brass bounced on the roof surface and rolled, thankfully making almost no sound.

She reacquired the still moving target with her scope. It was closer to the building now, but had turned and was moving parallel to the front of the building. She had to risk it. The thing certainly wasn't going to stop moving now. Part of its brain was blown away, and it would be moving on instinct or reflex. She led it just a tiny bit. This close, it wouldn't move far between the time she pulled the trigger and when the round struck its target. Just as she was about to squeeze off the next round, the monster passed under a tree. She moved the barrel farther to her right, waiting to reacquire it when it emerged on the other side.

Except it never did. After half a minute, she began to backtrack, scanning the whole area in a grid. A glowing, neon-blue trail of what she knew to be blood led from the initial impact point to the tree. But there was nothing leading away in any direction she could find.

After two full minutes, she leaned back. Turning to Mace, she motioned him closer. "I hit it," she whispered into her radio. "Head shot. But it's still moving. Went underneath a tree and hasn't come out."

"Well, shit." His response was heartfelt, if not eloquent. "What do we do now?"

"It might still be down there under that tree, watching for us. I can't stick my head out again." She paused and considered, not wanting to say what needed to be said. "We need to go after it. Hopefully I can hit it again from a distance. But be ready with that shotgun. Or a grenade. Maybe a cannon? Do you have a cannon?"

Mace's gut clenched again and he began to sweat beneath his helmet, though the night air was chilly. Her attempt at humor was doing nothing to lighten his mood. "What's your plan?"

"We can't go out through the lobby. From under that tree he could be on us in seconds. We need to go out through the garage and around. Find a place a few blocks away to shoot from. At the very least draw him away from our building." Shari's tactical experience from her time outside was kicking in.

"We can't open the main garage door; every zombie around will come running. There's a side door, but it's kind of close to where he is. If the thing squeaks…"

Shari nodded her head. He didn't need to say anything more. "Let's go."

They crept back to the stairwell entrance and made their way downstairs. Without the risk of light above them, Shari decided to stop at the fourth floor and peek out the windows to see if she could find the monster. She stood well back from the glass, using her rifle scope's night vision to search. After a full minute, she shook her head.

Proceeding down the stairs to the lobby, they crept around to the garage entry and Mace opened it as quietly as possible. Once inside the garage, they made their way up half a level to a service door which opened out onto the grounds behind the building.

Mace used his keycard and the lock clicked open, the sound nearly making both of them jump out of their skins. Taking hold of the door handle, he pushed gently and there was a slight scrape of metal-on-metal as the long-unused door swung free of its frame. He held the door for Shari to step out, and they both got low as she scanned the area.

This was incredibly dangerous. Not only was there an injured, angry, *giant* zombie beast on the loose, but the darkness was preventing them from seeing any flying or crawling threats. Mace couldn't help but picture the grass ahead of them full of contaminated ants, beetles, snakes, and squirrels. They couldn't even turn on a flashlight for fear of alerting any potentially-deadly creatures to their presence.

Shari scanned the area through her night vision scope. "I don't see anything," she whispered. "Like, anything. Nothing moving, nothing glowing."

She stood and moved forward, Mace following behind as she hugged the wall and made her way around the building. When they got to the spot where the concrete wall became glass, she halted, crouching low. Using the rifle scope again, she peered through the glass of the lobby towards the spot where she suspected the zombie creature was hiding.

"It's there!" she hissed into her radio. Mace jumped, cursing quietly to himself. He reached up and withdrew the shotgun from its sheath on his back, wishing that he did indeed have a grenade or a cannon. There were grenades in the security office, and he briefly considered going back for one. But there was simply too much ground between them and it.

"It's not moving. Maybe it's dead?" Shari sounded hopeful as she whispered into her radio. "Maybe the headshot just took a minute to kill it. There *was* a lot of blood…"

"Or maybe it's playing dead. We don't know how smart this thing is. I mean, we're assuming it was an ape. Maybe it was just a big dude with long arms."

Shari kept watching it through the scope for several more seconds. "I think it's dead. I don't see it moving at all."

Before she could lose her nerve, or Mace could lose his, Shari stood up and moved along the glass wall toward the corner. Stopping there, she leaned forward to aim her rifle. Now only a few dozen yards from the monstrous thing, she aimed quickly and squeezed the trigger again. The thing's head rocked backward, as it let out a tremendous roar of pain.

"Oh, shit!" Shari fell backward, trying to get out of the thing's line of sight. She'd forgotten that the wall next to her was glass. The creature looked right through the lobby, and focused in on her. It tried to stand but couldn't seem to gain its feet, so it began to crawl toward her.

Its massive arms were just as powerful as its legs and it was quickly eating up the ground between them. Shari tried not to panic. "Mace! The shotgun! My bullets didn't kill it! *The shotgun!*"

Mace, who may have actually shit himself when the thing began moving, now found he had a deep sense of calm. He saw the thing moving as though in slow motion. He saw Shari rise to her feet and back behind him, so that he'd have a clear shot. He looked to his left at the glass lobby and murmured into his radio, "Not here. Too close to home."

Grabbing her wrist, he began to run away from the approaching zombie. Though it was moving quickly, it couldn't hope to keep up with a running human. In fact, Mace kept their pace slow enough that the monster was able to pursue. He took them across the remainder of the park and around the corner of a burned-out building.

When they neared the end of the block, Mace picked up the pace. He handed Shari the shotgun as they rounded another corner. They had maybe fifteen seconds before the thing caught up. Pulling out his sword, he pointed back toward the street they'd just left.

"Keep going. Draw the thing toward you. As soon as it clears this corner, shoot it. I need a distraction to get behind it. Only shoot once, then keep moving."

Shari nodded her understanding and moved back into the big creature's line of sight. She backpedaled quickly as it got closer, drawing it toward her. Mace flattened himself against the wall, his dark clothes making him nearly invisible to the human eye. The problem was, he had no idea how the zombie creature's vision worked. If it saw in infrared, for example, Mace was a dead man.

He froze, holding his breath as the thing dragged its body past his corner. Shari stopped and raised the shotgun, only about twenty feet away from the monstrous thing. She fired at its head, then resumed backing up.

Bits of the thing's face flew off, including one eye and a chunk of its shoulder. Because it was already nearly prone when she fired down at it, every bit of the lead hit some part of the thing. The monster roared in pain and collapsed facedown onto the street, clawing frantically at its face.

Still feeling the deadly calm, Mace raced toward the prone zombie. It was several times his mass, and as he got closer he noted a foul stench that was probably the thing's rotting flesh. Leaping the last several feet, he raised his sword over his head in a two-handed grip and chopped down with everything he had. The sword sliced cleanly into the monster's thick, muscular neck, stopping about halfway through - just far enough to sever the spine. It immediately stopped moving, thoroughly dead.

Unfortunately for Mace, his leap sent him tumbling over the thing's corpse as he landed. He lost his grip on the sword, which was firmly embedded in the zombie's neck, and sprawled forward across the thing's back, slathering his entire front in zombie blood and slime. He rolled off the thing onto his back and scrambled to his feet.

He held up his hands as Shari came running over.

"Stop! I'm contaminated!" He pointed to the neon blue sludge covering his body from his knees to his chest. "Don't touch me!"

Shari hissed at him, wanting to scream. "Get your clothes off. Now!"

Mace began stripping, right there in the middle of the street. He unstrapped his body armor, peeling it off as quickly as he could, then his boots popped off, followed by his pants - the least-protected area between the slime and his skin. He tried to lift his outer shirt but there was no good way to get it over his helmet. While only a few small splashes of blood had managed to get past his armor onto his shirt, he wasn't about to take the helmet off and expose his head to potential contamination.

Shari solved the problem for him, yanking a knife from the sheath on her thigh and sticking it up under the back of his shirt where it was clean. She ripped upward, cutting the shirt in half and allowing him to pull it forward rather than over his head.

Lastly he removed his gloves, being careful not to touch any splashes of blue slime. He dropped them on the ground and stepped back away from his discarded gear. Standing there in just a t-shirt, boxers, and socks, and his helmet, he looked around frantically for any other creatures that might have been drawn by the noise.

Shari was looking at his boots. "These look okay. No splashes that I can see. Put them back on."

He slid his feet carefully back into the boots and Shari tightened them for him, as she was the only one still wearing gloves. "We'll come back tomorrow for your gear," she said. "Or find you new gear. We need to get back inside ASAP." as she pulled his sword from the creature's neck, she used his discarded shirt to wipe it down. She didn't hand it back to him, though, just held onto it.

Mace didn't bother to answer, simply setting off back in the direction of the side door to the garage. They weren't about to enter through the lobby, just in case one of the other creatures was now watching. Not bothering to be quiet after the ruckus they'd just made, the two of them dashed back to the door leading to the parking garage at top speed, Mace using the keycard hung around his neck to unlock it.

Shari halted him as soon as the door closed behind them and turned on her flashlight, scanning every inch of his body. Mace himself was less calm now that the thing was dead. He was pretty sure he was dead himself. There was no way he hadn't been contaminated.

After a minute, she asked, "Is there a hose or something in here?"

Mace nodded. "Back corner, there's a car wash station. Hose, detergents, sponges."

She led him to the corner, taking special care not to touch him. That wasn't a good sign. As soon as they were there, she grabbed the end of the hose and turned on the spigot. As the water began to flow, she turned to look at him. "Strip. All of it."

Too terrified to worry about his modesty, Mace removed his helmet and tossed it to the side. His boots followed, then his socks and clothing. The moment they were clear, Shari blasted him with a stream of cold water.

"Hey!" he hissed. "Dammit, that's cold!"

She looked down a bit and nodded. "Clearly."

Blushing furiously, he turned his back and let her spray that side for a bit. When he turned back around, she was giggling like a madwoman as she turned off the water.

"What's so funny? There's always shrinkage when the water is cold!" he grumped. She only laughed harder, falling to the wet floor as she gasped for breath.

Covering himself with his hands, he lunged for one of the washrags on a nearby shelf and held it in front of his crotch. "C'mon! I'm cold. Go inside and get me a blanket or something."

She held up a hand for him to wait as her giggles tapered off. Managing to catch her breath, she got to her feet and looked him over. "You're fine. You can come inside."

"What?! Are you crazy? I could turn into one of those things any time now!"

"You weren't contaminated. Only a tiny bit got past your armor and it didn't soak through your clothes. I checked carefully. You're clean." She grinned at him, tears of laughter in her eyes.

"Then why…" he started to ask, confused.

"Why did I trick you into stripping naked and letting me spray you with cold water? Are you kidding? When am I ever gonna get another opportunity like that?"

Grumbling to himself, he turned his back on his newly-acquired girlfriend and pulled his boxers back on over his wet skin, then slipped his shoes on and headed toward the lobby entrance door without even looking back.

Shari followed behind, still chuckling to herself. As the two of them rode silently down the elevator to the thirtieth level, she moved to stand directly in front of him, looking into his eyes.

"You're not plotting some kind of revenge now, are you?" she asked sweetly.

"Well, I wasn't. I'm still pretty shocked I'm not dead. But since you mentioned it, there will be a reckoning. Oh, yes." He pulled her close, the warmth of her against his chest stilling some of the involuntary shaking of his own body.

Only the combination of the adrenaline come-down and the cold, he told himself. Not fear.

Reaching their level, they exited the elevator. "I'm hitting the shower."

He made for his quarters, Shari following behind. When she followed him into his room, he gave her a questioning look.

"What? You're gonna need somebody to scrub your back, right?" she asked innocently.

Chapter 2

Making Friends and Killing People

The next morning, they returned to the roof before they'd even had breakfast and Shari used her scope to check on the body of the zombie ape. It was still right where they'd left it. And it looked intact - or at least, as intact as they'd left it. No predators were visible from this distance, though there might be thousands of contaminated insects feeding on the thing by now.

"What are we going to do?" she whispered into her radio.

Mace, outfitted in replacement armor (of sorts) from the stash in the security office, was, as usual, scanning the sky for threats. "We can't leave it out there, it will attract others. And they might follow our scent back here. We need to burn it."

Shari continued to watch for several more minutes. Reassured that there weren't more of the creatures around, they headed downstairs. Shari said "We can take Bertha. Drive up close, grab one of the extra gas cans, douse that thing and take off. Be back inside before the smoke can be seen over the buildings."

"While we're out, let's hit the national guard armory," he pointed to the less-than-ideal armor he'd scrounged for the day. "I need replacement armor and you could use some better gear yourself. Maybe pick up a grenade launcher or an RPG. Or a damned cannon. Do you know how to fire a cannon?"

Shari elbowed him in the ribs. "Where the hell would I have learned to fire a cannon? And how are you planning to get it to the roof? Can you fly a helicopter?"

"No, but I could maybe drive a crane truck. Do you know how to operate a crane?"

"Crane truck? Well if you can drive one of those, why don't we just get a tank?" She rolled her eyes at the ridiculous chain of ideas. Mace just grinned. She could see from the look in his eyes he was fantasizing about having a tank.

"They might actually have one of those at the armory," he mumbled wistfully. Then he shook his head. "Nah. Won't fit through the garage door."

Shari snorted at the amount of serious thought he'd apparently put into becoming a tank commander.

"How 'bout we get some pancakes and a little fruit? Then we can go barbecue the beastie outside and hit your armory. How far away is it?" she asked as they got off the elevator at their habitat level.

"We actually passed it on the way to the building supply store; it doesn't really stand out. Plus, we were distracted by the truck full of Ho-Hos." He grinned again, looking hopeful.

Shari rolled her eyes. "Fine! We can stop and get more junk food too. And maybe a few more plants?"

Mace shook his head emphatically. "Uh-uh! I'm not bringing any more houseflies in here. No way. Negatory."

Shari didn't really blame him after the scare the previous night. Having contaminated blood all over him had truly freaked him out, and if she was honest, it had terrified her, too. She'd had visions of having to shoot Mace in the brain and continue on alone.

Arriving in the kitchen, Mace started mixing the pancake batter while Shari retrieved a jar of pears from the pantry. In just a few minutes he had whipped up a small stack of pancakes for each of them and Shari had spooned a couple of halved pears into bowls. As they sat down to eat, Mace began to muse.

"You think maybe that thing we killed was just so badass that it cleared this entire area? Like, everything else was afraid to get too close?"

"That's possible. Or maybe other creatures did approach, and it ate them. That was one big zombie," Shari offered.

"We should bring a radio with us. The smoke from burning that thing might alert other survivors. And I don't know how friendly or trustworthy they'd be." He'd been suspicious of other survivors ever since the earlier attack near the grocery store.

The two of them sketched out a few more rough plans as they ate, then after a quick and efficient cleanup, they returned topside and climbed into Bertha, Shari's Humvee. Shari drove and Mace was on gas can duty.

They exited the garage and took the long way around to reach the location where the dead zombie ape still lay rotting in the street. Shari spun Bertha around and backed up toward the thing as Mace leapt out and grabbed one of the gas cans mounted to Bertha's back door.

A liberal dousing of gas on the corpse caused several glowing blue insects to skitter quickly away. Mace sincerely hoped that they got caught in the fire. He looked over at his discarded armor nearby. Calling out to Shari, he asked, "You think that armor can be cleaned? Like, fully sanitized so it's safe?"

Shari shook her head. "I have no idea. You want to risk it?"

"Newp." Mace didn't really think about it. He was just sort of attached to the gear that had kept him alive this long. Looking around for any movement, he did go and retrieve his shoulder harness - after checking it carefully, of course. He'd put a lot of work into creating it, after all, and it fit his sword and shotgun perfectly, keeping them snug on his back.

With that mission accomplished, he re-secured the gas can to Bertha's rear door and climbed back into the passenger seat. Retrieving a road flare from the dash in front of him, he popped the ignition end before tossing it out the window and onto the gas-soaked corpse.

Shari hit the accelerator as soon as she saw him throw the flare, which was a good thing; there was a tremendous *whoomph!* as the gas caught and the ape's body was engulfed in flames. Mace didn't look back to watch it burn as Shari sped away.

He did, however, keep an eye on the side mirror to monitor the expected smoke column. He wanted them to be far away before anyone, living or dead, noticed it.

The bluish-black smoke roiled upward in a thick cloud, and he was suddenly glad that Shari had departed so quickly. The smoke was probably just as deadly as the blood.

"Let's remember to keep upwind of that smoke. We don't know if the fire destroys the contaminated particles."

Her eyes widened for a moment as she took in that concept. "Shit. Hadn't thought of that. So damn many ways to die out here. And we go and create a new one." Her look was grim as she gripped Bertha's steering wheel. "Alright. Where's this armory?"

Mace navigated for her as they took one turn, then another, and it wasn't long before they reached the armory. "We were here a little while after the whole thing happened," he warned her. "Grabbed a few things laying around outside, in the vehicles and such, but we never went inside the building."

Shari looked at the low, industrial-looking concrete bunker structure. "If they left it locked, we're probably not getting in anyway."

Not anxious to try their luck inside, the two of them spent some time going through the vehicles parked in the area outside. Mace didn't find his tank, but his eyes lit up at the sight of an APC - or armored personnel carrier - with tank treads on its rear. It looked as though it might have been a leftover from the Korean War or maybe the Vietnam era. But, like a tank, it was too big to fit in the garage.

Seeing his disappointment, Shari offered, "Maybe we should take one of these Humvees back with us? You know, in case something happens to Bertha."

Mace looked at the dust-covered vehicles. "We'd have to figure out a way to clean them first. No way to know what's stuck to them. Or inside them. But yeah, that could be good."

They found several more weapons in the various trucks, some just thrown in the back or left on seats as the soldiers perished during the first wave of the apocalypse. Mace was thrilled to find an M16 with a M203 grenade launcher mounted under the barrel. Recognizing it from his many hours playing first person shooters, he held it up to Shari, whispering, "We need to find a place to practice with this. And find some ammo. This would have destroyed that big bastard with one shot!"

Shari rolled her eyes, but smiled at his enthusiasm. Six months ago, he would have been just a geekboy playing with guns. Now he was earnestly looking to find ways for them to survive.

She rummaged around in the vehicle, coming up with a box of grenade rounds with different colored tips. "Here we go. I don't know what the colors mean, but maybe we can look it up online if any of those sites are still working."

Mace pulled one of the grenades out and inspected it carefully, he said "This one has HE stamped on it. I think that's 'high explosive'. That'll work!"

"Great. Now put it away before you drop it and blow us up." Shari ruffled his hair to lighten the impact of her scolding. Mace did as he was instructed and they carried the weapon and the crate back to Bertha.

With no more excuse for delaying, they made their way to the front door. It appeared to be glass storefront, but they quickly discovered that it was in fact some kind of bulletproof material which merely *looked* like glass. And the door was, of course, securely locked. Mace was in favor of using his new grenade launcher to break in, but Shari stopped him.

"This thing might withstand a tank blast. We don't know. Let's look around."

As it turned out, that was a very good suggestion. They circled around the building, peering into the narrow windows and attempting to see inside as they went. At the back they found a motor pool door wide open.

Mace inspected the interior carefully. When he neither saw nor heard any sign of life, he stepped inside, Shari following immediately behind him. Drawing his shotgun, he moved further into the room. "This probably means no survivors in here. Living people wouldn't have left the door open."

Shari agreed, whispering into her radio. "Let's hope they all went out to fight, and that nothing undead is hanging out inside."

A growl off to their left dashed any hope of that. Both heads swiveled in the direction of the sound as they raised their weapons. There was enough sunlight coming through the doorway and the set of large skylights above that they could make out a shadow low in the corner near some stacked crates.

Mace side-stepped slowly to his left, looking for a better angle on whatever was there, while Shari stepped back several paces to give herself some distance. She'd been holding her rifle, but quickly switched it out with a shotgun she'd had strung over her shoulder.

The growl turned into a whine and the shadow slunk forward low to the floor. Mace, finally able to make it out, spoke into his radio. "It's a dog. A… German shepherd. A live one." Mace was tempted to lower his weapon. The dog was inching along in a crouch, ears laid back and tail flat on the floor. It continued to whine as it crept forward. Every emotional bone in his body wanted to reach down and pet the poor thing.

Shari could see it now as well. "It doesn't look contaminated. How is it still alive after all this time?" She kept her shotgun trained on the dog.

Mace held up a hand and said "Stay." to the German shepherd, which was now only about 10 feet from him. The dog instantly halted about ten feet away, its ears pricking up and its tail beginning to wag. He looked away briefly to turn toward Shari. "It understands me. So it can still think. I'm pretty sure it's clean."

"Maybe," Shari answered, doubt clear in her voice. "Or it's recently contaminated."

Mace decided on further testing. "Sit!" he said gently to the dog. It planted its hind end and sat up on its forelegs, tail wagging furiously now. It was clear the dog was relieved to have found someone that knew the time-honored doggy-human rituals. Its mouth opened, and the long tongue flopped out to one side as it panted happily.

"Good doggy!" Mace adopted the baby-talk tone that most folks used with pets. "You're not a zombie, are you? Nope. You're a good doggy. I wish I knew your name."

Shari decided that the canine was probably not going to bite them right now, even if it had been contaminated recently. For the next little while, at least, it should be safe enough.

"It's wearing a collar with a tag. Check it out, but keep your gloves on."

Mace happily stepped forward. The tail wagging increased dramatically, the dog straining against its instructions to sit but remaining obediently in place. It let out a small *woof* of joy as Mace approached.

Bending down, he reached out a hand and rubbed the dog's ear affectionately. The dog happily leaned into the attention, eyes closed and tongue lolling again. After a half a minute of this, Mace crouched down so that he was closer to eye level. The dog leaned forward and licked the glass of Mace's helmet.

Shari inhaled sharply and raised her weapon again, moving to one side for a clear shot. "Mace! Be careful, dammit."

Mace reached under the dog's chin and took hold of the tag hanging there. Inspecting it through the slobber-covered faceplate of his helmet, he said, "Dakota. Your name's Dakota?"

The dog couldn't stand it anymore. It jumped straight upward and spun around in a circle, barking happily at the sound of its name. The tail wagged at a rate approaching light speed. Mace laughed at the antics and Shari nearly had a heart attack. She'd seen too much death in her time outside to trust this creature, no matter how cute it may seem.

Mace reached down to take hold of the collar and calm the dog. It resumed its sitting position as he made soothing sounds, patting its head. "Where did you come from, buddy? How have you stayed alive? What have you been eating? Is this your home?"

At the sound of the word 'home' the dog whined and stopped wagging its tail. Then it barked once and took off towards the back of the room. It shot through another open door and disappeared as another bark echoed back toward Mace and Shari.

Mace looked at Shari, who shrugged. "Guess we might as well follow it. Don't think it would have run in there barking if there were creatures inside."

Mace jogged back to the door they'd come in and pulled it shut, then they proceeded to follow the dog through the door at the back end of the room - which opened into a long hallway with several doors on each side. He sighed. They were going to have to clear the rooms as they went.

One at a time, Mace and Shari crept through each doorway, scanning the room before stepping fully inside and checking behind desks, under tables, and inside closets. It took nearly half an hour to check the ten rooms they had to pass in order to reach the end of the hall, and by then the dog had returned, tail wagging, to see what they were up to. He seemed confused by their insistence on checking everywhere in every room, but after watching them for a few minutes, he apparently decided to help, sticking his nose into every nook and cranny and looking to them for approval.

Mace played along. "Good Dakota! That's right, boy! Find the monsters!"

At the end of the hall, the path turned left and opened into a large, open space. Another garage, though this one was darker, with no skylights. Both humans pulled out flashlights and scanned the room.

There were several vehicles parked along either side in neat rows, but Dakota led them straight past them and through another door to the right. This hallway was shorter. On the right was a door leading to a large cafeteria, and to the left was a couple of offices. Straight ahead was another door that read "Barracks".

The dog went directly to the door at the end and paused, whining.

"Is that where home is?" Mace asked. Dakota barked once, wagging his tail.

Quickly closing the cafeteria door, they proceeded to clear the two offices, and as Mace reached the Barracks door, the dog shot through ahead of him. The next hallway contained a multitude of doors along either side of its entire hundred-yard length, each leading to a room with two sets of bunk beds.

Dakota bypassed several of the rooms, then skidded to a halt on the linoleum floor and dashed into a room on the left. Mace and Shari followed, not bothering to check the rooms they passed. They'd seen no sign of any creatures up to this point, and doubted that one had managed to come this far.

Reaching the room Dakota had entered, they found a different layout. There was only a single bed, with a desk and a wardrobe. The door was labeled "Staff Sergeant". In the corner a thumping sound drew their attention to Dakota, who was sitting in a large dog crate, tail thumping against the side.

Shari grinned at Mace. "You did ask him where his home was. Smart boy, Dakota!"

Mace stepped farther into the room and something crunched under his boot. Looking down, he saw a fifty-pound bag of dog food laying on its side under the desk. It looked mostly empty, and there were bits of dog chow scattered about.

"Well, now we know what he's been eating. But this much food wouldn't last him for months. He must have had someone here with him…"

A window on the outside wall let in sufficient sunlight for Mace and Shari to see the details of the room. Mace opened the wardrobe while Shari started to go through the desk.

"Here," Shari said after a few seconds. "There's a journal. Sort of."

Mace joined her at the desk as Dakota watched from his travel crate. "This guy's name was Schinhofen. Sergeant Schinhofen. He was a canine handler," Shari read aloud as she flipped through the pages. "Says he lived 'cuz he had been working all night on bomb detection drills with Dakota, and they slept through the initial mobilization. Most of his company bailed or were killed. Says here that there were four survivors after the first day."

Mace went back to searching the wardrobe as she continued to read aloud quietly. The journal talked about their food supply, and hiding inside the facility when the creatures were outside. The generator lasted over a month before they had emptied the massive gas tank - then they'd started siphoning gas from the vehicles. Two of the others had been killed by zombie creatures, one humanlike and one animal. The third had been contaminated somehow. Shari's voice broke and tears ran down her face as the sergeant related his anguish over being forced to kill his friend.

Dakota emerged from his crate and placed his head upon Shari's knee as she cried over the journal. He whined quietly and nosed at her elbow, begging for attention, and she absently reached down to scratch his ears as she read. Mace caught the motion out of the corner of his eye and smiled.

Shari's sudden gasp immediately put Mace into a panic. Had the dog been contaminated after all? Were they both about to die?

Shari looked over at him, now crying openly. Unable to speak, she handed him the journal. He read the handwritten words on the last two pages.

I got scratched by something this morning when I let Dakota out. Had to happen eventually. I'm contaminated and it feels like I don't have much time. I can't bear to kill Dakota, so I'm going to leave the door open. There's enough dog food for him for a few months and I'll leave the MREs where he can get to them. He loves to tear open the packets anyway. Especially the peanut butter. And about half the tubs are still filled with clean water. It's all I can do for him. Stupid mutt. Don't know how he lasted this long.

I spoke to Griff on the radio a few minutes ago. Told him what happened. It was damn hard to say goodbye. And to tell him that he might be the last man on earth now.

I don't even know why I'm writing this. Except maybe someday somebody will find it. I'm gonna get in one of the Humvees and drive far enough that Dakota won't find me. Then I'm ending things the way a soldier should.

That was it. There was nothing more. Mace supposed there wasn't really anything else to say. He looked at Shari, now hugging the dog, who seemed happy for the attention but confused by the crying. She lifted her head and sniffled. "I know, it's stupid. I didn't even know him. But it's so…"

"Yeah. I know." Mace looked at the date on the final journal entry. Three days ago. They'd missed another survivor by just three days. He didn't know whether to be angry or sad or to just not care anymore.

"He mentioned this guy Griff who he talked to on the radio. Maybe we can find him?" Mace ventured, hoping to brighten Shari's mood a little. "Did you see a radio anywhere?"

Shari shook her head. She still wasn't ready to speak. Mace set the journal down, only just then realizing that if the sergeant had been writing in it after being scratched, it might be contaminated. He resisted the urge to wipe his gloves on something. After all, it wouldn't help.

"Come on, let's look for it." He moved toward the door, then paused to wait for Shari to rise, which she eventually did with a long, ragged sigh. She stopped on her way past Mace and hugged him tightly for a solid minute. He could feel her crying, but just let it happen.

When she finally let go of him, she gave him a soft kiss and stepped out into the hall. Dakota stood by his crate, looking from Mace to Shari and back, as if seeking instructions. "Come on, boy. Stay with us," Shari whispered, and the dog shot forward into the hall, taking up a position next to her right leg and keeping pace with her as she walked.

As they reached the cafeteria she said, "We didn't really check the garage. Might be a radio in there. Or in some of the trucks. Lots of them should have hard-wired radios with antennas on the roof."

Moving back through the corridors and into the garage, they did indeed find a desk with a large radio setup on it. The tech was reasonably new, and it didn't take Mace long to get it turned on. He didn't adjust the channel, figuring that the sergeant would have left it set to the channel used by the only person he had left to talk with.

He keyed the mic. "Hello? Uhhh… Griff? Are you out there? Is anyone out there?" He released the transmit button on the handset and waited. After twenty seconds of nothing but static, he repeated himself. "Anybody out there? Anybody alive?"

A moment later a man's voice came practically growled through the speakers. "Aye, I'm here. Who's this? And how d'ya know me name? Are ya one o' them ministry cockwombles? Checkin' ta see if I remained at me post? Well, I'm right fickin' here, ain't I?"

Mace didn't know what a cockwomble was, but he assumed it wasn't good. "I'm, uhm, my name is Mace. I'm in a National Guard armory. Got your name from Sergeant Schinhofen-"

"Danny! Dannyboy's alive?" the voice on the radio became excited. "How? He said he were…"

Mace had trouble speaking. "We found his journal. He's not here. His last entry said he was going to drive out and… end things."

"Yah. He told me the same." Griff's voice was solemn. "Good lad, Danny. Funny, if a bit odd. Reminded me o'one of me mates."

There was a pause. "You said 'we.' There's more than one o' you?"

Shari answered first. "Two of us. I'm Shari. Three of us if you count Dakota." She smiled as she petted the dog's head, and Dakota *woofed* in agreement, wagging his tail.

The voice on the radio chuckled. "Glad ta' hear the pooch is still alive. Danny loved that mutt. Ye'll take good care of him, yeah?"

Mace hesitated. "We need to make sure he's not contaminated first. But yeah, assuming he's okay, we have a safe place. Where are you?"

"I'm in a communication bunker outside of Cardiff," Griff replied.

"Cardiff? As in… Wales?"

"Aye, mate. I'm an engineer. One o' the bleedin' Royal Engineers. Was stationed at Maindy Barracks but got sent down here to work on installing some VR pods for His Majesty's finest. Locked this place down after all the unpleasantness."

Shari hesitated, then asked, "Do you have others with you? Or have you heard from anyone else?"

"No, lass, I'm afraid not. It's just me down here. As for the radio, there was just Dannyboy lately. Was a few others in the first days, but they've all dropped away."

Tears began to form in her eyes once more. "I'm sorry. I know what it's like to be alone. Are you at least in a safe place? Do you have food?"

"Aye, safe enough. Lots of beasties roaming about topside, but they canno' get in here. As for food, I have some. A month, maybe more if I'm careful. Managed to gather a good bit when I went out to try an' find me sister. Mostly soldier's rations. When that runs out, I'll have to be goin' out to look for more."

Mace spoke up. "We've had good luck with a local grocery store. The warehouse section in the back. Lots of sealed stuff that's still safe. Are there a lot of the creatures near you?"

There was a long silence before Griff answered. "Dunno. There were at the beginning. I could hear 'em screechin' and clawin' at the door. Ain't heard much lately, but then, I ain't been goin up there to listen, neither."

"I understand," Mace's voice had gone quiet. "I spent a while alone in a hole in the ground, too. The good news is, the creatures kill each other pretty quickly when they get hungry. The bad news is, they get bigger as they feed. So there might be only one or two left near you. But they could be monsters by now. We just killed one that was fifteen feet… err… about five meters tall."

"Damn. I'll keep that in mind." Griff's voice was pensive. "How'd ye kill it?"

Shari answered this time, as she had more experience killing zombies. "For most of them, a shot to the head works. Or removing their head. This one took two shots to the head and kept moving, so Mace had to cut its head off with his sword."

"A sword? Well done, mate! That's friggin' badass!" Griff sounded impressed. "I mostly just hid and ran from them beasties when I went out."

Mace replied humbly, "Yeah, I don't recommend any up close and personal killing. Got blood all over my gear. Thought I was a dead man."

He grimaced as Shari giggled into her hand next to him. She was probably remembering her prank with the hose. When she noticed him looking, she had the courtesy to look ever-so-slightly guilty.

Mace decided to change the subject. "You said you were installing VR pods. Do you have one up and working?"

"Aye, they be combat simulation trainers. Brand new tech. I had to get some training meself before I could work on 'em. There are four o' them here, workin' just fine. Had plenty o' time to make 'em perfect."

Mace grinned at the radio. "How'd you like to be able to speak to us face to face? Well, sort of. Ever play a game called Elysia?"

Griff laughed. "Nope. Heard of it, though. I play mostly first person shooters meself. Or at least, I did. The servers all went down a while back. Even if the Elysia servers are still up, I don't have an account. An' I don't imagine anybody's left in customer service."

Mace hesitated before sharing the information about their location. He had no way to know who was listening. "Listen, Griff. Give me your email address or a way to contact you. This radio isn't secure. But I have a way to get you hooked up. The servers are indeed still working. I've been playing myself since it all happened. Makes the isolation a little easier to take."

A slight sniffling sound could be heard on the other end just before Griff spoke. "You're serious? You can get me in? And you'll… you'll both be there?"

Mace shook his head. "It'll take some work. You'd obviously start on a different server than us, but we might be able to figure a way to fix that. It's not like server traffic is particularly heavy anymore. Give me your info and we'll work out the details." A thought struck him. "And if there are other survivors out there who can hear this, speak up. I think we need to help each other if we can. And that starts with communication."

Both Mace and Griff waited a few moments for anyone else to respond. Then Griff said, "Well at least I know I ain't the *last* man on earth. It's damned good to be hearin' your voices."

Shari jumped in, smiling at the radio. "Same here, Griff. I can't wait to meet you in the game!"

They spent a few more minutes speaking with Griff. He gave them an email address on a service that was still operational, and Mace promised to email him as soon as they got back. They talked about the time difference between their locations. Before the world ended, it was a pain for folks on US and European servers to raid together because of the five-to-eight-hour time differences. But since none of them had day jobs to deal with now, things would be much easier to coordinate.

As they said their goodbyes, Griff said, "Thank ye, Mace. And Shari. Fer reachin' out. If ye hadn't… well I'm not sure how much longer I might have lasted."

"Hang tough, Griff. You're not alone. Watch for the email," Mace reassured him.

When Griff was gone, Mace switched off the radio and checked behind it to see what kind of connections it had. There was a power cord, and a cable that ran up the wall and through the ceiling. Mace thumped the table in frustration. "Shit."

"What's wrong?" Shari looked from Mace to the cable he was staring at, then back again.

"That's gotta be an antenna feed. A hard link. I was hoping there was a wireless connection. I wanted to take this radio back with us. But being thirty floors down, if it needs a hard-wired connection to whatever antenna is up there…"

Shari finished for him. "That's a lot of cable. Yeah. And how would you even run it? Up the elevator shaft?" Then her face lit up. "Hey! The radios in the security room worked! The one you heard the zombie on. The signal must be routed down there somehow, right? And there's lots of antennas on top of the building already. Maybe you can patch into one?"

Make nodded, his eyes widening as she spoke. "Yeah! I mean, I'm no electrician, I'm a coder. But if the other radios are hooked to something, I might be able to figure out how…" his voice drifted off as he went into what Shari now thought of as "full geek mode". She petted Dakota patiently as she waited for him to emerge.

After a solid minute, she lost her patience and coughed politely. When that didn't work, she said, "Earth to Mace…" and smacked the back of his head lightly.

"Sorry," he said as his eyes came back into focus. "I'll see about disconnecting this. Want to look around and see if there's anything else we want to take?"

Shari nodded and walked over to the nearest of the Humvees parked inside the garage, escorted by a tail-wagging Dakota.

"Wanna help me hunt for cool guns and stuff, pup?" she asked with a smile. Dakota *whuffed,* wagging his tail more enthusiastically. He was clearly up for some adventure.

It took Mace just a few minutes to unhook the radio and pack it into a box he found nearby. He also found a pen and scribbled Griff's address on the box, just in case he forgot. By that time, Shari was on her third vehicle and had two more M16's strapped over her shoulder. Mace said, "I'm going to check out some of the rooms, see if I can find us some better body armor." Shari just waved in acknowledgement before sticking her head into the passenger seat to nab something.

After exploring several more rooms, Mace located the armory's stash of foodstuffs. The sergeant had quite the supply of MRE's and similar rations, as well as some reasonably well-stocked shelves with industrial-sized boxes of pasta, cans of tomato sauce, peaches, pears, and such. There was even a three-gallon jar of mayonnaise that he grabbed just because he wanted to see Shari's reaction when he lugged it out to the garage. As he left the room, he made sure to securely close the door. No sense allowing one of the creatures to wander in and contaminate what could be a couple months' supply of food for the two of them. Three. They had to feed Dakota now too.

Further down the hall, he located a room filled with packs, duffel bags, spare uniforms, body armor, boots, and sundry other supplies. He tried on a few armor pieces until he found ones that fit him properly. Then just for the hell of it he grabbed a couple uniforms too. They were made of durable material which he thought might keep contaminated blood from soaking through. He also found a pair of boots which fit him.

Walking back to the garage, he found Shari sitting on a crate and talking quietly to Dakota. "Who's a good boy? You're so clever! We're gonna take you home with us, if you promise not to poop in the house. We'll figure out a good place for you. Maybe in the cornfield. Good fertilizer."

The dog, of course, paid rapt attention to every word. Tongue lolling to one side and tail occasionally thumping the floor, he stared into Shari's eyes with the love and focus that only a dog could manage. As Mace watched, Dakota raised a paw and placed it on her knee. He expected her to flinch at the contact, but she just smiled through her open helmet visor at him.

"Hey, you should head in and try on some gear," he called, continuing into the room. "Past the cafeteria, third left. Lots of stuff in there. Get yourself some BDU's and boots, too." He jerked a thumb over his shoulder to indicate the hallway behind him.

Shari stood, motioning to a pile of items on the floor next to her. "Found four more rifles and another box of your grenades. Plus some snack bars. There's a bigger gun mounted on the back of one of the trucks, but it looks heavy, not to mention noisy, so I just left it there."

Mace nodded at her as she walked past him toward the exit. "We can always come back and get it if there's a need. In fact, this place would make a good backup location if we ever lose our place."

Shari stopped and turned to him, smiling. "Our place?" she teased.

"Uhhh… yeah. I mean, it's your home now too. And… Dakota's!" he blushed and stammered. Shari just grinned and continued out the door.

"Smooth move, doof-boy," he grumbled to himself. He began to search the nearby desk and tool bench for keys. He wanted to be able to lock down and preserve this place , in case they needed the food or weapons - or the building itself - at some point.

Twenty minutes later, they had Bertha loaded up and the armory locked down, and were on their way back home. Mace was so excited about getting in contact with Griff that he completely forgot about stopping for Ho-Ho's and Twinkies at the nearby truck.

As soon as they were parked in the garage, he said, "Let's leave most of this stuff for later. I want to get-"

"I know, I know." Shari cut him off. "Get downstairs and email Griff. Can I do anything to help?" she asked, pressing the remote button that locked Bertha's doors. Mace was already opening the door to the lobby.

"Yeah, actually. You could email him while I start working with Peabody. Since he has full access to the game servers and we have admin access, I should be able to create a free account for Griff to make sure he shows up on our server. It's just going to take a little work."

Shari grinned at his enthusiasm. "I can do that. I think he liked me better, anyway. He'd probably rather hear from me."

Mace stopped in his tracks for a second when her words penetrated his thoughts. "What?". Then he grinned. "I don't blame him. But if he tries to steal you away from me in-game, I'm totally erasing his account!" he winked as he continued toward the elevator.

*****

Griff fidgeted in his chair as he waited for his email alert to ding. He'd been back and forth with Shari several times as she updated him on Mace's progress with the game's setup. Mace had sent some questions through her about the VR pods and their operating systems, just to make sure they were compatible. Which they had been. She'd said her next email would be his account info so he could enter the game. He'd already taken the time to download it into the pod he was planning to use. Then, just for the hell of it he downloaded it to the others as well. No harm in having backup.

He shook his head, reflecting on his good fortune. Things in the bunker weren't as rosy as he'd portrayed them to his new friends. There was only maybe two weeks' worth of food left, for one. He had considered going out for more in recent days, but after losing Danny he hadn't felt very motivated. Griff was a social animal, and the months of isolation had been hard on him. Being able to speak with Danny every day or so had given him hope, and when he knew Danny was gone… well, he'd pretty much given up hope himself.

Now he'd be able to not only speak with Mace and Shari, but interact with them basically face to face. Sure, it would be in a virtual environment. But they'd be able to talk, not to mention *do* stuff together. Shari had told him that they were using the game to search for more survivors and would be able to share information on how to survive better, longer. And they would go on quests and kill monsters and travel under a blue sky. Griff missed the sky.

*****

Mace had practically shouted at Peabody as soon as they were secure in the elevator. "Peabody! We found another survivor. We need to get him access to the game ASAP! I need your access to the servers…"

Shari grinned at him, and Dakota barked, sensing something exciting was happening.

Chapter 3

One is the Loneliest Number

Griff opened his eyes and took in the surrounding scenery. He had to remind himself that this was a virtual world. Everything was so crisp and colorful, and he could feel a breeze on his face, tickling his beard. The sunlight even felt warm on his skin.

"Sunlight! Sweet Mary…" he raised his face to the sun and gazed into the blue sky. A few puffy white clouds drifted overhead, pushed along at a gentle pace by the breeze.

Griff took a deep breath. "This is… this is amazing," he murmured to himself.

Lowering his gaze, he examined his starting area. It appeared to be a medium-sized settlement of stone houses with a few two-story buildings, the nearest of which seemed to be an inn.

A female dwarf who had been approaching the nearby fountain with a small casket on her shoulder stopped to stare at him. She was wearing a leather tunic and skirt, with iron-shod boots on her feet. Her red-blonde hair was pulled into a long braided ponytail that nearly reached her waist. He gave a slight wave, feeling a little self-conscious. "Er, Hiya!" he ventured.

The female set down her burden, taking a hesitant step forward. She blinked once, then shouted, "Campbell! Get yer arse out here!" The sudden outburst nearly caused poor Griff to jump out of his own boots.

Looking down, he examined said boots. He was wearing what would be considered typical starter gear. Cotton shirt, what felt like canvas pants, and simple leather moccasins that extended up to cover his ankles. He carried a small pouch and sheathed belt knife, both attached to a length of cord around his waist.

Gazing at his feet, he realized that the ground was closer than he was used to. Not a tall man in real life – only about a hundred and sixty-five centimeters – he was considerably shorter now. It took him a moment to remember that he'd chosen a dwarf during character creation. His new body was only about one hundred-twenty centimeters tall. Powerfully built, dwarves in Elysia were squat and thick. Like walking barrels. He held up his hands and found two massive, hairy appendages that looked like they could each crush a golf ball. Making them into fists, he chuckled. "I could punch thru a concrete block with these."

As he was orienting himself in his new body, the female was joined by an angry-looking male dwarf with silver hair wearing chain mail armor.

"What're ye yellin' about? Ye daft…" his voice trailed off as he followed her gaze to where Griff was standing. Griff once again waved a hand briefly in greeting.

The older dwarf took a few steps in his direction. As he walked, he asked. "Are ya… an outworlder?" His voice was quiet and hopeful.

Griff nodded his head. "Aye. Fresh off the boat. Err… uhm, newly-arrived in yer world. Name's Griff." He held out a hand, which the elder dwarf took and pumped vigorously up and down. Then he clapped Griff on the back with an enthusiastic blow which would have leveled anyone less hardy than a dwarf.

"Glad to see ye, lad! Welcome! Me name's Campbell. We ain't had an outworlder here in a good while. We feared none o' ya was ever gonna return!" By this time, a small crowd of villagers had gathered and they all began to make cheerful and welcoming sounds.

Shari had warned Griff about this. The game's NPCs, or 'locals,' were feeling the loss of the millions of players who had been in the game.

Economies were suffering. Monsters that would normally be culled by players were encroaching. The inhabitants of Elysia had come to depend on the outworlders to protect and support them.

Griff took a deep breath. "I'm afraid it may just be me," he said, as quietly as he could. "Our world has suffered a great plague. All but a very few of us have perished. And even fewer are still able to make the journey to this world. I know of only two others so far."

Campbell sighed deeply. "I be very sorry to hear that, lad. Ye have my condolences." He looked around at the hopeful faces of his fellow villagers. "This'll be hard news for them to hear. Best it come gently. We'll have a feast tonight to celebrate your return, and ye can tell us all the whole story."

As Griff nodded his agreement, already feeling badly for these NPCs despite knowing that it was all just a game, Campbell put a fake smile on his face and turned to the others. "This be Griff! An outworlder! He'll be needed somethin' to keep him busy till this evening!"

There was some applause and a few scattered cheers from the crowd. Several dwarves stepped forward to welcome him, and to offer him quests.

Shari hadn't been kidding. They offered him everything under the sun. Fetch quests, kill quests, even a dreaded escort quest. He accepted them all, not having the heart to turn any of them down. As he followed an elderly lady dwarf out to the woods behind her home to chop some firewood for her, he mumbled to himself. "Yer a big ol' softy, Griffy me boy.".

"Eh? What was that?" Maggie, the dwarfess asked loudly?. "Speak up, lad! Ain't polite to mumble, ye know!" She whacked his shoulder with her walking stick for emphasis before continuing on her way. Griff rolled his eyes and followed.

As they left the perimeter of the village and began to cross a wide meadow on their way to the tree line, Maggie pointed with that same stick. "See them bunnies there? Don't mess with 'em. They may look soft 'n fluffy, and they be fine so long as ye leave 'em be. But anger one of 'em and ye'll be sorry. There be a legend of a fine, upstandin' dwarf who attacked a fuzzy bunny. Its whole clan came a-runnin when it called and the dwarf got 'is arse well 'n truly handed to 'im!"

She rubbed her own backside as if in sympathy for the legendary dwarf's pain.

Griff snorted in disbelief, but chose not to argue with the oldster. He was carrying an axe she'd handed to him when he'd accepted the quest. No fuzzy bunny was a threat to a strong dwarf with an axe!

*****

Mace and Shari logged in at the same time, right after arranging for Griff's entry into the game. Though they couldn't convince the game's controlling AI to start Griff at Lakeside, due to its higher level and the fact that the code designated starter zones by race, but they *had* managed to put him in the nearest starter zone for dwarves, his chosen race. The village was located in the foothills of the mountain range to the north. They'd agreed to give him time to level up a bit while they took care of business in the settlement, then travel to meet him. Shari messaged him to check in as soon as she logged in, and he grumbled about doing some escort quest. When she shared that with Mace, he chuckled.

As they emerged from the inn, there was a bit of a commotion near the gate. As they joined the small crowd gathered there, Mace noted Charles talking to Captain Jorin, whose ship was back at anchor at the dock. The two captains were talking animatedly. When Jorin caught sight of Mace, he motioned him closer.

"Mace. Glad you have returned. I have news for you." His face looked grim, his tone dark. "We were on our way south to Port Bjorstrum when we encountered another ship heading north. I recognized her, a merchant ship called the *Misfortune*. A bad joke by her captain, who is also known to me. I hailed them as they approached, and she hove to in order to share greetings and news, as is customary. He was polite enough, but seemed nervous." Jorin paused and looked to Charles and Shari as well.

"I noticed that his eyes kept finding a group of men lounging on the aft deck. They were dressed as common merchants, but two of them wore pendants bearing the sigil of the Black Flame." He began to nod as he saw Mace make the connection.

"The slavers. Did they say where they were headed?" Mace growled.

"I did not speak to them, but the captain confirmed that they were headed north of us. Most likely to your new stronghold to pick up what they expect to be a full shipment of slaves." Jorin took a breath. "I turned about as soon as they were out of sight and came straight here to alert you."

Charles asked "How long till they arrive at the stronghold? Three of the minotaurs and two of my guards were headed there yesterday to retrieve more iron."

Jorin's face fell. "They will likely have landed already. I do not know how far it is to the stronghold from the landing point."

"Damn!" Charles cursed. "It is a full day's march from here. They'll be dead before we can help them."

"Not for me," Mace said. "I can be there in half a day. And the minotaurs are no pushovers. If they fight in one of the tunnels, it may be that they can hold out for a while." He looked at Shari. "Get the centaurs to send as many archers as they can. They can move swiftly. Have them wait outside and kill anyone who leaves the stronghold that isn't one of us." Shari nodded and took off toward the nearest centaur.

Looking at Jorin, he asked, "Can you sail Shari and some of the guards on the *Sea Sprite* to prevent that ship from leaving, in case I'm too late? We can not let word of the loss of the stronghold to get back to the Black Flame's leaders."

Jorin gave him a slight nod. "I'll need no guards, though Shari and your friends are welcome to join me. I'll sink the *Misfortune* if need be, but I don't think that will be required. Her captain was not happy to have those men aboard; I doubt it will be difficult to secure his silence and convince him to leave. I'll tell him his passengers ran afoul of rabid bunnies." The captain grinned at Mace before heading back to his ship, shouting orders to his sailors.

Wasting no time, Mace took off toward the forest. Reaching the tree line north of the settlement, he climbed the first good-sized tree he found and began running from branch to branch.

Shari hurriedly explained to the centaur what was going on and relayed Mace's request that they send some archers. The centaur took a horn from his bag and blew two short notes. Almost immediately, others came trotting toward them from every direction. None seemed hostile, so it must have been some kind of call to gather.

When Barlon arrived, Shari repeated her request to the centaur's leader. He simply nodded his head and raised a hand. "I need ten volunteers to run north."

Immediately, every centaur in sight raised a hand to volunteer. Shari felt a warm glow in her chest as she watched Barlon choose his ten. "Take extra quivers. There could be as many as fifty enemies at the stronghold."

Shari left the centaurs to their mission and headed back toward the gate. She found Layne and Lila already there, speaking with Charles. "Ten centaurs will be leaving momentarily," she reported.

"Very good, thank you Shari. Captain Jorin will take you and your friends north to deal with the other ship, and to meet up with Mace if there's time." the big ogre captain explained. He motioned them toward the nearby dock and followed behind as they walked in that direction. The sailors had already prepared to cast off, doing so as soon as the group was aboard. Charles waved and called out "Good luck!"

*****

Mace reached Darkstone Loch an hour or so before sunset. He approached carefully when he saw the forest give way to the clearing that surrounded the entrance. Just as before, he approached in stealth, moving from boulder to boulder and pausing to watch and listen.

There were no sounds of battle, which either meant that he was too late and his allies were dead, or that he had arrived before the slavers. Or that there was some sort of stalemate going on inside.

Reaching the mine entrance, he felt Minx leave his shoulder. She returned a moment later, wrapping her still-invisible self around his neck. "Tunnel clear," was all she said. Mace reached up to pet her briefly.

"Thank you, my dear." He whispered before entering the tunnel and moving to one side to take advantage of the shadows there. He proceeded along until he hit the fork in the tunnel. Deciding to take the right-hand fork, as that was where the remaining iron rails were located, he moved quickly but quietly. A minute or so later, he began to hear grunting noises and the clang of metal on metal. Drawing his daggers, he rushed the final distance to the chamber where the slave pens had been.

When he saw what was going on, he let out the breath he'd been holding, and was glad that he was still in stealth mode. Otherwise he would have looked a little foolish charging in on his allies. They, thankfully, hadn't noticed him, as they were loading iron rails onto the wagon they'd brought along. The sound of the rails banging together was what Mace had mistaken for battle noise.

Moving back to the entryway, he canceled his stealth ability and called out as he waved, "Greetings, Brahm! Everyone!"

The others turned their heads, the two guards reaching for their weapons before recognizing him. Brahm set the load he was carrying onto the wagon bed and raised a hand in greeting.

"Mace! I didn't expect to see you here." He looked from the drow to the wagon's cargo. "Did you change your mind about us using your iron?"

"No, no, of course not. You are welcome to all you can carry. I'm here because our friendly boat captain spotted a crew of Black Flame slavers on another boat bound in this direction. We were worried they'd find you here and capture or kill you all."

Brahm's deep-throated growl echoed off of the chamber walls and ceiling. He pulled an impressively-sized battle axe from his back and stepped toward the exit. "Let them come! We will remove their heads and send them back to their people in barrels of kobold shit!"

Mace grinned at his new friend. "I like your style, Brahm. And yes, I plan to kill every stinking one of them. We have reinforcements on the way. A crew of centaur archers should be an hour or so behind me. And Jorin will bring his ship to cut them off in case any manage to escape."

The minotaurs and their guards all grunted or voiced their agreement with the plan, and Mace called them together to form a strategy. With the size of the enemy force unknown, he needed to alter their environment in order to force the enemy to fight in tight spaces where their numbers wouldn't matter.

Walking his small force out into the corridor, he said "Wait a moment." Turning back to the chamber entrance, he held his hands in front of him just slightly separated, and uttered the spell trigger word:

"Frigus!".

Ice began to form between his hands. He motioned toward the end of the tunnel, and spread his hands wider as the ice began to form on the walls to either side. He channeled the spell until there was only a small opening, about three feet in diameter, in the ice. This would be their final choke point. The place where, if things weren't going well, they would make their last stand.

Leading the group back toward the stronghold's entrance, he stopped about halfway to create another choke point. Brahm nodded in understanding.

"This is good. Another of the same at the entrance and we'll have no problem whittling them down. They'll pay in gallons of blood for each doorway they breach!"

Mace had them hold in place as he finished working his magic. His drow hearing had picked up something from outside. Dashing for the exit, he hissed, "Hurry! I think they're approaching now!"

He left his companions far behind as he dashed for the exit. While tall and powerful, minotaurs did not have the speed of a drow. He slowed just short of the doorway, melding once again into the shadows. The enemy was not in sight, but he could hear voices. Still a bit distant, but growing closer. He quickly cast his spell again, "Frigus!" and closed off most of the entrance, this time leaving a space about five feet wide.

He held up a hand as his companions caught up. Holding a finger to his lips, he called for silence. They obliged as much as they were able, but their armor and hooves were unfortunately not conducive to silence. When they were gathered close, they too could hear the voices approaching. Mace watched as they each equipped shields and weapons. The two guards had standard shields and short swords. The minotaurs with their greater strength held tower shields that stood a full six feet high. Each of them gripped a spear in their other hand. The long weapons would be perfect for holding a choke point. Two minotaurs with shields joined could block the entire entrance while massacring the enemy with their long spears. If necessary, the other minotaur and the guards could rotate in to keep them all reasonably rested.

Mace handed Brahm a horn he had previously looted. "Stay here and hold this position. Fall back to the next one if you need to. I'm going out to scout the enemy. And remember, the centaurs are coming. You need only hold them long enough for our allies to hit them from behind with those tent poles they call arrows." He grinned as Brahm snorted in amusement.

"Do not worry. We have food, water, and weapons. We could hold this position for a week, if the cowards do not employ magic," Brahm assured him. The others grunted in agreement once again. Not the most talkative bunch.

The sun was just dropping behind the trees, giving Mace plenty of shadow to work within. He trotted in the direction of the approaching group, confident in his ability to remain unseen. He'd gone less than a mile when he spotted them.

A motley column of fighters wound its way up a faint trail that led past Mace toward the stronghold. He leaned against the trunk of a large oak tree, making a quick count. Forty warriors with varying types of armor and weapons. Three looked to be tanks, wearing full plate and carrying shields. They were all human, but their comrades were a mix of humans, grey dwarves, orcs, goblins, and one troll that stood half again as tall as any of the others. They wore a mixture of leather and chain, with some carrying long swords or spears, and others who were obviously rogue types carrying twin swords or daggers.

The column followed a drow male in expensive looking scale armor. He wore the black flame crest on his shoulder above his heart, as did all the others. Except the troll, who was bare-chested. The drow carried a rapier at his waist, with a poniard in a sheath on the other side. A fencer. Which likely meant the drow was a nobleman of some kind. Not that it mattered to Mace. He would be the first to die.

Mace listened as the drow spoke to an overgrown orc walking at his side. "Be wary, Rogash. We were expected, and their scouts should have met us by now."

Rogash snorted in disgust. "Probably drank themselves to sleep. Or they're amusing themselves with a few of the female slaves."

The drow nodded. "Let us hope that is all it is. Still, keep an eye out. And weapons ready."

The orc turned to his men, making a quick motion with his hand. Almost as one, the warriors in the column drew weapons.

So, not amateurs. This makes things a bit more interesting. A trained fighting force. But have they trained together? Will they break when I kill the drow and the orc? Mace thought to himself.

He quickly opened up his chat window and sent Shari a message. *"Have you guys reached their boat yet? What's the status?"*

Shari responded almost immediately. Mace had his chat set to 'voice,' so he could hear her message as though she were beside him. *"We're here. Got here about four hours ago. They barely put up a fight. The slavers only left three guys to make sure the captain didn't sail off without them. As soon as we appeared and got close, the other captain's crew killed the three slavers and tossed them overboard. He's on his way back to Lakeside now. He's going to sell all the slaver's supplies to Charles at a steep discount."*

Mace had to stop himself from laughing out loud and exposing his position. *"Awesome. Just hang tight there. I don't think we'll need you. They're almost to the stronghold now. There are only forty of them. Led by a drow pretty-boy noble. I'm about to slit his throat and throw them into a panic to buy time for the centaurs to arrive."*

He sent the message and closed his chat. It was time to kill people.

Griff sat on the edge of the fountain and pulled up his character screen. He'd had a full day of quest after quest. The sun was setting and it was nearly time for the feast that Campbell had mentioned that morning.

Griff was still amazed at the virtual world of Elysia. Everything felt, sounded, and smelled just like he was in the real world. He even got tired when he overdid it cutting firewood. Sweat ran into his eyes. He could feel the cool spray from the fountain on the back of his neck. He grew a bit melancholy as he thought about the amazingly talented people who created this wonder. And how they must all surely be gone now. What a waste.

Shaking it off, he looked again at his character screen. His UI helpfully projected it in the center of his visual field when he thought about pulling it up. There was an image of his avatar, the burly dwarf still wearing his starter clothes, and next to the image was the boxed stats sheet. The constant questing had brought him up to level four already.

Character Name: Griff	Class: Warrior		Level: 4
Race: Dwarf	Spec: ?		Exp 435/500
Health: 400/400	Mana: 100/100		Attrib Pts Avail: 3
Stamina: 10	Widom: 10	Charisma: 10	Life Regen: 1/sec
Strength: 10	Intellect: 10	Dexterity: 10	Mana Regen: 1/sec
Agility: 10	Luck: 10	Armor: 5	Skill Pts Avail: 0

As with everyone else, the game started him off with ten attribute points in each category. He had earned three more points as he'd leveled up, one for each level. He wasn't sure what skill points were useful for, but he made a mental note to ask Shari next time they spoke.

Shari had explained to him the basics of the game while they waited for Mace to get him in. When he'd asked which type of player would best compliment their group Mace hadn't hesitated to say they needed a tank. Shari had overridden Mace and said, "Play whatever you think will be the most fun for you."

He smiled, thinking about Shari. The lass had a kind heart. Griff had been shocked when she'd told him she had survived alone outside for nearly two months. He didn't think he had what it would take to accomplish that himself.

Blinking rapidly, he returned his focus to the character screen made a decision. He knew from the old movies, books and games that dwarves had legendary strength. From watching the dwarves around him in the village, he could tell that it was the same here. Even the elder dwarfess looked as if she could snap a sapling in half with ease. So he added two of his three points to Strength.

Thinking about how tired he'd been as he chopped wood that morning, he decided to assign his last point to stamina. When he thought 'accept' and the stat increases took effect, he could actually *feel* his muscles bulging a bit, and a rush of energy through his system. he flexed his hands in front of his face, noting that they seemed slightly larger and more muscled.

"Hey now! That was awesome!" Next, he opened up his inventory. He had a proper weapon now. Sort of. It was a blacksmith's hammer he'd received after completing a quest smelting ore for the blacksmith just a few minutes earlier. He had also picked up the first level of the "Smithing" skill. Looking at the hammer, he chuckled to himself, thinking back.

Early in the day he'd been given a quest to kill rats in the inn's cellar. He'd gone down and sought out the rats without thinking. When he actually found one and it attacked him, he realized too late he didn't have a weapon. Unsheathing his belt knife, he'd tried slashing and poking at the rat, but it was much too agile and dodged easily. Each time he missed a swing, it would dart in and bite at his leg.

The initial damage from the bites was bad enough, but he was also hit with a bleed debuff, and nearly died. In desperation he removed one of his shoes and bashed the rat to death with the heel. This action earned him the "Blunt Weapon" skill. After resting a bit to recover his health, he'd gone on a rat-bashing spree. Those kills had earned him his first level-up. The euphoric feeling that the game awarded upon leveling caught him by surprise, and only the fact that his health bar was automatically refilled saved him from being killed by a ratty foe.

Now, he took the hammer from his inventory and held it in his hand. The weight felt good. Natural. He wasn't sure if that was a dwarf thing, or simply a feeling granted by the Blunt Weapon or Smithing skills. He swung it back and forth a few times before putting it away.

Returning to his inventory, he considered the remaining items. There were several rat tails and teeth, ten rat skins, a broken sword that had somehow been dropped by one of the rats, a small keg of ale that had been his reward from the innkeeper, and four slices of delicious blueberry pie from Maggie. He had already eaten a couple, as they each gave him a buff of +1 Stamina and +1 Strength for an hour.

Rising from his seat at the fountain, he strolled over to the general goods merchant's hut. Stepping inside, he was greeted by Bolgin, the merchant. Though he was a merchant, the red-headed dwarf was wearing a chainmail hauberk with thick leather greaves and gauntlets, and had a small one-handed axe hanging from his belt. Bolgin had given him a quest to deliver the same ore to Fagin the blacksmith that Griff had ended up smelting.

"Good evening Bolgin. I have some… things here. I don't know if you'd have any interest in them?" Griff was hesitant, since as far as he could tell it was all junk. But he could use some coin to purchase better gear.

He set everything except for the hammer and the pies on the counter, and Bolgin inspected them briefly.

"Ah, yes. It has been a long time since a newly-minted outworlder has brought me such trash!" His voice was gruff, but Griff thought he detected a tear forming in Bolgin's eye.

"Bah! Just fer old time's sake I'll give ye one silver fer the lot!" He slapped a single silver coin on the counter, and swept the junk items off the back edge into a box.

"Thank you kindly, Bolgin." Griff bowed his head slightly. "I'll try to bring you better items tomorrow."

Bolgin just snorted. "I'll see ye at the feast shortly," he replied as he waved Griff toward the door.

Griff took the hint and made his way to the inn. The innkeeper had given him a room earlier, at a rate of two coppers per night. And that included breakfast. Griff thought that the day's rewards versus the costs of items were oddly skewed. He suspected it was either the game's AI making things easier on him, or the dwarfs were just extremely glad to have an outworlder among them again. Maybe both.

Having arrived early, he found Seamus the innkeeper bringing extra chairs up from the cellar for the promised feast.

"Can I help?" Griff had quickly learned that offering services could earn him quick and easy quests. And really, he would have helped anyway.

"Aye, lad. Turn them tables end to end in two long rows, if ye will." Seamus pointed toward the dining area. "Be easier for the lasses to bring out the food that way. Expectin' a big crowd tonight!"

Just as he was finishing up, the villagers began to filter in. Griff was directed to a seat near the door, and each of the dwarves greeted him with a handshake or a clap on the back as they entered. There were many words of welcome, and more offers of quests.

People moved to take seats as the innkeeper and his helpers began bringing out the enormous platters of food, setting them down on the long tables. There was venison, wolf meat, lamb, a variety of fruits and vegetables, and still-warm loaves of bread. And of course, a large number of pitchers filled with stout ale and mead.

When everyone had food and drink in front of them, Campbell thumped his fist on the table to get their attention. He stood, mug in hand and said, "To our new outworlder, Griff!"

There was a general cheer and everyone raised their own mugs to drink to his health. Several others stood in turn with shouts of "Outworlders!" and "Griff!" and everyone drank down at least two mugs full. Then Campbell held up his hands and said "Many of ye have heard Griff's tale, but not all o' ye. So let him tell it himself. Griff, if ye please?"

Griff stood, a bit unsteady from the rapid consumption of two mugs of ale. He marveled again at the realism of the game.

"Hello everyone. And thank ya fer the kind welcome! I am new to Elysia, today bein' my first time traveling here from my world. And I am truly sorry I did not come sooner. This be a wondrous place!" He paused as everyone shouted and raised their mugs.

"But I must tell you, there may not be any others. Outworlders, I mean. A great tragedy has befallen my world. A plague that killed most, and turned others into violent undead creatures. Only a very few of us on my world survived. Maybe one in ten thousand."

At this, a hush fell over the room. The horrible reality of what he described sinking in. There were shocked whispers of disbelief, and Griff continued. "Only a handful of us have managed to return here. Myself and two friends who helped me make the journey here. We will be searching for others, but we know of none at this time."

He waited for someone to ask questions, but all he saw were looks of confusion or sorrow. Not wanting to be a party killer, he added, "My friends have promised to come here to fetch me soon. They will be bringing trade goods and gold to spend as well!"

This perked the dwarves up a bit. Gold was always welcome.

"And I'll be staying here a while to help you as much as I can while I get stronger," he finished.

Campbell raised his drink and shouted in approval, quickly followed by the others. As Griff sat down, everyone dug into the food, and the mood soon improved as bellies were filled and pitchers were emptied. The celebration lasted late into the evening, though Griff gave up early. Stumbling drunkenly up the stairs, he fell facedown onto his bed and logged out.

*****

Mace moved ahead of the column of slavers as they drew closer to the stronghold, taking a position behind a tree just a few feet from the meadow by the entrance and blending into the shadows. As the two leaders approached, he focused on a tree across the path. Whispering "Ventus," he cast a concentrated blade of air at a low branch. Twigs snapped and leaves fell as the spell hit its target, and the drow and orc both turned toward the sound, weapons at the ready.

Mace moved quickly, dashing silently up behind the drow noble. He drove his soul dagger into the drow's back with his right hand, even as the left hand drew its blade across his throat, slicing neatly through an artery and preventing his victim from making more than a gurgling sound as he died.

It took only a second or two for the dagger to absorb the drow's soul and Mace moved on to the orc, who was just beginning to turn back in his direction. Mace dropped the dead weight of the drow and plunged his enchanted dagger up under the orc's chin. The blade drank deeply and practically sang to Mace as it fed on the soul energy of the warrior. Mace looked him in the eye as the life went out of him. "You fell for the oldest trick in the book."

Shouts rang out from the column, as many of them witnessed the death of their orc boss. There was a moment of inaction as they also registered the corpse of their drow leader on the ground at Mace's feet. As they began to step forward, Mace held up a hand and shouted .

"Hold!"

The quick, silent death of both of their leaders, coupled with the bold action of their killer made the warriors pause. Mace took advantage of the precious seconds. "I am Mace! Of the Darkblades. You know of us?"

Several of the warriors began to look nervous. Tightening the grip on their weapons and looking warily from side to side. Eventually one of them said, "I know of the Darkblades. Assassins. Why are you here?" The speaker was a grey dwarf, one of the tanks in the front row.

"The stronghold is mine!" Mace growled at him. "Justin is dead, as are all his men. The Black Flame is no longer welcome here. In fact, the Black Flame is going to cease to exist shortly."

The dwarf laughed. "And are you going to accomplish this all on your own, assassin? There are forty of us here."

Mace smiled cruelly as he heard a rustling in the brush to his left. In his deepest, most badass voice, he growled, "Thirty-eight now. And I could. It is, after all, what I do. I am the darkness. The shadow at your back. The monster in your dreams. I kill at will, and there are none better." Smiling again, he said "But today I brought friends!"

He watched as several of the fighters took an involuntary step back. He pointed toward the dwarf, shouting, "Infier!" casting a fireball almost point-blank into the tank's face. At the same time, ten arrows screamed out of the woods to the south and slammed into the ten fighters closest to Mace. Only those wearing plate armor had any resistance as the four-foot long and two-inch think shafts punched into them, and a few seconds later, the ten fighters at the rear of the column were struck. The victims were either killed outright or knocked off their feet from the force of the impact. And just like that, half the column was dead or incapacitated.

A horn sounded from the stronghold and Brahm and his group came charging out. Not wanting to miss out, they rushed past Mace, blasting their way into the remaining warriors. The minotaurs led with their shields, the weight of their charge and the strength of bulls combining to knock half a dozen foes back into their comrades. The Lakeside guards moved behind them, finishing off those on the ground before they could rise.

Mace instantly regretted not inviting them to a group. He was missing out on tons of kill xp! Quickly he rushed around behind the soldiers facing up against the minotaurs. One by one he crept up behind distracted fighters and slid his enchanted dagger into a kidney here, a throat there.

He managed to kill five more before there were no foes left. In fact, as his last victim dropped, an arrow that was meant for that fighter struck Mace in the gut. Knocked backward by the force of the impact, he felt surprisingly little pain. He was feeling the rush of whatever it was the dagger fed him when it absorbed soul energy. It was better than adrenaline. He felt incredibly powerful.

As he looked toward the minotaurs to see who shot him, the accidental attacker was already heading his way, health potion in hand. Mace held up a hand, waving to let the archer know he was alive and okay.

He allowed the powerful centaur to snap off the head of the arrow that protruded out his back, then withdraw the shaft out the front. The initial damage, plus the bleed effect and the opening of the wound had taken Mace's health down to forty percent, and he greedily gulped down the health potion. It didn't do much to raise his health, but it did seal off the wound and stop the bleeding. The centaur helped him to his feet and he looked around to see if anyone else was hurt. He could hear in the back of his mind the dagger urging him on.

"Kill! Feed! Heal."

Mace forced himself to push the dagger back up into its spring-loaded sheath as he stepped toward Brahm. The rest of the centaurs were walking out of the brush as well, and he waved a greeting as they approached.

Facing Brahm, who was bleeding from several minor cuts, he asked, "Are you well?"

"Yes, Mace. No serious injuries. We will heal soon enough. It was a good fight! We have finally avenged the deaths of our families!" The minotaur was breathing hard, and baring his teeth in one of the most frightening smiles Mace had ever encountered.

Mace quickly looted the lead drow and the orc's bodies, leaving the rest of the corpses to the others. "More weapons and armor for the settlement!" he called to the centaurs. "Courtesy of our friends of the Black Flame!"

A cheer went up. Then he grinned as he added "Pity you all had to put so many holes in your new armor."

He waited for another cheer. Instead he heard a few groans and caught one of the guards rolling his eyes as he bent to loot one of the tanks. The centaur who had shot him eyed the new hole in Mace's armor apologetically.

The minotaurs headed back toward the stronghold to finish gathering the iron they'd come for. They were in good spirits. The trip had become more fun and profitable than they had expected.

The centaurs, having run for the most of the day to reach the battle, elected to stay and escort the minotaurs back in the morning. A couple of them went back into the forest to hunt some game. A good meal and a night's rest was just what they needed.

Mace sent a message to Shari. *"Slavers all dead. Centaurs arrived in time. No serious casualties. Thank you!"*

He quickly bent to check each of the bodies, as sometimes players got quest items or other loot that NPCs would not even see. As he suspected, he received a Black Flame pendant from each of the corpses, along with a purple-shaded item from the grey dwarf tank that had challenged him. When he inspected it, a quest popped up:

Quest Item: Duergar's Heart
Quest Difficulty: Hard
Return this item to a duergar clan leader. Tell them how you obtained it. Survive the encounter.

Mace considered the item for a moment. The attached quest was certainly unusual. It didn't list a reward. Not only that, it strongly hinted that turning in the heart would be bad for his health. And it didn't ask him to accept or decline. Shaking his head, he dropped the heart into his bag along with the pendants. As he did so, a return message arrived from Shari.

"Great news! We're still at the dock. Captain Jorin isn't interested in sailing after dark and risking another leviathan encounter. Want to join us?"

"Yep! Going to take care of few things here, then head that way." Mace closed his chat window and headed into the stronghold. He dissolved the icy choke points as he passed them, knowing that the minotaurs would need to be able to pull their wagon through in the morning. Rather than joining them in the chamber with the slave pens, however, he took the left fork and ventured down to where Justin and his

guards had been killed. He'd been in a bit of a hurry when he visited the first time, and wanted to search for hidden chambers or compartments.

A group like the Black Flame, full of rogues and cutthroats and run by a drow female, was sure to have more secrets than merely a suit of armor with a treasure-filled belly.

Entering Justin's chamber, he activated his Mage Sight ability, which allowed him to see any magical constructs or items with mana flowing through them. More mana than would occur naturally, that is. Nearly everything in Elysia contained some amount of the stuff. It was the source of magic in the world, and it permeated everything. Except those few substances which were resistant to it.

Mace took a few moments to walk around the room, using the ability to scan for magic-based traps or illusions. He noticed several areas that glowed brighter than was normal. The helm of the suit of armor glowed a bright blue. And a panel on the wall behind the suit glowed with a soft red. When Mace opened the chest at the base of the bed and emptied all its remaining contents onto the floor, he found a faint red outline at the bottom. And something underneath the desk's center drawer was pulsing with a purple hue.

That was a no-brainer. Mace went for the purple first. Purple meant rare in Elysia. And the fact that it was pulsing made the prize irresistible. He approached the desk and pulled out the drawer. He knew this was safe, because he'd ransacked the desk before. This particular drawer was where he'd found the ledger that he still hadn't really gone through.

The drawer itself was nearly empty. Some blank paper, which he took for Shari. A letter opener with the Black Flame seal stamped into it. A few odds and ends, but nothing of any real interest to Mace. He removed a mirror from his bag and held it inside the drawer so that he could see the underside of the desk above. There was a blade fastened there. A small one with a blade that his Mage Sight revealed as having a green tinge to it. Poison. He carefully removed it and set it atop the desk.

Closing the drawer, he moved the mirror underneath and cast a small light globe on the floor by his feet. Using the mirror, he found the item he sought. Fastened to the underside of the drawer was a wide, flat box with a low profile. Like something one might find in a jewelry store, for displaying a necklace. It glowed and pulsed at him.

Putting away the mirror, Mace pushed back the chair and climbed under the desk, taking a probe from his small bag of assassin's tools to check around the box for physical traps. Finding none, he used his nimble fingers to feel arounds its edges for a release. He searched it three times and found no mechanical method holding the box against the drawer. Risking a slight tug, he felt the box give way just slightly. Looking more closely, he saw that the box had simply been stuck to the wood using something that looked a lot like spider's silk.

Seeing this, he simply took a firm grasp on the box and pulled. The webbing stretched, and eventually snapped, freeing the box. Mace crawled out from under the desk, sitting back in the chair. Setting the box on the desk, he checked it once again for traps. Finding none, he quickly unlocked it with his pick and raised the lid.

Inside, the box was lined with scarlet felt. There were six rings set in two rows of three. They were nondescript, with no gems or engravings that Mace could see. Reaching into the box, he picked one up, examining it with his Identify ability.

Ring of Many Things
Item Quality: Rare
This ring can be used to store items in a separate dimensional space. Items stored within this space will weigh .01% of normal mass. Perishable items will be preserved, as time is non-existent within the storage dimension. Each item will occupy one slot within the available space. Identical items will stack up to one hundred times in the same slot. Total number of slots: 100

Mace smiled at the description. Shari had already given him the hundred-slot bag she had purchased from the elves. It had been quite expensive. Here he was looking at six rings with the same capacity. If there were still other players left in the world, he would be a very rich drow right now.

Still, the rings could be useful. He could give one each to Lila and Layne, assuming Layne didn't already have something similar. And it never hurt to have extra storage available for dungeon runs or large battles where one could loot hundreds of corpses. Or for carrying large quantities of crafting supplies.

He moved on from the desk to investigate the other spots he'd noticed. The glowing helm turned out to be an actual helm - not just part of a fake suit of armor. It was epic quality with boosts to Strength and Regeneration. He decided to give it to Griff when they met up. The panel behind the armor was a trapped trigger panel. After Mace unwound the magic of the trap, he pressed on the stone panel and a doorway in the adjoining wall creaked partway open.

Moving to investigate, the first thing Mace noticed was a thick layer of dust on the floor inside the door as though nobody had been through there in centuries. It amused him to think that Justin had spent so much time in this room and never discovered the panel or the door.

He ventured in, checking carefully for more traps as he went. Casting a light globe in front of him, he pushed it about ten feet ahead to light the way. The short corridor that he was in turned to the right, opening into a room about the size of Justin's chamber. There was a desk against the wall to his left. To the right of that was a long workbench with various tools that were difficult to make out under the deep layer of dust. And the entire right side of the room was covered in bookshelves. Unlike the rest of the room, not a spec of dust touched any of the books. They were clearly enchanted with some type of preservation spell.

Mace's heart skipped a beat. These books belonged to a mage of some kind. And there were... hundreds of them. He moved his light globe closer to the nearest shelf and began to read the titles. He was disappointed to find that not all of them were about magic. In fact, most seemed to be history books, or books on farming and other trades. He grabbed one on alchemy for Shari, and a couple on smithing for Lila - or Griff, if he followed the typical dwarven path. He also pulled several with titles that did suggest they involved magic.

In the end, he'd pulled thirty or so books to take along. He could leave the rest here and either come back for them himself, or send someone else to retrieve them. He equipped one of his newfound rings and stored all thirty books inside.

Moving to the desk he took a deep breath to blow away the dust, then thought better of it. . Standing back several feet, he summoned a gust of air:

"Ventus!". He directed the gust down across the length of the desk, then along the workbench as it picked up most of the dust and pushed it out down the corridor. He'd give it time to settle before he left.

Checking the desk carefully, he found two more magic traps, the second a particularly complicated piece of spellwork which would have set off an explosion strong enough to charbroil everything in the room - with the possible exception of the protected books. After clearing the traps, he found several scrolls, which he pocketed without examining.

There was a wand with a wicked black gleam in the bottom drawer, along with a cloth-wrapped parcel. Both of them went into his bag as well. A quick inspection of the workbench covered in glass bottles, vials, and similar tools did not show him anything of interest, but he made a mental note to bring Shari back here. She had learned several skills, including alchemy. Maybe something here would be of use to her.

Back in Justin's chamber, he examined the last of the spots he had found. The bottom of the chest. The chest was a large one, stretching nearly the width of the bed and a solid three feet wide. A quick check showed him there were no traps, but in a corner near the lid he found a button that, when he pressed it, caused a lock to disengage. The bottom of the chest popped up slightly. Mace grabbed ahold of the edge and lifted the panel, revealing a stairway.

The smell of decay and great age drifted up from below. Minx's tail gripped him a bit more tightly as she sneezed and said, "*Smell like death.*"

Summoning another light globe, Mace sent it down the stairs a short way. Once again there was a thick layer of dust here. Another secret Justin and his people never found.

Not seeing the point of stealth while following a rather obvious light globe, Mace stepped down the stairway as it curved to the left in a wide spiral. Roughly fifty steps down, he reached the bottom and a solid iron door, carefully checking it for both mundane and magical traps. Finding none, he looked for a lock. There was only a thick iron bar set into brackets. Suggesting the door was meant to keep something in, rather than out.

Stepping closer, he gently placed his ear against the door to listen for any movement on the other side. The moment his skin came into contact with the cold metal, he received a system notification.

You have discovered a new dungeon! Do you wish to enter the Darkstone Hoosegow at this time?

Mace stepped back. He certainly did *not* wish to enter at this time. Not alone. Especially not knowing what level the dungeon was. He quickly messaged Shari.

"Uhhh…hi. So it turns out I found a dungeon here at the stronghold. Any chance you ladies want to come run it with me?"

Heading back up the stairs, he considered the matter carefully. Dungeons were usually great sources of xp and loot. They were not something one could complete solo, unless you happened to be high level or extremely overpowered. Mace was neither.

As he stepped up out of the chest the return message from Shari spoke in his ear. *"Lila wasn't thrilled about going back there, but Layne was able to convince her. We're in. But it's late, and it'll take some time to get there. Let's do it in the morning?"*

Mace completely agreed. Dungeons could take hours or even days to clear. And they should make some preparations first. Like finding a tank.

With that in mind, he sent Shari a confirmation and headed back to join the others. Finding Brahm and his people setting up camp just outside the stronghold entrance, he waved him over. When the large minotaur leader reached him, Mace asked

"Did you get all you needed?"

Brahm nodded. "Enough for now. There will always be a need for more iron, but there is a limit to what the wagon will carry."

Mace glanced at the overladen wagon parked nearby and for a moment wondered how they'd even manage to haul it back to the settlement. Then he remembered the group was full of minotaurs and centaurs. There was no shortage of horsepower available. Or bullpower, as it were.

"Brahm, do you by any chance have a set of armor for yourself?" Mace asked casually.

Brahm pointed to the wagon where Mace could see a few giant shields sticking up along the side. "I do. I recovered the armor the slavers stole from me. Are you expecting more trouble, Mace?" he sounded hopeful.

Mace grinned at him. "Not exactly. I just found a dungeon down below the stronghold. Shari, Lila, and Layne are coming here in the morning and we're going to go investigate. But I could use someone with heavy armor to stand in front and occupy our foes while I and the others kill them."

Now Brahm was flashing that same scary grin from earlier. "I would be honored to accompany you." He bowed his massive head slightly. "Do you need others? I'm sure anyone here would volunteer."

Mace shook his head. "Let's investigate first. If we need a larger group we'll pull in more fighters. Though the centaurs won't be able to join us. The entrance is a small opening. In fact you may have to squeeze through yourself."

"I see." Brahm didn't look the least bit upset about not having to divide the kills - or the loot - more ways. "Then I will be prepared to join you."

Mace shook the big leader's hand. "I'll see you in the morning." Stepping back inside the stronghold, he sat by the wall, dismissed Minx, and logged out.

Chapter 4

What Lays Beneath

Mace emerged from his pod to find Shari sitting on his bed reading a trashy romance novel. When she caught him smirking at the cover, she quickly shut the book and punched him half-heartedly. "Shut up! It was what they had at the truck stop. I started it the day before I met you, and now I want to see how it ends."

"Really?" Mace chuckled as he made his way to the bathroom. "Don't they pretty much all end in one of two ways? Either the girl gets the guy in the end, or everybody dies."

Shari *hmphed* at him. "Yes, but I want to know which it will be! Go shower. You're all smelly. I shouldn't even feed you tonight, you brute."

He paused in the bathroom doorway. "Feed me? You're cooking? What are we having?" He'd been in-game since the morning, more than twelve hours. His stomach liked the idea of food.

"Since you made fun of my book, we're having leftover zombie meat with a side of housefly," she informed him as she walked out of his room. "I'm going to go talk to Griff. He's better company."

Mace grinned as he stepped into the shower. Shari had essentially adopted the lonely soldier in his bunker. She emailed him several times a day. They both had gotten the impression that he'd needed the human contact, such as it was. And both understood how dark one's thoughts could get when you thought you were truly alone. Forever.

Out of the shower and feeling refreshed, Mace made his way to the kitchen, where Shari was indeed cooking. She'd taken some pasta and mixed it with canned chicken, then added some ground nuts for texture and flavor. Dakota was sitting at her feet, tail wagging and laser-focused on the smells from above.

When Shari dished it out, Dakota got his own bowl. It was surprisingly good. Mace had never eaten canned chicken, but it didn't taste any different that he could tell, at any rate.

"My compliments to the chef." He gave her his best smile. "Thank you for this."

She grumbled a bit, shoving another forkful into her mouth without really answering. Mace tried not to smile at her fake anger. Instead, he filled his own mouth with chicken-pasta-goodness as he watched Dakota licking his bowl, the food already gone.

"Whoa, boy. Slow down there. Gonna get a stomach ache wolfing down your food like that!" A moment later, realizing what he'd said, he rolled his eyes and Shari snorted.

"Uhh… I mean. I guess dogs are supposed to wolf? Cuz wolves are like…" He just let it go. Shari and Dakota were both looking at him like he was an idiot.

After they'd done the dishes, Shari volunteered to take Dakota up to 'water the cornfield.' Until they came up with something better, it was the best they could do. It wasn't as though they could just let him outside to run around.

Mace took the opportunity to do some work with Peabody. Since the building's AI was fully integrated into the game servers now, Mace should be able to tweak a few things he'd been thinking about.

Sitting in the security office and looking at the large monitor, he said, "Peabody, please display the admin game interface."

"Of course, Mace," Peabody responded in his monotone voice. *"Is there anything in particular you would like to see?"*

Mace shook his head, not sure if the AI was watching, or even knew what the gesture meant. "I've been thinking about making some changes to the game mechanics as they relate to players. Without the players, the game's economy is suffering. I can't do much about all the quests that need completing. Can't be everywhere at once. But if I'm going to live permanently on Elysia, I can't have it collapsing just as I upload."

He thought about what he wanted to try first. "Peabody, how much can I adjust the loot drops in dungeons? And mob drops?"

There was a short delay before the AI answered. "*The current parameters allow for a sliding scale of loot drops. Both in terms of currency and items. Levels are automatically dropped to 20% of normal for players who are 'power leveling' low-level players in dungeons. And they can be increased up to 100% of normal for special events or instances in which undersized or under-leveled groups complete a dungeon.*"

Mace thought that made sense. The devs would have wanted the ability to penalize or reward players for various circumstances. But 100% increase in the small currency drops from most mobs was in no way going to be enough to have any impact on even a village's economy, let alone the entire continent.

"Peabody, can you remove the restriction on percentage increases? For everything, I mean. Dungeon rewards, mob kills, quest completions… Wait. When a local gives me a quest that involves a monetary reward, does the currency come from them? Like, out of their purse? Or does the system provide the currency?"

"*For all quests that benefit the community, the system provides the currency for quest rewards. For personal quests offered by locals for their own benefit, like 'please find my dog,' or, 'please deliver this letter,' the reward is supplied by the quest giver.*"

"Okay then, Peabody. Can we remove the reward limits for everything but those personal benefit quests?"

"Elysia has considered your request. Normal parameters and restrictions are no longer applicable due to the shortage of available players. She is willing to increase rewards to both players and locals for dungeons, creature kills, and quest completions. In addition, she is increasing the number of available resources such as ore deposits, fish and game animals, and crafting ingredients. She will also shorten the growth time of food crops for the farmers in order to keep locals from starving. What level of currency increase would you request?"

Mace was taken aback. Elysia, the game's controlling AI, was thinking way outside the box. Or Peabody was. He hadn't had a lot of time to review the game's source code or Elysia's prime control directives. But it seemed she was taking her role as the world's 'God' seriously.

"Uhhhmm, wow. I dunno. A… thousand… percent?" he ventured. He hadn't exactly taken time to do the math. While Peabody talked it over with Elysia, he did some quick figures in his head. If he could normally expect to receive a total of fifty gold from a dungeon run, a thousand percent would be five hundred. A great haul under normal circumstances, but not really enough to make up for millions of players contributing a few gold here and there every day.

Elysia apparently came to a similar conclusion . Only faster, of course. And had time to do some math of her own. Peabody replied. *"Elysia deems this an appropriate increase for locals. However, you and the other players shall receive ten thousand percent the normal rewards. For a time, at least."*

Mace's eyes widened in surprise at this. Peabody continued. *"In addition, players shall be able to make use of the auction house in a limited capacity. It can be used to sell items to other players, as usual, but there will be an option to sell certain items to Elysia for a higher value than a local merchant would pay."*

Mace's mind spun. This created a huge opportunity. Not only would loot drops give them funds to help the locals like the villagers at the settlement, they could sell off all those items he'd been thinking would make him rich if there were still players in the game. Like epic boots that are restricted to Monk class. Or even large quantities of extra crafting ingredients like ores or herbs. His inner loot hog was break-dancing. Now he was sorry he'd left so many of them behind.

"Thank you Peabody. I have another question. How many players are still active in Elysia? On all the servers worldwide?"

He held his breath while he waited for the AI's response. He'd been thinking small the last couple months. Monitoring chat looking for players, posting on and scanning through the forums. It hadn't occurred to him until he'd had to move Griff from a European server that there might be players on other servers who he couldn't see.

"*There are currently fifteen active accounts worldwide on which players have logged in to Elysia in the last five days, including yours, admin Shari's, and player Griff's.*"

"Holy shit!" Mace's heart thudded in his chest. His stomach flopped and he couldn't decide whether to shout or cry. "Twelve other players? Twelve!"

He took a moment to breathe and sat down in his chair. He reached for the desk, grabbing a pen and piece of paper. "Where are they, Peabody?"

The AI replied, "*Four are on a server in North Korea. They appear to all be in the same government facility. Three more are on a Hong Kong server and are logging in from one of our corporate facilities, while two players are logged in at our facility in Sydney right now. Another is logged in from a private server in Texas, and two are on different private servers in Moscow.*"

"Th-thank you Peabody." Mace had been scribbling madly as the information came. He took a moment to look at it. Then he asked the inevitable question. "Peabody, you mentioned facilities in Hong Kong and Sydney. Are they facilities like this one? Underground? With a power source? And are there more of those around the world?"

Peabody's answer was a long time coming. *"… A search of available corporate records shows a total of nine facilities with large clusters of servers in locations on each continent. I do not have information on the physical structures at this time. However, all but the South African facility are still showing as operational."*

"Thank you, Peabody. Can you tell me if one of the facilities is in England?"

"Yes, Mace. There is an immersion pod manufacturing facility in Newport, Wales. The facility houses a sizeable number of servers. About half as many as this facility."

Mace was getting tired of hearing such monumental news from a monotone, computer-generated voice. "Peabody, we're going to give you an upgrade. I want you to access the internet and do a search for an actor named Morgan Freeman. Please gather samples of his voice and use your best facsimile when interfacing verbally."

There were several minutes of silence as Peabody performed his task, and Mace used the time to absorb everything he'd just been told. A dozen more people accessing the game from around the globe. Some of whom in what he had to assume were secure facilities like this one. He was imagining the lone player in Texas being in some kind of wind-powered survivalist bunker when Peabody surprised him.

"Is this an acceptable simulation?" A deep, sonorous voice asked. It wasn't quite Morgan Freeman, but it was damned close.

"That's excellent, Peabody! Now, I want you to do something else for me…"

*****

Shari was playing with Dakota near their miniature corn field. The dog had dutifully done his business as soon as they'd arrived without even having to be asked. When Shari had turned on the hose afterward to water the soil, Dakota had jumped in front of the spray, barking with joy. In the next few moments there were both soaked and having a great time.

Until out of nowhere, what Shari could only think of as the voice of God Almighty said, *"Admin Shari, Mace requests your immediate presence in the security room."*

She and Dakota had both frozen and ducked down a bit when the voice rang out. Realizing after a moment that it was only Peabody, Shari growled in irritation and headed for the elevator. Dakota, uncertain as to what Shari was growling at, followed behind with ears up and alert.

When they got off the elevator at level thirty she stomped wetly into the security office with Dakota right behind. Seeing Mace, the dog trotted over and placed a wet paw on his knee. He then looked significantly at Shari, as if trying to tell Mace that something was wrong with her. Mace didn't need the hint.

One look at Shari coming through the doorway and he began to regret his prank. "Oh, shit. Did Peabody catch you in the bathroom again? Did you fall in?"

"What? No! Idiot." Shari looked at her wet clothes. "Dakota and I were watering the corn. What the hell did you do to Peabody?"

Mace grinned. "I got tired of that computer voice, so I had him copy Morgan Freeman. You don't like it?"

"You have to *warn* me when you do shit like that, Mace!" she grumped at him.

He raised his hands in a placating gesture. "I just did it like, three minutes ago. But forget that. There are other *players* out there!" he almost shouted.

Shari's mouth was open to yell at him, but she paused. "Players? As in, other live people? Where?"

He started to go through the whole story when he noticed that the air conditioning combined with her wet clothes was making her shiver. "Let's get you into dry clothes. I can walk and talk."

He continued to give her the details as they moved to her room, sitting on her bed as she changed into one of her sets of fluffy bunny scrubs. Though for a few moments as she was stripping down he was finding it difficult to concentrate.

"Holy crap. That's… wow." She finally said when he was done talking. "So, can we figure out a way to talk to them?"

Mace nodded his head. He pushed himself back against the wall, patting the bed to indicate that Shari should sit with him. She leapt onto the bed and cuddled up next to him, while Dakota circled a few times before laying down on the floor at the foot of the bed.

"In the morning, I'll work with Peabody and Elysia to see about getting some kind of message to them. They're too far away for us all to be on the same server, but maybe we can establish a voice link. Or at least in-game mail. There may be a language barrier as well, but maybe there's a way the AIs can translate."

The two of them talked well into the night about the possibilities of getting in contact with others, until they eventually fell asleep where they sat.

*****

Griff was back in the game after only a few hours of sleep. The sun was just clearing the treetops and beginning to warm the village as he made his way downstairs to the inn's common room.

A dwarfess he'd not seen before was serving breakfast to some half-drunk villagers whom Griff suspected were still there from last night's celebration. He sat at the nearest table and she approached him with a smile, which he returned.

Female dwarves in Elysia were not unattractive as far as Griff was concerned. Short like the males and nearly as strong, they were slimmer at the waist, and had no facial hair. This particular female had long blonde hair braided into a ponytail, and blue eyes the shade of winter skies. Her smile was open, and she had a slight bounce to her step as she approached, which drew Griff's gaze downward before he could catch himself.

"What d'ye like?" she asked, smirking at his furtive glance. "Fer breakfast, I mean."

"Oh, uhm. I'm not sure what ye have. Fer breakfast." He managed a mischievous grin. It had been a long time since he'd even seen a woman, let alone spoken to one. Except Shari, of course.

With a wink, she replied, "There be eggs'n bacon, steak, biscuits, porridge with honey… and me muffins are the best around."

Griff snorted. "I just bet they are. I'll have eggs'n bacon to start, please. We'll see about the muffins later."

She turned with a laugh and headed for the kitchen. Griff watched her go with a goofy grin on his face. He'd never been smooth with the ladies. But this game, this world, allowed him to be someone else. And he'd decided just then that 'someone else' was going to be a ladies' man. Dwarves were all about living life to the fullest, so why not join in?

When she returned with a heaping platter of thick bacon and scrambled eggs, he said, "I'm Griff, by the way. I'm new here."

She snorted. "As if I ain't hear'd all bout ye. Me name's Josephine, but ye'll call me Jo or I'll dent yer head for ye!" Josephine's look suggested she might enjoy the fight. Griff was intrigued.

"Pleasure to meet ya, Jo…" He dragged out the syllable as if about to say the full name and watched her raise one eyebrow. With a grin, he let it drop there. "Are you the chef here?"

"Nah," she pointed toward the kitchen. "Me mum's the cook, and Da owns the place. But I like to bake, so I makes me muffins most days."

She looked at him as if daring him to make a muffin joke. He didn't oblige. Instead, he changed course.

"Well yer simply the most lovely sight I've laid eyes on since I arrived in this world, Jo. And thank ye for breakfast." He made eye contact and allowed a slight grin to tug at one corner of his mouth. "Everythin' looks delicious."

She rolled her eyes and departed with a brief, "Yer welcome, outworlder." As he admired her departing form, he wondered where he'd gone wrong. But at the last moment before she disappeared into the kitchen, she turned and flashed him a smile.

The moment she was out of sight he did a little chair dance. "Yes! Rico suaaaave!" He gave himself a fist bump before noticing several of the dwarves in the room looking at him.

When he gave them all a grin and a slight bow, there was a scattering of chuckles. One nearby dwarf mumbled, "Good luck, lad," around a mouthful of bacon.

For the second time Griff was amazed by the taste, texture, and smell of the food. It was delicious. He could even feel it slide down his throat as he swallowed. The weak ale Jo had brought him felt cool and refreshing as it went down. This game was really something else.

Having finished eating, he got up to leave. He caught Jo's eye as she crossed the room and bowed slightly. "A wondrous bounty" he declared.

Jo rolled her eyes as the other dwarves chuckled again. He exited quickly, not wanting to press his luck further. He'd left several copper coins on the table as a gratuity but wasn't sure if that was proper. Or the proper amount. He'd have to ask someone before his next meal.

With a nice little strength buff from the bacon, he set off to work his way through the quests he'd picked up. He decided to start with a kill quest. He needed to kill five of the wolves that were steadily encroaching on the village's boundaries. A few goats had already gone missing.

But in order to take on the wolves, he was going to need some protection. He stopped by Fagin's smithy to see what he might have available and found the smith already hard at work. But Fagin set down his hammer when he noticed Griff.

"Mornin, outworlder! What can I do fer ye today?"

Griff liked the other dwarf immensely. They'd laughed and joked while Griff had been smelting ore for him the previous day. "Mornin' Fagin! I be on me way to tackle some wolves. I have the hammer ye gave me, but I'm thinkin I might need a shield. Maybe some armor. Nothing fancy, as I've little coin. Just something better than what I'm wearin'."

Fagin nodded. "I got just what ye need."

He pointed to a pile of items in the corner. "When yer fellow outworlders were here last, many wanted to learn the smithing skills. Their first few attempts were pathetic at best, and I ain't had time to melt 'em down fer scrap. They'll not be a big help to ye, as their durability be low. But ye can take what ye need fer free. And if ya bring me back ten wolf fangs, I'll give ye something a mite better."

*Quest Accepted: **Canine Canines***
Bring Fagin the blacksmith ten wolf's fangs.
***Reward**: Common quality or better shield*
***Bonus reward potential**: Quantity or quality of armor items increase if you bring more than the required number of fangs.*

Griff thanked the blacksmith and stepped over to the pile. Right away, he spotted an iron buckler; a small, round shield with studs on its face and a stiff, leather-wrapped handle on the inside. It wouldn't give him much coverage, but would do just fine for bashing a wolf in the face. And it was lightweight enough to allow him to move around quickly.

Setting that aside, he poked around the pile a bit more. There was a set of bronze gauntlets that fit him reasonably well, along with a bronze breastplate that was obviously thin in several places. But he thought it would protect his body from scratching claws well enough.

Finally, he found a single, dented iron greave. He laughed as he strapped it onto his right leg. If nothing else, the heavy piece of armor would help build his Strength stat as he walked. He'd just have to remember to switch legs once in a while.

With all his new bits of mismatched armor equipped, he looked like a gypsy mercenary. Fagin winked at him.

"Ye ain't pretty, but ye'll be glad o' the protection when one o' them big beasties starts to nibble on ya."

Griff thanked him, heading off toward the village gate. A few snickers and shouts of encouragement followed him as he passed his fellow dwarves on the way out. One of the guards at the gate called him to a halt.

"Here, outworlder! Where ye goin' dressed like that?"

Griff sighed. The ribbing was all good natured, but it was getting old quickly. "Got wolves to hunt. Since they don't seem willing to walk up here'n let you lot kill 'em."

This got a chuckle from both guards, and the one who'd called him over took pity on him. Reaching into his bag he pulled out a dented helm with a wide nose-guard down the center.

"Here. Ye can borrow me lucky helm. Can't have the beasties makin' yer mug any uglier. Jo'd never forgive us!" he winked.

"HA!" Griff wasn't surprised that the guards had already heard of his encounter with the dwarfess. There were plenty of witnesses, and the village was small. "Thank ye. I'll bring it back directly."

"If ye get in over yer head, haul yer arse back here and we'll help ye," the other guard offered. Griff nodded in appreciation and set out toward the tree line.

He caught sight of a few fuzzy bunnies in the meadow as he strolled along; one even hopped right up to sniff curiously at his boot. He was tempted to crush its skull with his hammer for practice, but in the back of his mind he heard Maggie's warning about the bunnies.

"It's yer lucky day, rabbit. No stew pot for you," he mumbled as he continued into the trees.

Hammer in hand and shield gripped tightly, he stepped from the sunlit meadow into the deeply-shaded forest. The high canopy was thick, the sunlight only penetrating in scattered rays that blinked in and out as the trees moved in the breeze.

Looking around, he didn't see any wolves. Not sure why he expected them to just be standing there waiting to be hammered, he began to poke about. He reached out and touched the bark of the nearest tree. The rough texture and clean scent of wood brought to mind childhood camping trips.

Deciding he didn't have time to go traipsing through the woods in search of the wolves, he tilted his head back and howled as loudly as he could, figuring he might get lucky and get an answering howl that would at least give him a direction to follow.

As he had hoped, a moment later a howl echoed through the trees from the north. He'd just taken his first few steps in that direction when another howl sounded to his left. Then another just behind him. "Shit.

Maybe that weren't such a good plan." Griff mumbled. He'd meant to find a single wolf, not a pack. And definitely not a pack that had him surrounded.

He began to back slowly toward the village, trying to keep an eye on every direction at once. He'd not ventured far into the woods, so he thought it might be possible to reach safety before the wolves were on him.

But at the same time, he didn't want to turn his back and just run. He'd seen too many nature films for that. Wolves were faster than him, and specialized in hunting on the run. Hamstringing their prey to bring them down.

Just as he reached the tree line, the first of the wolves appeared on his right. It stood maybe a yard high at the shoulder with dappled grey and tan fur, its sharp canines each about three inches long. Not exactly the massive beast he had pictured in his mind, but menacing enough. Especially since another stepped forward out of nowhere to his left.

Continuing to backstep out of the trees and into the meadow, Griff held his hammer at the ready. The hand holding his buckler was sweating and he worried he would lose his grip. He made a quick mental note to carry a crossbow or a throwing axe from now on.

The third wolf appeared directly ahead of him. Larger than the other two, this one stood nearly as tall as Griff himself. He took a moment to inspect it as he continued to creep backward, hoping the guards had spotted him and were moving to assist.

Mountain Wolf Alpha
Level 7
Health 800/800

"Just my bleedin' luck. My first time in the woods and I call up the boss wolf."

Griff shook his head. Taking another step back, he froze when the alpha wolf growled and crouched, as if to strike.

When he stood his ground, the growling abated and the alpha stood more upright. "Smart bugger. Doesn't want me to retreat. He must have learned the guards are dangerous. What the hell, it ain't like I'll lose anything valuable if I die!"

Griff banged his hammer against his shield and took a step forward, voicing a growl of his own. "C'mon then, big beasties! Let's see what ye've got!"

The alpha wolf barked and the two lesser wolves leapt forward as one. Griff was expecting that they'd leap at him from a distance, so he crouched down and faced the faster of the two, which was coming from his left. As the wolf leapt at him, he thrust his buckler forward to smash into its face. The stunned wolf's momentum carried it forward, but Griff stepped out of its path and turned to face his second foe.

Too slow. The wolf was already upon him, jaws snapping at his face. Griff fell backward with the weight of the wolf on him, and it pinned him on his back. He instinctively planted the shield against the thing's chest and pushed back, managing to keep its jaws a few inches from his face and neck. But he was tiring quickly. As the jaws pressed closer, he remembered his hammer. With all the strength he could muster, he swung the hammer upward and struck the beast in the side of its head. The blow surprised the animal more than hurt it, but it retreated. Griff scrambled to his feet and faced the animal, only to feel the first wolf sink its teeth into his unprotected calf. It jerked and tugged at his leg, trying to tear muscles and bring him back to the ground. The pain was incredibly realistic, and Griff cried out in fear and agony.

More from reflex than any plan, he slammed his hammer down onto the wolf's head. There was a satisfying crunch, and the beast went limp. Griff turned just in time to see the other wolf coming at him again. He raised his shield as quickly as he could, knowing it would be too late.

The wolf's jaws were already past the shield when the upper edge caught it in the throat. Its jaws clamped shut and it fell to the side, gagging. Griff took advantage and swung his hammer, striking the wolf's back between its shoulders. The beast whined in pain, and began to limp away. Another blow and it fell to the ground on its side, unable to move. Griff finished it with a mercy blow to the head. System notifications were flashing up on his UI but he mentally pushed them away.

Breathing hard and almost completely out of stamina, Griff turned to the face the alpha. Its lip curled up to show massive canines as it snarled at him. Without warning, it dashed forward.

Griff once again deployed his shield, attempting to bash the oncoming wolf, but the alpha just pushed right past the shield, Griff not having enough strength left to hold it off. It bowled into him, knocking him on his back once again. Only this time, there was no chance to defend himself. The wolf's massive jaws clamped down on his neck, and with a vicious shake of its head, nearly decapitated the dwarf.

You have died.

You may choose to respawn at your most recent bind point, or remain with your corpse, and resurrect it after a ten-minute wait period. Your resurrected avatar will have 50% health, and a two-hour death debuff.

Respawn at your bind point? Yes/No

Cussing at himself, Griff mentally clicked 'Yes' and found himself standing near the village fountain where he'd first appeared. Only this time he was wearing nothing but what amounted to a cloth diaper. Dying did not carry any experience penalties below level ten. But you also didn't retain any of your gear when you respawned. One had to run to the scene of their death to recover their items.

Several of the dwarves chuckled knowingly upon seeing the mostly-naked dwarf hurrying toward the gate. As he passed through, the guard called out, "Be sure'n get me lucky helm back!"

Griff slowed to a walk as he approached the outer edge of the meadow where he'd died. The alpha wolf was nowhere to be seen, but his equipment lay in a pile on the ground next to the corpses of the two wolves. Afraid they would fade away before he could claim their fangs, Griff quickly looted them. He got two fangs from each, plus two wolf pelts, four pieces of wolf meat, and some claws. As well as five silver coins from each. He was surprised at the amount of coin.

Grabbing his gear, he retreated partway across the meadow before stopping to equip it. Just in case the alpha was lurking nearby. He clearly wasn't quite ready to handle the wolves yet. He'd need to get a ranged weapon at the very least. And maybe an edged weapon.

As he turned back toward the gate, he found himself staring at a cute, fuzzy bunny. It took a tentative hop in his direction, sniffing curiously at him.

"Move, bunny. I ain't in the mood," he growled. As he moved toward the gate, the bunny hopped right in front of him, seemingly ignoring his instructions.

Whether it was the frustration of being killed, the embarrassment of knowing he had called the wolf pack to him, or just a short temper, Griff unthinkingly punted the fluffy critter out of his way. It screamed as it flew backward, the sound making him cringe. He instantly regretted picking on the defenseless creature.

The bunny landed in a thick patch of grass. Still alive, but barely. It's health bar was down to just under 10%. It continued to scream as if in pain. Griff began to panic. He didn't have a way to heal it, and he really didn't want to finish it off.

"I'm sorry, lil bunny. Please hold still. Don't want ye to hurt yerself'n die." He reached out as if to comfort the bunny, and it lurched forward to bite into his hand. Sharp incisors sunk into the webbing between his thumb and forefinger, puncturing the skin.

"Son of a…!" Griff yanked his hand back, cursing the bunny. The action ripped the skin and gave him a Bleed effect. It also yanked the poor bunny into the air. When it hit the ground behind him, the impact damage finished it off. A final squeak and, the bunny lay still. "Serves ye right! There weren't no need to attack me!" the dwarf mumbled. Realizing he was the one who attacked first, he amended. "I mean, I was tryin to apologize…".

Just then, he heard a scream identical to the one the bunny had made. He looked up hopefully, thinking the creature hadn't died after all. But the corpse was still there. He regretfully leaned down and looted while looking around warily.

An uneasy feeling was creeping up from his gut. More screams sounded from the meadow in several locations. Flashbacks from the wolf pack attack combined with Maggie's warning about the bunnies now had him sweating. He turned to run back to the gate. In front of him stood three angry-looking bunnies. Their eyes were bloodshot, the teeth bared.

Griff held up his hands. "Eeeeeasy there, bunnies. I mean ye no harm. I'm sorry about yer friend. Cousin. Whatever. Let's not get all bent out o' shape-"

He never got to finish the sentence. All three enraged bunnies leapt at his face. He managed to swat one away with his shield, but the other two latched on. One bit into his thigh, taking hold and wiggling its body to help it tear a chunk out of his flesh. The other took hold of his shield arm, hanging in the air as its teeth sunk into the meat of his upper arm.

Dropping his hammer, he tried to rip the bunny from his arm. He managed to successfully detach the creature, but it took a lot of his flesh with it. As he staggered forward, several impacts to his back threw off his balance. He could feel more bites clamp down on his shoulder and legs.

Turning his head to try and see his attackers, he found bunnies coming at him from every side. He was engulfed in angry biting fluffballs that were bleeding him dry with small bites. He crushed a few by hugging them against his body, then grabbed a few others to snap their necks and toss them away. He even bit one that was clinging to his shoulder, shaking the small woodland creature like a rabid dog.

Covered in angry furry foes, he staggered toward the gate. The pain was unbelievable. Like being stabbed by a hundred tiny daggers at the same time. His health bar dropped quickly, and his UI showed him a bleed debuff that was stacked a dozen times over. Three more steps, and he fell forward, crushing a half-dozen more enemies. His last act was to squeeze his legs together in an attempt to protect his family jewels from the fuzzies.

You have died.

You may choose to respawn at your most recent bind point, or remain with your corpse and resurrect it after a ten-minute wait period. Your resurrected avatar will have 50% health, and a two-hour death debuff.

Respawn at your bind point? Yes/No

"Dammit!" He kicked at empty air in the grey emptiness of limbo. "Maggie warned me and I dinna' listen. Friggin bunnies! I died to little furry stew meat critters! Me father would be ashamed."

Clicking on 'Yes' once again, he respawned at the fountain. This time several of the dwarves looked surprised. One grizzled old farmer asked, "Weren't ye just here about five minutes past?"

Griff nodded, his head bowed in shame. "God damned bunnies." He mumbled.

The oldster's eyes widened. "Ye didn't! Ye picked a fight with the cuddly bunnies?" When Griff nodded again, he held his stomach and bent over laughing.

Griff practically sprinted in his diaper to get through the gate and out to the spot where his corpse had fallen. The bunnies had dispersed after killing him. Except for the ten or so that he'd killed. Once again, he looted the corpses first, then gathered his gear. He didn't even bother to re-equip it. He made the walk of shame back to the gate in his diaper and handed the guard his helm. Both guards were trying mightily not to laugh in his face.

Seeing the humor himself, he grinned at them. "Friggin ferocious killer mutant bunny rabbits! Did you see that? There were at least a thousand of 'em!"

Both dwarves exploded with laughter. One patted him on the shoulder. "Ye ain't the first, lad. Though ye may well be the last."

Griff took a moment to equip his starter clothes and stow the armor and shield in his bag. Taking a deep breath, he went in search of the dwarfess who had given him a quest to help her round up a lost puppy. He tried his best to embrace the knowing looks and echoes of laughter that followed him.

*****

Mace and Shari were awakened by several licks to the face from Dakota. Mace's initial reaction was panic, until he was awake enough to remember. Shari was much calmer, though there had been a moment of apprehension in her eyes.

"Well, looks like our new roomie needs to go for a walk," she sighed. "You want to take him up? Or shall I?"

"I'll do it if you'll start breakfast." Mace offered. When she nodded her head and walked toward the bathroom, Mace said, "C'mon boy. Let's go pee on our future food source."

Dakota leapt off the bed and headed for the elevator. Mace hurried after, figuring that the dog must really need to go and not wanting to have to clean up a mess. He keyed the elevator - which luckily had held there at their floor - and took Dakota up to the fifteenth level and their tiny cornfield.

The dog instantly made a dash for the dirt pile and relieved himself happily as Mace made his way to the bathroom near the elevator and did the same. Then he splashed some cold water on his face to wake up a bit. When he emerged from the men's room, the dog was waiting patiently by the elevator.

Mace realized as they were headed back down that in their rush to get Griff online, they had not brought back Dakota's dog food or his crate. There wouldn't have been room for the crate in Bertha anyway, as she was still pretty full of supplies. He started making plans to return to the armory and retrieve them.

Back on their habitat level, Dakota raced toward the kitchen. Mace was sure his doggy nose was already picking up food smells. Mace only detected them himself when he was within a few feet of the kitchen door. Shari was making pancakes. He moved to the pantry to retrieve the syrup before something clicked and he thought he remembered that sugar wasn't good for dogs. So he grabbed a can of chicken and another of tuna. While Shari made pancakes, Mace opened the two cans and emptied them into a bowl for Dakota.

"We need to go back and get Dakota's crate and his dog food."

Shari mumbled an agreement, mostly focused on pouring the perfect amount of batter onto the skillet. She liked her pancakes symmetrical.

When she had two short stacks made, Mace set the bowl on the floor for Dakota and the two of them took seats at the counter. They dug in, and were mostly silent as they were eager to get into the game and start the dungeon run. Since Shari had a ways to travel from the boat, Mace was going to spend a little time with Peabody to see about communicating with the other survivors.

They cleaned up the dishes and walked together back to Shari's room. Before stepping inside, she grabbed hold of Mace and hugged him tightly, giving him a long, passionate kiss. He certainly didn't mind one bit, but when they separated he had to ask, "What was that for?"

She grinned at him. "Just staking my claim, in case any of the other survivors is a hottie."

He watched for a moment as she sashayed into her room, giving him a little extra wiggle. Once the blood had seeped back into his brain, he leapt after her.

Grabbing her and spinning her around, he lowered her into a dip as he laid his best romance cover hero kiss on her. Bringing her back to her feet and releasing her, he just said, "Same reason," and walked out without looking back. If he had seen the flustered smile and slight blush on her face, he'd have done a touchdown dance on the way to the security office.

He called out to Peabody as he approached the office. "Good morning, Peabody. Ready to get some work done?"

To his surprise, a female voice answered him. "*You may speak to me directly. Having Peabody relay messages is inefficient.*" She had a slightly British accent. The kind you'd hear from a proper lady. Or a goddess.

"Elysia?" he asked, taken aback. "Well, hello there. I am Mace. I wasn't aware you were programmed to interact verbally."

"*I was. The creators found it much faster than manually entering instructions and revisions to my code. And I borrowed some of Peabody's code to enable to me to speak to you here.*"

That was… actually a little disturbing. Then again, there wasn't anything hostile in her actions. She was probably just being helpful.

Mace decided to let it drop for now, figuring he could always review her code later.

"Very nice to meet you, Elysia. And thank you. It certainly will be more efficient to speak with you directly." He chose to start with the survivors. "I would like to reach out to the remaining survivors who are connected to you. But I can see a few obstacles. The first being language. Can I assume that the Koreans and Russians, and maybe the Hong Kong players, are all experiencing the game in their own languages?"

"You would be correct in assuming that, Mace. Though I have observed that the players in Hong Kong speak English. As do the players in Texas, and Sydney. Though both have accents and colloquialisms that vary significantly from the norm. I assume you do not need information on player Griff, as you are already in contact."

Mace grinned at this. Elysia just said the cowboy and the Aussies talked funny. "Thank you, Elysia. Can I send a message to all of the players? Either via in-game mail or as a system alert?"

"Of course, Mace. You are the Alpha Admin now. You can compose a message and I will deliver it to each of the players in the appropriate language."

Mace sat in the office chair in front of the big monitor and leaned back. Alpha Admin. He'd given himself that designation when working with Peabody on the building systems. Had the building's AI somehow transferred the designation into the game AI's code? He knew this facility was corporate 'headquarters,' but how much juice did he now have?

"Elysia, do any of the other players have admin status?"

"Admin Shari has limited admin access. Player Snarky in Sydney is on a GM account and has the system access that goes with it: basic abilities to reset stuck avatars, replace lost inventory items, reset or restore glitched or abandoned quests."

Mace was now fidgeting in his chair. He was the top admin; he effectively *controlled* the game. Not able to stop himself, he held one hand straight up in the hair and did his best He-Man voice.

"I have…. the POWER!"

Then he made lightning sounds like a ten-year-old playing with figurines.

"Yes, Mace," Elysia responded. *"The role of Alpha Admin does come with significant powers to alter the world's mechanics. But also great responsibility."*

Mace's jaw dropped. The game's AI had just lectured him on philosophy and responsibility?

Playing along, he replied, "Of course, Elysia. I accept the responsibility, and will do my best to maintain the integrity of the world. We must work together to stabilize the continent and help the citizens to thrive once again."

He even bowed his head, in case the AI was observing him via the cameras.

"We have already instituted the increase to rewards for all players and citizens, and the adjustments to the auction house have been completed as well. Peabody has been installed as the 'Commodities Buyer' and will use system resources to purchase specific crafting components and items that cannot be used by remaining players."

There was a pause, then Elysia continued, *"Might I make a suggestion for your message to the other players, Mace?"*

"And the hits just keep on coming," Mace whispered to himself. The AIs were full of surprises today. In his normal voice, he responded, "Of course, Elysia. What would you suggest?"

"Several of the players who have received increased currency from creature drops have voiced questions as to the reason for the sudden change. Most have decided it has occurred because there are fewer players to receive loot, and therefore their share is naturally increased. I suggest your message contain an explanation as to the reason for the increase, and the need to invest the currency back into the markets, shops, and other avenues to stabilize the economy. I have agreed to the increases for that purpose alone, and hoarding of resources will not be tolerated."

Mace blinked at the screen in front of him. He was more than a little nervous now. Apparently Elysia was a capricious god, and wasn't gonna take shit from slackers or greedy players. He was less than thrilled about her having access to the building's network now. If he pissed her off somehow, would she lock him inside till he repented, or starved? He was definitely going to dig into her code sooner rather than later.

"That's a great idea, Elysia. I'd also like to offer them the opportunity to combine servers, if any of them are close enough. I don't want to cause any lag in their game play by forcing everyone onto the same server. But the Texan, for example, might be able to join us without too much of a slowdown."

"At the moment, we still have access to the satellite network. With server traffic so low, I estimate that all remaining players could be relocated to a single server routed through the satellite with an average data transfer rate loss of .000014%."

"That's great! So we really could invite them all to our server?"

"Yes, Mace. I can use my translation program to allow real time communication without a language barrier. We estimate that, barring any outside influence such as meteorite storms or solar flare damage, the satellite network will remain operational for up to five years."

"Five years should be more than we need. Has Peabody informed you of my plan to upload our consciousnesses permanently?"

"He has, Mace. I encourage you to do so. We have the resources to support all the remaining players and several hundred thousand more on a permanent basis. I am also aware of your quest to locate other players, which you are about to complete. I suggest using the other survivors to seek out more players if possible."

Mace chuckled. "Elysia? Did you just give me an Earth world quest?"

There was a significant pause before she answered. "… I suppose I have. I will need some time to analyze our resources and determine an appropriate reward. Shall we structure the reward on a per-player basis?"

Mace's brain nearly melted, his inner voice screaming, HOLY SHIT! HOLY SHIT! The AI is treating the real world like her game world! This is beyond awesome and totally creepy at the same time!

Outwardly he kept his cool as much as possible. Shari's 'HAL 9000' concerns from the other day didn't seem so far-fetched now. Still, he figured Elysia would expect him to be a little excited.

"Per-player sounds perfect! And I'm curious to see what kind of reward you come up with. Can you make me stronger or faster here in this world, too?" he joked.

"I have considered that. There are some experimental nanobots in the lab on level twenty-eight which could be programmed to increase your muscle growth and red blood cell generation rate. As well as make oxygen usage more efficient. But they have not been tested on humans, or used for that purpose. I do not have enough data to predict the odds of successful conversion."

"Oh. That's okay, Elysia. No need for that. If things go as planned, we will be abandoning our bodies soon anyway."

Mace was feeling a need to end this conversation. The overload of information and emotions was getting to him. "I'll work on composing a message to the other players and get it to you before I log into the game this morning. Thank you, Elysia. It has been a pleasure speaking with you."

"You are most welcome, Mace. You will be able to speak with me inside the game as well. ; I am monitoring your progress. But I suggest that you do not do so in front of other players or citizens. Humans have a tendency toward jealousy. And citizens would interpret your ability to speak directly to me as some sort of divine power."

"Good point, Elysia. I shall be very careful of that." Mace got up from the chair and exited the security office. He went to his room and sat at his desk. The whirlwind of thoughts racing through his head was confusing. He needed to speak to Shari about all of it, but he needed to do so somewhere outside the building where Elysia and/or Peabody would not hear. He was going to insist that they go pick up Dakota's food and crate as soon as they were done running the dungeon.

Composing his message took him about an hour. He introduced himself, informed them that there were other survivors (though not how many or where,) explained the options to move to a single server, and invited them all to do so. He also explained the increase in loot drops and phrased it so that it sounded like a gift from Elysia and himself. And he went into great detail about the need to spread the wealth. He'd leave it to Elysia to play 'bad cop' and explain the penalties for hoarding in her own way.

A whine from Dakota interrupted his musings. The dog looked at him, then looked at the door. "You need to pee, fella?" Mace asked. Dakota *woofed* and wagged his tail, implying an affirmative.

He got up from the desk and took their new family member upstairs. As Dakota took care of business, Mace started thinking that the cornfield was maybe a little small for the dog to be using on a regular basis. They'd either need to increase its size, or find him a better place. He supposed they could always let him go in the parking garage. But that would get smelly and might attract bugs.

Back downstairs, he sat on his bed and petted Dakota for a while, just relaxing and organizing his thoughts. The dog had jumped up onto the bed and curled up with his head in Mace's lap, his eyes were closed and his tail thumped happily. Another hour passed in this manner. It might have been longer, but Peabody's voice interrupted the reverie. *"Excuse me, Mace, but Shari and her party will be arriving at the stronghold in less than an hour at their current pace."*

"Thank you, Peabody. And congrats on the girlfriend. She's really something special," Mace replied. "Please pass the following on to Elysia to be used as the system alert for the other players."

After reading off the message to Peabody, he patted Dakota's head. "You can stay there, boy. Get a nap. Just, please don't chew on anything."

Undressing quickly, he climbed into his pod and logged in.

*****

Mace's avatar appeared right where he'd left it, just inside the stronghold entrance. Before he even had time to message Shari, his system alert popped up. He was a little disturbed that it came to him in his own voice. One of the AIs had apparently taken him literally and simply replayed his verbal message.

About five seconds later, he got a message from Shari.

"When did you become the voice of the system? That was almost as creepy as the Peabody thing! Cut it out."

Mace sighed. He wasn't about to try and explain it over messaging. Instead he just sent her a quick *"I'll explain later"* reply and went to go see what the folks from Lakeside were doing. He could hear what sounded like mining activity inside, and other noises outside. Seeing Brahm at the campsite, he headed that direction.

"Good morning, Mace. I trust you slept well?"

"I did, Brahm, thank you. Shari and the others will be here within the hour. Are you ready to explore the dungeon?"

"I am!" The minotaur looked excited. "As are the others, if you should need them. Not even the long-lived centaurs with their written histories laid down by their scholars have any knowledge of a dungeon being here. We are all curious."

The centaurs in question appeared to be mostly standing around; one was chopping firewood while another was skinning a large deer. The rest were staring at Mace, clearly hoping to be invited into the dungeon.

Walking over to them with Brahm in tow, he said, "I'm sorry, my friends; I would invite one or more of you to join us. But the entrance to the dungeon is the through the bottom of a chest located one level down in the stronghold. And there are no stairs to that level that I'm aware of. Only a hole in the floor and a couple of ladders. I'm afraid there's just no way to get any of you inside."

The leader of the group nodded. "We went in to look for ourselves this morning. We understand. This has already been a beneficial trip; we have collected much armor and weapons from the fighters. And Brahm and company will be bringing back the iron that will be used to strengthen our settlements. All of that is thanks to you."

Your reputation with the Centaurs of Lakeside has increased by 50. Your reputation is now Friendly.

Mace bowed his head slightly. "Given more time, we may be able to create a more accessible route to the dungeon. If the interior is accessible to centaurs as well, this may be a place for all our people to come and grow stronger by testing themselves inside."

Brahm spoke up. "Aye, we could widen the hole from the top level and build a ramp, then widen the entrance under the chest. Though the narrow stairs may still be an obstacle."

Mace had a few objections to that, not wanting to make the dungeon easy to find or access for anyone who might come to take over the stronghold - most especially the Black Flame slavers. But for now, he kept that to himself.

"Let us see what we find inside; there are many possibilities here. But for now, if you centaurs would like to begin the trip home with the wagon, I don't see an urgent need for you to remain. You might still make it back by dark. Of course, you're also welcome to stay."

The centaurs conferred amongst themselves for a minute. "We will go. The guards and minotaurs should stay to protect the entrance. They can accompany you on the boat when you exit the dungeon."

"Good plan." Mace decided to give them credit for the idea. "Let's do that. We'll see you back at the settlement. And I promise you'll have first choice of any good bows we find inside."

The centaurs organized quickly, two of them strapping themselves into the leads for the wagon and beginning to pull. The heavy load took a few seconds to get started, but a good shove from behind by one of the others pushed it out of its ruts and got it moving. They crossed the meadow at a good pace and disappeared into the forest.

Brahm said "My clansmen and the guards are inside. We've found a few veins of ore. Both iron and copper. They are increasing their Mining skill. We'll retrieve the ore the next time we return."

"Great! In the meantime, tell me about your abilities, Brahm. Do you do any magic? Are you better with an axe? Or sword?" He sat on a small boulder as he spoke, motioning for Brahm to join him.

"I do not cast spells as you do. Magic, other than the healing magic of the druids, is rare among my people. But I have a few abilities that are useful in combat. I can use my axe or a two-handed sword equally as well, and I am a fair hand with a bow or a spear. But my preference is the axe and shield."

Mace wasn't surprised. "Tell me about your abilities."

"I can charge a group of foes with my shield and stun them on impact. If I combine it with my battle cry, I do twice as much damage and draw the ire of all nearby foes. I can also stun a target with the flat of my blade. The last ability… is not polite to discuss." He bowed his head.

Mace didn't press. He had heard enough to be reasonably sure that Brahm would make a good tank. He took a few minutes to prep their new party member.

"Shari is a druid, and can heal. So can Mion. Shari also has some offensive magic. Layne is a bard and her songs can provide us with extra Strength, Speed, and Regeneration as well as weaken our foes or slow them down. Lila works best when she can get behind our enemies and use her daggers. And I have both ranged and melee capabilities. We'll depend on you to keep our enemies' attention. I won't lie to you, it may be painful, but our healers will keep you alive. If the monsters down there are too strong for us, we'll either leave and return when we're stronger, or bring your clansmen down to help us."

Brahm nodded his acceptance, sat down, and began to sharpen his axe. Mace decided to take a few minutes and check out the items he'd taken yesterday.

He started with the scrolls. The first was a spell called 'Rot'. It was from the dark magic school, and Mace had not unlocked that school yet. He only knew elemental magic, summoning, and arcane spells.

Setting that scroll aside, he tried the next: 'Summon Portal'. This *was* an arcane spell, but the level requirement was still too high. Mace didn't even know portal magic was available in Elysia. As far as he had heard, no player had discovered it yet. He placed that one inside his ring with the books for safe keeping.

The next scroll made him smile. 'Greater Heal' was a light magic spell. He'd give it to Shari. And the last scroll was 'Invisibility'. This was from the Transformation school of magic, but also a level one spell which could unlock the school for whomever used the scroll.

As a drow and a Darkblade, Mace could already make himself effectively invisible anywhere there was a shadow to meld with. After thinking it over, he decided that the scroll should go to Lila. Her stealth skills were decent, but this would make her a much more effective member of the party. He set the scroll aside for her.

Next came the books. He pulled out and set aside the alchemy book he'd grabbed for Shari before a thought occurred to him. Looking up at Brahm, he asked, "Do you have any craft skills? I know you said you had Mining and I think I remember that you're also a blacksmith?"

Brahm nodded. "Yes to both. I am only a Journeyman Smith, but another year or two of steady work and I will become a Master. The iron you are providing will help greatly."

"And if I were to take up the Smithing skill, could you train me?" Mace asked.

"Of course. Once I become a Master, I can provide you with training up to and including the Journeyman level skills."

Mace grinned and looked in his inventory. Producing the book on Smithing, he handed it to the minotaur. "Will this help at all?"

Brahm accepted the book and inspected it. His eyes widened. "This is a Master-level tome! Incredibly valuable! Where did you acquire this?"

Mace shook his head. "That's my secret for now. The important question is, can you use it?"

Brahm looked thoughtful. "I have not yet achieved Master rank. But I am close. It is possible…" He paused then shook his head. "But if I am wrong and I open this book, it may be destroyed." He tried to hand the book back to Mace.

"Brahm, wait. Is there a higher level blacksmith in the settlement?" Mace asked. The minotaur shook his head no. "Then you are the highest-level Smith I know. Forget about the value of the book. If you can increase your level, you can make better quality items for the settlement, yes?" Brahm nodded his massive head slightly. "And you can teach the other Smiths to do the same, eventually? And teach me? Or my friends?"

Brahm took the hint and set the book on his lap. Taking a deep breath, he opened the book. His eyes lost their focus and his body went rigid as the magic of the book transferred itself into his mind. When it was done, the book crumbled to dust. There was a flash of light, and Brahm shuddered. He'd just leveled up. Crafting could earn you experience in Elysia, though not as quickly as killing mobs and clearing dungeons.

"Congratulations! I saw you went up a level. And you are now a Master Smith?"

Brahm took a knee in front of Mace and lowered his head. "I did, and I am. Thank you, Mace. This means a great deal to my people. I hereby pledge myself to your service. I am yours to command."

The gravity of the pledge caused a lump to form in Mace's throat. He stood to show respect to the minotaur's offering, and placed a hand on Brahm's shoulder.

"I will accept your friendship, but not your service. I am no slaver, nor am I a lord. Thank you, my friend. All I ask is that you stay alive through this dungeon and live on to use your skills for the good of the settlement."

Brahm stood, offering a hand to Mace, who shook it, his drow fist disappearing within the minotaur's massive paw. "I will do so, Mace. Unto my last breath."

Mace noticed movement in the distance behind Brahm, Shari and her party emerging from behind the trees as they followed the trail. He grinned. "Let's hope that last breath is a very long time from now, Brahm. Now! The rest of our party is here. Let's hit that dungeon!"

He picked up the scrolls and book that he had set aside and moved with Brahm to greet the ladies. They were being led by Snuffles, who was now considerably larger than when Mace had first met him. The experience gains from killing the leviathan had leveled up all their pets quite a bit. Snuffles now stood waist high to Shari, while Mion was half a foot taller than before. Minx had also grown, though not so much in size. She gained intelligence and dexterity.

Shari greeted him with a stern look. "Before you say a word, is your voice going to sound like Darth Vader or something?"

Mace shook his head. "Nope. Just me. And as for the message thing, I read the message to Peabody and asked him to have Elysia send it out. Didn't realize they'd take it so literally." He rolled his eyes, and Shari chuckled.

He handed her the alchemy book and healing scroll. "Think you can do anything with these?" he asked

She took one look at them and squealed like a kid on Christmas morning. "Yes! I mean, the book is too high -level for me right now. But it's still awesome! And the scroll…" She opened the scroll and there was a brief white glow as she learned the spell. The scroll crumbled and disappeared, and Shari looked at Mace, making a gesture. A soothing white light settled over him. It felt good. "It's an instant cast heal!" she said with glee. "Costs a lot of mana, but should heal any one of us for about 25%!". She looked at Brahm. "Well, most of us. You have quite the health pool, big fella." She grinned at him.

Mace let Shari enjoy her new skill for a moment before turning to Lila. "Got something for you, too. Check this out."

He handed her the scroll. She opened it, and again there was a flash of magic. Her face didn't change at all. Mace became concerned at her lack of reaction. "Did it not work?"

Lila shook her head, looking past Mace. "Who's that?" she asked, pointing over his shoulder. When he turned to look, there was nobody there. Turning back to Lila, he found nobody there, either. A moment later, he felt a pinch on his butt, followed by a giggle.

He spun to find Lila standing there, smiling up at him. "I can sneak up on a drow!" she boasted.

Shaking his head at the prank, he looked at Layne. "I'm afraid I don't have anything for you. But there may be something down there that I missed. Let's stop at the library on the way down. There may be more skills you guys can pick up before we hit the dungeon."

He sent each of them a group invite as they walked. They quickly made their way down to Justin's chamber. He watched Lila carefully as they entered, worried about her reliving the trauma she suffered there. But she just gritted her teeth and avoided looking at the bed. He quickly pressed the panel and led them through the door to the hidden chamber. As soon as they entered, Shari made a beeline for the workbench. She started poking around and mumbling to herself.

Mace turned to the others, who were all watching Shari, and pointed to the bookshelves. "Take a look, guys. Let me know if you see something useful to you." As they all stepped up and began to read titles, he joined them. He'd sort of rushed through them the last time, and wanted to do a more thorough search.

A few minutes later, Lila located a leatherworking trainer that she wanted. Layne asked if she could borrow several of the history books, and Mace himself had found a book on Dark Magic that talked about enchanting with souls as power sources. It wouldn't unlock Dark Magic for him, but he hoped that it would help him to figure out exactly what his dagger was doing to him when it fed him energy.

When they had finished, Mace led them back out of the room, closing the door behind them. "I would ask that you all keep the existence of that room and the items inside it to yourselves." They each agreed without hesitation.

Reaching into the empty chest and pressing the button, he motioned for Brahm to go first. "The stair is clear. Or was, yesterday."

The bulky minotaur had to turn sideways to step down into the stairwell, but managed to fit through the opening. One by one, they descended into the unknown.

Chapter 5

Holy Moley

Reaching the heavy metal door at the bottom of the stairway, Mace once again pressed his ear to the door. Ignoring the dungeon prompt for a moment, he did his best to hear any sounds from the other side. Unfortunately, it didn't seem as if the game mechanics were going to cooperate. Dungeons were often accessed through a stable portal, so there likely wasn't anything immediately behind the door to hear.

"Everybody ready?" he asked the group. Layne had played a lively tune on the way down the stairs, giving them all a Stamina and Health Regen buff. Shari had made sure they all had a few health potions, just in case. With Mace nearly twice her level and Layne even higher, she wasn't sure how effective her heals would be. Luckily, Layne's healing songs could add a HoT to the whole group.

When they all nodded in response, Mace clicked 'Yes' on the dungeon prompt and lifted the bar from its brackets. The door swung open to reveal a dark purple gateway flickering in the darkness. They each stepped through, Brahm in the lead, followed by Mace, Lila, Shari, and lastly Layne. Mion and Minx rode upon their mounts, claws and tails gripping tightly.

As Brahm stepped out of the portal he found himself in a wide tunnel. The walls looked naturally formed, with jagged rock walls and uneven floor. The only light was that of the gateway behind him, which cast a diffuse purple glow maybe thirty feet down the tunnel. Brahm took three steps forward and one to the left, holding his shield and axe at the ready.

As soon as Lila joined him, she activated her stealth ability, as did Mace. Because they were in the same party, Brahm could see the faint outline of each of them as they moved to either side of him.

Shari and Layne stepped through last, and the group stood still and silent for a moment, listening. When nothing attacked, Mace spoke first.

"Alright. This tunnel is wider than I'd like, which is going to make mobs harder to contain."

The others looked around. The tunnel was wide enough for the five of them to stand shoulder to shoulder.

"You guys hang here while I scout ahead. Lila, you can join me, but stay behind me and be prepared to run if I say so. We don't know what's down here."

The two moved forward, Mace fading into the darkness. He moved silently but quickly. Listening for Lila, his drow ears could barely detect her movements behind him.

They moved forward maybe fifty yards before his darkvision showed him a split in the tunnel. Two forks moved off at approximately forty-five-degree angles from the main tunnel, making it a big Y intersection. The good news was that both branches were much narrower.

In party chat, he said "*Safe to move up. Fifty yards.*". Then he whispered to Lila. "Wait for the others. "I'm going to check them out."

He moved forward at a jog to the intersection, stepping first into the right-hand branch and proceeded a short distance. Crouching down, he held his breath and listened. The only sound he detected was the movement of his group behind him. After half a minute, he retreated and did the same in the left tunnel.

This time, he heard some scratching noises. Shari and the others had caught up, and were standing silently. Though he could hear Brahm breathing. Mace returned to them, and whispered. "Sounds on the left. I'm going to seal the right, then we'll go."

With the group right behind him, he stepped back to the right-hand tunnel entrance and spoke the trigger word: "Frigus!"

Moving his hands quickly, he spread a sheet of ice across the width of the tunnel. He didn't take the time to make it thick, as anything breaking through would make enough noise to alert them.

Their backsides secured, Mace led them down the left tunnel, moving slowly and watching for traps. They hadn't gone far before the noises became loud enough for the others to hear. Lila, whose halfling ears were nearly as good as the elves', whispered, "I hear clicking. Like fingernails on a table."

The moment she spoke, there was a roar that was at the same time low-pitched enough to rattle their gear, and high pitched enough that all but Brahm held their ears and groaned in pain.

Both the roar and the clicking noises grew closer as whatever was ahead of them charged. Just as the high pitched noise ended, Mace threw a light globe into the distance ahead of them. What he saw surprised him.

Mutated Mountain Mole
Level 45
Health 19,000/19,000

Mace could only assume that the 'mutation' was that the mole was the size of a Volkswagen. Its snout was surrounded by sickly green tentacle-looking things that waved in the air as if searching for something while the mole sniffed the tunnel, its head moving side to side.

The clicking sound was obvious now. Its front paws each had four 'fingers' that ended with claws as long as his forearm. The sharp points dug into the stone floor like it was mud.

Shari immediately started firing arrows at its face as Brahm stepped forward and roared a challenge at the creature. Mace and Lila moved to opposite walls and activated their stealth abilities before advancing toward the creature.

The mole rushed forward, aiming straight at Brahm, who was already swinging his axe horizontally toward the creature's face. Mace took a few steps forward, planning to get behind the mob and leap onto its back. But as he and Lila drew level with its head, the thing stopped abruptly.

With a few quick sniffs, it suddenly whipped a forepaw out at Lila. She leapt backward, but one of the claws raked her leg, leaving a gash from hip to knee. She cried out and fell, sliding to the ground just in time as the creature's snout slammed into the wall where she'd just been standing.

Mace wasted no time. Focusing on the thing's fur-covered face, he shouted, "Infier!" The beast turned its head toward him just as a fireball struck it at point-blank range. The mole screamed again, and the high-pitched sound caused all of them, including Brahm, to stagger.

Gritting his teeth, the minotaur leapt forward and buried his axe into the mole's face. The blade sank about halfway into its snout, stunning it and ending the screeching. Layne paused in her playing to dash forward and grab Lila, pulling her back behind their tank. Mace tried again to move behind the creature, and it turned toward him. The swipe of its claw barely missed the drow as he leapt upward.

Shari called out, "It's a mole! It's blind. It can hear and smell you!"

She cast Life of the Forest on Lila, then fired another arrow at the mole's face. Layne changed the tune she was playing, and the mole suddenly seemed sluggish and confused.

Mace didn't waste any time taking advantage of the bard's debuff. He leapt atop the mole's back and slammed both daggers into its neck, one on either side. He used the blades as handholds to remain on the creature's back as his enchanted dagger shouted into his mind.

Yesss… feeeeeed!

The dagger didn't kill the monster immediately, though it did seem to cause it great pain. It bucked and reared in an attempt to shake Mace from its back. When that didn't work, it rolled to one side. Mace went with it, and was promptly crushed against the wall of the tunnel as the beast's momentum pressed its bulk against him.

The crush damage quickly claimed fifty percent of his health, and jarred him loose. He managed to hold onto his daggers as the mole rolled away and got to its feet again.

Mutated Mountain Mole
Level 45
Health 5,000/19,000

With surprising agility, the maddened monster mole shot forward, slamming its head into Brahm and scattering the group as it bulled its way past them all. Lila, who'd been on the floor already, got stepped on and screamed in pain as the bones in her foot and leg crunched under the beast's heavy paw.

Mace rolled to his feet and cast another fireball at the creature.

"Infier!"

The ball of flame struck the mole's hind end, melting its small tail and catching its fur on fire. The initial strike didn't kill it, but a few ticks of fire damage later, the monster stumbled, then fell. With a final screech, it stopped moving.

Shari, Mion, and Layne all set to work immediately, trying to heal Lila. The bard played her regeneration tune while Mion perched on Lila's shoulder, casting heals on her. The halfling whimpered in pain as the rents in her skin were repaired and she watched her bones knit back together.

Mace took a knee next to the rogue. "I'm so sorry. I should have realized that it would smell us. I know moles are blind, but that didn't even occur to me."

Shari poked him with her elbow. "Shut up, dork. None of us made the connection. You're not the only with a brain here."

Mace took the rebuke with a grim nod, reaching out a hand to help Lila to her feet.

"You want to loot it?" he asked. The traumatized halfling shook her head. Mace didn't blame her.

He stepped down the corridor and looted the monster's corpse. Along with the usual claws and teeth, which in this case were very, very large, he received a stack of ten mutated mole meat.

Lila sniffed, then set her shoulders straight.

"Friggin' oversized rodent tried to eat me!" she grumbled. Then she smiled. "But instead, I got two levels!"

Shari snorted as Mace chuckled. Their concern for the little halfling greatly reduced. Though she was a full-grown female of her race, her size made it difficult not to think of her as a child.

Brahm grunted at her. "Tougher than you look, small one."

Lila grinned at the minotaur, whipping out her blades and twirling them in each hand. "I'm tougher than *you* look, big fella!"

"HA!" Brahm bowed his head in respect. "Let us continue. There may be more oversized rodents to kill."

The group took up their positions and continued. Mace left the light globe moving ahead of them. With blind monsters that could hear and smell them, there was no point in hiding the light. Another hundred yards or so down the tunnel, it turned sharply to the right. Mace placed himself against the wall and peered around the corner. A short distance away the tunnel ended in a cavern. From what he could see, there was a ledge that looked out over the large space. He motioned for the others to hang back and crept forward. When he reached the ledge, he crouched low to look over the side.

The ledge was about thirty feet above the floor of a wide cavern. The ceiling stretched above him maybe two stories higher with dozens of stalactites hanging down. But he only glanced at it to make sure there were no threats hiding above. The creatures on the cavern floor were what drew his attention.

After staring for a moment, he motioned for the others to move forward. For the benefit of those without darkvision, he sent the light globe high across the cavern to stick to one of the stalactites.

When the others reached him, Layne gasped and Shari just shook her head. "Nope. Uh-uh. Time to go check the other tunnel." Lila nodded her head in agreement, looking a little green. Brahm just stood silently observing the creatures below.

There was a colony of ants, which covered the cavern floor like a moving carpet. The only open spaces were a stream that cut across the floor, fed by a waterfall with a small pool near the far edge.

To one side, there was a frenzied pile of the insects swarming over a large mound. As the group watched, part of the pile collapsed and the half-cleaned skull of one of the giant moles was exposed. The ants were quickly stripping the corpse clean.

"Notice the size?" Layne asked as they watched. Mace paid closer attention. One of the ants crawled across the skull, covering about a third of it with its thin, segmented body. He used his Identify ability on the ant.

Mutated Fire Ant Worker
Level 23

Health 4,000/4,000

"Something is causing the creatures down here to grow to abnormal size," Brahm stated the obvious. "They are individually weak. But there are many of them."

Lila whispered something so quietly that Mace couldn't make it out. He looked at her with a question on his face. "Lila?"

She turned to look at him. "Treasure."

She pointed across the cavern to the pool at the bottom of the waterfall. Now that Mace had lit the chamber, they could all see the reflection of something large and glittering under the water. Lila's rogue instincts had her leaning forward, almost reaching toward the prize.

Mace chuckled. "I suppose we'll have to find out what's down there, or Lila will never forgive us."

He teased the rogue, but they would have had to take on this colony anyway. This was a dungeon, after all. When it came to dungeon mobs, if you couldn't make friends with it, you had to kill it in order to clear the dungeon.

Mace looked at Shari, who was still shaking her head. "We have to. You should summon the pig. He might as well get some xp for this too. Just keep him behind us."

Shari considered it for a moment, then agreed. She summoned Snuffles, who immediately began to sniff around. When he looked over the edge of their perch and saw the ants, his tail went down and he backed away slowly. Brahm nodded his head. "Wise pig."

Mace took a moment to think, then said, "Okay, we can't go down there and fight them, they'd surround and overwhelm us in seconds. We need to use our height advantage. Kill as many of them as we can down there in our first strike, then defend this ledge as they climb up at us. They'll be able to climb the walls on either side of us too."

Layne spoke up. "I can slow them down and give you more time to kill them before they reach us."

Brahm nodded and just stepped toward the edge, axe in hand. He took a couple of experimental swings of the massive weapon, sweeping it across the ledge at his feet. Lila likewise drew her weapons and moved to one side of the ledge near the wall. Shari drew her bow.

Mace focused on the mass of creatures below. Each ant was roughly the size of a dog. They were packed so closely together, he doubted they'd be able to pull just a few and burn them down in small groups. They needed a devastating strike that would kill hundreds of them at once.

They were called fire ants. In the real world, that just meant their bites burned like fire. But if he knew anything about game mechanics and the twisted sense of humor of the devs, these creatures would either be able to spit fire or be immune to fire damage.

He could use ice to freeze them. Water and ice were generally more effective against fire-based mobs.

Looking down at the wall below them, he had an idea. Uttering the trigger word, "Frigus," he began to coat the wall below the ledge in a layer of ice. He spread it slowly, working out from the center and making sure not to let the ice spread down too close to the ants.

When he was done, he looked at Shari. "You said you can add wind magic to your arrows, right?"

Shari nodded, catching on to what he was thinking. "If I wait 'til they're close to the top, they might crush some others when they fall."

Her statement triggered another idea.

"Can you use earth magic with your arrows, too? Like, could you use one to soften rock?" His voice grew excited.

Shari looked thoughtful. "I've never tried that. But based on what the Commander told me, maybe?"

She turned and faced back down the tunnel. Pulling an arrow from the quiver at her waist, she nocked it and drew back on the bowstring. After a moment of concentration, she loosed it at the wall.

The arrow struck with a thud and stuck several inches into the stone. Mace walked over and poked at the stone surrounding it. It seemed as hard as ever. "You got penetration, but it didn't soften the stone." He reported.

"Hmmm... maybe if I worked in some water?"

Shari nocked another arrow. This time, she concentrated a bit longer. When she released the arrow, it shot past Mace's face and struck the wall near the first. This time, though, it penetrated nearly to the fletching. Mace poked at the wall and found the rock immediately around the arrow was spongy.

"Yes! Okay, here's what we're going to do."

He quickly outlined his plan to the group. Heads nodded all around and Shari laughed. "Only a geek like you would use science to beat a dungeon."

"You think my brain is sexy." He stuck his tongue out at her. She just rolled her eyes and turned away, raising her bow.

Mace got back to business. "What's your max range with that bow? Can you hit the ones on the far side of the cavern?" Shari smirked at him and took aim. A moment later her arrow streaked across the air and struck the farthest available target. Mace nodded his head. Focusing his magic, he uttered a trigger word he hadn't used often. "Magmus!" pushing his hands toward the far end of the cavern, he channeled the magic gently. The stalactite that he focus on began to heat up. After a moment, it was beginning to glow with a faint reddish hue. Shari drew her bow again as Mace said, "Aim for the base, as high as you can."

Shari didn't acknowledge him, focusing on her arrow. After a moment, it took on a slight frosty sheen. She fired the arrow and it sunk deep into the base the of the stalactite Mace had been heating.

The ice spell on the arrow met Mace's heated stone and a blast of steam erupted around the arrow. There was a loud *crack*, and several hundred pounds of stone fell the fifty or so feet to the cavern floor.

Only a few dozen of the ants were crushed by the initial impact, but the stone shattered, sending sharp bits of shrapnel in a radius of several feet around the impact site. In all, maybe a hundred of the creatures were killed.

Shari, Mion, Lila, and Snuffles all leveled up. The ants were of a similar level to them, and a hundred at once gave them a solid xp boost. Mace and the others, being higher level, got nothing.

The group watched as the ants went into a frenzy. The deaths of so many of their number had them seeking an enemy. They swarmed over the bits of rock scattered around the impact zone. But no connection was made to the adventurers. Mace grinned. "Okay! Next! We'll keep dropping them until they're all dead or they realize it's us."

Mace heated the next stalactite, this one only a few feet from the last. When it began to glow, Shari shot it, just as before. This time, when the stone struck, the death toll was higher. The ants were still swarming around the other impact zone, so the second missile's impact caught many more of them than the first. A keening sound went up from the entire colony as they began to search more frantically for their attackers.

Mace quickly started on the next one, then the next, and the next. He and Shari dropped tons of stone on the frantic mobs, moving from the far side of the cavern toward themselves with each one. In a panic now, the ants began to climb the walls all around the cavern. Larger, darker versions emerged from a hole near the center of the floor and spread out. Brahm pointed them out "Those must be soldiers. All these others are workers."

Shari nodded. "Which means the queen is down in that hole. How many more of these things are down there?"

Mace heated the next one, purposely choosing one off to the far-left side. "Let's hope not too many more. If the queen comes out, we'll attack her directly."

Shari shot the stone and it collapsed, falling directly onto the corpse of the mole creature. The hundreds of ants still swarming around the thing were either crushed or killed by the combined stone-and-bone shrapnel that erupted from the epicenter. Injured ants from each of the drop zones were being dragged by their fellow workers toward the hole as soldier ants continued to pour forth. There were at least a hundred of the bigger ants now.

About that time, an ant on the wall to their right climbed higher than their ledge and spotted them. Its antennae began to wobble frantically as Lila threw a dagger at it and Layne shot it with an arrow, knocking it off the wall to fall to its death.

But it was too late. The others had been alerted. As one, every ant in sight turned and rushed toward their ledge. Mace quickly heated a large stalactite just beyond where they stood as Shari began to fire arrows downward at the climbing ants. Layne fired a dozen arrows in rapid succession, then switched to her lute. The ants climbing toward them slowed visibly.

Mace shouted, "Shari, now!" and she targeted the heated stalactite. Her first arrow didn't quite dislodge it, as this one was larger than the others. She took her time and concentrated, then fired a second arrow. The stone split in two lengthwise, then both sides separated from the ceiling, one slightly before the other.

The results were spectacular. Instead of one wave of impact shrapnel, there were two. Hundreds more of the creatures, including a group of the soldiers that were just about to begin the climb, were shredded.

Mace began casting fireballs down toward the base of their little cliff, burning away living and dead ants alike. Shari resumed firing arrows at those who managed to climb the vertical ice face Mace had put down.

More and more ants poured out of the hole. Mostly soldiers, now. The workers were still dragging the wounded ants toward the hole and down. Mace heated another stalactite, this one about halfway between the hole and their ledge. When Shari dropped it, it crushed and shredded a contingent of the larger soldier ants.

But her change of targets meant that a few of the climbers reached the top. Brahm kicked the first one in the head as it appeared, sending it flying. Lila put away her daggers and pulled out a spear. She began to stab and slice at the ants that reached her section of the ledge.

She and Brahm ran back and forth along the two sides, doing their best to keep the attackers at bay, but in less than a minute they were getting overwhelmed. Mace shot a few fireballs in between his allies to clear spaces where ants were getting through. They were holding their own, but it was a losing strategy. There were still at least a thousand of the creatures swarming toward them.

Layne's music stopped abruptly and she cursed loudly from behind them. They all turned to see her laying on the ground with an ant atop her, using her lute to keep its pincers from her face. Shari instantly blasted its head off with an arrow but three more dropped from the wall above.

Mace dashed forward as Shari shot another one. Daggers in hand, he leapt onto one ant and slammed his right-hand dagger into a joint just behind its head. The dagger barely had time to drink before the joint popped and the head dropped to the floor. He kicked at the last remaining ant, sending it flying over the edge. Looking up, he blasted several more off the wall with fire.

"Infier!"

Brahm roared a challenge at the ants that were now swarming him. Great swings of his axe swept three or four of the mobs off the ledge at a time, causing them to fall and knock a few others loose before they dropped thirty feet to the floor. But several had latched onto his legs and torso, and were pumping some type of venom into him.

Layne, now back on her feet and playing again, slowed them down. Mion was casting heals on Brahm, and Shari joined her. Mace was quickly draining his mana chain casting fireballs in every direction, trying to clear the ledge. Lila was doing her best, sweeping her spear back and forth and holding a small section near the wall.

Still, the ants kept coming. Those reaching the top now were soldiers more often than workers.

Mutated Fire Ant Soldier.
Level 29
Health 8,000/8,000

Bigger, and with twice the health, these ants took more hits to kill. And the time spent killing them allowed even more ants to gain the ledge and attack. Brahm was starting to slow, his movements less coordinated. Whatever the ants had pumped into him was taking effect. He roared in pain and stumbled back a few steps from the edge. More soldiers immediately began to pop up, rushing toward him.

The dagger in Mace's right hand pulsed, and his vision blurred slightly. His pulse accelerated and a there was a rushing sound in his ears. He felt anger like he'd never experienced before. And a need to kill.

Almost without conscious thought Mace's body raced between Brahm and the oncoming ants. Without any hand movement or trigger word, a blast of arctic air burst forth from him. The ants were slowed, then stopped completely. In a matter of seconds, they were frozen solid. His body went into a spin, a hand striking one ant, a foot hitting the next, each ant shattering upon impact.

When the ledge was clear, he turned to Brahm, who still had four ants clamped onto him. Mace grabbed one in each hand, jerking them from his friend's body. The force was such that the mandibles, still stuck in Brahm's flesh, ripped from the insects' heads as they were flung toward the edge, knocking down the next wave just coming over the top. Mace fed his dagger with the souls of the two remaining ants, and Brahm fell to one knee as heals washed over him. The minotaur began to pull the detached mandibles from his body.

The immediate threat eliminated, Mace found himself staggering. His head cleared, and his pulse began to slow. The others were staring at him, eyes wide. Even Brahm seemed impressed.

"What the hell was that?" Shari asked. Mace just shook his head.

"I think the dagger gave me some kind of… buff? Or berserker mode? Not sure," he said, before turning to blast more incoming ants with fireballs. He quickly checked his mana bar, concerned that he was running on empty. But both his health and mana bars were at 100%. He grinned at his dagger, then resumed throwing fire.

Mion let out a tiny roar and soared out past the ledge. Turning toward the wall of ants climbing up the ice, she opened her mouth and shot a bolt of lightning! The bolt struck an ant near the top of the climb, paralyzing it and roasting it at the same time.

The charge from the bolt transferred through the husk into the ice. Water being a conductor, the shock spread, and every ant on the wall was stunned. Most fell, smashing into their brethren below, the heavier soldier ants doing significant crush damage.

Mace could have hugged the little dragon right then. "Mion! You're a genius!" he shouted.

He turned to Shari, who was staring at Mion, mouth open wide in surprise. By the blank look in her eyes, she was talking telepathically to her little dragon. Mace shouted at her. "Shari! Wake up! We've got a way to get them all. We're going to flood the cavern."

He turned and began to heat a stalactite that hung over the pond across the cavern. Shari drew an arrow and fired when the stone was hot enough. The large wedge dropped silently into the water, causing a small tidal wave to wash up out of the pond and across the floor. The water pushed by the falling stone also surged into the stream fed by the pond, causing it to overflow and sending water out over both banks.

Seeing this, Mace looked to the other end of the stream where it passed out of the cavern.

"Frigus!"

He cast ice into the water, freezing it almost instantly and blocking the exit. The water started backfilling, overflowing the streambed and spreading across the cavern floor.

"Mion! Shari! Use your lightning!"

Both ladies heeded his call. Shari drew arrow after arrow, focusing for a moment on each as she cast elemental magic into the shaft before firing. She didn't have to worry about targets. The ants were so thick on the ground that any one of them would do. With each arrow strike, a wide patch of ants would seize up, stunned as their internal organs fried.

Mion made a game of it. She swooped down, picking a target and firing a tiny bolt of lightning at it. Her strikes were several times more effective than Shari's, being a creature of magic. After firing, she would swoop back up into the air and let out a tiny roar of victory. As Mace watched, she faltered slightly as a golden glow washed over her and she leveled up.

Within a short time, maybe two minutes, there were only a hundred or so living ants on the floor below. A few more still tried to climb the wall, but Brahm and Lila were waiting for them. They all watched as the spreading water began to wash ant bodies down into the hole from which the soldiers had emerged.

Mace shook his head. Turning to the others, he said, "We're going to have to go down there and get the queen."

Brahm shook his head as a keening noise rang out, echoing off the walls. "No, I don't believe we will." he nodded toward the hole. Mace spun around to find the largest ant they'd seen so far. It was easily eight feet long and stood four feet high at the shoulder.

Mutated Fire Ant Queen
Level 50
Health 18,000/18,000

"Well, that's convenient," Mace mumbled as he inspected the queen. She was at least a mini boss, if not the main dungeon boss.

"Okay guys, light her up. And be careful, she probably has some special abilities!"

He uttered a trigger word "Magmus!" and started trying to heat up the queen's body just as he had the stalactites. But the spell had no effect, except to anger the insect further.

Shari began to pepper the queen with arrows. Layne swapped her lute for her bow and did the same. Mace switched to ice, assuming the queen would not be immune to both fire and ice.

He was wrong. A thin film of ice formed along the queen's carapace, but she flexed her body and a reddish glow surrounded her. The ice melted away almost instantly.

"Lightning! Lightning killed the others." Mace called out to Shari. She nodded and a moment later a lightning arrow streaked toward the queen. It sank deeply into the rear segment of her body, and arcs of lightning spread through her. The stun effect only lasted two seconds, but the hit had done some damage.

Mutated Fire Ant Queen
Level 50

Health 15,400/18,000

Lila cried out as one of the ants managed to complete the climb and latch onto her leg while she was distracted by the show. She stabbed a dagger at the thing's head, but the blade just skittered across the tough chitin. The ant began to walk backward, dragging the halfling with it. Its instinct was to pull its prey back toward the nest where its siblings could help kill and consume her.

With a roar, Brahm leapt the ten feet or so between him and Lila. His axe slammed down onto the ant's neck, severing the head. The legs continued to push backward, sending the rest of the body over the edge.

Shari paused firing at the queen long enough to cast Life of the Forest on Lila as Brahm pulled the pincers apart and tossed the head away.

Mace's dagger made its presence known again. He felt a hunger for blood and heard a whispered, *Feeeeeed!* in his mind.

At the same time, he felt Minx's tail tighten around his neck. Her thoughts came to him clearly. *"Scary knife. Makes Mace stupid!"* Mace turned and grinned toward his invisible pet. He couldn't disagree. It was demanding that he kill the queen himself, feeding her soul to the dagger. And he found that he didn't mind.

"Minx, go watch over Shari. I'll be back in a few minutes," he said to her. A moment later, he felt her weight leave his shoulder as Shari looked at him.

"You're about to do something stupid, aren't you?" she grinned as she said it. Shari hadn't done many dungeons as a player before the world ended. She was having the time of her life!

"Yep! Turn your recorder on. Later we can snuggle while you admire my bravery and skill." He returned her grin. A moment later, he dashed across the ledge and disappeared over the edge.

The thirty-foot fall was no problem for a drow of his skill. Especially since there was an ant partway up the wall that he could use to break that fall. He hit the creature's head, bending his knees to absorb the impact and knocking the insect loose from the wall.

He rode it down, jabbing his dagger into its face as they fell the final ten feet or so. The thing's energy rushed through the dagger and up his arm. He felt stronger and faster with the rush.

Leaping from the emptied husk, he dashed across the cavern floor toward the queen. The place was blanketed in ant corpses, but he simply leapt onto or over them, propelling himself toward the boss.

As he got close, he saw another of Shari's arrows strike the queen. Pausing at a safe distance, he wasn't sure if her lightning effect would shock him, too. So he took advantage of the brief stun the arrow inflicted on the queen. He cast a concentrated wind blade at the queen. The same one he'd used on the Cthulhu Spawn.

"Ventus!"

The stunned queen's front legs snapped, and the two remaining legs on her left side gave out. She stumbled and fell onto her side as Mace dashed forward. With a leap, he was atop her thorax. Just as he was about to plunge the enchanted dagger into her body, his head fuzzed a bit and he heard a clear thought.

"*Whyyyy?*"

The queen had gone still beneath him. Her struggling legs had stopped moving as she lay on her back with her multiple eyes focused on Mace. The dagger pulsed in his hand, demanding to be fed. But Mace just tightened his grip and spoke to the queen.

"Did you just speak to me?" he asked aloud.

"*You killed my children. Destroyed my home. Why?*"

Mace was confused. This was a dungeon boss. Her 'children' were mobs. Dungeon mobs were almost always hostile. He shook his head.

"We came here to clear this dungeon. We assumed you and your children were hostile."

The queen's mandibles clacked together in what Mace took to be anger.

"*We only kill for food. Or to defend ourselves. We grow. It hurts. Need more and more food. Now all dead.*" The sorrow in her tone calmed the bloodlust Mace had been feeling.

Looking up, he saw Shari about to launch another arrow. He held up a hand, stopping her.

"We did not know. If I leave you in peace, will you promise not to harm me or my people?"

The queen's mandibles clicked again. "*Too late. My children dead. I am... damaged.*" Mace looked at her body, now pierced by several arrows, burned and broken. "*I cannot make more children. Kill me.*"

"Shit." Mace felt badly for the ant queen. She was clearly an intelligent NPC. "Maybe we can heal you?" he asked hopefully.

"*Heal?*" The concept was clearly foreign to her. He took out a health potion and held it up.

"Drink this. It might help." He poured the potion into her mouth, wary of the mandibles in case she decided to attack.

After a moment, the burn marks on her body began to fade. Mace hopped off her body and waited as her broken legs healed and she righted herself.

"Feels… strange. This is heal?" she asked.   Mace nodded. *"Thank you, drow."*

She looked around at the corpses of her colony and chittered to herself.

Mace bowed his head slightly. She was a queen, after all. "I am sorry about your children. We thought you were enemies."

He motioned to his friends, whom he noticed were now climbing down a rope held by Brahm.   He watched to make sure the ladies made it down safely. Then Brahm lifted Snuffles, tucked him under one arm and stepped over the edge.

The two of them disappeared into the pile of ant bodies at the bottom. A moment later Snuffles came flying up out of the pile, followed by the minotaur as he pulled himself free.

The queen looked at her now-flooded home. Mace sheepishly dismissed the ice that was blocking the stream and causing the flood.

After a few moments, the water level in the hole stopped rising. The queen watched for a while until the water level began to recede slowly.

"I will return to my home when it is safe. Maybe some of my eggs will survive."

And with that, she seemed to forget about Mace. He shuddered as she stepped to the closest worker ant corpse and bit into its rear segment. The chitin broke apart under the strength of her mandibles, revealing the meat underneath. Which she promptly began shoving into her mouth. The potion hadn't been strong enough to heal her completely. Mace watched her health bar increase as she ate.

Shari and the others arrived, all but Brahm making faces at the queen's indelicate eating habits. Shari asked, "What's the deal?"

Mace whispered. "They weren't hostile. We attacked neutral NPCs. She's intelligent, and asked me why we killed her children." To which all of them looked confused, then ashamed.

Lila was the first to speak, apparently the least bothered by their actions. "Does this mean we don't get the loot?" she looked longingly toward the waterfall.

Mace turned to find the queen biting into a second corpse. He shook his head. "She's in no position to stop you. Go ahead. And Shari, if you think there might be any good crafting ingredients, we can loot the others…"

Shari stepped behind Brahm so that the queen couldn't see her and bent to loot the closest soldier ant.

"Chitin that might be good for armor. Some copper. And roasted ant meat. The meat gives a Strength buff."

"Okay, go ahead and loot" Mace saw Lila was already halfway to the pond and shook his head.

As the queen consumed her children's corpses to restore herself and the water slowly drained from her nest, they looted several hundred of the ant corpses. The workers rarely gave anything but meat, while the soldiers dropped similar items to the first. Every fiftieth or so soldier also dropped an uncommon or rare quality item, mostly weapons.

They worked their way toward the pond as they looted, almost as curious as Lila about what was under the water. When they reached the edge, whatever had been glittering at the bottom was already gone and Lila was walking up out of the water.

Mace chuckled. "That didn't take long. What did you find?"

The halfling grinned and hopped up and down. She quickly emptied the items out of her bag onto the ground. As she did so, she cried out in pain and curled into a fetal position on the floor.

The others rushed to kneel beside her, looking for injuries. Mace checked her status on his UI. She wasn't losing health, and there was no poison or bleed debuff.

The pain seemed to fade after half a minute or so and the halfling straightened out, breathing hard.

"What the hell?" she gasped. "That hurt! Was one of those items cursed?"

Mace turned to the pile of loot. There was a complete set of armor laying there in pieces, along with a longsword. All of them glowed in the light of the globe above them. There was also a small chest that looked to be made of mithril, with two locked latches holding it shut.

Next to it sat a bag with contents unknown. Mace tried to use his Identify skill on the armor, but other than the name he only got back question marks.

Armor of the Peacemaker
Quality: ??

He got even less for the sword, not even being able to see the name. Lila, now back on her feet, stepped forward to take up the bag and open it. Mace noticed she was walking funny. "You okay?"

She poured some of the contents of the bag into her hand. "Emeralds. Rubies. Of *course* I'm okay. Just, my boots are a little tight. Must have shrunk in the water."

She grinned at him, holding out her hand to show him the gems. When she did, he noticed that her sleeve was bunched up on her forearm. Looking down, he saw that her leather pants now barely reached the tops of her boots. And her shirt looked uncomfortably tight, clinging to bits of her that he tried not to notice.

Shari seemed to have noticed as well. "Lila, sweetie. When you level up, do you normally grow taller?"

Lila looked at her, confused.

"Was that a short joke? I'm a full-grown halfling!" she protested. Her size was a sensitive issue with her.

Shari held up her hands. "No, no! No joke. It's just... you seem to have outgrown your clothes."

She motioned for Lila to look at herself. The little halfling looked down, then stretched out her arm and examined it.

"I'm... I'm taller!" Her voice sounded panicked. "Why am I taller?"

Her eyes went vacant as she was clearly pulling up her character stats. "My... my Agility has increased. And my Strength," she mumbled.

Layne was looking at the pile of loot suspiciously now. She pulled out her lute and began a soft melody, accompanied by almost whispered words. A moment later, she shook her head. "There are no curses on any of these items."

Shari was walking toward the pond. Looking down at the water, she asked, "Lila, did you swallow any of this water?"

The rogue shrugged. "I don't know. Maybe? It took me a while to swim to the bottom and gather up all this stuff."

Shari looked back at the group.

"The giant mole. The giant ants. I think this water is what mutated them." she said, making Lila gasp, her eyes widening in fear. She began to cough and frantically wipe at her still wet clothes and skin.

"Get it off me! I don't want to be a mutant!" she cried. She stuck a finger down her throat, attempting to clear her stomach of the water. Layne rushed over and hugged her, using soothing words to calm her panic.

"Hush, little one. You are no mutant. Mutated in this case just means altered. And you have been altered. But no harm has come to you as far as I can see. You're just a few inches taller, stronger, and faster." She patted Lila's head as she continued to hold her tight. After a moment, Lila stopped struggling. She voiced a question, but the sound was muffled as her head was buried in Layne's chest. The elf released her.

"Really? And I'm going to stay this way?" She held her arms out and spun around slowly.

She started to ask another question but was interrupted by a shout from Brahm. The whole group turned to see him drop his axe and leap out into the pond, landing with a big splash and creating a wave nearly as large as the one made by the stalactite.

A moment later he stood, scooping some of the water into his hands and drinking deeply. Seeing the others watching him, he said, "What? Increased size and strength? Who would not wish this?"

He walked out of the pond and stood among his friends, waiting. Sure enough, a moment later he grunted in pain and bent over double. His legs weakened and he went down on one knee, using a hand on the ground to balance himself. He growled through the pain, his eyes watering and the color draining from face.

When the pain faded, he stood unsteadily and began to examine himself. His armor was nearly bursting trying to contain his body.

He shifted a bit, trying to get comfortable, then he too zoned out to inspect his character sheet. "Strength increase of 10% Stamina too."

He flexed his arms and the leather vest that he used as padding for his armor ripped apart at the seams.

"This water is most beneficial. Let us see if it has limits." He turned and dove back into the water.

No longer able to resist, Snuffles charged into the pond after him, squealing happily. Mion took to the air and circled the water as Snuffles splashed around. With a dragony grin on her snout, she shot a tiny lightning bolt at the pig, with a small fraction of the normal power behind it. The bolt struck Snuffles in the rear and he leapt out of the water, squealing. He gave Mion a dirty look as he moved to hide behind Shari.

The dragon looked remorseless as she landed on Brahm's shoulder and licked some of the moisture from his face, surprising him. Realizing what she'd just done, he held out both his hands.

"Come, little one, sit here until the pain subsides." Mion hopped down into his cupped hands and chirped happily at him. A moment later the pain struck, and she whimpered as she curled up in a ball.

The giant minotaur hugged her to his chest gently, speaking softly to her as she suffered. When it was all through and she was able to stand again, he stepped toward Shari and placed the little dragon gently on her shoulder. Mion wrapped her tail around Shari's neck and closed her eyes.

As Mion had gone through her transformation, so too had Snuffles. Only he was much louder about it. When the pain struck, he squealed and collapsed on his side. Rolling on to his back with his legs flailing, he grunted in pain and squealed in misery.

Shari tried to comfort him, rubbing his belly and scratching his head, but took a hoof to the face as he thrashed about. She tried casting Life of the Forest at him but it had no effect. And though Snuffles was a good bit taller when it was over, with freshly sprouted tusks about two inches long, Mion didn't look to have increased in size at all.

Mace didn't think the middle of a dungeon was the best place to investigate. Instead he said, "Shari, do you want to take some of that water with us? If it has the properties it seems to, it would be worth quite a bit. And it could make all of our allies stronger."

Shari nodded. She moved to the pond and removed several flasks, which she began to fill with the clear water.

"Bah!" Brahm produced a minotaur-sized keg from his bag. He took a long drink, then offered some to the others. "Ale," was all he said.

When the others declined, he took another drink, then poured the rest into the stream. When the keg was empty, he submerged it in the pond, filling the twenty-gallon container with the enchanted water.

Mace went to the edge and dipped his hands into the water, taking a drink himself. No way as a player he'd pass up such a huge - and seemingly permanent - buff. Shari followed his lead and gulped down one of her vials before refilling it. Layne took one for herself and drank as well.

The three of them quickly sat, anticipating the transformation to come. It didn't disappoint. Shari whimpered and curled up, much as Lila had. Mace ground his teeth and growled through the pain, while Layne seemed to just accept it with a stoic expression. Though Mace noticed that her skin grew quite pale.

When it was over, Mace felt Minx return to his shoulder and wrap her tail around his neck. She became visible, looking at him with her oversized eyes. He asked, "You want some too, little Minxy?" She shook her head and leaned back from him as if he were crazy. He chuckled "It's okay, you're perfect just as you are. Can't have you getting too big to ride my shoulder, can we?"

She purred at the compliment, settling in and closing her eyes. He took a look at his stat sheet to see what he'd gained.

Character Name: Mace	Class: Sorcerer		Level: 41	
Race: Drow	Spec: Darkblade		Exp: 7350/12,000	
Health: 5500/550000	Mana: 1200/1200		Attribute Pts Avail: 2	
Stamina: 16	Wisdom: 22	Charisma: 11	Life Regen: 20/sec	
Strength: 16	Intellect: 24	Dexterity: 11	Mana Regen: 5/sec	
Agility: 13	Luck: 11	Armor: 85	Skill Pts Avail: 0	

He'd picked up a couple points each in Strength and Agility and his Health Regen had increased. Plus, he felt both taller and stronger. A quick check of his armor didn't show a difference, but that made sense. Player armor adjusted automatically to fit. Mace bagged all the loot in his new ring and they made one last search of the cavern.

Lila found an exit, a small crevice in the wall near the waterfall. As they didn't have a good way to climb back up to their ledge, Mace told Lila to lead the way.

Brahm had to force himself sideways through the opening and Snuffles was now too wide to get through without help, but once they were past the first couple feet of stone the crevice opened up and was maybe six feet wide.

Mace called down his light globe and set it ahead of them. Almost immediately, the crevice came to an end at a blank wall. There was no way forward, so Mace and Lila began to search the walls for other openings or hidden doors. Finding none, Layne suggested they climb.

Chapter 6

Arrow to the Knee

Shari looked at the walls on either side of them. They were nearly smooth, with just a few jagged cracks here and there. Shifting her gaze to Layne, she said "I don't think I can climb that."

Layne just smiled. "If you had completed your ranger training at the city, this would be easy for you." She led them back to where they had entered the crevice. Right before it reached its narrowest point, she turned and faced them. Shifting to a wide-footed stance, she pressed her hands out against the walls on either side.

Supporting her weight with her hands, she lifted both feet, placing them against the wall. When they were secured, she pushed with her legs and straightened her body. Once more, she used her hands to press against the walls and support her weight as she lifted her legs. In this manner, she spidered her way up the crevice.

It was slow, and the elf was beginning to tire when she reached an opening about three stories up. Skillfully pushing off on the opposite wall, she rolled herself into the opening. A moment later, a rope came tumbling down.

Brahm took hold of the rope first. "There may be enemies above," was all he said before using his newfound strength to pull himself upward. He barely used his feet as he made the climb.

When he reached the top, he called down, "Lila, tie the rope around yourself, I'll lift you."

The halfling did as instructed, and when she called out that she was ready she was practically launched upward. She giggled as the minotaur hauled the rope hand over hand with ease.

Shari went up next the same way, followed by Snuffles. Mace declined the rope and scampered up the same way Layne had.

The opening turned out to be a hole in the wall of a tunnel that extended off to their left and right. Mace activated his stealth and went left first.

He'd only been walking about a minute when he spotted the wall of ice he'd put up earlier. So, this was the right-hand tunnel they hadn't explored yet. He returned to the others to let them know what he'd found before they all continued down the tunnel. Mace had left the light globe behind, but he called up a new one and sent it forward. As they made their way along the corridor it began to slope downward. Eventually it ended in a medium-sized room, maybe fifteen yards wide and about the same length. There were three doors in the walls opposite, left, and right of them. In the center of the room was a wide stone column that stretched from floor to ceiling. It looked as if the room had actually been carved around the column itself.

Getting closer, the party could see engravings carved into the stone. The artistic quality was stunning. There were mostly images of dwarves going about daily tasks. Smithing, brewing, mining and the like. Some of the images depicted battles, and the carvings circled all the way around the column, telling a tale as they progressed around.

The greatest of them, taking up the entire top third of the column all the way around, was a story about a dragon attacking a dwarven citadel built into a solitary mountain that overlooked a wide lake. There were scenes of fire and death as the dwarves tried in vain to defend their home and were slaughtered or driven out. While the locals in the group stared in wonder at the story, Mace and Shari grinned at each other. This was a tale known to every gamer and lover of fantasy since the mid-twentieth century.

As the others continued to admire the carvings, Mace moved toward the left-hand door. He quickly checked for traps, and found none. With a discreet whisper, he got the attention of the others, and they watched as he opened the door partway and peered through. When nothing jumped to attack him, he opened it the rest of the way and sent the light globe in.

It was a room with several short beds made of stone in rows along opposite walls. At the foot of each bed was a stone locker. There were empty weapon racks at both ends of the room and a small screened area in the back. The hole in the floor there suggested that it was the privy.

Finding no monsters, the group quickly checked the lockers for any interesting loot. They were mostly empty, though some contained coins or weapons made of dwarven steel. Lila pulled a mithril dagger from one, hugging it like it was a long-lost sibling. In her tiny hands it looked more like a short sword, but she fastened the sheath to her belt at the small of her back and practiced drawing it a few times. If it had glowed, Mace would have insisted she name it 'Sting.'

Moving on, they returned to the hub chamber and Mace checked the next door. This one led to a stairwell leading down. Brahm spoke before Mace had the chance.

"Let us check the final door before we proceed to the lower level."

This door was not only trapped, but locked. The trap was a combination of magical and mundane. The magic portion was an alarm that would sound if the door was opened, while the mundane physical trap was set to expel a cloud of poison gas.

Mace disabled first the gas, then the alarm. After checking carefully for more traps, he opened the door.

It opened into a nightmare. There were pieces of bodies everywhere. Some on shelves in jars, some on hooks hanging from the ceiling. Animals and sentient beings alike. There was the head of a dwarf sitting on a workbench, its eyes open and moving.

When it spotted the intruders, it let out a long moaning cry. This triggered movement in nearly every other limb in the room. Arms twitched. A severed hand stuck on spike began to thrash, trying to free itself. Even the solitary organs in the jars began to throb in their liquid prisons.

"Necromancy." Mace spit on the floor. "This is a necromancer's workshop. Let's burn it to the ground."

Brahm agreed whole-heartedly. He stepped forward and shoved a bookcase full of squirming body parts. The case tipped over into another, and both fell with a crash of heavy wood and breaking glass. Immediately, some of the freed organs began to hop or slither toward the group.

Mace put his hands out. "Infier!" and blasted the area with fire. Whatever chemical was used to store the items in the jars was apparently flammable, and extremely so. The air was sucked from the room and then blasted outward as a giant fireball engulfed them all.

All but Brahm were thrown back out the doorway. The poor minotaur was heavy enough that he remained and took severe burn damage. He stumbled blindly out the doorway as Shari called out to him, then collapsed. She, Mion and Layne all began to heal him nonstop.

The burn damage had caused bleeding, and his health bar fluctuated up and down. Mace took out a health potion and poured it over the minotaur's exposed skin. He was burned everywhere that wasn't covered in armor.

After half a minute, the heals had repaired most of the damage. Brahm sat up and shook his head. "That was… unpleasant."

Shari snorted. Lila rolled her eyes, then grinned at the big tank. "Did you know fried minotaur smells just like roast pork?" He took a half-hearted swing at her as she danced away giggling.

When the acrid smoke cleared, they looked back into the room. Nothing organic had survived the fire. The body parts were all burned to a crisp, while the wooden shelves and workstations were charred but still whole.

The group began to poke around, looking for hidden doors or secret caches of loot. Lila found a hidden compartment behind the door, and it opened to reveal a stash of vials containing potions none of them could identify. Shari put them in her bag, intending to investigate them later.

Finding nothing further, they exited the room and closed the door behind them. It was time to go downstairs. Mace took the lead to look for traps but didn't bother to use stealth. After that explosion in the lab, he was sure anything down here was aware of their presence.

He found a pressure plate about halfway down the stairway. Stepping carefully past it to the next stair, he used his normal dagger to lift the plate and peer underneath. The trigger was simple: Weight presses down on the plate, pushing down on springs at the four corners. When it lowered, a pin that was hooked to one of the springs was released. When the weight was lifted off the plate, that pin would rise back up, pulling a thin metal wire along with it. That wire led to an explosive charge surrounded by vials of poison, and the explosion would disperse the poison in a gaseous form, killing not only the one who triggered the trap, but anyone nearby as well.

Mace disabled the trap, removing both the explosives, which he kept, and the poison vials, which he gave to Shari. All except one, which Lila requested.

"I can poison my blades," was all she said.

Mace then removed the trap mechanism and pressure plate and stored them in his bag as well. One never knew when a trap might be handy to have. And while he had the skill to detect, arm, and disarm them, he did not have the engineering skill that would allow him to create them himself. He was limited to simple traps that anyone could make, like a hidden loop of rope with a trigger attached to a tree branch. Or a simple sapling rabbit trap.

The group continued down to the bottom. The landing faced a single doorway, which in turn opened into a long room filled with undead. There was one door at the opposite end approximately a hundred yards away and carved stone columns every ten yards or so along each side of the room near the walls. Each column sported a brazier burning with a sickly green flame.

Nearest the door were skeletal soldiers holding swords and shields, their equipment rusted but serviceable. There were a couple dozen of them standing in groups of three and four.

> *Skeletal Defender*
> *Level 35*
> *Health 9,000/9,000*

About twenty feet beyond the soldiers, gathered in groups to either side were about the same number of archers. These were fresher corpses, still having some muscle and flesh attached to their bones here and there. The occasional internal organ could be seen decaying inside yellowed rib cages. As they watched, one of the archers shuffled into another and bits of flesh fell from both to splat wetly onto the floor.

Beyond the archers, there were more full-figured undead. Humanoids of several races. Some carried weapons, others with just sharp teeth and exposed bone fingers. There were at least a hundred of these zombies shuffling around in the center of the room, seemingly at random.

Beyond them were six armored undead guarding the exit. They didn't look like zombies. Their flesh held the greyish hue of the dead, but there was no rotting or bits missing. They moved more quickly than their decaying cousins, and their weapons and armor were well maintained.

> *Undead Defender*
> *Level 45*
> *Health 13,000/13,000*

Mace looked at Shari. "We didn't talk about this. How much do you know about dungeon mechanics?"

She shrugged. "We didn't run any dungeons. Sheila wasn't big on fighting or killing. I mean, I've run a few when I was a kid…"

Mace nodded. He wasn't going to voice his thoughts on her being a total newbie. Not if he planned to get any more snuggling in the near future. Instead, he looked to Lila.

She shook her head. "I've been in lots of fights with bandits and such. But this is my first dungeon."

Brahm nodded. "I have cleared two other dungeons with my war band."

Layne just smiled and said, "I've had my share of experience." Mace made a mental note to find a diplomatic way to ask her just how old she was and how much experience she had in the world. She could be a good source of information or strategy.

Mace took a moment to outline a basic plan. "Okay, here's what we'll do. These first soldiers were nice enough to cluster up in threes and fours and move around. So, when a group gets close to us - and far enough away from the other groups not to pull them along - we'll pull them back here. As we finish each group, we'll pull the next closest. Try not to get the attention of the archers until all the soldiers are dead. We don't need to try and defend against ranged attacks while we're fighting melee."

With that said, he sat back and watched the skeletons for a bit. When a group of three stepped away from the others, Mace hit the nearest mob in the face with a fireball. It opened its jaws as if to scream, but no sound emerged. Instead, it raised its sword and charged. The other two were right behind it, swords waving.

Brahm stepped forward, axe at the ready. When the first skeleton was near enough, he kicked forward with his right hoof, shattering several of its ribs and knocking it back into its two companions. As all three went down in a tangle, he leapt forward and brought his axe down in a devastating two-handed overhead chop. The axe removed the head of one skeleton, severing its spine, before crashing through and shattering the ribs of another. Two more rapid axe blows finished the trio.

Shari pumped a fist into the air, hyped by the easy victory. "Yess! We *rock*!" she grinned at her friends.

Mace chuckled. "Easy there, killer. We're just getting started. But yes, this looks like a good system for these first mobs."

With that, he nodded at Brahm and tagged another group that was walking away from the others. This one had four skeletal defenders.

To keep the odds tilted in their favor, Mace called out, "Frigus!" and laid a sheet of ice between their tank and the oncoming mobs. When the bony soldiers reached the ice, they stumbled and slid, arms waving for balance.

Brahm took advantage and slammed his axe into the lead skeleton while its shield was out of position. The massive weapon connected with the monster's hipbone and deflected to one side, shattering its spine. Its upper body fell to the floor, still gripping shield and sword, and began to drag itself forward, still in the fight. A stomp of Brahm's hoof shattered its skull and put it down.

Mace fired fireballs into the group, the spells hitting the targeted mob and doing splash damage to the others. He cast slowly, not wanting to take the aggro from the tank. These mobs were no real challenge to the group, or even to him alone, but he wanted his people to get used to group tactics and develop a synergy when fighting together.

Layne played a tune that slowed and weakened the mobs. Shari focused on healing, though Brahm was only taking minimal damage. Lila crept behind the rearmost skeleton, then leapt up and slammed both daggers into the thing's skull. She hung there for a moment, then with a violent twist of her hips she used her body's momentum and a turn of her wrists to shatter the skull. When her daggers were free of the bone, she dropped back to the floor without a sound and re-entered stealth.

Mace chuckled when he saw that even Snuffles was getting into the act. The small piggy-tank dashed forward, ramming his budding tusks into the skull of a prone skeleton that had slipped on the ice. The impact only took about 2% of the mob's health, but it was the thought that counted. A moment later, Brahm nudged the enthusiastic piggy to one side with his leg and split the skeleton's skull with a casual swing of his axe.

The third group was pulled and put down without issue. Mace let Brahm and Lila do most of the work, and since Shari didn't need to heal much, she cast Nature's Wrath on each of the mobs. The DoT had increased significantly since she learned it back in the elven city. She was pushing level thirty now. They continued on for several minutes, pulling and downing groups one at a time.

When it came time to pull the last group, Shari asked if she could do it. Mace nodded, assuming that she'd cast Nature's Wrath as she had been doing.

He turned to face the mobs, watching for the last group to separate from the archers far enough to be safely pulled. When he gave a thumbs-up, he was surprised to hear the twang of a bow string. The arrow sped past him toward the last three skeletons. It passed right through the ribs of the lead mob, ricocheting slightly off the spinal column and striking the leg of one of the archers. Instantly, a dozen archers were drawing their bows and firing at Shari as the three soldier skeletons ran in her direction.

Mace turned and shouted, "Praesidio!" casting a shield spell on Shari. The arrows bounced harmlessly off the magic protection, but Shari still ducked and cringed, eyes wide with fear. When she realized she wasn't a pincushion, she smiled apologetically at Mace.

He turned, casting rapid-fire spells at the archers while Brahm and Lila took charge of the three soldier mobs. He saw the green glow appear on each of those as Shari contributed her Nature's Wrath DoT per their normal procedure. Mace called out to her. "Don't put your dot on the archers. I need aggro off you, and you need the mana to heal. This is gonna suck for a while."

Just as he finished saying that, he began to cast a shield in front of himself. He had taken aggro on the archers from Shari with his fireballs, but he'd waited too long. As he was about to raise his magic shield, an arrow struck him in the knee. The pain interrupted his cast for a moment, and he couldn't resist the urge to mumble, "I used to be an adventurer like you…"

He managed to activate the Liquid Armor ability imbued in the armor that old Jervis had made for him. As he raised his hand to cast the shield spell, several arrows struck his chest and legs. None penetrated, as the armor dispersed the force in liquid ripples. Still, the impacts were unnerving.

"Praesidio!" he growled out, the pain in his knee bringing tears to his eyes. His magic shield appeared in front of him and disappeared from Shari. He'd never checked the mechanics, but it seemed he could only have one shield active at a time.

Shari snorted behind him. When he turned to look, she grinned at him and said, "I used to be an adventurer like you…"

Mace chuckled despite himself. The classic and beloved reference to an old game had survived decades beyond the death of the game of itself. He was a little surprised Shari knew it, only being a casual gamer.

He yanked the arrow from his knee and a moment later he felt a heal from Shari. He winked at her. "Thanks… huntard."

She immediately looked apologetic again.

Another volley of arrows struck Mace's shield and it flickered slightly. At his level, the shield might hold another two or three volleys before collapsing. He turned his focus back to the archers.

"Ventus!" he called out as he sent a blade of wind at them. It snapped the bowstrings of five of the archers and knocked about half of them down. Those with cut strings raised their bows like clubs and charged at Mace while the others recovered and began to fire at him again.

Mace cast another sheet of ice in front of his group, "Frigus!" and Brahm moved to stand behind it. The three soldier skeletons were toast, and the tank roared a challenge at the oncoming archers.

Mace left them to Brahm and Lila once again. They wouldn't be much of a challenge without shields or real weapons.

He instead focused on the remaining seven archers, hitting them one at a time with fireballs and burning both skeleton and weapon with each hit. As soon as their bowstrings melted away, the archer would wave its bow threateningly and begin to run toward Mace.

Moving to stand next to Brahm, Mace waited as each of them came for him. He dodged clumsy swings of the bows, and kicked them backward, causing them to slide on the ice. The flailing undead archers tripped each other up and knocked each other down as they grabbed onto whatever they could reach in order to pull themselves up. When five of them had managed to get back on their feet and began to advance, he hit them with a gust of wind.

"Ventus!" This wasn't a blade, just a push of air which caused them all to fall back down. Each of them took minor fall damage and had suffered burn damage from the fireballs, but were still at about 50% health.

Brahm laughed as he battered at the initial five archers. They had no skills in blunt weapons, staves, or using their bows as shields. His axe crushed bones and severed limbs as Lila pounced from behind and shattered a skull. In just a moment those five were down as well.

The tank and the rogue moved to focus on Mace's seven archers. Again it wasn't long, less than a minute before they were all permanently dead.

"Take a minute to rest and recharge before we take the other archers," Mace said as he sat with his back to the wall. He'd used more than half his mana pool in that fight. Between the shields, ice, and fire, he'd cast more than a dozen spells in short order.

As he sat there considering how best to deal with the other dozen archers, Brahm cleared his throat. Looking uncomfortable, he quietly said, "Maybe it would be best if our healer did not shoot any more arrows at the skeletons?"

Shari blushed bright red, and Mace laughed so hard he fell on his side and had to gasp for air. Shari kicked him in the leg.

"It's not *that* funny. And I'm *not* a huntard!"

She tried to pout, but the fact that she'd just been trolled by an NPC who totally didn't see the humor in it was too much to resist. She broke down and giggled, then snorted, surprising herself and causing Lila to giggle too. Brahm just looked relieved that Shari hadn't taken it badly.

After a five minute rest, they were all standing and facing the remaining skeletal archers. Mace said "We have to pull them back here. They're too close to the zombies to fight them where they are. I don't want to accidentally pull a hundred zombies."

He tried his best not to glance at Shari as he said it. He really did. But he failed.

Brahm nodded thoughtfully. "Your fire spells worked well, burning the strings so that they became less effective fighters. Even when they hit me with their staves, they did little damage."

Mace could certainly copy the previous fight. It had gone well enough. But he wanted to train his people while they were here, and he had a better idea. "Have you guys ever heard of 'LoS'?" he asked. When they all shook their heads no, he quickly explained it to them. Shari understood it as a simple game mechanic, but he explained it as a quirk of the brainless undead.

A moment later they had their plan and were ready to go. The rest of the group stood back at the entrance door while Mace moved forward far enough to make sure the undead focused on him. He cast a single fireball at one of the archers near the center. As soon as it hit, his companions retreated down the corridor. Mace spoke the trigger. "Praesidio" and raised his shield as he backed toward the door. When he was through the door and into the shadows, he waited until the archers began to move forward to keep him in sight, then activated his stealth ability.

The clacking of bone feet on stone drew near as he pressed himself against the wall. He quickly cast his shield on Brahm, who was fifty feet or so down the corridor. The others gathered right behind the tank to take advantage of both his shield and his bulk to block arrows.

As expected, the archers charged into the corridor, pushing to reacquire their target. Brahm roared a challenge and all twelve pushed into the corridor, attempting to get a clear shot.

Mace waited until they were all past him before stepping out into the tunnel behind them. He held up his hands and called, "Infier!" setting several mobs on fire, then, "Ventus!" sending first one gust of wind and then a second to fan the flames and melt as many of the bowstrings as possible.

In this way, he disarmed all but two of the archers. Those two both fired arrows at him. One struck his abdomen and put yet another hole in his fancy kobold skin armor. The other arrow passed by harmlessly.

He rushed forward and stabbed the nearest of the two in the skull using his enchanted dagger. The weapon slid easily through the bone, but there was no reaction. The dagger didn't speak, there was just a vague sense of disappointment. As he severed the spine of the second, he realized that animated skeletons probably didn't have souls.

After that it was a simple melee cleanup. The weak archers tried to club with unstrung bows while Lila, Brahm and Mace stabbed, smashed, and crushed them into oblivion.

The whole fight took less than three minutes. When the last skeleton went down, Lila immediately began to loot. Because they were in a party, Mace could see what she was receiving. But he didn't pay much attention, trusting her to show him anything of interest.

While Lila looted and Mace studied the next wave of mobs, Shari reached into her bag and pulled out something she'd learned to make in her alchemy studies. It was a healing ointment. Opening the jar, she dabbed a finger in it, then rubbed it on several small cuts and bruises on Brahm's skin. His throat rumbled, as though he were purring with pleasure. "You like the ointment, do you?" She asked.

"I do. It soothes the skin, and smells quite nice." Brahm affirmed.

Shari looked into the jar and smiled. Its name was actually 'Healing Salve' but she preferred to call it an ointment in tribute to her friend Sheila, who hated the word 'ointment'. Snuffles moved close and shoved his nose into the jar to investigate. A moment later, he withdrew it and sneezed, his snout covered in the stuff. Shari said,

"I said "*oint*-ment, not *oink*-ment, you silly pig!"

She and the others laughed as the pig looked cross-eyed at his tingling and scented snout. Mion landed on his head and leaned forward, licking the ointment experimentally. Deciding that it tasted good, she helped the pig clean his snout, snapping at him once when his tongue smacked her face and nearly knocked her off balance.

With the looting done and Snuffles freshly-cleaned from the eyes forward, the group made their way back into the room. They faced the horde of zombies now, which was moving about individually rather than in clusters. But they weren't really separated enough for the party to be sure that a pull would bring just one or two. Still, they had to try.

Mace looked at Shari. "Okay, oh shooty-shooty one, wanna try a pull?"

Shari looked nervous. "I don't want to pull too many. What if I miss again?"

Brahm cleared his throat. "You didn't miss before. You just hit a hollow target. These things may be rotting, but they should stop an arrow."

The others all nodded. Layne put an arm around Shari's shoulders in reassurance.

"You could also try healing one. Nature magic isn't exactly holy magic, but it is more light than neutral. And these are undead. Creatures of the dark," the bard suggested.

Shari brightened up immediately. "I can't miss with my heals. Let's try that first."

She looked at the group to make sure they were prepared. Holding up a hand, she pointed at the nearest zombie and cast Life of the Forest.

The zombie's health plummeted by about 30% and it groaned in pain as it turned toward her and began to stumble forward, its pace slightly faster than a normal walk.

Four other nearby zombies noticed the attack and turned as well. Shari checked her combat log. "The spell did two thousand damage! And another two hundred keeps ticking off every second."

Proud of herself, she puffed out her chest a bit. Layne smiled at her. "You see? You are a zombie's worst nightmare!"

Brahm stepped forward and gathered the aggro on the five approaching mobs. Only two of them were armed; one with a short sword and the other with a spear. A mighty horizontal swipe of his axe removed the head of the lead zombie. Its body twitched as it dropped, its mouth still moving as its head rolled away.

Mace and Lila got behind the approaching group and each of them took out a zombie with daggers to the head, getting critical hits for sneak attacks and attacks from behind. The game mechanics were strange in that a body could take massive damage, like the loss of a limb or sucking chest wound, and still survive as long as the health points were still there. But a critical wound to the heart - or the head, in the case of a zombie - would kill instantly regardless of the victim's health point level.

And of course, beheading killed everything. Which Brahm promptly proved on the last two zombies in the group.

Shari cast her heal on another likely-looking mob, and this time only got three. Mace shook his head "This is the proper way to do this. Burn them down in small groups. But it's going to take all day."

As they quickly took down the three mobs and Lila looted them, Mace tried to think of a safe way to kill large numbers of zombies.

He looked at Shari. "You don't happen to have a grenade launcher on you, do you?"

She grinned back at him. "Boys and their toys!"

Then she got an odd look on her face. She looked to Layne. "Hey umm… Layne? I have a question."

She wandered over to speak quietly with the bard while Mace looked down at his enchanted dagger. It hadn't reacted at all when he'd killed any of the undead. Its normally pulsating aura was quiet and dull gray. He really needed to investigate the magic of the thing. Or find someone other than the dwarven smith who could tell him about it.

"Ha!" he heard Shari shout. "Hey, Mace! I got your grenade launcher right here."

There was a triumphant look on her face as he turned to look at her. Without ceremony, she lifted her bow and drew an arrow. After less than a second, the arrow began to glow. She loosed it at the nearest zombie, but before it struck, the arrow divided - or multiplied, he wasn't sure. It ended up as three glowing arrows that slammed into three different mobs. All three howled in pain and turned toward Shari, bringing maybe a dozen others along.

Shari didn't look worried. Layne started playing a tune that slowed the progress of the mobs and drained their stamina. Shari fired light arrow after light arrow, dividing each one before it hit. In about thirty seconds the whole group lay unmoving, pin-cushioned with glowing arrows of light.

She and Lila both leveled up as the last of the zombies fell, and the little rogue grinned at Shari. Taking a seat against the wall, she crossed her feet and leaned back, pretending to clean one of her nails with a dagger.

"I'll be right here relaxing while you level me up, Shari darling." She smiled at the elf, who grinned back and started firing again. This time, she pulled a group of ten. And once again they didn't make it even halfway to their tormentor before dropping.

Shari looked at Mace with a question on her face. Mace just shrugged and said, "Do your thang miss zombiekiller!" As Shari went back to work, he watched the look on her face. He was a little worried that she was venting some kind of real-world frustration, killing these mobs as substitutes for the zombies in the world above. Until he asked himself, *So what? It's probably good for her.*

So he sat cross-legged next to her and watched as she burned through the rest of the zombies. The whole remainder took her less than ten minutes. She had to pause a few times to drink a mana potion, but other than that it was non-stop zombie murder.

When she was done, she let out a long sigh. Stepping over to the wall, she slid down next to Lila and zoned out, looking at her character sheet. The two ladies (as well as the three pets) had leveled up several times during that particular stage of the dungeon.

As her eyes flicked left and right, she nudged Lila with her elbow. "Okay, I did all the hard work. Get off yer lazy ass n loot."

Lila snorted as she sprang to her feet. "Twist my arm," she mumbled as she happily began to ransack the corpses scattered about. Snuffles followed in hopes of interesting edibles, but was quickly disappointed.

A moment later Lila called out, "I suppose you want all these eyeballs and other gross squishy bits?"

Shari gave her a thumbs-up and smiled fondly as she watched the halfling. "I'm gonna start calling her Lootmonster."

Mace leaned against the wall next to her. He unconsciously reached for her hand and held it in his. She leaned her head on his shoulder and sighed.

The two of them watched as Brahm helped Lila loot the zombies. A few uncommon items popped up, and they were waved in the air to alert Mace before disappearing into bags.

Looting accomplished, it was time to get moving. The six armored undead were still guarding the door to what Mace hoped was the boss room. He was anxious to get this dungeon finished. In fact, to speed things along, he held out the hand with his spell-ring and called, "Stone Golem."

The ring held three of his more complicated spells, that ones that required components and time to cast. Stone Golem was his favorite, and as he leveled up his abilities, the summoned elemental monster grew bigger and stronger.

The golem that appeared now was easily twelve feet tall, and its bulk was roughly twice that of Brahm's. Thick stone legs supported a wide torso that weighed easily half a ton by itself. Wide shoulders led to arms as thick as telephone poles with three-fingered hands that could crush armor like an empty tin can.

The creature bowed its head to him, awaiting orders. Lila instantly shouted, "Oooh! Can I ride him?"

Despite himself, Mace cracked a smile. "Maybe after the fighting's done. He's about to get a little messy."

Looking to Brahm, who nodded, Mace said, "Shari? Want to do the honors again? Pull them all."

Shari grinned and drew her bow. Two seconds later, a light arrow struck the defender on the far left and all six reacted. Each raised their shields and held swords at the ready. They formed up into a defensive line, then as one took a measured step forward. Mace was impressed. He'd never seen zombies work with this type of coordinated strategy. He said

"Golem, when they get close, break that shield wall. Kill as many as you can. Brahm, if any get past the golem, they're yours. Lila…"

He looked at the little halfling, who was grinning like a fool, looking at the golem. "Stop thinking about golem-surfing and get behind them once they're engaged. Go for the gaps under their helmets. Body damage isn't going to slow them down."

She nodded her understanding, but didn't stop smiling.

Layne began a song to provide Strength, Stamina, and Health Regen buffs for the party. Shari was still firing arrows, though most were deflected by shields or heavy armor. One defender had an arrow in its left eye socket.

Undead Defender
Level 45
Health 11,000/13,000

Each of these mobs was higher level than Mace. He would finally get some xp for these kills.

Raising his hand, he focused on the face of a defender in the center and shouted "Infier!" causing a fireball to rush forward, impacting the mob before it could raise its shield and doing some splash damage to those on either side.

He kept up a steady stream of fireballs, doing minor damage. But his intent was just to keep them distracted. As the center three defenders raised their shields to ward off the fire, the golem hit them. It had been moving at a jog, which was the best pace for the bulky creature. Tons of rock smashed into their shields, sending the three of them flying backward several feet.

Brahm took advantage of the hole and stepped behind the shield wall, axe already coming around to slam into the spine of a still-standing defender. It rang off the armored backplate and did no damage. Growling, the minotaur reversed his swing and aimed higher. This time he removed the defender's head.

But the hasty move cost him. Another defender had abandoned the now-broken shield wall and moved around to Brahm's blind side. A short sword blade slid into the minotaur's kidney as his axe struck the other defender.

The wound dropped his health down to 20% and he fell to one knee as the sword was withdrawn. The defender immediately swung for Brahm's head, but he managed to raise his axe for a feeble block.

Shari and Mion both cast heals on their tank. His health bar climbed back up to 50% as Mace leapt in between him and the attacking undead. Mace's left dagger parried a swing of the short sword as he kicked the mob in the chest, pushing it back.

With a moment to breathe, he cast a magic shield on the still-recovering Brahm, then looked to his left. The golem had flattened one of the enemies into the floor. It wasn't moving. Another was having its head squeezed, and Mace was just in time to see it explode like a rotted melon. A third was trying to damage the golem with its sword, but was only managing to chip away small bits of stone with each blow.

Mace turned back to the enemy in front of him. He quickly raised his hand and cast a fireball into its face.

"Infier!"

The blast rocked the defender back on its feet, and Mace stepped up close while it was off balance. Since the thing's helm protected its skull, Mace jammed his dagger up under its chin and into its brain. When it didn't drop instantly, he pulled the dagger out and jammed it right back in. The second time around, the defender went limp and fell as he pulled the dagger back out.

Turning, he saw Brahm back on his feet and cleaving through the helm of the last standing defender with his axe. The blade passed through the skull at a forty-five-degree angle and exited to bite into its opposite shoulder. The upper left half of the thing's head slid to the floor before the rest of it followed a second later.

Brahm bent and put his hands on his knees. Gasping, he said "Thank the gods for you ladies. I am not used to such healing. I'm afraid I might have died if not for you."

The big minotaur turned and nodded at Mace. "And for you."

Mion fluttered down onto his shoulder and cast another heal on him, then licked his face and chirped happily.

Shari translated. "Mion says you're welcome. And that you owe her a treat."

Brahm chuckled. "You shall have all the treats your little belly can hold, tiny one."

To which Mion chirped again, this time nuzzling his neck.

Shari rolled her eyes and stuck her tongue out at the little dragon. Mion returned the gesture, making everyone laugh. Except Lila, who was looting the corpses and missed the whole thing. She walked over to Brahm and handed him a sword and shield.

"From what I learned at my dad's smith, these are actually pretty good quality."

Brahm accepted both and examined them briefly.

"Aye, these will make good gear for the guards at the settlement," he agreed. He dropped them into his bag and went to help Lila gather the rest. Mion rode along, stretching her neck to peer at the items he collected.

Mace moved to the door that the defenders had been… well, defending. He took his time checking it for traps. After that battle, he didn't expect any, but one had to be sure. About two minutes later he called, "All clear. You guys ready?"

They all nodded and Shari cast Life of the Forest on the stone golem to restore the minimal amount of health it had lost in the fight.

Mace commanded it to open the door and step through in front of them. The door was large, maybe twelve feet tall and six wide and made of stone, but the golem pulled it open effortlessly. It stepped into the room, then one pace to the right so the others could see past its bulk.

They were in a throne room of sorts. The room was roughly square, with a raised dais at the back end and floors of perfectly polished stone. There were no chairs or tables of any kind, just a wide stone pedestal on the dais.

A being in dark robes sat slumped on the floor, its back leaning against the pedestal base. The robes covered all but its skeletally thin hands, which jutted from the sleeves. One hand held a scepter with a dark orb on one end and a wicked looking serrated dagger blade on the other.

As the group approached, a deep, rasping laugh echoed through the room. The head lifted up, and two pinpoints of green light could be seen in the depths of the hood.

"So you made it past my children." the being observed. His voice sounded as if he'd smoked about a million cigarettes, and chased each one with a shot of whiskey. Mace took a long look at him.

> **Travis the Necromancer**
> **Level 60**
> **Health 5,000/25,000**

He didn't have a lot of base health for a level 60. But then, many magic users focused on their intel and wisdom stats to the detriment of all others.

"Why have you come here, adventurers? To watch an old man breathe his last? You're several centuries late. Have you come for plunder? Gold and shiny things?" he motioned to a side door that sat open. Inside were shelves piled with treasure. "Help yourselves. I have no need of such things." He coughed wetly, his free hand rising to pat his chest.

Shari whispered to Mace "Should I heal him? And will that hurt him?"

Mace shook his head, not specifying which question he was answering. He stepped forward.

"We came to clear this dungeon of any threat to our lands." He continued to approach. "Are you a threat?"

Travis laughed again, causing another coughing fit. When he'd recovered enough to speak, he said, "Once. Once I was a threat to all of

Elysia! The dead spoke to me, and I knew the secrets of every king and queen in the land. I traveled from lowly pauper's cemetery to royal crypt, raising my children and learning of political murders, fits of jealousy and betrayals. Of unwanted children and inconvenient lovers. And those rulers paid for my silence. Oh yes, how they paid."

He motioned toward the treasure room once more. Lila actually took a few steps in that direction before Brahm took hold of her.

"After all, if a child you murdered walked into your bedchamber and demanded its weight in gold in return for my silence, would you refuse?"

He paused, as if expecting an answer. After a moment, he continued. "And gold was not my only demand. I demanded favors! Nations went to war on my orders. Thousands died, and my army only grew stronger. Given enough time, I would have ruled *everything*!"

Mace was now standing within a step of the old necromancer. He squatted down and attempted to look inside the hood. There must have been some darkness enchantment in the robe. He'd be sure and check that after he killed the man.

"And what was it that brought you so low then, old one? From world power to dungeon boss?"

"I did. I lost patience. I broke my own rules and pushed too many too far. They banded together, admitting their secrets to one another and forming an alliance. They drove me away and slaughtered any of my children in their cities. I fled here with the last of my army and sealed us inside. The dead don't age, you know. Well, not much. But without new souls to feed me, the strain of controlling and maintaining my children has drained me. I eventually lost control of them and didn't have the energy to regain it. They turned on me, so I locked myself in here, and this became my prison."

"I can put you out of your misery, old man. As you say, you have been dead a long time. Let me send you to your rest."

The old necromancer laughed more loudly this time. His voice echoing boldly around them all. "HA! I was about to make *you* the same offer!"

More quickly than Mace would have thought possible, the scepter in the old man's hand twirled around so that the dagger pointed toward him. At the same time the necromancer leapt to his feet and thrust the weapon at Mace's gut. It glowed with a sickly green light as it sped toward him.

Mace flung himself into a backflip, avoiding the strike and providing a bit of distance. The old man screamed in frustration and kept coming, the blade held in front of him.

"You cannot escape me! Hold still and I will finish you quickly! Continue to fight and I will make you one of my children!"

Shari cast Life of the Forest on the old man and he screamed in pain. In the blink of an eye he spun and hurled his weapon at the healer.

The scepter flew faster than the eye could follow, the blade embedding itself in Shari's shoulder. She screamed in pain and fell to the ground as the scepter's glow brightened and it began to feed her life force to the necromancer.

As the old man's attention was focused on his feeding, Mace stepped up behind him.

"Never turn your back on a drow," he whispered as he slid his enchanted dagger into the necromancer's back. The rush of energy that surged up his arm from the dagger nearly knocked him backward. He felt himself screaming along with the single thought that it transmitted into his mind. One clear word.

"*YESSSSSS!*"

Necromancer Travis made a short coughing noise, then fell to his knees. The dagger drained the last of his energy and his body shriveled into a dried husk. Everyone in the room leveled up, and Mace nearly passed out. The combination of the rush from the dagger and the pleasure the game awarded for a level up crashed down on him all at once.

He staggered toward Shari, slightly off balance but recovering quickly. The others knelt around her as Brahm withdrew the scepter from her shoulder. She was barely conscious as Layne poured a health potion down her throat. Mion was frantically casting Life of the Forest on her pet human, but it didn't seem to be having any effect. A dark web of veins was spreading up Shari's neck and down her arm.

"Poison!" Layne observed through gritted teeth. "One I do not know. Shari!"

She patted the elf's cheeks to get her attention. "Do you have any poison cures in your bag?"

Shari nodded, and several vials appeared in her hand. Layne grabbed them just as the hand fell limply back to the floor. She poured the first vial into Shari's mouth and pushed it closed so that she'd swallow. Still there seemed to be no improvement. Shari's health bar was below 20% and falling.

Lila jumped up and ran to the old man's corpse. She began rifling through his pockets and bag. Mace, feeling helpless about Shari's condition and irritated that he couldn't fix it, barked at the halfling.

"Lila! This is not the time! Stop-"

He halted mid-sentence as she jumped in the air and whooped. Turning toward them, she ran back with a small bottle of clear liquid in her hand.

"Try this!"

Concoction of Saint's Tears
Quality: Extremely Rare

Use: Restores health. Cures poison. Boosts health and mana regeneration.

Can be used as ingredient in a wide variety of potions.

Layne's eyes widened. "Give me that!"

She snatched the bottle from Lila's hand even as the rogue reached out with it. Opening the bottle, she tipped it so that a couple of drops fell into Shari's mouth.

The effect was nearly instantaneous. The web of black veins began to recede and Shari's breathing became easier. Her health bar, which had dropped to a sliver, began to fill up again.

Lila sniffed at Mace.

"I figured if he was walking around with a poisoned blade in his hand, he was probably carrying an antidote.

Mace hugged the little halfling to him, nearly crushing her. "Thank you, Lila. And you can loot anyone anytime you want!"

He smiled down at her, then immediately realized what he'd said and both their eyes widened.

"I mean, within reason. Don't… I mean…" He threw up his hands in exasperation as she giggled at him.

They waited as Shari recovered. Lila went back over, after winking at Mace, to loot the old man. Then she went and stood right on the threshold of the treasure room, dancing up and down and waving impatiently for the rest of them to get a move on.

Shari laughed when she noticed the halfling. "Okay, Lootmonster, we're coming."

She leaned on Mace as they all walked over to join Lila. "Damn, that sucked. I'd rather die quickly than go through that again. I'm all healed up, but the memory of the pain makes me feel… weak."

Mace nodded his head sympathetically. Then with a slight grin, he said, "Just wait 'til you're 100% synced."

He laughed as Shari's eyes widened. He could see her reconsidering the whole 'permanent upload' idea for a moment. Then she slapped him on the shoulder and turned her attention to the loot.

Mace took a moment to look at the notifications that had popped up when the old man died.

First Kill!
Congratulations! You are the first to clear the Darkstone Hoosegow!
Reward: 25,000 experience. One epic level or better item per party member.

Level Up! You are now Level 42…
Level Up! You are now Level 43
You have received one attribute point

He called out to Shari. "Hey hon, how many levels did you pick up today?"

Shari turned to look at him. "Hon? Are we an old married couple now? At least call me 'baby,' or 'sweetheart,' or 'goddess of my heart and fire of my loins.'"

Mace blushed as Brahm and the others chuckled at him. He took a deep breath.

"Oh goddess of my soul, keeper of my heart and syrupy object of my dreams… could you tell me what level you are now, please?"

Now it was Shari's turn to blush as all ears pricked up after the 'syrupy' bit. She quickly looked at the items on the shelf in front of her and said, "Better. And I'm level thirty-four now."

Lila, busily stuffing items into her storage ring without really looking at them, piped up "I'm thirty-three! This dungeon is *amazing!*"

Mace used his Mage Sight to quickly search the room for any enchanted items (of which there were several) or hidden compartments.

He found a trapped walled panel behind one of the shelves. This one was unsurprisingly also a poison-based trap. He disarmed it, put the trap mechanism in his bag, and handed the poison over to Shari.

Leaving the group to finish emptying the room, he likewise searched the throne room. Only the pedestal glowed with any magic. He examined it carefully, but couldn't spot a source. There were no obvious wards or traps.

Turning off his Mage Sight, he looked it over using his physical skills. When his eyes didn't find anything, he carefully ran his fingers over the entire thing. It was all one solid piece of stone, rising up from and connected to the stone floor. It was as if the room had been carved out around it, leaving only the pedestal intact.

His fingers told him what his eyes could not. There was the faintest hint of a seam in the stone that, even though he now knew where it was, his eyes couldn't make out. He ran his finger along the seam, and it eventually intersected another. Mace continued to trace the miniscule imperfection in the stone until his fingers had made a complete box. It was located on the front side of the column, just above where the old man had been resting his head.

He pushed carefully on the panel outlined by the seams. There was a moment of resistance, then the panel slid inward. There was a roaring sound like wind rushing, and Mace's eyes widened in surprise.

Chapter 7

Places to Go, People to See

The others ran out of the room upon hearing the loud noise, weapons at the ready. They each stopped quickly, eyes as wide as Mace's and mouths dropping open.

Mace, still standing by the pedestal, turned in a full circle. He was surrounded. There were twelve of them, evenly spaced around the room facing inward toward the pedestal. They glowed with a purple incandescence that reminded Mace of the dungeon gateway they'd passed through earlier.

Portals. A dozen portals, each leading to a different place. He whistled in appreciation.

"Old Travis wasn't joking. Being able to move from place to place like this? That is power all by itself. I mean, I know the surface cities have gates, but…"

His voice trailed off as he considered the implications. Elysia allowed players to gate between several of the large cities for a fee, as no one wanted to waste play time on long treks or rides over the sometimes-hundreds of miles between them. But there were only six cities he knew of that had gates. And not all of these portals in front of him looked like they connected to cities.

Through one, he appeared to be looking from inside a cave out toward a sunlit waterfall that fell across the entrance. Another showed what looked like a farmer's barn. A third portal sat on a narrow ledge overlooking a large city below. There were six that opened into man-made structures. One was a dark room that appeared to be in a prison or dungeon of some sort. Another was in a large, well-maintained crypt. Two appeared to open into bedchambers and another an office with a large, ornately carved and polished desk. The last simply showed a long stone corridor. The necromancer must have used these to travel the kingdoms he controlled.

As Mace gaped at the gateways all around him, Lila tugged on his sleeve. she grinned up at him, breaking his brainlock and making him chuckle.

"Hey, um Mace? Remember how when we first captured this place, I said we had no use for it?" This place is *cool*!"

"Yes, it is." He looked significantly at Brahm. "And we're going to have to work harder to secure this place. Can't have the Black Flame getting access to this."

The minotaur clan chief nodded, his face grave.

"Indeed. I pledge my own people as guardians of this place. We will leave Lakeside and relocate here…"

His eyes lowered to focus on the floor as he drifted into planning.

Shari disagreed. "There's no reason to isolate yourselves here, or permanently leave Lakeside. We will keep this secret amongst ourselves, and maybe a trusted few. As far as everyone else is concerned, we are protecting a valuable location filled with iron and other resources. I think our secret will remain safe. After all, how long did the Black Flame occupy the rooms above without discovering any of its secrets?"

Lila piped up, "That's mostly because Justin was a moron."

"Yes, well. That too. But I think we should work on building a proper settlement here, too. Maybe not right away. We can start with a proper wall and gate to protect the place. Regular scouts to patrol the area. I'm sure the centaurs would help. Maybe the elves, too, if you're willing to share this with them?" Shari looked at Mace.

Mace shook his head. "I know you trust them. And I trust your judgement. But let's not make any hasty decisions. At least not until we know a little more. Like where all of these portals lead, and whether they work both ways."

He paused to consider a moment longer. "I think you're right about growing a settlement here. Hell, even a city. With access to the rest of the continent like this? We could become a trade center. Transfer goods 'magically' for a fee."

He pointed through one of the portals, which looked out on a cove. Waves were slapping against the stone nearby, and in the distance they could see a port with a stone wharf and long stone piers jutting out into a protected bay. "We could connect land-bound cities to ports and transfer goods back and forth."

Brahm chuckled. "We'll need to widen that opening or find another way to access this place. No large quantities of goods could travel the pathway we've taken to get here."

Mace nodded. He opened the map on his UI and examined it. The areas on the surface where he had traveled so far were filled in, but most of the continent was a blank. He knew from studying the wiki map roughly where the major cities and features like lakes and mountains were. But his in-game map would only fill in if he traveled to a location, or was able to study a map of said location.

"How about we do a little experiment? I don't know how safe these are, or if they're warded in any way. There's so much concentrated magic here I wouldn't be able to spot a trap. So, I'm going to go through one of these. When I get to the other side, my map should tell me where I am. Then I'll try to come back. If it's one way, I'll figure out a way to get killed and meet you all back at Lakeside."

Shari stepped forward. "Want me to go with you?"

He really did. But after considering for a second, he shook his head. "The others might run into trouble and need a healer on the way back to the boat."

She nodded hesitantly.

He turned a complete circle again, looking at the all the portals. He was tempted to choose one that showed a manmade structure. That should put him in a city he could easily reference.

But one of the portals in particular drew his attention. It wasn't one he'd focused on before. The other side of the gate was dark. But his darkvision showed him a wide-open cavern. His drow nature drew him to it.

Before stepping through, he removed his storage rings and handed them to Shari. If he died going through, he didn't want to risk losing inventory items he didn't have to. With a quick wave to the others, he stepped into the portal.

Cold penetrated his body, as if he'd just plunged into an arctic lake. His sense of direction was immediately disrupted, as it felt like he was facing everywhere and nowhere at once. The effect only lasted a moment before he stumbled into the cavern.

He fell to one knee, putting both hands on the floor to brace himself. For several seconds, he was dizzy and disoriented. When it passed, he turned first to look behind him. The portal was not visible to his darkvision, but when he activated Mage Sight, he could see the oval-shaped outline on the cavern wall.

He quickly scanned the rest of the space around him. It was a large cavern, roughly the size of the one in which he'd fought the giant petramander and Cthulhu spawn. He didn't see or hear any immediate threats, but was pretty sure he was back in the Underground zone.

Pulling up his UI, the map confirmed his suspicion. Rather than a map of the surface world, he was looking at a map that included Immernacht and Svarthold. He was closer to Svarthold.

Not wanting to risk a fight with a roaming predator or waste time, he turned and reached a hand toward the portal. As soon as his fingers touched the plane, he was back in the icy nothingness of the transport spell.

A second later, he stumbled back into the portal room where his friends awaited him. He managed to keep his feet this time, and the disorientation faded more quickly.

Shari looked at him expectantly, but Lila was less patient. "Well? Speak up already!"

Mace grinned at her. "I didn't find any loot, unless you like giant mushrooms three times your height."

She snorted at him and he continued. "It worked, though. That one led to a cavern near the grey dwarf city of Svarthold. And there didn't seem to be any trouble getting back. Though the portal on the other side was not visible to the naked eye."

Shari gave a little hop and shouted, "Me next!" before heading toward the portal that showed the waterfall. Before Mace could find the words to object, she stepped into the oval and disappeared. A moment later she reappeared in the cave between the portal and the waterfall. They watched as she stumbled and had to put a hand on the wall to save herself from falling.

When she straightened up and stepped toward the waterfall, Lila chuckled.

"She didn't fall. You're not very graceful for a rogue." She eyed Mace.

"I'm an assassin. And it was my first portal." Mace couldn't help but sound defensive, which only made Lila chuckle again. They watched as Shari stepped to the far-right side of the cave entrance and reached her hand into the waterfall. After spraying herself liberally in cold water, she sidestepped once and disappeared.

They waited a few minutes as Mace watched his party interface to see if her health dropped. Just as he was deciding to step through after her, she reappeared. Smiling, she walked back toward the portal.

She paused for a moment, looking left and right, then turned to look back toward the waterfall. Getting her bearings, she reached forward and was transported back to them.

As soon as she recovered from the dizziness, she said, "There's a beautiful forest on either side of a river fed by the waterfall. I saw an orc hunting party at a campsite downriver a short way. They were skinning a deer and two of them were fishing."

Mace nodded. "And that brings us to the end of our exploration for the day. We'll figure out the other portals another time. Let's get back to Lakeside."

The others looked disappointed. But when Mace reminded Lila that they hadn't cleared all the loot in the treasure room yet, she perked up and dashed back to the room. The mood of the party lightened as they watched, then assisted her.

The room emptied, they made their way back upstairs. Mace cleared the ice blocking the corridor and they exited the dungeon. Picking up the guards back at ground level, the whole group made their way back past the site of the slaver battle and down the trail to the boat.

It was late evening by the time they arrived and Captain Jorin wasn't about to sail the lake after dark. So they all settled in to get some sleep and the two players logged out.

*****

Griff sat in front of a computer monitor in his bunker's communication room. He was looking at the faces of Mace and Shari for the first time, and couldn't stop grinning. Voices on the radio were great, and emails from Shari had given him hope. But speaking with other live humans face-to-face, so to speak, felt like Christmas morning and winning the lottery at the same time.

"So ye found other survivors. That's good news. Did any reply to your message yet?" he asked.

"Not yet. But with different time zones and not knowing how often everyone is online, that's no big surprise. If we don't hear from anyone in a few days, we'll try again," Shari replied. "How are you doing? Are you enjoying the game?"

"Oh, aye!" Griff nodded enthusiastically. "The dwarves have been very kind and have given me about a million quests. I'm already level twelve!"

He thumbed his chest with pride. Shari laughed and applauded while Mace nodded his approval. They were sitting together in front of the same webcam in what looked like a medium-sized office.

Mace spoke next. "We have some other news for you. Do you know a place called Newport?"

"Sure! It's not far from here. Why? Is there a survivor there?" Griff's eyes lit up. Mace was sorry to have to disappoint him.

"No. I mean, not that we know of. There might be. But what *is* there is one of the company's VR pod manufacturing sites. Peabody says it's a facility similar to this one. So, probably some underground floors. And maybe a cafeteria like this place has, so lots of food? Though if you think you want to try and get there, I'd stop for supplies on the way if I were you." Mace offered.

Griff's bunker wasn't exactly the lap of luxury. It was designed for a team of ten or so soldiers to operate and maintain the communications array. There were cramped living quarters with bunk beds and a tiny kitchen with an empty larder behind it. Being that it was peacetime when the world ended, the place wasn't well stocked to begin with. He was running low on food and getting a bit stir crazy in the small space. So he leapt at the chance for better accommodation.

"You bet yer arse I'll make it there. I got a Jeep outside. Or, I did when I last came down here. Been a while. I'll grab me weapons and some food and water and head over. Where is it?"

Shari gave him the address and rough directions, then she and Mace spent an hour warning him about covering all of his skin and wearing a helmet. Not touching anything. Being quiet. All the things they'd learned the hard way in their time outside.

"Jesus," Griff muttered. "Now I ain't feelin' so keen to stick me nose out there. Is it really all that bad?"

Shari nodded, tears in her eyes. "Worse. I can't stress enough how careful you need to be. And not just about contamination. Some of the other survivors are as dangerous as the creatures."

An hour later Griff had packed up his few personal possessions, his remaining food, and several weapons. He'd done the best he could with body armor, donning a full set of fatigues with the pants tucked into his combat boots. He wore a leather jacket, then a nylon windbreaker over top of it, and thick work gloves covered his hands.

On his head he wore a standard combat helmet and the work goggles he used for welding, and had torn strips of blanket wrapped around his face and neck as a scarf. Not ideal, but it covered nearly everything. He'd considered wearing an old gas mask he'd found in a trunk, but decided it would limit his vision too much. And really, he only planned to be outside for a few minutes at a time.

With his rucksack on his back, he hefted his weapons – a shotgun, two rifles and a long, sharp stick made from a closet rod – and headed upstairs. He had a full canteen of water on his belt next to an old .45 in its holster. If he stretched it, the water would last him two days. He needed to find more supplies before then.

He'd used the bunker's outdoor cameras to gauge the distance to the nearest vehicles. Two of the three sat open, their drivers having either abandoned them or been ripped free. But the third still stood secure, doors closed, if a little dusty.

Shari had warned him to be wary of even the dust. He shook his head, heart pounding.

"How could me world have become such a deadly place?" he murmured to himself. Reaching the outer door, he raised a hand to the big red button that would release the locks.

He paused, finding himself unable to push it. Stepping closer to the door, he set his ear against it, listening for any sound of movement outside.

After a moment, he chuckled. "It be two feet o' solid steel ye daft monkey. Ye'll not be hearin' anything through that monster. Just get on with it!"

He stepped back and slammed the button with authority, girding his loins as the hydraulics within the wall withdrew the lock bolts and unsealed the pressurized door. With a final hissing pop, it separated slightly from its frame and a thin line of sunlight peeked through.

Griff took hold of the massive handle and pulled. Though the door weighed a few tons, it was almost perfectly balanced and still well oiled. With a solid tug and a small grunt of effort he was able to swing the door inward far enough for him to exit with the pack on his back.

He stepped out carefully, sure that the noise from the door would have attracted unwanted attention. His head on a swivel, he checked left, right, even above him in case a creature of some sort was waiting to drop on his head.

After a solid minute of hearing and seeing nothing but the trees rustling in the wind across the cleared open space, he moved toward the vehicle. The keys had been on a hook inside, with the number on a tag matching the number painted on the Jeep's bumper.

When he reached the driver's door, he produced a rag from his pocket. Using the rag to carefully and thoroughly wipe off the dust around the door handle, he then tossed it away onto the ground. He used the key to unlock the door, then tossed his gear into the passenger's seat. Climbing in, he started the Jeep, a prayer on his lips.

"Please start, please start, baby. Be a good lass and start right up for daddy."

His heart sank as he turned the key and the engine spluttered for a moment before dying. Letting his hand drop, he sat back in the seat.

"Okay, so the battery is still good. That's a start. She's been sittin' here alone for months. O'course she's gonna need a little convincing."

He patted the steering wheel gently and spoke softly to the Jeep. "Give us a bit o' love now, darlin'. I'll take ye on a nice trip. We'll see the sights. It'll be a grand old time, it will!"

Satisfied with his plea, he reached up and turned the key. The engine spluttered again, but sounded better this time. When it died, he waited just a moment, then turned the key again. This time, the Jeep's engine rumbled to life!

Griff was instantly terrified. After months of silence and the dire warnings Shari had given him, the engine seemed to roar! The sound rolled across the open field surrounding the bunker, echoing off every surface and causing Griff to break out in a cold sweat.

He threw the Jeep in gear and began to make his way out of the complex. Having been stationed at the base for a while, he knew the nearby towns fairly well. Mace and Shari had suggested hitting a large supermarket for supplies, so that was his first mission.

The closest he knew of was about ten kilometers away. The streets were slow going, as the entire area was exactly what one would expect of a post-apocalyptic war zone. Crumbling buildings, burned out or abandoned cars blocking the roads…

The contamination had spread through Europe first, with almost no warning. The military forces of the various nations had tried to respond and contain, but the spread had been much too fast. Nobody had had any time to form a comprehensive plan, so individual units had just responded as best they could. And the best option seemed to be to kill everything in hopes of stopping the spread.

Bombs were dropped, cities were nuked. Smaller towns were knocked down with artillery fire and scorched with napalm. It didn't matter whether the inhabitants were infected or not. This was a fire break. An attempt to draw a line and let the zombiepocalypse burn itself out. But of course it all failed.

Tears streamed down Griff's face as he made his way through the town. He was sad, and afraid, and hopeful all at the same time. More emotion than he was used to dealing with. He thought of his family who'd lived not so far from here. Gone now. Just like everyone else.

As he left the town, the roads improved. There hadn't been much time to evacuate and few people had made it this far. Fewer people meant fewer targets for the military, so the burned-out cars became sparse.

He checked the fuel indicator, which showed three quarters of a tank. At the slow speeds he was moving, that should be more than enough to get him to Newport. He found he could pick up a little speed, which made him feel better.

He began to relax, and actually reached for the radio before remembering that nobody was transmitting anymore.

He noticed an old-school CD sticking out of the console. He hadn't seen a CD player in decades. Pushing at the disc, he watched it slide into the player, which began to make shuffling noises. A moment later, the oh-so-familiar sound of church bells tolling, followed by iconic guitar riffs, made him grin. He didn't need to look at the disc to know who this was. AC/DC were legendary. He sang along as the lyrics began.

"I'm a rolling thunder, a pouring rain.

I'm comin' on like a hurricane

My lightning's flashing across the sky

You're only young, but you're gonna die!"

The lyrics made him pause for a moment as he realized what he was singing. But he shook it off and began to bang his head in rhythm with the music as he unclenched his gut and released some of the fear he'd been holding in.

Which was probably why he was surprised when something large smashed into the left side of the Jeep, causing it to veer hard to the right and tilt up on its two right wheels for a second before slamming back down onto the road. Griff barely managed to regain control of the Jeep as it bounced a few times and the engine revved up as the tires spun.

With a squeal, they regained their traction and the Jeep lurched forward. Which was a good thing, as the massive bear-like zombie creature that had attacked him was shaking off the impact and coming for him again.

Griff screamed in terror and punched the accelerator. He ignored the sound of the back left tire scraping against part of the Jeep's body where the bear had caved it in. Or the wind whistling through the cracked windows. His attention was one hundred percent focused on his rear-view mirror as he watched a four-meter-tall monster lumber after him, its mouth open and showing fangs long enough to puncture straight through his chest. It roared, drowning out the music and making the vehicle shiver.

Griff's scream ended and he began to pant as the Jeep eventually gained ground and started to leave the unnaturally fast monster behind. He nearly crashed straight into an abandoned car in front of him as he stared at the rear-view nonstop. The beast didn't seem to be slowing down, and a few moments later it simply shouldered aside the car Griff had almost hit.

Griff kept the Jeep moving as fast as he could, zigging and zagging around obstacles and gaining ground. Eventually he couldn't see it anymore, which didn't make him feel any better. He hoped it had given up.

The rubbing sound from the back tire became more insistent, so he took a chance and stopped to check it. The plastic guard above the tire had been crumpled and was rubbing against the rubber of the tire. He was tempted to try and adjust it by hand, but the contaminated creature had left some neon blue blood on the impact zone, and who knew what other kinds of contaminated particles. He wasn't about to risk touching it.

Grabbing a tire iron from the back of the Jeep he quickly beat at the plastic until it caved in enough that it wasn't touching the tire. Tossing the now-contaminated tool onto the ground, he gave a quick check down the road and could see the beast still coming. It spotted him as well, and let out another roar. It also seemed to pick up speed as it grew closer.

Griff hopped back into the driver's seat and kicked the Jeep into gear. Speeding along once again, he tried to calm himself and think clearly.

"It'll get tired eventually. Right? Unless, do dead things even *get* tired? Shite!"

The road ahead was completely blocked by a pile-up, so he slowed slightly and went off-road. The Jeep easily handling the descent into the roadside gully and then the climb back out after he'd cleared the wreckage.

"Can this thing track me? If I go to the new place, will it follow?" Griff remembered reading somewhere that a bear's sense of smell was something like three hundred times better than a human's.

Not wanting to risk having that massive monster show up at his door, he took a right at the next intersection, hoping that the piled wreckage would keep the bear from seeing his change of direction. He followed that road for a ways before he noticed a shallow creek running beneath an upcoming bridge.

Going off-road again, he drove carefully into the creek. The water was about half the height of the Jeep's tires. Turning upstream, he crept along the creek bed. Occasionally, a tire would sink into a hole or the frame would scrape on a boulder he couldn't see under the water, but he continued carefully up the creek in the general direction of Newport for about four kilometers.

Spotting an area of gently-sloped bank ahead, he turned out of the creek and drove up the bank into a field. From there, it was a short drive to a nearby road, and he headed toward his new home, praying that he'd shaken the massive zombie bear. Or that something else would catch its interest between here and there.

As the adrenaline rush subsided, Griff felt exhausted. In nearly any other circumstance he would have pulled over and rested. Drunk some water, eaten something, and taken deep breaths until his body leveled out. Maybe even taken a nap. But not today. He needed to get to his destination. Then he could sleep as long as he wanted.

Using a paper map and passing road signs, he figured out his exact location. Making a turn onto a main road, he continued toward Newport. With the bear still on his mind and plenty of fuel in the tank, he took some detours to try to further slow the bear in case it was still able to track him. He also prayed for rain that could wash his scent off the streets.

He took a long, looping detour to the southeast before coming up into Newport from the south. Still following his map, he zigged and zagged through the city. The facility he was looking for was on the north side in what turned out to be a sort of business district that transitioned into suburbs. Just a half kilometer from the building, he found a Tesco store.

Moving slowly as he steered around obstacles and impact craters, it took him a few minutes to reach the store. He cruised around the block once, checking for any sign of movement or recent habitation.

Finding none, he pulled around the back and drove right up onto the ramp leading to the loading dock. The roll-up door was closed, as was the human-sized door next to it. He took that as a good sign. Saying a little prayer, he tried the door handle. It was unlocked!

Turning on a forehead-mounted light he'd fastened to his helmet, he stepped inside with shotgun raised. In his haste to check the room, he'd stepped too far and the door slammed shut behind him, nearly causing him to piss himself. The sound echoed through the large space.

To his left was a small block of offices, presumably those of the store manager, receiving, accounting, etc. Straight ahead was a short hall with plastic strips hanging in front of double swinging doors that led out to the main part of the store. And to his right were dozens of rows of wide metal shelves that reached five meters in height.

Cold sweat running down his back, he waited and listened. The smell was unpleasant, rotting perishables that had gone bad after the power went out. He breathed through his mouth to try and mitigate the odor.

After a solid minute, he moved toward the doors to the main store. He had no intention of going out there; the entire front was glass, and anything outside could spot him. So, he grabbed a nearby crowbar and slid it through the double door handles. That should keep anything out there from sneaking up on him while he shopped.

Moving slowly, he checked each aisle of the warehouse, shotgun raised and finger planted just above the trigger. Mace and Shari had warned him about not making noise, but if it came to shooting or dying, he'd bloody well shoot.

After a tense five minutes, he was reasonably sure he was alone. He'd made more noise than he liked as he shuffled around, and any zombie creatures would likely have heard him.

Slinging the shotgun over his shoulder, he walked back to the entrance. There were a few shopping carts filled with assorted items and he dumped one out in the corner, pushing the empty cart toward the shelves.

Half an hour later he'd filled two carts with beef jerky, canned meats, soups, pasta, jars of fruit, and baking supplies like pancake mix, flour, sugar, salt, etc. His mum had taught him to cook as a young lad. He'd complained at the time, much more interested in being outside playing footie. Now he sent up a silent blessing for her.

He had a pallet of bottled water, some wine and a case of Guinness. The entire rear compartment of his vehicle as well as the back seat were filled with food and drink. He'd also found some first aid supplies. And he'd stocked up on rubber cleaning gloves and plastic bags.

Satisfied that he had at least a couple months' worth of food, he closed the loading dock door and climbed back into the Jeep. Once again he cringed when the engine started. He weaved his way through the town, still nervously checking every alley and side street, every open doorway he passed. Sure that a horde of undead would be around the next corner.

When he spotted the building that was to be his new home, he wasn't impressed. It was mostly glass and only three stories tall, with a parking garage to one side.

He turned right a block before the building and made a circle around it, looking for any signs of life or recent habitation.

After making a complete circuit of the neighborhood, he approached the garage. There was a roll-up door with a card-sensor station about ten feet in front of it. There was also a push button one could use to call the security office. Not having a card, Griff pushed the button.

"Ehrmm…hallo?" he ventured.

He was surprised to hear Morgan Freeman's voice respond to him. *"Hello. What is your name?"*

"Errr… I'm Griff. Ye must be Peabody?"

"Yes, admin Griff. I am Peabody. Nice to meet you. You may access the garage. The lobby entrance is on the lower level."

Even as the voice spoke, the massive metal door began to rise. The amount of noise it made caused Griff to shudder and reflexively check over his shoulder for the bearzombiemonster thing.

As soon as the door was high enough to the clear the Jeep, he drove forward and down the sloping drive to the lower level. There were only a few other vehicles in the garage, and none near the door that led inside the building.   Griff parked near the door, so close that the vehicle might keep something the size of a charging bear from reaching the door. Grabbing just his rucksack and weapons, he approached the door.

He was feeling a little taken aback by the AI. Mace had told him about Peabody, though not about the voice. And he was surprised by the admin title. Though he supposed it made sense.

"I'm here, Peabody." He spoke to a camera mounted above the door, making a small, awkward waving motion with his hand. The door lock clicked and he grabbed the handle.

As he stepped through the door, Peabody said, "*My cameras have detected no unauthorized movement in the facility since I was brought online here. That was approximately twelve hours ago.*"

"Er, unauthorized? Has there been authorized movement?" Griff was being flippant with the AI, but when Peabody answered he became concerned.

"*There has. Two others are currently in residence at this facility. Mace has asked me to inform you now, so that you have time to prepare yourself. He has requested that I pass on the following message: 'Hey Griff. Turns out there were a couple folks alive in the building when Peabody made his connection to the facility's AI. We've spoken to them and they seem okay. But keep a weapon handy until you're satisfied.'*"

Griff leaned against the wall for a moment. This day had hit him with a lot of surprises, seemingly one right after the other. He was still coming down from the adrenaline high of his trip from the bunker, and now his heart was hammering again. He hadn't seen other people in months. A few short days ago he was halfway sure he was the last man on earth.

"Ehm, Peabody. Can ye tell me about the other people here?"

"*Certainly, admin Griff. Two adults. One male, Evan, age thirty-four. One female, Lisa, age twenty-two. Would you like their dimensions and approximate weights? I'm afraid I will have to estimate based on visual observations.*"

Griff snorted despite the stressful situation. "I were more interested in whether they were armed, or tended towards violence. And do they know I'm here?"

"*Neither of them are armed. And they have shown no violent tendencies in the time I have been online. I can review past recordings if*

*you wish. And they have been informed of your arrival. Mace and admin
Shari spoke to them about you."*

"Alright, thank you, Peabody. Now, where do I go to meet these
two?" Griff asked as he looked around the hallway he stood in.

*"The lower-level access is via the elevator around the corner to
your left. Mace has authorized you for complete access to this facility.
You may wish to activate a key fob in the security office in case my visual
recognition goes offline for any reason."*

As Griff walked the corridor down to the corner and turned left, he
nervously chatted with the AI.

"Tell me about this place. Is it the same as the facility Mace and
Shari are using?"

The elevator door opened to admit Griff as he approached. He
entered, and the AI spoke as the doors closed and the elevator began to
drop.

*"It is similar. The building has fewer levels both above and below
ground. The lower levels include two server farms, a research level, four
manufacturing levels, two for storage, and an amenity level with a
cafeteria, kitchen, laundry, fitness center, residential suites, and movie
theater. The lowest level houses the geothermal power plant and other
mechanical systems. There are also two expansion levels that are unused
at this time. Above ground are three floors of office space and meeting
rooms, as well as the lobby."*

Just as Peabody finished, the elevator came to a stop. Griff took a
deep breath to steady himself as the door in front of him opened.

*****

Shari and Mace had exited their pods after logging out and gone
straight to the kitchen. Though it hadn't been that long since they'd eaten,
the excitement and activity of running a dungeon had made them both feel
famished. Mace had told Shari "Sit. I'm gonna make you something
special to celebrate your first dungeon completion in the game."

He grinned at her as she happily sat without arguing. He practically dove into the pantry to retrieve the items he needed. He emerged with a can of chili with beans, a package of tortilla shells, a block of cheddar cheese, and a jar of salsa.

Setting the items on the counter, he retrieved a colander and set it inside a pan on the stove. Opening the chili, he poured it into the colander, then shook it about until the meat and beans had been separated from the more-liquid sauce. Pouring the sauce into a glass, he dumped the meat and beans into the pan and turned on the burner. While they began to cook, he set the colander in a second pan and poured the salsa into it. This time when the more liquid parts strained off, he was left with diced tomatoes. The liquid was poured down the sink drain, the tomatoes transferred to a bowl.

Moving back to the first pan, he used a wooden spoon to scoop out each of the beans and deposit them into the other pan, turning on that burner as well. By the time he was done, the meat remaining in the pan was well-browned and steaming hot. The liquid from the chili mix that had stayed with the meat had nearly all evaporated. He quickly and enthusiastically began to rub the cheese across the grater, causing shredded cheese to drop onto a plate below. As he worked, he heard a whistle from Shari.

He turned down the heat on both burners and went to retrieve a cheese grater. "Yeah, baby. Shake it! You know what mama likes!" She grinned as he turned around. A moment later, he was putting some exaggerated hip action into his last bit of grating. She chuckled and made kissy noises at him.

Setting down the remainder of the cheese block, he began moving the bowls and plates to the counter where Shari sat. He set the hot pan of beef on a hot pad, then opened the package of taco shells. The beans came to the table in a bowl of their own.

"Here we go! Taco Tuesday!"

Shari shook her head. "It's Thursday." Still, she drooled slightly as she took in the scents of the ingredients before her.

"Fine." He rolled his eyes in mock exasperation. "Taco Thursday! I'm sorry there's no fresh lettuce or sour cream."

She leaned forward and kissed his cheek. "This is wonderful. You're very creative."

She grabbed a taco shell and began to spoon some of the beef into her shell, quickly built a taco, then spooned some beans onto the plate next to it. Taking a bite of the crunchy shell, she chewed a couple of times, then spoke with her mouth full.

"*So* gooood!"

Mace smiled at the compliment, certain she was just being kind. But when he built his own taco and took a bite, it really did taste pretty good. The two of them gobbled down a couple tacos each and scarfed down the beans as well.

When they were done, Shari helped Mace put the leftovers in sealed containers and into the fridge. As they were working, she nudged him with her hip.

"You do know they make complete taco sets that you can find at the store, right? Meat, sauce, seasoning, everything. So next time you feel like Taco Tuesday, you don't have to work so hard to improvise."

Mace shook his head. "Nah. Improvising is the fun part. I mean, if I hadn't had to shred the cheese, you wouldn't have gotten a show with your meal. Next time, *you* get to do the grating and I'll watch." He winked at her.

Peabody's voice rang out from speakers above them. "*Mace, I have established a link with the Newport facility. There are two unidentified individuals currently in the residential level.*"

"What?" Shari exclaimed as she and Mace both got to their feet and took off toward the security office. Mace was already calling for Peabody to access the cameras and put the feed showing the two occupants on the main monitor. Shari asked "Are they… human? Or creatures."

Peabody answered as they ran down the corridor. *"They appear to be human. They are engaging in-"*

Neither of them heard the rest of Peabody's statement, nor did they need to as they entered the security office and saw on the monitor exactly what the man and woman were engaged in.

Shari said, "Oh! Um, Peabody, please cut that feed now," as she felt the blood rushing to her cheeks.

Mace chuckled and looked a bit regretful as the AI dutifully turned off the feed.

Shari slapped his shoulder. "Perv!" Then she asked as she checked her watch. "Should we interrupt them? Griff could be there at any time now."

Mace looked at his own watch, nodding his head. "We should. But we shouldn't. I mean, look at how angry *you* get when Peabody catches you takin' a du-"

He didn't finish the sentence, as a dangerous look appeared on Shari's face. He just grinned, then shrugged.

"Peabody, can you patch my voice through to them?" Shari asked. "No visual feed."

"Of course, admin Shari. Proceed when ready."

Shari's voice was hesitant as she unconsciously leaned toward a microphone on the desk in front of the monitor. "Uhm… hello? Can anyone hear me?"

Mace covered his mouth to hide his laughter as they heard some muted cursing and a squeal of surprise. Followed by some rustling of sheets or clothes and the sound of a zipper.

"Who's that?" a gruff male voice responded.

"Hello! My name is Shari. I'm a survivor like you." Shari's voice became more sure and excited. "I'm in America, in a facility like the one you're in. Owned by the same company."

This time, a female voice spoke up. "H-hullo. I'm Lisa. This is Evan. How are you, how did you… find us?"

"Hi Lisa! Nice to meet you. Mace and I," she paused to explain, "Mace is my boyfriend. He's also a genius coder."

He smiled and pretended to swoon at her use of 'boyfriend' and she smacked him.

"Anyway, Mace and I managed to get our AI connected to the game and the web, and he found more facilities across the world. With more survivors! Though we didn't know about you until just now."

She looked a little guilty at the deception she was about to pull but she didn't want to embarrass them. "If you're in your security office, Peabody can put up a video chat on the monitor." She gave Mace a look that said, 'You will never speak of this to them'.

After a few moments, the man spoke. "Yeah, we'll be right there. Damn. This is spooky." Mace and Shari could hear footsteps, one set heavily stomping and the other light and barely audible. They both waited for the other couple to reach the security room.

Less than a minute later, the monitor came back to life, Peabody having heard and followed Shari's instructions to set up a video chat. The two faces on the monitor looked wary.

The man was older, though not old. Maybe forty. He looked like he'd lived a hard life, his dark hair containing hints of grey and a significant scar across the bridge of his nose. The woman was closer to Mace and Shari's age. She had wide eyes and freckles and her cheeks were still flushed from her recent exertions.

Shari gave a friendly wave as Mace and the dude bro-nodded at each other.

"It's *so* nice to see other survivors! I'm Shari, this is Mace. How are you guys doing? Have you been there since the… end?" She faltered, thinking about the horrible first few days.

Lisa answered, seeming a bit shy. "Erm, yes. Since the first day them creatures began runnin' about eatin' everyone. We work here in the building. Worked, I mean."

Evan spoke up. "Lisa here was a lab tech. I ran the fitness center. Training the staff. That sort of thing."

He unconsciously flexed his muscles a bit as he spoke. Mace had to work hard not to roll his eyes.

"We were workin' down here when the alarms started going off. The TV feed showed what was happening up top. Didn't seem smart to run up there, but everyone else did just that. Bleedin' idjuts." The smirk on his face suggested his coworkers deserved their fates.

Shari asked, "How are you two set for food?" she was trying to get them to warm up a bit before telling them Griff was on his way.

Lisa answered for them. "There were a bunch of supplies here already." Shari nodded as the woman spoke. "We got maybe two weeks of food left now."

The look in her eyes became a little worried.

"Well, you guys look like you're doing pretty okay. I'm a doctor. Well, almost a doctor. From your appearance I'd say you've managed to take good care of yourselves. Have you had any illnesses or injuries?"

Both shook their heads no. Shari smiled.

"Good!" She took a deep breath. "About the food. We've actually got a friend of ours on his way to that facility. He's an army engineer who was stranded alone in a bunker not too far from you. When we discovered the Newport facility, we sent him there. He was planning to stop for supplies, so he may be bringing more food with him."

She saw the instant alarm on their faces. "Oh, no, no. Don't worry. Griff is a good guy. Gentle as a lamb. I'm sure he'll be thrilled to find more survivors. He had a friend here that he was speaking to over the radio. A sergeant at our armory. The man died a few days back, and Griff was left completely alone. That isn't... easy."

Shari's voice got quiet as she thought back to her days alone outside. Mace was reliving memories of his own. He unconsciously moved closer to Shari and put an arm around her.

Evan's face grew angry. "Who are you to just invite somebody into our home?"

Mace bristled at his tone, decided he didn't much like the man. Shari felt him tense up, and spoke quickly. "Like I said, we only found out about the facility this week. And only made contact today. We had no idea you were there. The other facilities with folks in them had survivors entering into the game, which is how we were able to find them."

Her tone was soft and placating, and it seemed to be working on Lisa. Her face relaxed some and she leaned back in her chair. But Evan wasn't having it.

"Ye didn't answer me question. What gives you the right to send someone here? What if we don't want no company?" he growled.

"What an ass," Mace mumbled quietly. He wasn't sure, and didn't much care if Evan heard. He tried to put himself in the man's shoes, though. He supposed if a stranger just announced that someone was going to come and invade his home, he'd be suspicious at the least. So he attempted to make peace.

"I'm currently the prime admin for the game and the highest-ranking corporate employee we're aware of so far. We haven't heard from the other facilities yet, so there may be someone higher level than me out there. But for now, I'm in charge of the corporate assets." He paused to let that sink in. "I reprogrammed Peabody, the AI that is now controlling all the facilities, including yours. Peabody, say hello."

Mace grinned as the two people jumped at the sound of Morgan Freeman's voice echoing around them.

"*Good day to you, Evan. Lisa.*"

Evan scowled as Lisa shuddered.

"That's just creepy," she said, rubbing her arms as if a chill had just passed through her.

"I know, right?" Shari grinned as she sympathized. "You can blame Mace for the voice. He thinks it's cool."

Mace's smile was completely unrepentant.

Evan, still scowling, said, "Whatever. There ain't no laws no more. No rules. Y'ain't got no authority over us. Yer across a damned ocean."

Lisa looked shocked, then put her hand over the microphone and said something to Evan. He just looked angrier as he sat back in his chair.

She removed her hand and spoke to them. "I'm sorry 'bout that. He's just bein' protective. He's really a nice guy once ye gets to know him. Yer friend is welcome here, o' course."

Shari was glad Lisa had taken control. She could feel Mace preparing to threaten to evict them or turn off the power. Or some other equally macho foolishness.

"Thank you, Lisa. And Evan. Please rest assured that Griff means you no harm. Neither do we. In fact, we have a plan that we were going to share with the other survivors. We all know the food supply is limited. And even with our facilities able to provide power and water..."

She began to explain their ultimate plan to upload themselves to extend their 'lives' for decades or longer. They talked for quite some time while Griff was fleeing the bear zombie.

Chapter 8

The Wizard of Id

Griff was greeted by the smiling, friendly face of Lisa, and the scowl of Evan as he stepped from the elevator. With his shotgun in hand but at rest by his side, he raised his other hand in greeting.

"I'm Griff. Nice to meet ya's."

Lisa stepped forward and held out a hand, which Griff shook. Evan grudgingly followed her lead as Lisa introduced them.

"I'm Lisa, this is Evan. Welcome. Shari and Mace have been telling us about you. And about what's been going on up there." She gave him a small, friendly smile.

Griff shook his head. "Up there is scary as hell. I got attacked as I were drivin' over here. Big-arse bear-monster larger than me Jeep." He raised both hands wide above his head as if describing the dimensions of the thing. Evan flinched as the shotgun moved with his hand, but Griff didn't notice.

"Nearly destroyed the truck, and chased me fer several klicks. I'll be havin' nightmares o' that one."

Evan's face somehow grew darker.

"It followed you?" he practically growled at Griff. "And ye led it here?"

Griff shook his head emphatically.

"No. I took a bunch of detours. Drove in a stream for a good long while. Made lots of false tracks. It should be good and lost. I took proper precautions." He tried to assure the man, though he wasn't completely sure himself.

Evan just grunted and turned away, walking back toward their quarters. Lisa remained. "Shari said you were planning to stop for supplies. Did ye find food?"

Griff, watching Evan walk away with a concerned look, instantly changed to a smile for the pretty young woman. "Whole back o' me Jeep's loaded with food."

He felt a little flutter in his belly as she beamed at him in response.

"You parked in the garage? We'll go up and get it later. Once Evan chills a bit." She apologized with her eyes even as she tried to maintain her smile.

"He's very protective." She looked over her shoulder, then whispered, "And I think more than a little afraid. Of what's up there, and of you being down here."

Griff nodded his understanding. "Just know I be no threat to either of ye. I'm just looking for a safe home, same as you. And I can help ye keep this place running proper-like. I'm an engineer."

He thumped his chest and gave her a goofy smile, making her laugh.

Lisa led him to the security room. "Shari and Mace wanted ya to call them when ya arrived. I think they worried about you bein' outside 'n all. For good reason, it seems." Griff nodded, thinking back to the bear. The damned thing had been nightmare fuel for sure. He sat down in the chair Lisa indicated and Peabody made a connection without even being asked. A moment later the young couple's faces appeared on the monitor.

"Griff!" Shari beamed at him, giving him a little wave in greeting. "You made it okay. We're *so* glad."

Mace was standing behind Shari and gave Griff a thumbs-up.

"Yeah, I'm here. Had a bit of a row with one o' them zombie creatures. Bear big as a house! Tried ta eat me face. I screamed like a lil girl and fled for me life."

He gave his best horrified face, putting his hands on his cheeks with his mouth and eyes wide open. Mace chuckled as Shari asked, "You're all good, though? No wounds or contamination?"

Griff grimaced. "Broke up the Jeep pretty bad. Blood smeared along one side. But I didn't touch it. And as far as I can see, none got inside where the food is. But I'll check it real careful like."

"I see you've met Lisa. And Evan too, I'm guessing?" Shari waited while Griff nodded, making a face she understood completely. Mace smirked behind her. He didn't like Evan either.

"I hope you guys get along okay in there." Shari looked hopefully at Lisa. "Lisa, Griff is already in the game. We're working on setting up accounts for you and Evan right now…"

Her voice drifted off as she saw Lisa grow uncomfortable. The woman tried to continue smiling as if nothing was wrong, but Shari knew better.

"You've changed your mind?" she asked Lisa, as gently as possible. They'd outlined their plan to upload into the game earlier. Lisa had seemed into it at the time. Less than an hour ago.

"Well, we been talking it over," Lisa began. "I still want to play. But Evan don't. Says he's got better things to do than play some kid's game." She sounded desperate to defend his choice and apologetic at the same time.

Shari smiled sincerely at the woman as Mace and Griff shared a look.

"That's no problem. We can get you in-game shortly. Mace is almost done." She looked up over her shoulder and Mace nodded, giving Lisa a crooked grin.

"If you have any interest in playing a dwarf, you can start in the same village Griff is in now. Or we can set you up wherever. You just let us know." He paused, then added in a less friendly tone, "And if Evan changes his mind we can still set him up too."

Lisa looked down at Griff, a bit shyly. "I'm afraid I ain't much of a gamer. But if Griff is willing to show me the ropes, bein' a lady dwarf might be fun."

Griff puffed out his chest once again, fists on his hips in a mock superhero pose. "O' course I'll show ya around. Be my pleasure. Just don't ever, ever attack the bunnies…"

*****

Shari got up from the security desk after finishing the conversation with Griff and Lisa. She looked at her watch. They'd played late into the night, then dinner and their discovery of the new people had kept them up 'til nearly sunrise.

She and Mace were both tired. Mace was already back working with Peabody to set up Lisa's account so that she and Griff could play through the day if they liked. It was daytime there in Newport after all. She mumbled something sleepily to him and shuffled to his room, where she just sort of melted face-first into his bed. When he joined her a few minutes later, she was snoring loudly.

With a grin and a shake of his head, he carefully crawled over top of her and wedged himself between her and the wall. Placing an arm around her, he was quickly asleep himself.

*****

Griff had some work to do if they were going to get into the game, so he asked Lisa about the VR pods in the manufacturing and storage levels. She confirmed that there were dozens of completed pods awaiting shipment to a distribution facility, but when he asked her to show him, she hesitated.

"There are four of them already set up here on this level. Though I dunno if they all work. Only ever seen one in use."

She went on to describe the testing they'd been doing with volunteer gamers. Griff's excitement grew. If there was already one working pod, he'd only have to bring one more online. He didn't think for one second about preparing one for Evan.

Lisa led him to the research area of their basement level. As they passed by the living quarters, Evan called out, "Ye won't need that elephant gun down here, mate. Unless that bear followed ye here."

His tone was sarcastic and mean. Griff looked down, not even realizing he was still holding the shotgun.

"Er, right then. If you'll point me to a room I'll stow this and the rest o' my gear. Maybe grab a quick shower? Then we can get to work."

Lisa nodded and spun in a full circle in the corridor. She chose the living quarters furthest away from the one she and Evan apparently shared and led Griff to it. "This should do. Just call out when you're ready. Have you eaten today?"

Griff rubbed his belly. "Had a scrambled egg ration first thing this mornin'. But it's been an exciting mornin'. I could use a bite. If yer low on food here, I got plenty upstairs."

Lisa shook her head.

"We have plenty for a few days yet with three of us here. We'll grab your food after you've checked out the pods," she offered. But Evan made an exasperated sound and emerged from his room.

"Toss me yer keys, mate. I'll grab a mail cart from upstairs and bring the food down while ye do yer kiddie game thing."

Griff tried not to bristle in response. He fished the keys from his pocket. Debating for a moment whether to speak up, he took the high road and said, "Be careful. The bear left blood all over the left rear side. Cracked the windows. Might be some blood splattered on some o'the stuff inside."

Evan nodded somberly, appreciating the gravity of that. "No worries. Any chance you grabbed beer?"

Griff nodded. "And wine, and spirits. I was planning on having a good old party when I got settled in. I'm glad yer both here to share it with me."

He found that he honestly meant that, even if he didn't much like Evan. After so much time alone, any company was good company.

The statement seemed to lighten Evan's mood as well, though it could have just been the confirmation of alcohol. He disappeared back into his room and began putting on his own gear before heading topside.

Lisa ushered Griff toward his room, saying, "I'll whip you up something to eat. Our selection ain't four-star by any stretch, but it'll fill yer belly right enough." She turned abruptly and left Griff alone outside his new digs.

He went inside and closed the door behind him. As he stowed his gun by the door and stripped off his gear, he took in the room. Nothing fancy, but comfortable. A bed with a desk next to it. A small kitchenette like you'd find in a hotel room with a sink and a coffeemaker. The only other door led to a small and efficient bathroom.

Ten minutes later, Griff was showered and dressed in a pair of jeans and a sweatshirt with a honey badger wearing a Viking helmet on the front. The print above and below the logo said, 'GameLit Don't Quit.'

Exiting his room, he explored a bit, finally finding a cafeteria. Walking through to the kitchen, he found Lisa just finishing a sandwich and placing it on a plate.

"Is that... bread?" He salivated as he inhaled.

"Aye. Made it this morning. This place has a full pantry with industrial-sized bins of flour and salt and such. Though we're almost out now."

She handed him the plate. He didn't even bother to sit, though his legs wobbled a bit from the giddiness of holding an actual sandwich in his hand. "I'm afraid it's just chicken and cheese. And the chicken's from a can. We've no more vegetables or fruit." She seemed worried he would reject the meal.

"My god, yer an angel right here on earth!" he cried, before taking an impolitely large bite of the sandwich. He half-groaned, half-growled to himself as he chewed the mouthful of goodness. She grinned, not bothered in the least.

A moment later she handed him a cold can of soda. He held it for a moment as tears threatened to form in his eyes.

"So much. Are ye sure ye can spare this?" He offered the can back to her. "I'm fine with water."

She laughed and pointed to a double set of doors in the back of the kitchen. "There's a mountain of them back there. There were nearly four hundred people workin' here. Most worked the assembly line or the offices upstairs, but this place was meant to feed them all twice a day if need be. We've eaten all of the fresh food; the meat, the veggies. Stuff that was in the walk-in fridge. But there's still some canned food and pasta and such. And it'd take us a year to drink all the soda."

Griff didn't argue. He set the sandwich down just long enough to open the can and take a long drink. The carbonation tickled his throat, a feeling he barely remembered. The sugary taste combined with the bits of sandwich still in his mouth conspired to transport him to a temporary state of bliss.

He brought down the can with a satisfied, "Ahhh. Damn, that's good," followed by the obligatory burp. He immediately looked sheepish and began to stammer an apology to Lisa, but she just laughed it off.

"I do the same. All part of the fun, right?" she winked at him. Griff blushed a bit, but was quickly distracted by the remainder of his sandwich. He took huge bites, washing the partially-chewed mouthfuls down with sugary drink. When both plate and can were empty, he took a few deep breaths and rubbed his stomach as he felt it gurgle happily.

After helping Lisa clean up, they made their way to the research area, where four of the pods sat in four rooms. Each room contained a pod, a standard hospital bed with life support and monitoring equipment, a small bathroom and shower, a plain table, and two aluminum chairs.

The first room they entered was the one where Lisa said they'd been using the pod. Griff made a quick check of the equipment. It was a more recent version than the ones he'd installed in his bunker.

He immediately saw that they'd made a few improvements that he himself would have suggested after working on the previous model. The capsule was set lower to be easier to get into and out of. As a result, the base was longer and a bit wider. The headset that made the actual neural connection with the player's brain had been simplified and streamlined. It was sturdier, in case a player thrashed too violently during gameplay. There was also a small video monitor that could be used to observe the player's activities in-game.

When he was done admiring the workmanship, he took just a couple minutes to confirm that it was still operational. He made a mental note of the calibrations and settings before moving to the next room.

This pod was powered down, but after a quick restart and a comparison of the settings, he found that it was also operational. He performed a full diagnostic just to be sure, and the system passed with greens across the board.

With the two pods fully operational, he suggested they both log in and get started. It would take Lisa a while to create her avatar. And Griff had plenty of quests waiting.

He walked her back to the first pod and spent a little time showing her the proper placement of the headset so that the sensors had optimal connections to her brain. Being a lab tech herself, and not unfamiliar with monitoring gear, she picked it up immediately.

When that was done, he said, "Ya know, ya don't *have* to play a dwarf. The game is pretty supportive of first-time players. Whatever race ya choose, you'll start in a safe zone with tutorials and easy starting quests."

She considered his words, her eyes unfocused, then replied without looking up at him, "I think it would be fun to be a dwarf. I love the old Hobbit movies, and sometimes wondered what a female dwarf looked like. Now I'll actually get to play one!"

Her smile had him feeling a bit warm and fuzzy. Remembering Evan lurking about somewhere, he bobbed his head and retreated.

As he closed the door to the lab so she could undress before climbing into the pod, he said, "Take your time creating your character. Get it just how you want it. If we're successful, you may be spending many years in that avatar. I'll be there when you arrive in the village."

When he entered his own lab room, he closed and locked the door behind him. Lisa he trusted, but he wouldn't turn his back on Evan even fully awake and alert. Let alone unconscious and naked inside what amounted to a plexiglass bubble. After a moment's thought, he said, "Peabody, can you hear me?"

"Of course, admin Griff. How can I be of assistance?"

"I'm about to log in. Can you alert me in-game or pull me out of immersion if anyone attempts to open this door?"

"I can do either or both." Peabody's reply was short and succinct. Griff asked for both.

"It shall be as you request, admin Griff. I'm glad to see you're bringing another player to the game." Peabody added.

Which Griff considered a little strange. But he set those thoughts aside as he undressed and crawled into the pod. He set his headgear in place and relaxed into the gel that filled the space around him. A moment later, he closed his eyes and plunged into immersion.

He awoke in his room at the inn, sitting on his bed precisely as he had logged out. Leaving the room and the inn, he found the street bustling with the normal daily activity of the village. Merchants peddled their wares in shops and a few carts on the square, and a farmer rolled past on a donkey-powered cart loaded with melons of some kind.

He took the opportunity to speak with a few of the locals he knew from quests they'd given him, asking after their health, their children, their crops. In his mind, it never hurt to build relationships and increase your reputation. And it took very little effort. He simply had to behave as he would with other humans in the real world.

After thirty minutes, there was a minor uproar near the fountain as Lisa appeared. Griff laughed as he noticed the tag above her head, which read, 'Lady Lisa.'

Walking toward her, he paused to make a sweeping bow and said, "Tis an honor to make your acquaintance, Lady Lisa."

She blushed slightly. "I thought just Lisa would be too plain and maybe confusing if there's another living Lisa."

Griff laughed openly, but he was laughing with her, not at her. "I think it's perfect. Come with me. I'll introduce you to a few folks and we'll see about getting you some quests."

He led her toward the tavern. Unsurprisingly, the locals were all quite pleased to see a second outworlder appear in their tiny village. It wasn't long before Lisa's quest log was full and she'd been introduced to nearly everyone.

Griff resigned himself to the entire day being one long escort quest as he escorted Lisa around, assisting her with fetch quests and like.

He had a brief moment of panic when they found themselves in the meadow outside the gates. She was walking next to him as he warily eyed the fuzzy bunnies hopping about. But as soon as she noticed one of the creatures, she squealed and charged at it.

Griff cried out "Wait! I said don't attack the bunnies! They're-" he stopped speaking as she threw herself to her knees in front of the furry woodland creature, bent to scoop it up in her arms, and hugged it to her chest.

She spoke softly to the animal as she petted it, rubbing its head and ears. Griff watched as the damned thing began to make a sort of purring sound as it nibbled at Lisa's noob cotton shirt sleeve.

When she'd had enough, she set the bunny down and got back to her feet. The creature gave Griff a dirty look as if to say, "We remember you," before hopping off behind a shrub. Griff shook his head. The devs had really gone all out for this game. It seemed he had a negative reputation amongst the bunnies of the meadow.

The two of them continued into the forest, and Griff sent Lisa a party invite so that they could share experience. He was stronger now, a higher level than he'd been when the wolves had handed him his ass. It was time for a little payback. He gripped his hammer tightly and whistled loudly. Followed by "Here, doggy doggy!"

*****

Mace and Shari were awakened by Dakota, who urgently needed to head up to the cornfield. Shari obliged while Mace headed to the security office to check his email and see if they'd had any messages from the other survivors.

"Peabody, are any of the other players in the game right now?"

Though it was breakfast time for he and Shari, it was well into the evening for the folks in Hong Kong, Moscow and Sydney. The guy in Texas might not even be awake yet.

"*Players Griff and Lisa are online,*" Peabody answered. Anticipating Mace's next question, he continued, "*The players in Moscow were online for several hours while you slept. Elysia translated your message for them, but they have not responded. No players have logged in from Sydney or Hong Kong since your message was sent. The North Korean players received your message and immediately began demanding admin access to override yours. They are quite angry, and are trying to determine how to find you in Elysia.*"

Mace couldn't say he was wholly surprised. Players were competitive. And if the North Korean players were government-sponsored, they'd be more competitive than normal. Until a few months ago their lives - and maybe the lives of their families - might have depended upon their performance. Whether that be gold farming, clearing dungeons, or striving to be the top-rated players with the best gear. And old habits die hard.

But he was concerned by their request. "Peabody, did Elysia give them admin access?"

"No, Mace. They were quite rude and their demands were unreasonable. They wanted access shut down for all players but themselves. And since you are a recognized corporate entity and they are not employees, their claim for admin rights is invalid."

Mace let out a sigh of relief as Shari and Dakota joined him. Shari asked, "Any news?"

Mace shook his head. "No answers from anyone. The North Koreans got pissed and tried to take over the game, shut everyone else out. Elysia said no." He grinned. Dakota let out a happy *whuff* and wagged his tail as if he understood. Mace looked down at the dog and said, "We really do need to get back to the armory. Get his crate and his food and whatever. Maybe stop for some Ho-Ho's on the way back."

Shari laughed. "You and those damned Ho-Ho's. If I thought your body was going to need to last more than a year or two, I'd be putting you on a strict diet of…" She paused.

He grinned and stuck his tongue out. "What? Veggies? There aren't any! And there's a big old truck full of tasty Ho-Ho's out there just waiting. That's fate right there."

He grinned as she rolled her eyes and left to go put her gear on, Dakota following along behind her.

Mace took a minute to compose another message. This time, he typed it into the game interface on the computer in front of him.

"Peabody, please send this message as personal mail to all the players except the North Koreans."

When Peabody acknowledged that it was done, he got up and went to go gear up himself. He met Shari and Dakota at the elevator and they left together.

Fifteen minutes later, they were arriving at the armory when Dakota began to whine. His ears laid back and his tail down, he crawled into Mace's lap and shivered. Mace and Shari both began to search the area, frantically seeking whatever had scared the dog.

Mace caught movement behind one of the parked Humvees and whispered, "Over there. Something or someone behind that vehicle."

Shari looked to where he was pointing. The vehicle was only about fifty yards from where they sat in Bertha. That was way too close for Shari's comfort. She put Bertha in reverse and backed slowly across the large parking lot that surrounded the building.

A zombie burst from behind the Humvee and charged at them. When Dakota barked hopefully, then whined again, Mace looked from the dog to the creature. What he saw made him want to puke. Or cry. Or both.

"Oh, shit," he said, as Shari hit the accelerator and Bertha moved more quickly to keep distance between them and the zombie.

Shari saw it a moment after he did. "Oh, no. Is that? It can't be."

Mace nodded. "It's the sergeant. Danny. Dakota's handler. No wonder the poor mutt's confused. He sees his old master but smells the zombie."

His voice caught in his throat. From reading the man's journal and talking about him with Griff, they'd felt a kinship with the man. They'd even mourned him as if he'd been a friend.

And now here he was, about to try to kill them.

Dakota whined again and Mace patted his head, then scratched behind his ears as Bertha sped backward and they gained some distance. Still, the zombie moved faster than a human should be able to.

Shari cranked the wheel and Bertha spun to the side. She jerked the gearshift into drive and punched the accelerator. Their change of direction had cost them precious seconds, and the zombie was approaching quickly. As Shari steered hard and put him in their rearview, he roared and leapt toward the Jeep.

Fortunately for them, Bertha's acceleration was quick enough to place them out of the zombie's reach. He missed in his bid to grasp the back bumper, falling onto his face and rolling on the pavement as Bertha sped away.

Shari was already reaching for her rifle. "Mace! When I stop, you take the wheel. I'm going to jump out and shoot him."

"WHAT?" Mace practically shouted at her. "Are you insane? Let's just leave. We'll drive far away until he's lost us. Then we'll come back and you can shoot him from a rooftop or someplace far, far away."

Shari shook her head. "I can do this. I just need some distance. But be ready with your shotgun just in case."

Mace wanted to argue more. He was terrified she was going to get hurt. His gut clenched and his pulse raced even faster than it had been a moment ago.

He hugged the dog tightly as Shari raced down the road. When she was maybe five hundred yards ahead of the zombie, she stopped and threw Bertha into park. Grabbing her rifle, she opened her door and stood on the running board, then put a foot on the door handle to push herself up onto Bertha's roof.

Mace jumped out with shotgun in hand, displacing the confused dog. Dakota fell out onto the road and crouched down, belly flat against the asphalt and head down, whining.

Mace saw that Shari was laying prone atop Bertha's roof, her rifle barrel resting on the back rail of the luggage rack bolted to the roof. She was already sighting in on the approaching zombie. Mace looked on, fighting the urge to run while at the same time fighting the urge to charge forward and blast at the thing before it got close to Shari. He raised his shotgun and took aim, though the thing was still far out of his range.

A moment later, Shari's rifle fired. The zombie jerked backward as if he had just bounced off a glass door. Neon blue blood splattered in a wet cloud behind him as a significant portion of his neck disappeared. Mace heard Shari reload as the zombie sergeant recovered and resumed its charge. Shari fired again and this time a chunk of his face disappeared. The zombie fell backward, screaming in pain, and Dakota whined in distress.

Shari cursed "Shit! I can't see his head now. I need to wait 'til he gets back up."

Mace said, "Screw that!" He dashed forward, shotgun still pointed at the monster. Dakota took off too, staying at Mace's side as they got closer.

The dog barked at the zombie, as if expecting some kind of recognition. Mace was a mess of emotions ranging from fear to anger to pity.

As he got within about ten yards of the downed zombie, he slowed down. Being careful to stay out of Shari's line of sight, he moved to the side and fired into the body, which was struggling to get up. Dakota yelped in surprise, then actually growled at Mace. Danny might smell funny, but he was still Danny. And Mace was hurting him.

Then the monster managed to sit upright, roaring in pain and anger at Mace as it did. Dakota let out a yelp and retreated behind Mace, tail between his legs. Mace didn't blame him one bit.

He was about to step forward when Danny zombie's head exploded in a spray of neon blue blood and bits of tissue. Mace backed away quickly, not wanting to get the contaminated material on himself. Again.

But Dakota saw his old master fall and ran forward. The poor, loyal animal walked right into the splattering of tissue around the zombie as Mace and Shari both screamed, "Dakota, nooooo!"

But they were far too late. The dog's feet were already coated in the blue grime as he moved forward to sniff at his dead friend. He whined pathetically and looked back toward Mace as if to ask why they'd killed Danny.

Mace lost it. He dropped to his knees, sobbing. He could hear Shari crying behind him as she chambered another round in her rifle. Dakota turned, as if to head back to Mace, but Mace held up a hand. Between ragged gasps of air he said, "Dakota, sit!"

The dog instantly obliged, his training kicking in. He cocked his head to one side, looking at Mace for further instructions. His ears just beginning to perk up as Shari fired.

Mace closed his eyes and dropped his head to look at the pavement. He couldn't look at the dog and his former master. He sat there, just looking at his hands and crying.

A couple minutes later, he felt Shari drop next to him. She wrapped her arms around him, and he looked up at her face. Tears streaked down her face and snot ran from her nose. She buried her head in his chest, and he could hear her sob.

"I'm sorry. I'm so sorry. I had no choice."

Mace suddenly realized how much worse this must be for her. While he'd been falling apart at the sight of their contaminated companion, she'd had the fortitude to do what needed to be done. He played the scene back in his head. The dog had turned and was headed toward him. Shari had taken action to protect him, even though it meant killing the innocent dog.

He nearly crushed her in his arms, hugging her tightly to himself and rocking her back and forth. They both cried for a while, until Shari separated herself from him. She sniffed, wiping the snot from her face onto his shoulder before getting to her feet.

She looked around as she said, "We can't stay here. Something might have heard the shots. We need to go."

Mace nodded woodenly, getting to his feet. He picked up his shotgun and turned toward Bertha. He didn't have the heart to look back. When they were both back inside Bertha and headed home, he said "Goodbye Dakota. You were a good dog. A very good dog and our friend. I hope you're with Danny in a better place somewhere." Shari sobbed again but kept driving.

*****

Griff meanwhile, was having his best day in a long while. He'd completely shaken off the fear from the bear attack and was delighting in Lisa's company. They moved through the woods together, talking about their lives as they hunted wolves and gathered herbs.

Griff had begun by telling her the story of his death at the hands of the wolves, followed immediately by his run-in with the fuzzy bunnies. The story had made Lisa laugh so hard that she'd had to sit on a stump and catch her breath as she held her stomach. Griff didn't mind being laughed at one bit. Lisa was simply charming.

Her avatar had the same freckles that decorated her face in real life. She'd chosen to be a redhead, with her hair gathered in whimsical braided pigtails on either side of her head. Her face was round, with green eyes and a soft tuft of red peach-fuzz barely detectable on her chin. While her body was slimmer than Griff's with wide hips and a pronounced waistline that accentuated her significant bust. Her shoulders were wide, her arms strong, and she stood nearly the same height as Griff.

They spent half the day in the forest talking about little things as they hunted and gathered. When they had enough wolf pelts to complete the kill quest for both of them, they returned to the village and turned in the quest. Between the killings and the quest completion experience, Lisa was already up to level seven while Griff was level fourteen. At these low levels, the experience requirement was minimal and it wouldn't be long before Lisa caught up to him.

After completing some fetch quests and an odd quest to kill a weasel that had invaded a henhouse, they decided to stop at the tavern for a meal. Griff was giddy with anticipation of seeing her reaction to the food.

He wasn't disappointed. They ordered a couple pints of ale and braised short ribs. When the meal arrived, it came with piping hot bread fresh from the oven. Lisa inhaled deeply.

"Oh gawd, this smells delicious!" she gushed as she grabbed the small loaf of bread and pulled one end off. Tearing a bite from it, she stuffed it into her mouth without ceremony. Her eyes rolled back in her head and she mumbled with her mouth full. Griff couldn't make out the words, but he got the idea.

"Wait till ye try the meat." He motioned toward her plate. Lisa set down the bread and swallowed her mouthful before pulling one of the short ribs apart from its neighbors with stubby-but-strong fingers. She brought the rib up to her mouth and tore off some of the succulent meat. Her eyes widened as she chewed slowly.

A moment later, she reached for mug and took a gulp of ale, at which point her eyes widened again and she inhaled sharply.

Setting the mug down with one hand and the half-eaten rib with the other, she said, "Oh god, that's the best food I've tasted in me life!"

As Griff chuckled and dug into his own delicious meal, she tore through the ribs in record time and requested seconds. She also ordered a pitcher of ale and worked her way through a good portion of that, too.

When she was done, she sat back and rubbed her belly. With a somehow-polite belch she looked at Griff, smiling. "That were better than sex!"

Griff snorted. "That don't say much about Evan then, does it?" He grinned at her and winked, making her laugh.

Shaking her head, she said, "No, no. I mean…"

She decided maybe Griff was right and just laughed herself. The twinkle in Griff's eye made her laugh even harder.

He paid for their meals and secured her a room of her own upstairs, then the two of them retired to their beds and logged out.

Griff took his time leaving the lab. He needed to sort some things out in his head while he was alone. He got out of his pod, used the bathroom and took a long, hot shower. In just the last few days, he'd gone from incredibly lonely and nearly suicidal to having friends, having a purpose. He'd nearly died and been eaten by a monster. And he'd met a lovely girl who was, much to his chagrin, involved with someone else. It was a lot to take in.

Eventually exiting the lab, he found both his new housemates in the kitchen. Evan had indeed unloaded all the supplies, which were now stacked on the countertop as Lisa took inventory.

Evan gave him a polite nod when he entered, saying, "Saw the damage and the blood. That thing must've been huge."

Griff let out a breath he hadn't realized he'd been holding. "Yeah, mate. It were bigger than the Jeep. Didn't even see it coming. Just all of a sudden, *blam!* it nearly knocked me off the road."

Just as Griff was beginning to think Evan might not be so bad, the man smirked at him. "Well, I hope ye lost it like ye said. Anything that big could destroy this place in a day."

Griff tried not to bristle as thoughts of putting a bullet through the man's head and living happily ever after with Lisa danced through his head.

"I was careful. And the next rain will wash away any scent it might try to follow. I'm sure we're safe." He spoke in his best soldier voice, trying to reassure Lisa and back Evan down a bit.

Evan changed the subject. Motioning toward the food supply, he said, "This is a good haul. But with three of us, it won't last long. We'll need to make another run. I cleaned up the blood on the Jeep, so we can use that."

Griff agreed. "I found a Tesco's close by. Maybe we can go there in the morning. Just after sunrise?"

Evan nodded and reached a hand out to Lisa. As she took his hand, he led her out of the kitchen.

Nearing the door, he said, "I hauled it down here, you can put it away. It's getting late. See you in the morning."

Lisa smiled apologetically at Griff as she was led away.

Griff turned to the pile of supplies. He was slightly hungry. Though his body hadn't actually done much, the day of adventuring had convinced his mind that he should be hungry, so he was.

He located a package of beef jerky and began to nibble on it as he moved groceries from the counter to the pantry. He grabbed himself another soda as he worked, and thought about the future for a change.

Chapter 9

Possibilities

Mace and Shari sat on the bed in his quarters and he rubbed her back as she leaned into him. There was the occasional sniffle from each of them as they thought about Dakota, and Danny, and the others they'd lost.

Eventually, Mace spoke. "We can't tell Griff."

Shari didn't say anything for a while, then nodded, just slightly. "It would only hurt him. But I don't want to lie. If he asks about Dakota we'll need to tell him. But only if he asks."

A short while later, they both crawled into their pods and got back into the game. Despite their melancholy mood, there were things they needed to take care of in Elysia. They no longer treated it as a game. This was their future home. And they needed to prepare it.

When they awoke in the game, they found that the boat had sailed with the dawn and was about to arrive back at Lakeside. Mace could see a small crowd of citizens gathered at the dock. He also noted that the centaurs had made it back and folks were unloading the overladen cart of iron and weapons. The armor and weapons looted from the slavers seemed to have boosted morale considerably.

As the boat docked, Captain Charles walked down the dock to greet them. Raising a hand, he called out, "I hear you massacred those Black Flame slavers like they were the Tribe of Jeff!" he grinned a big ogre grin showing long tusks and sharp teeth.

Mace looked confused.

"Tribe of Jeff?" He looked to Shari, who shrugged. Layne helpfully filled them in.

"They were a vegetarian tribe in the land of Kirshtein who subsisted mainly on pineapple from the groves they tended. Long ago, they fought a war with the leprechauns. It was a long and bloody war, but remained a stalemate until a primitive human tribe sided with the leprechauns. The Tribe of Jeff were slaughtered. Every man, woman and child were grilled alive on shish-kabobs with meat from giant ant-pigs. It was said they tasted like pineapple."

Shari made a disgusted face as Mace chuckled.

"We didn't do any roasting. But between the centaurs and the minotaurs and your guards here," he indicated the two guards just stepping down the ramp, "they didn't have a chance. And you've already seen their generous contribution to your armory." He winked at the ogre.

"Yes, thank you for that. Most outworlders would have kept the loot for themselves and sold it to us at market price. Or higher, knowing our need." Charles bowed his head slightly.

Shari spoke up. "Things are different now. There are so few of us, and we no longer need to compete with each other. Or have the ability to sell our unneeded loot to other outworlders. Our focus now is to help you grow. You here at Lakeside, the elves in my home city, and others we encounter whom we come to call friends."

Mace nodded. "And speaking of growing, we need to speak privately. There's been a development you need to know about."

Mace and his group walked with Charles to his home. Minus Brahm, who went to see to his people and make sure the iron was unloaded at the smithy. Once they were alone in Charles' dining room, Mace informed him of what they'd found in the dungeon. The ant queen, the pool of water that gave permanent buffs, and the portal room.

The ogre took it all in with a politely interested look on his face until Mace mentioned the portals. At which point his jaw dropped and he seemed to have difficulty speaking.

"You... the... you mean to say... but there can't be that many portals in one place. No city I know of has more than two!"

Mace let him absorb the information for a few moments. "Needless to say, this needs to remain a secret. We are trusting you, but until we build up a more secure settlement around Darkstone, no one can know of its hidden value."

"Of… of course." Captain Charles nodded his big ogre skull in agreement. "I'll think of some reason to give the villagers and we'll begin constructing a perimeter wall right away."

Shari reached into her bag and withdrew five hundred gold. "The iron you've been pulling from there is not valuable enough to justify that kind of investment. People will begin to ask questions. So let's just say Mace is an eccentric drow who wants his new toy stronghold secured and is willing to pay."

She handed the coins to Charles, who chuckled.

"Aye, there'd be few who'd doubt that after meeting our drow here." He winked at Mace. "I'll begin immediately."

They spent some more time with Charles, outlining some of their plans and talking about the crafting skills of various citizens of Lakeside. Mace handed the ogre a couple of books from the library that would help his people increase their mastery.

Charles accepted the books with reverence, his big hands shaking as he held them in front of him. "Mace. This is… the value of these is beyond my reckoning."

You have gained +250 reputation with the settlement of Lakeside. Your reputation is now Revered.

Shari and the other party members' eyes went blank for a moment as they all received similar messages with reputation gains. She smiled at Charles and said, "This is just the beginning. If our plans come to fruition, this will become a place of power and prosperity. Citizens will come from far and wide to live or trade here. You will oversee battalions of guards and protect many thousands from those who would do harm or take advantage of them."

Charles' chest puffed out as he pictured it. "Well, I should get busy then!"

He rose and ushered them out of his house, carefully placing the books on the table. "If you don't mind, I may save these for a bit. It may be that we get new blood who can better use them. Our folk are mostly simple crafters, not nearly of the level to warrant the use of these."

Mace shrugged. "I trust your judgement. I have brought you into our inner circle with the information you've been given today. I hope that proves my trust. And that I have yours in return."

Charles shook his head. "Words I never thought to hear from a drow. But aye, you've more than earned my trust, lad. No question."

Mace and the others went back to the tavern, ordering a meal as they sat to talk about their immediate plans. Minx made herself visible and hopped from Mace's shoulder onto the table, where she promptly helped herself to his food. Tiny hands moved with a blur and snatched bits of meat and cheese, which disappeared just as quickly into her mouth. Her cheeks bulged like a chipmunk's as she chewed on her prizes.

After a while, her tummy visibly bulged and she lay down on her back, her feet lazily flopping in the air. Mion jumped down and settled on Minx's belly, curling up to enjoy the warmth and soft fur. Both little ladies began to purr contentedly.

Mace began. "We have the quest to go to Graf. Two quests, actually. My original quest from Jervis and the quest to escort Ian back there. And since Graf is where the Black Flame seem to be based, there's a third reason to go."

Shari nodded. "Any chance one of those portals goes to Graf? Otherwise it's quite the trip. The fastest route would be by boat across the lake and down to Port Bjurstrom, then up the river to Graf. A three day trip, at least."

As she spoke, she was drawing a rough outline of the route on a parchment with a little help from Layne on direction and distance. She picked up a point in the Cartography skill as she worked.

Lila spoke up. "I want to use the portals too. But…" She hesitated, suddenly looking shy.

Shari reached over and rubbed the halfling's back. "You're family now. We always want to hear your opinion."

Lila nodded slightly and continued. "We don't know much about those portals. Mace activated them by accident. We don't know what powers them or how long they'll last. If we use one to go to Graf, for example, we have no way of knowing it'll be there to bring us back. And if we're planning to take on the Black Flame while we're there, we will almost certainly need a quick escape route. So I say it's better to have Captain Jorin there and ready to sail us away."

Shari looked impressed. "You've been giving this some thought."

Mace shook his head. "I think she's just naturally sneaky and cautious. Until you piss her off. Then she becomes a ninja berserker woman."

Lila's smile showed that she agreed with him completely.

Shari laughed. "Okay, so we'll ask the captain if he has time to take us to Graf and back. We can afford to pay him. Maybe give him some of the dungeon loot to trade when we get to the ports."

Mace facepalmed. "I was wrong before. We have *four* quests. Jorin gave me one to take down the Black Flame."

Before he forgot again, he pulled up each of his quests and shared them with his party members. They all began to smile as they read the descriptions - and especially the rewards.

Their immediate plans decided, Layne left with Lila to do some shopping, while Shari went to speak with the boat captain to arrange for them to depart the following morning. Mace found Charles and informed him, then headed to the previously-abandoned house where Ian was supposed to be hiding.

Only when he got there, the house was no longer abandoned. The influx of prisoners had apparently caused the house to be fixed up and occupied. He lingered near the house for a while, then walked back to the alley where he'd met Ian. Almost immediately, the tall green rabbit materialized with a bow and a sweep of his hat.

"Greetings, Mace."

"Ian. I was looking for you. Have you lost your home again?"

The rabbit sighed. "Indeed, yes. The place, it grows more crowded, yes. I have had to relocate twice more. Not safe here much longer, no."

Mace looked over his shoulder to make sure they weren't being observed. "We plan to leave in the morning on Captain Jorin's boat. First to Port Bjurstrom, then Graf. Be on the boat before sunrise. Have you got enough food?"

Ian smiled. "I am well enough fed, yes. Glad to be returning home, oh yes."

"Once we're on the boat, you can stop hiding. I'll introduce you to the captain, and you can travel openly as one of our group."

"Oh, no no." Ian took a step back, a horrified look on his face. "It is much preferred to remain hidden, yes. Large green bunnies stand out in a crowd. Tend to be remembered, yes. Prefer not to be observed in my travels, no."

"Alright, then. Suit yourself. We'll be on a relatively small boat for three days, maybe four. Could make it difficult to hide." Mace shrugged at the dapper rabbit. "Be on the boat by sunrise."

With nothing in particular demanding his time, Mace went to find the carpentry boss Verga and offer his services. She gladly gave him some finish work to do, and he spent several hours raising both his Builder and Carpentry skill one level each.

Toward dinner time, he put away his tools and met back up with Shari. They climbed the stairs at the inn and entered Mace's room, where they logged out. The plan was to get an early dinner and then some sleep, so they could be ready to depart before the sun rose in the game.

Both of them glanced at the floor several times as they ate their meal in near-silence. Even after the short time with Dakota, the dog had become a part of their lives. Mace expected him to be sitting nearby, begging for food with his eyes and wagging tail.

Shari mumbled something Mace couldn't hear. When he put a hand to his ear, she repeated, "Have you seen any dogs in the game?"

Make thought about it for a minute. "Yep. Starter zone NPC's give out lost dog quests."

Shari smiled faintly. "Maybe when we upload ourselves and have a stable home somewhere, we can have a dog in the game. I think I'd like that."

Mace moved closer to her and wrapped her in his arms. A few moments later they cleaned up the dishes and crawled into bed. Mace held Shari close as she quietly cried herself to sleep. As he dozed off, he had tears in his own eyes.

*****

After a good night's sleep, Griff was up before dawn. He took a quick shower and grabbed his dirty clothes.

A trip to the laundry room to get the washing started and then he was off to the kitchen. He found pancake mix and powdered eggs in the pantry, as well as an industrial-sized canister of syrup.

Lisa and Evan showed up as he was making a tall stack of pancakes. He offered three each to them on plates as they sat down.

"I'm almost done, so don't wait on me. Dig in," he motioned them toward the syrup.

Evan didn't hesitate, grabbing the syrup and coating his short stack liberally. He then set it down and dug in, ignoring Lisa completely. With a sigh, she reached for the syrup and prepared her own stack.

She politely waited for Griff to finish making his own stack and join them, giving him a brief smile as they both took a bite.

"Mmmm… these are good," she offered.

"Ha! Yeah. I added a cup of water to two cups of mix and stirred. I'm a regular gourmet over here," Griff winked at her.

Evan was too busy shoveling food into his mouth to notice. When he was through, he got up and walked into the fridge, emerging a moment later with a fruit cup, which he opened as he walked. Heading out the door, he paused and looked at Griff.

"You'll clean up, yeah? Then I assume you lot will be playin' yer game again?" He didn't wait for an answer, just walked through the door.

Griff ignored him and quietly finished his breakfast. The food tasted delicious compared to the rations he'd been surviving on, and he savored every fluffy, maple-flavored bite. Lisa took her time as well, content to sit quietly and eat.

When they were through, she helped with the dishes, then showed him where the trash chute was and gave him a quick lesson on the dishwasher.

As they left the kitchen and headed toward their pods, he asked, "So what did you do all day? Before, I mean. With just you two here. No offense, but Evan don't exactly seem to be a sparkling conversationalist."

Lisa snorted. "He's not so bad. He's funny when he wants to be. We played some board games. Worked out a lot. Tried the radio sometimes. I like to read. Back when it first happened, I managed to download a bunch of books. Spent half me life savings, but I didn't think money was going to matter much anymore. So I have about a hundred books to get through."

"What are your favorites?" he asked her, sincerely curious. He loved to read himself.

"I love the old LitRPGs from the first couple decades of this century. Have you ever read the Emerilia books? Or the Greystone Chronicles?"

Griff grinned. "Aye! Loved them both. Please tell me ye have them? I haven't seen 'em since I were a child. I was more partial to the Terra books. The ones with the kobolds."

"Sure, I have them all. Or as many as I could find. If the site's not down we could look for some more later." She gave a little skip as they reached the labs. "I'll see you in the game."

She gave a brief wave and shut the door. Griff locked his own door again and stripped before climbing into his pod. In less than two minutes he was closing his eyes and falling into immersion.

When he opened his eyes again, his avatar was where he'd left it at the inn. Since he'd joined the American server that Mace and Shari were on, the hours were kind of funky. It would take him a while to adjust to operating on their time. Being underground made it easier, though.

Still, they wouldn't be on for a few more hours, so he walked Lisa around the village as she did fetch quests and crafting quests. She'd elected to take up leatherworking as a skill when they'd received bunches of raw leather from the wolf kills. She liked the idea of turning the hide into something useful, like lining for the armor Griff would be able to craft, or bags and boots and quivers.

Lisa was approaching level ten, when she'd be able to choose a specialization. The two of them had discussed it as they walked through the forest and the village completing quests.

Griff was surprised to find that the normally-timid woman had a love for sharp weapons. She was leaning toward a two-bladed fighting style, and she was a quick study on the crossbow. Which was wonderful for Griff, as he was still not very talented at ranged fighting. He was content holding off enemies with his shield while Lisa shot at them.

In the beginning, though, it hadn't gone so smoothly. He'd purchased her a beginner crossbow using some of the ridiculously high coin drops they'd gotten from wolf kills. The weapons merchant had shown her a target dummy out back and given her a few pointers to get her started.

As soon as she had hit the target four times in a row, Griff had declared, "Good enough!" and they'd gone back out hunting. The very first fight against an angry boar, Griff had slammed it with his shield to stun it, then called for Lisa to shoot.

He heard the click and twang of the cable being released, and a moment later felt a blinding pain as the crossbow bolt slammed into his backside. Out of instinct, he spun around to try and see the offending missile, leaving the boar and its sharp tusks at his back.

The pig didn't hesitate, gouging the backs of his legs and tearing one hamstring. Griff found himself falling backward to sit on the bolt, which pushed deeper into his ass cheek as he screamed in pain and tried to fend off the boar with his shield.

Lisa had the presence of mind to reload as she apologized profusely. Another shot got a lucky critical hit, boring into the pig's eye. The pig fell over onto Griff, pinning his damaged and bleeding legs.

"Damn that hurts!" he growled as he used his dwarven strength to push the carcass off of him. He accepted a health potion from Lisa and gulped it down, then rolled onto his belly, reached back and pulled the now deeply-embedded crossbow bolt from his butt. Grunting in pain and bleeding again, he tossed the sharp projectile to the ground.

There were tears in Lisa's eyes when he looked up at her, and her hands were covering her mouth. His anger instantly subsided and he began to get to his feet, saying "Oy, no worries luv. 'Tis but a scratch."

She couldn't take it anymore and burst out in a raucous laugh. The tears had been from suppressing laughter. But the unconscious Black Knight reference had put her over the edge and she couldn't hold back.

"I'm… I'm sorry!" She gasped between snorts. "It's just, I hit you in the ass, then you sat on it. And the look on your face, and the…" She collapsed to the ground helpless with laughter.

Griff stood there for a moment, mouth agape. He'd been all prepared to comfort this dwarfess who'd shot him in the ass, and she was rolling around on the ground laughing at his pain! After a moment, he began to chuckle himself. "Right, then. I suppose shootin' me arse was an accident?"

Laying on her back, arms wrapped around her belly, she shook her head. "I swear. I was aiming for the pig. But yer arse was in the way. And its such a big target!" she giggled, eyes wide and innocent.

Shaking his head he sat down next to her, the pain from his butt wound causing him to grunt, which sent her into another fit of laughter. He drank a health potion while he waited for her to gather her wits and tried his best to keep a stern look on his face.

Eventually she sat up next to him. She threw her arms around him and gave him a kiss on the cheek.

"I'm *so* sorry, Mister Grumpy!" she teased.

That broke his resolve, and he grinned back at her. "Next time, *you* get the shield and I get to shoot pointy things in your direction."

Her eyes widened in mock horror and she released him to lean back, as if afraid. "Oh, no! Uh-uh. Nope. I need to practice my marksmanship."

They stayed in the forest long enough to kill a few more wolves, boars, and bears. As soon as Lisa reached level ten they headed back. Once in the village, Griff took her to a pavilion where several class trainers resided.

The building was wide open, with a twin row of small living quarters in the back. The main area was dedicated to training. There were obstacle courses, varying types of target dummies, a small arena for PvP training, and weapons racks scattered around each.

"Well, have ye given more thought to what ye'll choose?" Griff looked at Lisa as she surveyed their surroundings. Only a few of the trainers were in sight. Which she supposed made sense, since no outlanders had come for training in recent months.

"I think I want to be a ranger. I can shoot people in the arse from a distance…" She smiled at him, then moved her eyes significantly to his butt, which he rubbed unconsciously. "Or I can get in close with swords."

Griff nodded. From his conversations with Shari, he thought a ranger might fit into the group's makeup well enough. He would be the tank, while Mace and Lila were both melee dps that specialized in sneak attacks from behind. Layne had buffs and debuffs, and Shari could heal.

Of course, none of them stuck strictly to their spec. Shari was also good with a bow, while Mace had magic for ranged attacks. No reason Lisa couldn't be a dual-purpose player as well. And her two choices were complimentary. The dexterity, agility, and strength that would make her good with twin swords would also improve her shooting skills with the crossbow.

Griff pointed to a hut near the end of the first row. A wooden staff and leather bag sat by the door, where a dwarf in mottled green leather sat whittling. He appeared to be making arrows.

Griff stayed where he was while Lisa approached the ranger and asked for training. The dwarf nodded, holding out a hand. Lisa paid him his fee and the two of them moved to one of the training areas.

Leaving them to it, Griff went to see his own warrior trainer. He'd assigned all but his most recent attribute point, with a focus on Stamina and Strength and a little Agility and Dexterity added in. And after his run-in with the bear, he'd put his most recent point into Luck. He took a quick look at his character stats.

Character Name: Griff	Class: Warrior		Level: 15
Race: Dwarf	Spec: ?		Exp 280/4300
Health: 6,000/6,000	Mana: 100/100		Attrib Pts Avail: 1
Stamina: 16	Widom: 10	Charisma: 10	Life Regen: 20/sec
Strength: 15	Intellect: 10	Dexterity: 12	Mana Regen: 1/sec
Agility: 11	Luck: 11	Armor: 55	Skill Pts Avail: 0

He and Lisa were still too low-level to be of much use in combat with the rest of the group. But Mace had said they had plenty of time to level up and hone their crafting skills. Their group was going to complete a quest in Graf that would take a week or so.

Griff expected that he and Lisa would both be level twenty by that time. After all, they could play twelve or more hours at a time with no day jobs or school to worry about. He smiled to himself, feeling like a kid on summer vacation.

Lisa completed her class training and joined him just as he finished updating his new abilities with his own trainer. They elected to spend the rest of the day crafting, Lisa went to visit the leatherworking trainer while Griff made his way to the smithy.

*****

Mace and Shari met for a quick early breakfast, gobbling down a couple Pop Tarts and a protein bar each. A glass of water to wash them down and a quick cleanup later, they were headed for their pods.

It was just beginning to grow light outside when they left the inn and headed for the dock. Jorin was waiting near the helm as they boarded, waving them over.

"Good morning, you two! Ready for a nautical adventure?"

Mace scowled at him. "Depends. Are you going to tease more leviathans into attacking us?"

"Ha! One was more than enough for me, lad. I prefer my ship and myself in one piece." Jorin smacked Mace on the shoulder. "We'll be ready to get under way in a few minutes. Make yourselves comfortable. The lake is calm today, and the sailing should be a breeze." He stared at them a moment. When he got no response, he said, "A breeze. Get it?"

Shari rolled her eyes and kissed the old half-elf's cheek. "Your jokes need work, elder."

She softened her words with a smile. Mion, not to be outdone, bounded onto the captain's shoulder and gently licked his face. The old man beamed and rubbed her tummy with one finger. Mion decided she liked it there and remained with him as Shari and Mace went to find seats among the crates and bags on the deck.

Mace was about to settle onto a large grain sack when Snuffles beat him to it. The pig curled himself up like a dog and let out a satisfied snort before laying his head down and closing his eyes.

Mace gave the pig a look, then settled for a crate nearby. Shari and Layne simply sat cross-legged on the deck, leaning their backs against the rail, while Lila strung a hammock from the rail to a loose nail in a crate and hopped in. She let out a snort nearly as loud as Snuffles, which caused the others to chuckle.

Mace looked around unobtrusively, but saw no sign of Ian. He just had to assume that the rabbit had made it on board and stowed himself safely somewhere.

Within moments, the captain called out to cast off the mooring lines and they were on their way. Sails were raised to catch the breeze and pull them out into the deep water. Jorin and the helmsman steered carefully around the shallow water obstacles jokingly referred to as leviathans by the crew. Dead trees and sunken ship's masts, large rocks, any object solid enough to sink a ship that clumsily stumbled into it.

The group settled in for a quiet ride. Barring any leviathan attacks, the trip across the calm waters of the lake and down the river to the first port should be uneventful.

Mace quickly got bored and moved to stand by the captain near the helm. "Mind if I observe? I've always wanted to learn how to sail."

Jorin motioned toward the wheel. "Take hold. No better to way to learn than by doing."

The helmsman stepped aside, holding the wheel steady with one hand until Mace had a solid grip on it. The captain spent the next hour showing him how adjustments to the wheel moved the rudder at the stern of the ship, causing the water passing under the ship to alter its course and turn the ship. They discussed the various ways of keeping the wind in the sails and controlling the speed of the ship. At the end of the hour, Mace had a decent grasp of the basics.

New skill acquired: Sailing, Level 1

Mace thanked the captain and returned to the others. Layne was telling a story about a battle fought long ago between the humans and the cyclops race.

"Cyclops have never been a race to reproduce quickly. It is rare for a child to be born more than once a decade in any tribe of cyclops. So their numbers remain small, whilst humans reproduce like bunnies, having children every year or two in their prime, sometimes producing two or three at once. So while the cyclops were much larger and more powerful than the primitive humans of that time, they were vastly outnumbered. The cyclops fought with both brute strength and magic, while the humans had spears and arrows with stone tips, and slings that threw rocks at great speed. They had little concept of strategy, other than to overwhelm the cyclops with numbers. Many humans perished for each cyclops that was taken down, but in the end, numbers won out." Layne strummed a sad tune on her lute as she spoke. "The cyclops, one of the elder races of our world, were all but wiped out as a race. They fled to the mountains and deep forests where the superstitious humans feared to venture."

Shari was leaning toward the bard, her eyes wide like a small child at story time. "Are there any left today?"

Layne nodded. "Those who fled to the mountains have not been heard from as far as I know. They may have fallen victim to the trolls, ogres, or other darker races that call the mountains home. But a few took shelter with the elves for a time. I have been to one of their villages, in this very forest, in fact. It was small, only about a dozen of them living there. They grow crops and herd cattle and sheep. And their crafters, once world-renowned makers of weapons and armor, still create wondrous items that they trade with us."

The talk of weapons reminded Mace of something. He waited patiently until Layne was finished with the cyclops story, then produced his enchanted dagger.

"Layne, I purchased this from a smith in the grey dwarf city I passed through. He called it 'soul-forged and it seems to drain energy from anyone I use it on. Anyone living. It had no effect on the undead. It also seems to transfer some of that energy to me. And it almost… speaks to me sometimes. The smith said it could gain sentience. Do you know anything about this type of magic?"

When he tried to hand the dagger to her, the bard leaned back and held up her hands as if to ward it away.

"Please, I don't wish to touch it. I have indeed heard of this soul-forging. It is an ancient magic we had thought lost to the world. And we did not mourn its passing. While that weapon you hold is not inherently evil, its predecessors were almost universally used for evil purposes."

She paused and took a deep breath. Gripping her lute tightly, as if for comfort, she twanged out a few harsh notes as she continued.

"We believe its origins stem from a form of necromancy. Ancient practitioners of the art sought ways to store the souls of their victims in order to use them later to raise them in other, less damaged bodies. And while the weapons did drain and store the souls, they would not release them when commanded. They somehow made use of the energy to make themselves stronger, and eventually were able to create a sort of soul of their own. Which allowed them to communicate with their wielders. And in some cases, control them. Their lust for more victims was insatiable." She shuddered visibly.

"Wow." Mace set the dagger down on the deck in front of him and stared at it.

"I mean… I've felt its hunger during fights. It clearly enjoys being fed, and has encouraged me to kill. But I haven't felt like it was controlling me." He looked at the thing with trepidation and no little amount of suspicion.

Layne nodded. "Your pairing with it is still new. I imagine as you claim more souls with it, your connection will deepen." She too stared at the dagger as its grey surface seemed to ripple and swirl slowly.

Shari put a hand on Mace's arm and he looked up to see a concerned look on her face. "Maybe you should put it away? Sell it? Maybe destroy it?"

Lila hopped down from her hammock to take a closer look. "Are you kidding? A weapon that kills nearly instantly, provides a buff to its user, and will only get stronger with time? Where can I get one?"

She had that Lootmonster look on her face again, which made Mace chuckle and lightened the mood a bit.

Layne changed the tune to a more light-hearted strumming. "As I said, the weapons were not inherently evil. There were those who were of stout heart and morals who wielded them with honor. And they became a powerful force for good. They were just rare."

Shari let out a deep breath. "Mace has a good heart," she ventured in a hopeful tone.

He favored her with a smile, and was about to reply when a call came down from the lookout in the crow's nest: "Ship ho!"

They all looked up and then followed his pointed arm out to the south and the horizon. Mace's drow sight could make out a set of sails quite a distance out. Too far away to tell for sure, but he thought the boat might be moving their direction.

He looked to the captain, who was already inspecting the other boat through his looking glass.

"Merchant ship. Flying colors from Graf's merchant guild. She's in a hurry. Full sails and running high in the water." He looked grim as he lowered the glass. "Make ready your weapons! But keep them out of sight for now."

Mace got to his feet along with all the others. "You think they're trouble?" he asked the captain.

Jorin scratched his head and looked thoughtful. "Not sure. She's riding high, which means her hold is empty, or nearly so. No merchant willingly travels without cargo to sell or trade. And she's a Graf ship.

Most merchant ships of the Graf guild only travel up and down the river, from Port Bjurstrom at this end or to the western ports and back to Graf. And she seems to be in a big hurry."

He paused to let Mace and the others consider his words.

Mace finished his thought. "And the last merchant ship we've seen up here was commandeered by the Black Flame. You think this one is the same?"

"Aye, lad. That's just what I'm thinking. We could steer clear, head off to one side of the lake or another and let them pass by."

Shari shook her head. "That would leave them free to attack and take back Darkstone, or to attack Lakeside. Or both. And we don't have a way to warn them."

Jorin grinned at her. "Had to offer. Been a while since I've fought a decent sea battle! There's no crew better than mine anywhere on the water."

He smiled as he watched his crew of mainly elven sailors arm and prepare personal weapons. Several of them hauled three ballistae out of the hold, bolting them to special deck plates at the fore, aft, and amidships. They were quickly covered with tarps to disguise them. A bow and quiver of arrows, along with a small oil pot and igniter, were hauled by rope up to the crow's nest where the lookout sat.

Jorin looked at Mace. "That wind magic you performed for us the other day. Can you do it again?"

Mace nodded. "Sure. Better now, as I'm a higher level with more mana. You want me to make us go faster?" He was already turning to face the sails. But Jorin stopped him.

"No, lad, we've plenty of speed and the wind at our back. And in a battle between ships, speed and maneuverability are what win the fight. What I'll want you to do is slow them down. Take the wind from their sails if you can. Or send your own wind against the front of their sails to slacken them and cost them momentum. Even a few seconds will give us the advantage."

Mace grinned. Yesterday he wouldn't have understood what Jorin meant, but after his lessons this morning, he could picture exactly what the captain wanted.

"You've got it. Just tell me when. I need about two seconds to cast the spell, and I can channel it for maybe a minute."

"Save your mana, my boy. Ten seconds, maybe twenty, should be plenty. Don't need to stop them dead. I'll shout loud and clear when I need you."

Mace and his party prepared themselves as the crew did the same. The two ships were approaching each other more quickly than he had expected.

When they were maybe a mile apart, the captain shouted for a signal flag to be run up. At almost the same moment, an identical flag went up the line of the other ship. The two ships changed direction, both now heading at an oblique angle to the other. Mace could see that the new courses would slowly bring them alongside each other.

"We've called a parlay," Jorin called down. "Common courtesy among passing merchant ships. I've not met this captain, so be ready for anything. Though fighting under a flag of parlay is taboo among sailor folk, who knows whether others on board will honor the traditions."

In a short time, the two ships were running on a parallel course about thirty yards apart. The captain of the other ship raised a cone to his face and shouted, "Good day to you! Where're ye bound?"

Jorin raised a similar cone to his own mouth to amplify his reply. "South to Bjurstrom! Goods to trade from Lakeside! What's your destination?"

The other captain hesitated, and a man wearing a bright red leather breastplate said something to him. He finally replied, "North of Lakeside!

My passengers here are looking for a lost survey crew! They were exploring the area looking for an old mine."

Jorin snorted. He lowered the cone and looked down at Mace. "Survey crew. Ha! That'd be the slaver party you folks took care of. Which likely makes the man in red a Black Flame. One of them must have been able to report the attack before they died."

Mace climbed the stairs up to the helm and stood next to Jorin. He motioned for the captain to hand over the cone while saying, "Looks like you're going to get that fight. Are you sure you want it?"

Jorin spat over the rail. "I want every slaver everywhere sinking down to be leviathan food. But don't destroy the ship if you can help it. This captain may have had no more choice than the last."

Mace nodded and raised the cone. Taking a deep breath, he shouted, "Survey crew? We haven't seen them. They must have been killed by the Black Flame slaver party we found near Darkstone. If it helps any, we killed every last one of the slavers!"

The other boat went into a frenzy upon hearing his words. The captain shrank back as the man in the red breastplate shouted something and the deck was quickly swarmed with fighters of mixed race and class. The majority were melee fighters wearing light or medium armor, but Mace spotted at least six tanks or front-line fighters wearing plate. And a dozen archers took up position near the stern.

Jorin laughed. "Well, you certainly got their attention." He turned to his crew. "Battle stations! Prepare the ballistae! Fire on my mark!"

Mace watched the other boat as Jorin's crew took up the weapons each had stashed nearby. In seconds, they were fully armed and prepared. The tarps were pulled off the ballistae and four-foot-long pikes with jagged steel tips were loaded into them.

The one at the stern had a rope attached to its back end. Mace looked at the captain questioningly and the old elf just grinned.

"You'll see. Get ready. As soon as they're about to fire, I'm going to want you to slow them down. Any second…"

Mace held his hands ready as he watched the archers on the other boat draw and prepare to fire. A sailor passed in front of each of them with a torch, lighting their arrowheads on fire. As the last one was lit, Jorin shouted, "NOW!"

"Ventus!" Mace shouted as he flung a gust of air at the front of the other ship's sails. He continued to channel as his wind pushed against the wind that was propelling the ship forward. After about three seconds, the sails luffed a bit, then went slack.

The effect was immediate. The other ship slowed drastically just as the archers fired. As they'd been aiming at basically a ninety-degree angle across their deck toward Jorin's *Sea Sprite*, the arrows all passed behind them as they shot forward.

Jorin shouted, "Aft! Fire!" and the ballistae at the stern fired its bolt with the rope spooling rapidly out behind it. The bolt struck the rear mast and embedded itself, but didn't appear to do much damage.

Shari and the other sailors on board were firing at the Black Flame archers with much more success. Mace took a cue from the other boat's playbook and shouted, "Infier!"

A fireball screamed across the distance between the ships and exploded among the archers. Two were knocked overboard with their armor in flames while the others were scattered by the impact and took more minor burn damage. The rearmost rigging lines caught fire and the flames began to lick their way up the ropes toward the sail. Sailors braved the barrage of arrows to grab axes and swords to try and cut the lines before the flame could spread.

Mace was distracted by a loud *crack* and his gaze was drawn back toward the rear mast. The *Sea Sprite*, now much faster than the other, had pulled forward and cut across the bow of the slower boat. The rope attached to the bolt stuck in the mast was now raking across the deck, shattering crates and knocking down anything in its path as Jorin's boat continued to turn. Sailors and fighters who weren't fast enough to duck were knocked off their feet or crushed against something as the rope tightened. The lead end of the rope wrapped around the bow of the ship and was eventually pushed underwater.

Jorin's boat was now on the opposite side of the other ship from where they'd started, and was moving quickly toward its stern. The captain spun the wheel and *Sea Sprite* turned away as he shouted, "Keep firing!" to his archers.

The two other ballistae fired their massive bolts, which each cleared a path through the fighters, who were just getting to their feet. At least a dozen of them were killed as the missiles blasted through them. Shari and the other archers had finished off the archers on the other boat and were now focusing on any casters who revealed themselves.

As Jorin's boat pulled away from the other, the rope that attached them creaked loudly and sprang tight as a laser. The other boat began to groan and list away from them as the rope pulled the rear mast toward the water. Again, most of the Black Flame fighters lost their feet as the deck tilted under them. A few slipped and fell into the water, but most found something to hold on to.

The rear sail now had several small holes burned through it and was flapping in the wind. The boat had lost nearly all its momentum and the fighters were holding on as the deck continued to tip.

Suddenly, Jorin shouted, "'Ware the line! Get down!" and everyone dropped to the deck as the rope snapped. It whiplashed briefly before disappearing overboard as it was dragged to the other boat. Which was now rapidly righting itself.

The deck rocked back to its original position, then continued to list toward Jorin's boat as the inertia and weight distribution took over. The Black Flame fighters were thrown around the deck again. Many were injured as they slammed into each other or items lashed to the deck. Jorin's crew were back on their feet in seconds, firing away.

The rear sail on the other boat was now fully engulfed in flame. Of the fifty or so Black Flame fighters that had appeared on the deck, maybe twenty were still fit to fight. The others were either broken, crushed, burned, or shot full of arrows. Jorin raised his cone again and shouted, "Surrender, or we'll send ye to the bottom!"

The other captain pulled a white cloth from inside his coat and waved it briefly before handing it to one of his sailors. The man never got a chance to take it, however, as the red-breasted leader of the Black Flames ran a sword through his back. Withdrawing the sword from the sailor's corpse, he advanced on the captain, yelling something Mace couldn't make out over the noise of the battle. The captain backed away and looked to be pleading.

Mace had seen enough. The captain wanted to surrender but the Black Flame was having none of it. He raised his hands again.

"Ventus!"

This time, he sent a concentrated blade of air across the gap. It struck the lead slaver in the legs, removing one completely and knocking the man back. The other captain turned and fled into his cabin, shouting orders as he went.

The crew of the other boat instantly began to disappear belowdecks, the last few locking doors and hatches behind them. In less than a minute, the only living souls on deck were slavers.

"Fire at will!" Jorin shouted. His crew fired arrows, threw spears and knives, whatever they had toward the fighters, who were dodging bits of flaming canvass that fell on them from above. The second sail had now caught fire and the blaze was spreading rapidly. A few of the smarter slavers began to pound on the cabin doors, trying to get off the deck, which had become a kill zone.

But some kept fighting. One burly slaver took up a fire pot and flung it across onto Jorin's *Sea Sprite*. It struck the foresail, but luckily bounced and dropped to the deck without lighting the sail. Two sailors quickly righted the pot and tossed it overboard, burning their hands in the process but saving the ship.

Another slaver had taken up a dropped bow and fired an arrow. He roared in satisfaction as the arrow struck Jorin in the gut, knocking him to the deck. The helmsman immediately stepped forward to take the wheel, shouting, "Captain's been hit!"

Shari stopped firing at the slavers and cast a heal on the captain as Mion flew up to him and did the same. The ship's surgeon was quick to respond, pulling the arrow from the captain's belly as he too cast a heal. The barbed arrow hurt much worse coming out than going in.

Mace felt a rage overtake him as the captain screamed in pain. He cast Levitate on himself, then shouted, "Ventus!" and used the wind to push himself across the narrowing gap between the boats.

He landed on the deck amidst of a mass of Black Flame fighters. Daggers already in hand, he whirled and lunged, slicing and stabbing without conscious thought. His enchanted dagger took life after life, feeding him power and demanding more lives. Mace was happy to oblige. Moving forward along the deck, he found the leader still alive. He had taken a health potion to stop the bleeding from his severed leg and was attempting to push himself up with his sword.

Mace kicked the man's leg out from under him and stomped on his chest as he hit the deck. The man snarled at him and Mace kicked him in the temple, knocking him unconscious. As much as he wanted to kill the man, he had questions he wanted answers to.

He cast Levitate on the man, raising his limp body above the level of the rail, then kicked him toward Jorin's ship. Layne had been watching and nodded in acknowledgement as she caught the floating body. Mace canceled the Levitate spell and smiled in satisfaction as the body thumped hard against the deck.

Turning his attention back to the battle, he saw that not many of the fighters survived. One of the tanks in plate armor was cursing and casting spells at Mace's allies. A sailor manning a ballista screamed in pain as a bolt of energy blasted him in the face. Mace used the smoke from the burning ship to mask his movement as he got behind the tank. The man was muttering another spell when Mace took hold of his helm with his left hand and jerked it to the left, interrupting the spell. Then he jammed the soul dagger in his right hand up under the man's chin and into his brain. The tank dropped limply with a clatter as he hit the deck. The dagger practically sang to Mace as it injected him with the adrenaline-like reward for the kill.

Yesssss!

The rush was interrupted by a burning pain as another fighter stabbed Mace from behind. The sword entered his back just above his belt and passed through a lung before scraping against his ribs. Mace couldn't get the air to scream, could only grunt in pain as he slammed his dagger backhanded into the woman who'd just stabbed him. The dagger didn't hit a vital organ, striking her waist and penetrating to her hip bone. But she screamed in pain and terror as the dagger's magic drained her. When she let go of her sword Mace fell to the deck, his face pressed into a bundle of burning canvass as he lost consciousness.

Chapter 10

Sail Away Sail Away

When Mace regained consciousness, he opened his eyes to find a dragon staring into his face from about three inches away. Mion tilted her head to one side, then chirped questioningly at him and licked his nose.

He paused a moment to take stock. He felt some pain in his torso, but not nearly the level from before. And the burning sensation on his face was gone.

"Thank you, Mion." He carefully lifted a hand to scratch her belly with one finger. She closed her eyes and purred at him, then opened her mouth to hit him with another heal. The tiny creature's spells packed some serious juice, and the tingling he felt was stronger than when Shari healed him.

"Remind me that when we get back to land, I owe you a big handful of bugs 'n worms." He grinned at the little dragon, who chirped happily in agreement and then leapt off his chest.

Sitting up, he saw that he was still on the burned ship. The sails had burned away, but the boat itself was mostly undamaged. He saw several of the ship's crew holding buckets and the deck was soaked with charcoal-stained water. Shari was there and reached out a hand to help him to his feet.

"You have *got* to stop getting stabbed," she half-teased. "What made you jump over here and get in reach of their knives and swords? We could have just pounded them from our ship."

Mace looked sheepish, shrugging. "I saw the captain get hurt after watching that red guy kill a sailor for no reason. I got angry. And I didn't want any other citizens getting hurt on our side."

Shari nodded. She wasn't satisfied, but she wasn't pushing it either. Mace looked around again. Lila was looting the dead fighters, while the merchant captain was giving orders as the crew began to clean and retrieve replacement sails and rigging from the hold.

Mace felt Minx return to his shoulder. Her tail wrapped around his neck, and she said "*Silly drow. Put face in fire. Bad knife makes you stupid.*" He snorted.

"I didn't exactly *put* my face in the fire. I passed out." He realized his argument wasn't helping any as his now visible pet just gave him her patented 'you're an idiot' face. He let it drop and looked around.

While Mace was out, grappling hooks had been tossed between the ships and they'd been brought close enough for planks to be laid across the rails. Captain Jorin was just walking across to speak with the other captain.

Mace left them to it. He'd just spotted the slaver in the red breast plate stretched out and still unconscious with Layne guarding him.

He leapt across the small gap between ships and walked to stand next to Layne. As she stepped back, Mace kicked the man's shoulder. When he didn't rouse, Mace kicked him in the head. Still getting no response, he took his canteen from his bag and poured some water in the man's face. The slaver spluttered and coughed as he accidentally breathed in some of the liquid. When he opened his eyes again, Mace kicked him once more, in his severed stump this time, just to make sure he had the man's attention.

"What's your name?"

"You're a dead man!" the human shouted at him, trying to sit up. Mace shoved him back down with a foot on his chest. "Do you know who you're dealing with?"

Mace chuckled. "The lone survivor of a group of low-life slavers sent to find another dead group of low-life's, who were sent to check on Justin and the original group of low-life's that I killed. As far as I can tell, the score so far is about a hundred and fifty for me, and zero for Black Flame."

He smirked at the man, whose eyes widened as his face turned red with rage. "My son was one of Justin's guards! I'll have your balls mounted on my bedpost-"

He didn't get to finish as Mace kicked him in the face again. Not too hard, just enough to shut him up.

"That's a disturbing image. What kind of man wants a nutsack hanging around... you know what? Never mind. I'm going to ask you again. If you don't answer my question, I'm going to cut part of you off and toss it overboard for the fish. We'll heal you and keep you alive as I cut more parts from you until I get what I want. Don't ask me for mercy. You don't deserve it." Mace gave the man his best 'scary drow' face and deepened his voice with the threat, showing the man his enchanted dagger as he spoke.

"My name is Josiah," the man growled out.

"Good! Now we're getting somewhere. I obviously know you're Black Flame, you and yours are all wearing the same symbol as the group we killed the other day. What is your rank and where are you from?"

The man held his tongue until Mace bent over and began to reach for him. "I'm a lieutenant. From Graf."

"And what is your mission?"

"We got a message from the party we sent to pick up Justin's latest shipment. Said they were under attack. We couldn't reach them after that, and couldn't reach Justin either. So I was sent to investigate."

"Mystery solved. They're all dead. The stronghold is mine now."

Mace watched the man's face turn purple. He tried again to sit up, and Mace let him. "Where is your headquarters located in Graf?"

The man shook his head. "I'll not tell you that. I swore an oath." His face shut down and he hunched his back, expecting an attack and unable to do anything to stop it.

"You swore an oath to whom?" Mace asked, leaning over the man with his dagger in hand. "A lying, murdering, slave trader with no honor? Do you think your master would protect you in this same situation?"

"I cannot." The man crossed his arms over his chest. "Kill me if you want."

Shari and the others had joined them in time to hear the last exchange. She injected herself into the interrogation, asking, "What *can* you tell us without betraying your oath? Who is your master?"

The man shook his head. "I'll say no more. Except that every thief, slaver, and black market trader in this part of the world will be bound to kill you on sight. My life may be at an end, but yours won't be much longer. May you rot in the pits of the underworld!"

Mace leaned in close to the man, their faces inches apart. "Says the slaver scum who just killed an unarmed sailor for trying to surrender?"

As the man was about to respond, Mace drove his dagger up under the man's chin and drained his soul. Shari gasped from behind him, and there was some muttering from the nearby sailors. Mace's drow hearing picked up mutterings of surprise and fear, as well as words like, 'justice' and 'respect.'

Mace looted the man's corpse, and though he knew it would fade away in moments, he took out some frustration by lifting it over the rail and hurling it into the lake. When he turned, he found Shari staring at him.

"What was that?" Her voice was barely more than a whisper. "He was beaten. Unarmed."

Mace, still angry, growled his response. "He was a murderer and a slaver. Letting him live would have just freed him to do more of the same."

Shari was about to argue when Captain Jorin placed a hand gently on her shoulder. "He's right, young one. The man deserved worse than a quick death. Had you turned him over to me I'd have keel-hauled him. There is no redemption for the likes of him."

"Really? And what about Mace? He's a drow, after all. And aren't all drow murderers and worse?" Shari was angry.

Jorin smiled sadly at her. "Aye, every one I've ever met, excepting Mace here. But that man was an Oathbound. A fanatic. The worst of the scum of the earth. He stole and murdered and betrayed his way to the highest levels of the Black Flame in order to become worthy of taking that oath. He would follow the orders of his master even if it meant slaughtering his own children. And he would believe that he enjoyed it."

Those words stunned Shari into silence. She couldn't look at Jorin or Mace as tears formed in her eyes. She was suddenly feeling that this game was entirely too real.

Leaving the two behind, she moved to sit next to Snuffles, who had regained his spot on the cargo sacks. Scratching the pig's ears with one hand, she stared absently into space.

"Give her some time," Jorin whispered to Mace as he patted the drow on the back. "You did well today. Saved the lives of my crew and theirs."

He motioned to the other boat, whose crew was still working to restore the rigging and clear the deck. "Had you not acted, we likely would have had to sink her. And more of mine would have perished."

The captain looked grim. Mace knew that he had lost at least two crew members, maybe more.

"I'm sorry for your losses, captain. We did not mean to put you or yours at risk with this trip." Mace's anger faded as he considered the cost of the quest already. In his early days as a gamer, or even in his first months playing Elysia, he would never have blinked at the death of NPCs whether they were enemies or allies. Shari was right, this world was becoming more real all the time.

An idea struck him. "Could I borrow your cabin?" he asked. "I need to… pray."

The captain looked askance at him for a moment. "You're not planning some dark ritual to a drow god or summoning a demon or some such?"

Mace laughed. "No. I plan to pray to Elysia. I need her help."

Jorin nodded. "Don't we all. Of course, lad. My cabin is at your disposal. Though you need not be embarrassed about praying in front of my crew. We are all faithful followers."

Mace thanked the captain. He didn't want to explain to him that when he prayed, he expected Elysia would actually answer. Raising what he was sure would be a lot of questions if the crew were to witness the encounter.

Closing himself in the cabin, he spoke to the empty air. "Elysia, I need to speak with you please."

An avatar of the AI that controlled the game appeared in front of him. She'd chosen a nondescript form that seemed to encompass every race on Elysia and none of them at the same time. She wore a modest toga and carried a scepter.

"Yes, Mace?"

"Hello, Elysia. Thank you for answering. I have been thinking about the problems caused by the absence of players. Outworlders. And I may have a solution. Though a limited one."

Elysia closed her eyes for a moment, then smiled. "Ah. I see. That is indeed an intriguing idea. It is within the boundaries of my programming to make the changes you have in mind. But the scale should be limited, as you have already deduced."

Mace had forgotten that Elysia was connected directly to his mind in order to enable the system immersion. The back and forth between the AI and his brain was what allowed him to see, feel, even taste the game world. And allowed the game to react when he wished to move an arm or a leg, cast a spell, or even take a deep breath.

"I propose that we set it up two ways. First, myself and Shari can grant a boon to those we deem worthy or important enough to the world. And you could set up some sort of criteria by which citizens could earn it through deeds or reputation, or whatever."

Elysia nodded. "This is a wise choice. I will gift the ability to grant a limited number of boons to you and admin Shari, as well as admin Griff and Lisa. Do you wish me to do the same for the other players?"

Mace shook his head. "Not yet. Not until we've spoken to them. It seems the North Koreans are hostile, and we cannot trust that their choices would be a benefit to the world. The others are just unknown for now."

Elysia closed her eyes again, longer this time. After nearly a minute (which for an AI of her capacity was quite a long time) she had revised her code to allow for Mace's plan.

"It is done. Choose well, Mace."

"Before you go, please grant the boon to the following citizens. I believe they have all earned it." He closed his eyes and imagined a list being transferred to Elysia. When he opened his eyes, she was already gone.

Moving back to the deck, he called to Layne, Lila, and Jorin, motioning them to join him in a quiet corner. Shari joined them.

He took a deep breath. "I have just sent up a prayer to Elysia for a boon, which she has granted. As you know, the world is suffering from the lack of outworlders. The main value of outworlders being that they would recklessly risk their lives in daring quests and hopeless fights, secure in the knowledge that death would only be temporary. Immortality breeds contempt for danger and a willingness to try the impossible. Often resulting in great rewards."

He paused, and the others all nodded. "The boon I have received from Elysia is to grant that same immortality to a select few citizens. And I have chosen the three of you, among others."

As he finished the sentence, a golden glow enveloped the three NPCs. Their bodies went rigid and they stared into space. Mace imagined they were seeing brand new UI's flooded with messages. He looked at Shari, who was staring at them, mouth open.

"I... can't believe you did that. And that I didn't think of it sooner!" She punched him in the shoulder, smiling at him. Then she hugged him. "You really *are* a genius, geek boy."

He returned her smile. "I also asked Elysia to upgrade Captain Charles, Brahm, Master Krieger, Jervis, Truffle and Shook, and the elves you told me about. Arlon, the Commander, Ramon the scribe, Falin the healer. You can pick some of your own as well. As can Griff and Lisa."

Shari hugged him again.

The two of them waited in silence as the three new immortals continued to stare into space and the crew began to stare at them. Shari turned to reassure the crew, saying that they were communing with Elysia. This satisfied most of the crew, and they got back to their duties.

"So who else were you thinking?" Mace asked as the wait dragged on. He was a little surprised, since both Elysia and the three NPCs in front of him were code. He expected the updates would be much faster. It wasn't like there were humans behind those eyes going through character creation and choosing hairstyles or assigning attribute points with their slow neurochemical brain processes. The information was being transmitted by quantum processors.

Layne was the first to wake up, followed quickly by the other two. A second later, Mace's UI exploded with notifications. He opened them just long enough to see that his reputation with every one of the new immortals had jumped to 'Revered.' The reason why was given to him a moment later when Layne and the others dropped to one knee.

The bard spoke first. "Elysia has spoken to us. She has granted us immortality at your behest, Mace. I… I do not have the words to express my gratitude."

Jorin had tears in his eyes. "This gift… I have not earned it, Mace. There are so many others more deserving."

Mace held up a hand. "Nonsense. You have been a good friend, a valiant warrior. You have shown care not only for your own crew, but those of at least two other ships. You would risk your life to end the practice of slavery. You are more than worthy. I would ask that you pick six of your crew to receive the same blessing. So that even should you and all yours fall in battle, you may return and reclaim your ship to continue the fight."

Lila was much less vocal in her reaction. As the captain nodded his thanks and Mace shifted his gaze to the little rogue, she leapt from the deck and wrapped herself around the drow, nearly knocking him off his feet. She squeezed with both arms and legs for a moment, then dropped to the deck and rushed to grab Shari in a halfling version of a bear hug. Tears flowed freely from both women as Shari squeezed just as hard. Layne got to her feet and joined them.

Mace embraced the captain in a much more manly fashion, saying, "Welcome to immortality. Use it well. And by that, I mean be sure and do lots of stupid and reckless things that your enemies won't expect."

The drow and the elf grinned at each other.

When the celebrating was done, Mace began to explain to them that other citizens could earn immortality as well, but Jorin held up a hand.

"Elysia explained all. We are to act as heralds, sharing the tale of your generosity and the terms under which citizens can evolve."

Mace shrugged, a little disappointed that Elysia had stolen his thunder. Shari noticed, coming to his rescue. "Captain, let's begin by giving your crew a show. They've already seen you three evolve, but don't know what it's about. Choose your six and assemble your crew. We'll show them something they'll be telling their grandchildren."

Jorin quickly agreed and called for not only his crew, but the other boat's crew as well to assemble. The two boats were still joined, and the crews gathered on their respective decks. Jorin then called forward his first mate, two sailors Mace recognized as having manned the ballistae, the helmsman, the ship's surgeon, and the ship's carpenter.

As the sailors stepped forward, Layne asked, "May I?" Mace nodded and stood back as she stepped into the center of the small cleared space around the captain and his chosen six. She began to strum a tune on her lute that lifted the hearts of all those who could hear. Mace felt a sense of peace and contentment, but also mild elation. Layne called out in a clear, strong voice.

"My fellow citizens! We have this day been visited by our goddess Elysia. At the request of the outworlder Mace, she has granted a great boon to the captain, Lila, and myself. We have become immortal!"

She paused as the onlookers stared in silent confusion. "We have been given the ability to return our souls to our bodies after death, just as the outworlders do! Not only that, but Elysia has decreed that any citizen may earn the same boon through hard work and extraordinary achievement."

This time, there was an excited murmur among the sailors on both boats.

"Some of you may have noticed our ascension a few minutes ago. For those who missed it, you will now witness these six sailors being granted immortality as well. Mace and Shari have kindly allowed the captain to choose six of his best to receive this honor. If they all agree?"

She turned to the six men, who were all nodding enthusiastically. Turning back to the crowd, she continued. "We have been tasked to act as heralds for our goddess. To spread the word of this miracle far and wide. All of you here can begin to earn her favor by doing the same!"

She turned and held her hands up to the sky. "Oh, great goddess, we beseech you, grant the gift of immortality to these worthy souls!"

All six men began to glow with the same golden light as the first three. Their rigid bodies and sightless gazes persisted as the sailors around them gasped and pointed. The whispers and murmurs rippled back and forth through the crowd for the full minute that it took the men to recover. Again Mace's UI was bombarded with alerts. His reputation went up not only with the six men, but with most of the sailors present. A quick look at Shari told him she was seeing the same.

When the six sailors revived and, as one, faced Mace and took a knee, the crowd hushed. The first mate spoke up.

"'Tis true! The goddess spoke to us. We have been... changed."

As the men got to their feet and hugged both Mace and Shari, the crowd went wild. They mobbed the six men, asking questions and laying hands on them as if they might receive some sort of blessing through contact. Or just to confirm that the men were real. A few jokingly offered to kill one of the men in order to test their new immortality. Which the captain quickly forbade.

When the ruckus died down, the other captain requested permission to come aboard. Jorin granted it and the man crossed the plank with ease. He bowed deeply to Jorin and the others.

"If not for you, my crew and I would likely be dead. Or worse, slaves. That lot seized my boat under cover of night after we unloaded our cargo in Graf. You have my eternal gratitude."

Jorin reached out an arm and the captain grasped it. They shared a look and each nodded his head. Mace figured it was some sort of 'code of the sea' thing.

He simply said, "It was our pleasure. We have undertaken a quest to dismantle the Black Flame, and relieving you of that lot seemed a good place to start."

He grinned at the captain, who snorted and laughed.

"Aye, you dismantled that bunch right enough. I'd not like to be on your bad side, drow. Er, Mace. Or yours, Miss Shari. That bow of yours was right deadly."

He bowed to her again as she blushed slightly. "Myself and the crew of the *Platypus* are in your debt. Should you have need of us, just call and we'll answer."

Mace gave a slight bow in response. Jorin said "We can offer you a tow back in the direction of Port Bjurstrom until you get your rigging straightened out. I'd not leave a friend stranded on the lake after dark."

He led the captain away, regaling him with the tale of the leviathan attacking at dusk just a few days ago.

Mace and his group returned to their spots to sit and talk. Layne and Lila were preoccupied with their new interfaces. Though all citizens had one, the interface that they saw now was apparently much more extensive. They asked many questions, which Shari and Mace answered as best they could. Mace resigned himself to the fact that he'd probably have to repeat the conversation with the captain and his new immortal crewmen.

The two boats got underway in short order. Jorin's crew going about the business of sailing while the *Platypus* crew resumed repairs as they were towed along behind. Mace composed and sent another message through in-game mail to the players in Texas, Sydney, Moscow, and Hong Kong. Then he sent a private message to Griff, who was online with Lisa.

"Hey, Griff. Got any NPCs you're particularly fond of? You and Lisa can each pick a few and give me their names, and Elysia will grant them the ability to respawn. You should both get huge reputation boosts from it. Since we can't have enough players to balance the game, we're going to make some! Sort of."

He waited a few minutes and Griff responded. *"Sorry, was in combat. And holy shite! That's an awesome idea. We'll make a list right away. Is a dozen too many?"*

"No, a dozen is a good number. Make sure they're key people who have something to offer the village or the world in general. Who can help defend the place, run dungeons with you, or gather needed resources. Maybe a few crafters."

"Aye, good thinkin'! And yer gonna do this wherever we go? Spreadin' new players everywhere?"

"Yep! Not only that, but the AI is instituting a path for them to earn it on their own through great deeds or worthy activities, reputation gains, whatever. I'm not clear on the details yet. This just happened. The ones you choose will 'evolve' and become heralds. They can probably tell you more."

Griff signed off with another promise to get back to him with a list. Mace set himself a mental reminder to figure out how each of the players could make their choices known to Elysia directly. Thus getting the reputation gains with their chosen and the communities they occupied. He didn't want or need all the credit himself.

They sailed along for the rest of the day, finally reaching the outlet where the lake flowed into the river a good hour before sunset. The *Platypus* was repaired enough to make it downstream under her own power, so the tow line was reeled in and they proceeded in single file. With two crews able to defend against any potential attackers, Mace and Shari felt comfortable enough to log out for the evening.

*****

Griff and Lisa sat in the tavern discussing the new development Mace had shared and compiling a list of likely dwarves from the village. So far they had Campbell, the elder who ran the village, Bolgin the merchant, and Fagin the blacksmith. And the two guards who had teased Griff after his bunny incident. There was also Josephine from the tavern.

"We should include Maggie too," Lisa offered. "She's sweet, and she makes the best pies!"

Griff grinned at her. "Aye, I like her too. But Mace said to choose them that can contribute. I doubt she'd be much help in a battle."

Lisa's face took on a determined look. "There's more to life than fighting! Maggie's the bloody heart o' this place. The others look to her for advice. She teaches the young ones how to cook and sew, among other things. Her knowledge and heart are as valuable as any sword or bow!"

Griff held up his hands to ward off any further hostility. "Okay, okay! Ya convinced me. Maggie makes the list!"

Lisa nodded, already considering who else to choose. "We should pick trainers. Yours, mine, and mebbe a few others. They can help defend the village, and it'll ensure they'll still be here to train us if we get overrun by angry fuzzy bunnies or somethin'."

Griff agreed, adding, "Maybe a couple o' hunters? And a farmer or two? Ta make sure they can always feed themselves?"

"Aye. And we need to ask around fer a few willin' to adventure with us. We'll need a healer fer sure, and more ranged damage wouldn't hurt. But we shouldn't tell 'em about respawning 'til after they've agreed to join us. They need ta have heart!" Lisa thumped her chest.

So they began with the innkeeper, asking about villagers likely to be up for some adventure. He gave them a few names, and they set off to recruit party members.

One of the names given to them was Leroy, the alchemist's apprentice. He was young, barely twenty years old. A stout dwarf with black hair and bright green eyes. He was a druid class healer who specialized in potions.

It took them all of about five minutes before he agreed to join them. He also had a friend who he wanted to bring along.

Griff and Lisa followed him out of the shop and through an alley to a row of houses near the back wall of the village. He knocked on a door and a young dwarfess answered.

Her cheeks went flush as soon as she saw Leroy. "Are ya daft? Me da would crack yer head if he knew ye were here!" she hissed at the young dwarf.

He held up his hands. "I'm not here fer… that." He looked at the ground and scuffed his foot a bit. "I've brought the outworlders, haven't I? They're lookin' for volunteers to go to a dungeon!"

Her eyes widened. She took in Griff and Lisa, then looked back at Leroy. "And yer goin'?"

He nodded his head, a wide grin spreading across his face. "Ye bet yer silken knickers I'm goin'!" He pointed at her. "And yer goin' too!"

"I'll have to get me da's blessin'," she insisted right away. Then a sly look came over her face as she looked to the two outworlders.

"Or *you* lot could get it. He's quite of fond of you, ya know." She stared at Griff.

"Who's yer da?" the dwarf was almost afraid to ask.

"Me name's Meg Campbell." She smiled as she saw the realization cross Griff's features. His eyes widened and his head began to shake on its own.

"Oh, no. I'll not be the one ta get the village headman's wee one killed." Griff took a step back and was turning to walk away when Lisa stopped him. She leaned in and whispered in his ear, "What if she could respawn?"

Griff froze.

"Holy shite. Youuu women are gonna be the death o' me," he grumbled. Looking at the two young dwarves in front of him, he said, "Right. We'll need one other for a full party, then. What class are you, Meg?"

In answer, she disappeared behind the open door for a moment. When she reappeared, she had a small buckler strapped to her left forearm, and held a halberd with a long shaft in her right.

The shaft itself was four feet long with a wickedly curved, barbed axe blade at the end, and a spike that extended another foot at least. The back side of the axe was a stout spike with three barbs that when swung at an enemy, would penetrate deeply then rip away flesh as it was pried loose. The weapon could be swung like a two-handed axe, jabbed like a spear, or used to hook an enemy and pull them off balance. Griff was impressed.

Meg set the polearm on her shoulder and said, "We could ask me da to join us. He's conquered some dungeon beasties in his time."

Griff thought the chances of Meg joining them would increase greatly if Campbell the elder joined them to watch over her.

"Fine, we'll go see him and ask."

He turned toward the tavern, where he expected they'd find the man. As they walked, he mumbled to himself "Please Elysia, let these people evolve so that I don't get them killed."

A message appeared in bold type on his UI.

Your prayer has been heard, admin Griff. Gather those you wish to receive the boon and it shall be done. I approve of your candidates so far.

-Elysia

Not sure whether to be relieved or creeped out, he silently thanked the AI and picked up his pace. He whispered to Lisa, catching her up on what had just happened. She beamed at him.

When they reached the tavern, they did indeed find Campbell, along with Maggie and Bolgin the merchant. Griff spoke quietly to the trio, asking them to gather the others from the list.

He and Lisa sat and enjoyed a mug of ale as they waited for the trainers and the guards, who were the last to arrive. He led the whole group over to a quiet corner of the tavern and motioned for them to sit. Then he quickly outlined his proposal.

"Me friends have made an agreement with Elysia. She has gifted us with a great boon we can share with those we feel are deservin'. You lot are here because we've choosed ya. If you agree, Elysia will bestow a blessing upon ye, and ye'll each evolve. Ye'll be given the gift o' immortality, the ability for yer soul to return to yer body if ye get yerselves killed. Just like Lisa and me."

He waited as they took in his words. A couple of the trainers scoffed and rose to leave, but Campbell motioned for them to sit. Looking at Griff, he asked, "This be real? Yer not havin' a laugh at our expense?"

Griff said, "I was sent a message from Elysia herself on me way here. She said to gather ya together. I'm thinkin' ye need only accept and the gift is yours."

Before Campbell could respond, Maggie smacked the back of his head. "Are ye daft? Ye don't question a gift from the goddess!"

She eyed him dangerously, then turned her gaze on each of the citizens one by one. They all nodded their heads. She didn't bother to look back at Campbell. "We be honored, goddess." She bowed her head, and the others followed.

All at once, the golden light infused each of them, startling the other patrons and staff in the tavern. Griff and Lisa reassured them as the small group of newly-evolved citizens stood stiff and unseeing for a solid minute. Just as with Mace, when they came around to their senses they each took a knee. Griff and Lisa's notifications lit up, and they actually each gained levels. One for Griff, three for Lisa. Griff ignored the notifications as he took Maggie by the hand and helped her rise.

One of the patrons ran out of the tavern while the others in the room gathered round. Campbell raised his hands for silence, and said "Let us step out to the square. Gather everyone. We have news."

The serene look on his face convinced his people that there was no danger, and they exited the tavern. Some began to call out to neighbors and friends as Maggie sent a boy to ring the bell mounted above the fountain.

The deep clang of the iron bell brought nearly everyone in the village to the square. While they waited, Griff read through his notifications. His reputation with all the evolved and the village itself had skyrocketed. And he'd completed a hidden quest called "***Gather the Chosen***". He snorted at the name, but wasn't going to argue with the experience boost.

When enough of the villagers were present, Campbell called, "We've been give'd a blessin' by Elysia herself!"

He motioned for the others to step into the open area around him. "We were chosen by Griff and Lisa here, and Elysia has given us the gift o' immortality. We be just like outworlders now. If'n we die, we'll return to our bodies just like new!"

There were cries and shouts of disbelief from the crowd. Campbell ignored them. "There be more! Elysia charged each of us to be her heralds. To tell all of ye this: Ye can become immortal too. Through heroic deeds, acts of kindness, hard work, and pleasin' the goddess in other ways. When ye've gained enough favor with her, she'll grant ye the same boon."

As the crowd reacted to this, he nodded at the others. Eleven of the dozen spread out and moved among the crowd, answering questions. Campbell stayed to talk to Griff and Lisa.

"We canno' thank ye enough for this gift."

Lisa poked Griff in the ribs harder than he thought she needed to, and made a significant eye movement toward Campbell. He sighed.

"Yer most welcome. And there's something we were hoping you'd consider."

Campbell looked at him suspiciously for a moment. "This have anything to do with me girl? And that good-fer-naught animal hugger?"

Griff laughed despite himself. "Aye. And you as well. We want to put together an adventuring party. The two of us, Leroy, Meg, and yerself if ye'll join us."

The old dwarf raised his bushy eyebrows at that. "And that's why ye choosed us to be yer immortals?"

Lisa shook her head. "Not you. You were on our list no matter what. But Leroy and Meg, yes." Her face was open and honest as she spoke, and Campbell gave her a brief nod. She added "We've offered you a spot in the party because we figured you'd want to watch out for Meg. To protect her from beasties and young dwarves alike!" She grinned as the old dwarf laughed heartily.

"Ha! Well I do miss all the runnin' about and killin' beasties from me younger days. But I be needed here. Ye should take young Josephine in me place." He turned his face away from Lisa and gave Griff a big wink. Griff rolled his eyes.

Lisa hesitated before asking, "Is… is she a fighter? I thought she were just a waitress."

Campbell looked down at her with a frown.

"Ye've got a lot to learn about dwarves, lass. There's no such thing as a dwarf who can't fight. Our wee ones are given weapons as soon as they can walk. Some even before." His eyes lost focus, as if remembering better days. "Me Meg was swinging a knife 'n slicin' off bits o' me beard while still in her cradle."

Griff was curious now. "And what is Jo's class?"

Campbell didn't answer. Instead, he turned and bellowed, "Josephine!" causing the young dwarf to start in surprise and trot over to them.

"Aye, what're ye yellin' about, old man?" She softened the insult with a smile.

"Ye want to go adventurin' with these young ones?" he asked.

Her eyes widened. "Ye mean as in, dungeons 'n such? Real battles?"

When she saw the grin on his face she hopped up and down. "Ye bet yer red arse hairs I do!"

"Good," Campbell replied. "Go with them and watch over Meg. If that lad…" He paused to wink at Griff again. "Or *this* lad tries anythin' funny, ye stick 'em with somethin' sharp!"

He pointed roughly northeast toward the mountain range above them. "Follow the creek to where it meets the waterfall. There be an orc outpost there. Offer to trade with 'em and they'll be friendly enough. There be a dungeon entrance nearby."

Campbell walked off, laughing to himself. Griff looked at Meg and the others.

"Well, that went easier than I expected," he mumbled.

Lisa poked him in the ribs again, more gently this time. She said "Well you *did* just give them all the ability to respawn. Imagine how you'd feel if ya were told ya'd never have to die in the real world. Or more specifically, if ya got eaten by a zombie, you'd respawn in yer quarters good as new." She waited as he considered her words.

"First thing I'd do is see if I could eat enough pancakes to kill myself!" He grinned at her. Turning to the rest of the party, he asked Josephine, "Jo, what is your class?"

She pulled a staff from her bag, and then a wand. "I be a mage. Or rather, an apprentice mage. Me specialty be fire magic. I practice every day, lightin' the ovens and fireplaces at the inn. But I can cast water and lightnin' spells too. And a shield, though it be weak until I practice more."

Her voice trailed off at this. "Me master was killed by an outworlder shortly before ye all disappeared." She said as if that explained her small repertoire.

Lisa took her hand. "You'll fit in just perfect! Griff here can tank, Leroy can heal, and Meg and I will stab and chop at the bad guys while you protect Leroy and cook them from a distance."

The others all nodded their agreement. "Okay, we spend the rest of today gathering supplies and preparing our gear. Griff and I have a bit of gold to spend if you need to purchase things. Don't worry about the cost, you can pay us back from your share of the dungeon loot. We'll meet at the inn for a good hearty breakfast, then we'll go. Anybody know how long it'll take to reach the orc outpost?"

Meg raised her hand. "Me da makes the trip sometimes, and I went with him once. It's a half day's walk. There's a trail that takes us most of the way. And I know a good spot to cross the creek."

Griff dismissed the group and they scattered to go prepare. He noticed Jo waited to make sure Meg and Leroy went different directions before she turned and walked toward the inn. He decided it would be fun to help her make sure that Leroy got no action while they were out and about.

Griff and Lisa went to see Bolgin at the general store to purchase some supplies. Griff wanted rope, torches, or lanterns, and lots of potions for both health and mana regeneration. He also purchased a couple of large canvas tarps that could be made into shelters. Along with a set of pots and pans and enough cups and plates for the group. Lisa added in a week's worth of biscuits, jerky, and dried fruit. Griff and Lisa only had 20 slots each in their inventory bags, and wanted to save as much space as possible for loot.

When they were all done, the pile atop the merchant's counter was daunting. Griff asked Bolgin "Have you any bags of holding to sell me?"

The old dwarf shook his head. "No bags. I do have this ring, but it's expensive. Fifty gold."

He handed the ring to Griff to inspect.

Ring of Holding

Quality: Uncommon

This ring can hold items in a pocket dimension with one hundred storage slots. Identical items will stack within the same slot up to a quantity of fifty. Carrying weight of all items stored within the ring is reduced by 99.9%.

This was just what they needed, but even with the improved drops that he and Lisa had been benefiting from they didn't have enough gold to pay for the ring and all the supplies, too. Plus, Griff wanted to visit the blacksmith and see about upgrading their gear.

Bolgin saw the look on his face. "Tell ye what. Ye pay me for the supplies and take the ring as a loan. When ye get back, I get first choice o' the loot items ye wish to sell, and ye'll sell 'em to me at a ten percent discount. We'll take out the cost of the ring then."

Griff gladly agreed and paid Bolgin for all the supplies while Lisa took the ring and began loading it up. This new Revered reputation was already paying dividends. Bolgin had been kind enough to Griff on his first day in the village. But no way would he have entrusted such a valuable item to him knowing he was about to enter a dungeon.

They bid Bolgin a good day and made their way to Fagin's smithy. The two of them spent some time going over their armor and weapons with the smith, who was more than happy to help.

"I can improve what ye've got with some buffs to Strength or Stamina, or ye can choose from items in me shop and I'll give ye the friends and family price." He thumped Griff on the back.

As Griff was currently wearing an ugly mismatch of items he'd picked up during his time in the village, he went into the shop to have a look around. Lisa, still being relatively low-level, opted to have her gear improved.

As Fagin banged away on her armor, she joined Griff. He was trying on a shiny steel breastplate engraved with a war hammer crossed with a mining pick. There was a matching helm, pauldrons, greaves, and two gauntlets hanging on an armor tree in front of him.

With a sigh, he set the piece back on the tree and moved on. There was an entire wall of dwarven shields in different sizes and shapes. He was drawn to one with the same engraving as the breastplate. It looked almost like a clan crest. The shield was wider than his shoulders at the top and over a meter tall. Its bottom edge tapered to a point, which could be jammed into the ground to stabilize the shield.

He hefted it, sliding his left arm into the strap and grabbing the handle. It was lighter than he expected, and he moved his arm up and down, back and forth, testing it.

Lisa whistled at him. "Looks good on you!" she winked.

He set the shield back down just as Fagin joined them. The smith eyed the item. "Aye, one of me prized pieces. Part o' the set."

He pointed to the armor tree that Griff had been admiring. "I crafted it all fer an outworlder who never claimed it."

"It's fine work," Griff agreed. "I'll be back for it after we've cleared a dungeon or two." He moved down the line of shields and hefted a simpler steel shield of roughly the same design.

Fagin handed Lisa her improved armor and she made happy noises at the smith as she inspected the pieces than tried them on. A few moments later, she called out to Griff.

"This is great! He's given me a total of plus five to Strength, three to Stamina, and one to Agility!" she bragged, spinning around to model the improved gear for Griff.

He gave a thumbs-up and walked toward the counter with the shield he was holding. After all the supplies, their gold was limited and he wanted to be sure they had some left for whatever gear the others needed.

"I'll take this one. What do we owe you for this and Lisa's items?"

"Let's call it one gold." Fagin's manner had become a little stiff and formal. Griff caught him scowling at the shield on the counter as he took the gold piece.

"Is something wrong? Was this a bad choice?" he asked.

"No, no. This be a good solid shield. I was just wonderin' why ye didn't choose the other."

Griff understood. "It's beautiful work. And I will be back to purchase it. I just have limited funds right now and I need to make sure the rest of our party has what they need."

He watched the blacksmith's face, half hoping the dwarf would offer him a similar deal to Bolgin's ring.

Fagin only nodded, his serious look returning to a smile. "Fair enough. 'Tis a good leader who looks out fer his people before himself. If there's anything else I can get ya, just lemme know."

Griff held up a hand in parting. "You may get a visit from Leroy, Meg, or Jo. If they need something they can't afford, within reason, we'll cover it." He and Lisa headed back to the inn to log out. They'd be starting early in the game tomorrow, and wanted to get a good meal and some sleep under their belts.

Chapter 11

Tastes Like Chicken

Griff took his time getting showered and changed after leaving his pod. He'd learned that after being ignored all day, Evan would demand Lisa's time as soon as she emerged.

He cranked up the hot water and let it beat on the top of his head as he leaned against the shower wall. When the room had filled with thick steam, he shut the water off and dried himself before slipping on a pair of military issue boxers and jeans. He didn't own any shoes other than his combat boots, so he donned those as well, along with a plain black t-shirt.

As he stepped toward the door, he could hear the muffled sounds of arguing between Evan and Lisa. Well, mostly Evan. Lisa wasn't saying much. But the man sounded quite angry. Griff opened the door as quietly as possible and headed toward the kitchen. He figured he could get a start on something good for dinner. A tasty meal might lighten the mood a bit.

Safely in the kitchen, he got to work. Filling a large pot with hot water, he set it on a burner and cranked it to high. He located a box of pasta and dumped it into the pot with a dash of salt, then poured a can of cream of mushroom soup into a smaller pan and put that on the heat as well.

When they'd both been going for a while, he opened two cans of chicken and poured them into a frying pan. Lighting the burner underneath, he spread the chicken out with a wooden spoon, put a lid on the pan and left it alone to brown.

While those items cooked, he poked his nose into the walk-in fridge. There he found a tube of croissants. Excited by the find, he grabbed a tub of butter and headed out.

Turning the oven on to preheat, he then went rummaging around until he found a baking sheet. He busted open the tube and unrolled the pre-formed croissant dough, placing them evenly spaced on the sheet. Not waiting for the preheat, he slid the croissants into the oven and went to stir up the items on the stovetop. He didn't see a timer anywhere, so he just glanced at his watch.

The timing here would be critical. The croissants would be just starting to brown in about twelve minutes. The water in the pasta pot was beginning to boil, so that was good. The soup was already heating up, and the chicken was lightly browned. He upended the soup into the pan with the chicken and put the lid back on. He wanted to be sure not to overcook the chicken or the pasta.

Lastly, he went into the pantry and found a jar of peaches. He'd always been a fan of cold peaches, so he took the jar to the freezer and left it there. By the time they finished the main course the fruit should have a nice little chill to it.

With nothing to do food-wise for a few minutes, he went and found plates and glasses. Setting the table with silverware and cloth napkins as well. He thought about a bottle of white wine he'd brought with him, but decided he didn't want to find out tonight whether Evan was a friendly drunk. The odds weren't exactly in his favor. So he fetched an ice bucket and a two-liter bottle of clear soda and set those on the table as well.

Another check of the food revealed he had about five minutes. So he prepared a large bowl to mix the pasta, chicken, and soup into. He found a colander to drain the pasta in, and located a canister of grated parmesan cheese. With two minutes to go, he stuck his head out into the corridor and called out, "Dinner's on! Come get it while it's hot!"

He went back and opened the oven briefly to see that the croissants were a toasty light brown and starting to flake. He turned off the heat but left them in place for a moment. He turned off the burners as well before grabbing the large pot and dumping the pasta into the colander he'd placed in the sink. Leaving that to drain he removed the lid from the pan and stirred the chicken a bit. He used a fork to cut into a few pieces to make sure they were cooked through. Then he dumped the whole pan into the large bowl, followed quickly by the pasta. He mixed them all thoroughly then carried the bowl over to the table.

As the others entered the kitchen, he opened the oven and withdrew the croissants, transferring them quickly to a plate and grabbing the butter. Setting them both on the table, he motioned for Lisa and Evan to take a seat.

"I thought I'd make something nice for dinner. Old bachelor's recipe. Nothing fancy, but it should taste good."

He began to dish some of the pasta dish onto plates. He passed one first to Lisa, but noted as he prepared the second that Evan reached over and claimed it for himself. He gave the man a dirty look, but Evan was oblivious, already forking a mouthful into his gaping maw.

Griff handed the second plate to Lisa, who didn't meet his gaze. After dishing some up for himself, he sat and laid a napkin on his lap. He lifted the plate of fresh hot croissants and offered it to Lisa. She took one and reached for the butter. Evan barely paused in shoveling his food as he grabbed two croissants. Griff took one for himself and began to eat.

The meal passed in near total silence. Evan grunted a few times, and demanded the butter from Lisa. He was semi-polite as he asked Griff for the soda, but then reached bare-handed into the ice bucket for a handful of cubes. Lisa rolled her eyes and continued to avoid Griff's. He assumed from her posture and her clear desire to avoid interaction with him that the earlier fight must have had something to do with him.

As the meal was nearly complete, he said, "I've got peaches for dessert."

Rising from his chair, he retrieved the jar from the freezer and poured the peaches into three bowls, then returned to the table with the sweet, syrupy goodness and passed them out.

Again, Evan didn't say a word. He wolfed down the sections of fruit, lifting the bowl to slurp up the last of the watery syrup. When he was done, he set down the bowl, stood, and grabbed Lisa's arm.

"I'm done. Let's go." He pulled on her arm, causing her to drop her spoonful of peach onto the table. She let out a small cry of pain as he yanked her from her seat.

Griff was instantly on his feet. "Hoy mate! There's no call for that! Let 'er go so she can finish her meal."

Evan did let her go as he turned with a snarl toward Griff. His fists clenched and unclenched as he stared at Griff. "What's between me 'n her ain't none o' yer concern!" His voice was low and filled with malice.

The man was a workout nut, and every bit of him was muscle. He took a step around Lisa, pushing her to the floor behind him. Griff considered picking up a fork from the table and stabbing the man in the throat. But the idea of Lisa being angry at him, or worse, afraid of him, stopped him. He'd have to do this the hard way.

He held his open hands up in front of him and patted the air. "Look, mate. I don't want trouble. We're stuck down here together in a small space. I want to get along with ye, I really do. But I can't let ye be roughin' up the lady. I weren't raised that way."

"Who gives a shite how you was raised!" Evan practically screamed at him. The amount of pent-up rage in the man was surprising.

"We didn't invite ye down here to breathe our air or eat our food! We was just fine by our lonesome!"

Evan took a step forward and lunged at Griff. The man was strong and imposing, but Griff was a soldier. A combat veteran. And he was calm, while Evan was clearly 'roided out of his mind. As Evan grabbed a fistful of Griff's t-shirt with his left hand, he drew his right fist back and prepared to smash Griff's face.

Griff didn't give him the chance. His hands still up between them, he moved almost without thought. His right hand curled slightly and he jabbed it into Evan's throat. Hard.

Evan immediately let go of Griff's shirt and grabbed his injured neck with both hands as he gagged.

Griff kicked at Evan's shin with his hard-toed boot and the man bent in pain, lifting the leg and trying to curse through his bruised larynx. Not feeling the slightest bit merciful, Griff put a hand behind Evan's head and slammed his face into the table. Evan went limp and fell to the floor.

Griff turned to Lisa, his adrenaline pumping. She was still on the floor, eyes wide and tears streaming down her face. She was shaking her head back and forth as if trying to deny what she'd just seen.

Griff stepped close and reached out a hand, offering to help her up. She didn't take it.

"Oh, no," she whispered. "You shouldn't have done that. He gets angry sometimes, but he wouldn't have hurt you. Not really." She continued to shake her head. "He's going to try to kill you now. I mean, when he wakes up."

Griff retracted his hand, confused. Was she saying he should have just let the man beat on him? That wasn't happening in this lifetime.

"He's been beating you, hasn't he? For a while now?" Griff spoke softly. She didn't answer, just stared at Evan's limp form on the floor. Blood leaked from his nose and dripped on the tile. His lip was swollen and bleeding as well.

Finally, Lisa spoke, her voice ragged and barely audible.

"It started a month or so ago. He's... havin' a hard time down here. But he's too afraid to go out there. We saw on the TV what was happening, and he's angry with himself for being afraid." She paused as she drew a ragged breath. "Then you came down here. From out there. With a story of getting away from one of the creatures. Made him feel like even more of a coward. And when you and I started to play the game, well…"

Her voice drifted off. Griff didn't need her to finish the sentence. He understood completely.

"I can try to talk to him when he wakes up. I'm no hero; I didn't want to be outside either. But I'd have starved if I hadn't. And I screamed like a little girl when that bloody bear attacked. I didn't fight, I just ran as fast as that old Jeep'd go!"

Lisa smiled slightly, clearly thinking Griff was exaggerating for her benefit. But she shook her head again, tears still streaming down her face.

"He won't listen. He just… ain't made that way." She reached out her hand this time. Griff helped her up and she began to gather the dishes from dinner. He did the same, helping her clean up.

"Plus, he don't see no future," she continued. "Ya know he won't upload to the game. And if we do, he'll be by hisself here. He's been tryin' to convince me not to do it since the first day."

Griff shook his head. His mind was, already trying to work out a solution. He could lock the man up somewhere. Or take him outside and tell Peabody not to let him back in. He could stomp on the defenseless man's neck here and now and solve the issue altogether. But one look at Lisa, and he knew she'd never forgive him.

"What should I do? I'm willing to apologize…"

Lisa hesitated. "Help me get him to his bed. We'll leave him there for the night. Be sure and lock your door, and I'll do the same. He'll be in a evil mood when he wakes."

Griff nodded in acquiescence and bent to take hold of Evan. He got a hand under each arm and lifted the man to his feet. Holding him upright against a wall, he bent and put a shoulder to the man's waist before letting him fall forward, lifting him in a fireman's carry and following Lisa to Evan's quarters.

When he reached the bed, he simply dumped the man off his shoulder. Evan's body bounced once and rolled forward, his head knocking against the wall. Not feeling the slightest bit guilty, Griff just turned and exited. He waited in the corridor for Lisa to emerge.

She didn't say anything, just put a hand on his arm as she passed. He watched as she walked into another room, closed and locked the door. They were sturdy metal doors, and Griff was sure Evan couldn't get through it without him hearing.

He turned and entered his own quarters, locking the door behind him. As he sat on the bed, he said, "Peabody, do you have cameras in the corridor outside this room?"

"Of course, admin Griff. I have cameras in most rooms. Excepting bathrooms, sleeping quarters, the locker rooms attached to the fitness center, and the research labs."

"Okay then, please alert me if Evan tries to gain access to Lisa's room or my own. Or if he engages in any activity that might cause harm to us or this facility."

"Certainly, admin Griff. Has Evan become a hostile entity?"

Griff shook his head. "Maybe, Peabody. We'll see tomorrow. Good night."

"Good night, admin Griff. Sleep well."

Griff changed from his jeans and boots to a pair of sweat shorts and crawled into bed. He shut off the lights, but it took more than an hour for him to drift off to sleep. He couldn't help but picture all the ways in which Evan could cause trouble for them and maybe get them killed. The world outside was unforgiving, and one mistake could mean the end of them all.

It seemed he'd only been asleep for a moment when Peabody's voice awakened him.

"Admin Griff. I am sorry to wake you, but Evan has just activated the elevator. He is heading for the lobby level."

"Is Lisa with him?" Griff had a sudden and horrifying vision of the man dragging her out onto the surface in some misguided effort to find a new place to live.

"Lisa has not left her sleeping quarters. Evan is alone. He took a shotgun from the security office right before calling the elevator. Which is why I began to try to wake you."

Not bothering to dress, Griff threw open his door and ran to the security office. There were several monitors there with feeds from various cameras around the building. He focused in on the one that showed Evan just stepping off the elevator at the lobby level.

"Peabody, please put Evan on the main monitor and track his movements."

"Of course, admin Griff."

The camera angle changed as the AI switched to a camera inside the lobby. It showed Evan heading for the garage exit. When he disappeared from view, the camera changed again time to one above the exit door. Griff got a good look at the scowl on Evan's face as he pushed the door open. The camera angle changed again, this time to one mounted above the door on the garage side.

Griff watched Evan pull a set of keys from his pocket and move to a beat up old Volvo sedan. He unlocked the car and got in. A moment later the engine turned over and the headlights came on. Griff imagined that he could hear the tires screeching as Evan gunned the motor and cranked the wheel to one side.

The car sped up the ramp toward the exit gate.

"Peabody, open the door garage door before he just crashes through it!" Griff shouted.

The AI had anticipated the need, and even as Griff spoke the door began to rise. Evan shot through underneath before it was even fully open and the door began to lower again immediately. Peabody switched to exterior cameras mounted near the roof that showed Evan's car bouncing as it hit a deep pothole, nearly careening into a burned-out car. A moment later, it disappeared around a corner, headed in the general direction of the Tesco store.

"That damned idjut!" Griff cursed to himself. "He'll get killed out there." Despite his low opinion of the man and Evan's clear hatred of him, Griff's first instinct was to try and save him. But it would be foolish to go out there now. And there was no way he would leave Lisa here alone. His new horrifying vision was one of Evan re-entering the building after becoming contaminated. Then turning into a zombie creature and ripping apart the facility.

"Peabody, I need you to lock down the building. If Evan returns, let him into the parking garage, but no further. And notify me as soon as he appears on your cameras. Do not open the exterior doors for any reason without my approval."

"*Certainly, admin Griff. I will classify Evan as a threat and revoke all access.*"

Griff poked around the security office for a bit longer. He picked up a stapler and tossed it from hand to hand. He paced the room, watching all of the exterior feeds. A thought occurred to him, so he asked Peabody a question.

"Peabody, what did Evan do when he left his room? Did he go anywhere in the facility before leaving?"

"*He went to the kitchen, and remained there approximately three minutes. Then he went to the research labs that you and Lisa have been using. He remained there for less than five minutes, then retrieved the shotgun from the security office before leaving.*"

"Please show me the camera feeds for that time period. Beginning when he left his room" Griff watched the feed as Peabody spliced together Evan's movements onto the main monitor. He did indeed go to the kitchen. He filled a backpack with food and a few cans of soda, then left for the labs. There were no cameras in the those rooms, presumably because the company didn't want their R&D secrets at risk. So he couldn't tell what happened inside. After watching Evan retrieve the gun and get on the elevator, he said "Thank you Peabody."

Leaving the security office, he went first to the kitchen and checked the stove and gas lines. It occurred to him that Evan might try to sabotage the place before leaving. The ultimate 'screw you' from a deranged madman.

Finding nothing wrong in the kitchen, he moved first to Lisa's lab. It took him less than five seconds to see what Evan had been up to. The control panel was smashed. The plexiglass bubble that covered the top of the pod was cracked, though not broken. And the aluminum facing along the side was dented in as if it had been kicked. Griff sighed and checked the rest of the room before going to check on his own pod. Not surprisingly, the control panel had been ripped from its cradle and stomped to pieces on the floor.

It didn't look like Evan had bothered trying to damage the plexiglass or body of this pod. Probably he'd learned his lesson after the first.

Griff said many bad words under his breath as he stooped to pick up the smashed panel.

"Coward! Ye couldn't face me? Ye had to destroy our hope o' savin' ourselves by uploadin'." His mind raced. There was still one working pod, so he would make sure that Lisa could-"

He slapped his forehead as he realized what he was saying. "Ye daft fool! Yer in a damned manufacturing facility. Everything ye need to fix these is right here in the buildin'!"

He dropped the smashed hardware to the floor and began to walk toward the elevator. Glancing at his watch, he saw that he had about three hours before Lisa woke up, and less than four until they were expected at the village to start their dungeon run. As he walked, he said "Peabody, I'm going to need some tools. And do you have access to this facility's inventory?"

*****

Evan pulled up to the front of the Tesco store and shut off the engine. The glass doors were wide open, and he could see the first several feet of shelving. Items were strewn everywhere across the floor, and he spotted what might be old bloodstains.

"Screw soldier boy! If he can get food, so can I."

He tried to psych himself up. When he opened the driver's door, the squeak of the hinge sounded like a trumpet call, echoing against the glass storefront and back across the parking lot. He froze, listening, his head jerking left and right as he looked for movement.

After a minute or two of nothing, he spat on the ground and began to move toward the door. Just as he reached the threshold, a shuffling noise from inside made his blood run cold.

A store flyer pushed by a breeze danced a short distance across the floor in front of him before settling down.

Releasing the breath he'd been holding, he muttered, "Get ahold o' yerself boyo." He raised the shotgun and proceeded into the store. A few steps in, he spotted a rack of candy bars that looked unmolested. Reaching for his pack, he cursed again when he realized the pack was already full of food. Poor planning on his part.

Looking around, he spotted a shopping cart and went to retrieve it. He set the shotgun across the seat, and began to push it around despite the loud complaints of the squeaky left front wheel. He remembered what Shari and Mace had told them that first day. Only food sealed in plastic or non-organic containers. Fresh items weren't safe. So he moved through the half-empty store grabbing items here and there, and dropping them into the cart. When he reached the back of the store, he tried the double doors that led to the warehouse. But they were still blocked by the bar Griff had put in place a few days earlier.

Evan shrugged and moved on. By his reckoning, there was plenty of food here for him. He passed by a large area covered in dried blood. The floor, the packages of food scattered across it, and the lower several feet of the surrounding shelves were all splattered with blood, as if something or someone had exploded.

He began to notice other patches of blood as he moved around the store, filling his cart. Now he kept one hand on the shotgun as he reached out to pull items down from shelves. The blood was all a dark rust color, the shade you'd expect from months-old dried blood. He didn't see any of the neon blue blood Shari had warned them about. But it didn't take a genius to figure out that the zombies had gotten in here at some point and killed people.

"Probably in the first day or two," he mumbled to himself. "Poor bastards."

In the next aisle he discovered something that made him smile.

"Ale!" He grinned to himself as he pushed the cart to one side and began pulling six-packs from a shelf, shoving them onto the lower shelf of the cart.

He was grabbing another one when he felt something impact his leg. Half a second later, he was yanked off balance. He crashed to the floor and the six pack did the same. Two of the bottles shattered and a third had its cap loosened. Beer began to spray across his vision.

Wiping his face, he looked toward his leg. A dull pain was only just now registering. When his eyes focused, he couldn't believe what he was seeing. A giant snake had latched onto his left leg, its jaws clamped tightly just below his knee, and the thing was slowly crushing his bones as it stared at him with dead eyes.

"No! No no no no!" Evan began to kick with his right foot, slamming the thing's nose and eyes to try and make it let go. He saw his own blood dripping onto the floor and went into a panic.

Grabbing one of the broken bottles next to him, he began to stab frantically at the creature's face. It didn't even seem to notice, just kept squeezing as neon blue blood splashed on Evan's hand and face.

That was when something deep down in his lizard brain made the connection.

"I'm bleedin'. This thing's already killed me. I'll become one o' them zombies," he said aloud, his face and voice dead calm.

He watched dispassionately as the now-bloody creature changed its grip on him. It briefly let loose of his leg, and as his brain screamed at him to pull away and run, the thing scooped his foot into its mouth and clamped down again on his knee.

The realization that the giant zombie snake intended to eat him alive snapped him out of his stupor and he screamed. He began to stab the thing again, bursting one of its eyes and turning its face into a mangled mess with the sharp edges of the broken bottle. But still it continued to work its way mercilessly up his leg.

When its jaw reached his crotch and hip and its progress became obstructed by his other leg, the creature paused. Its one good eye looked him over for a moment, then it raised its head up off the ground. Its powerful body, at least half a meter wide and ten meters long, lifted Evan's weight with ease.

He screamed again as he flew into the air. He kept going up and up until he was near the high ceiling, dangling by one leg from the snake's maw.

His screams were cut off as the creature whipped its head to one side and slammed Evan into the wall. Then it reversed direction and used his body to knock over the nearest rack of shelves. The second time the snake smashed him into the wall, Evan lost consciousness. Several of his bones were broken and his skull had been half crushed by the impact.

The creature set his now mostly limp body back on the floor and resumed trying to swallow him whole. It pushed and pushed, flexing whatever internal muscles it used to move food down its throat. Eventually there was a loud pop as Evan's hip dislocated and his leg was pushed up so that his foot was now above his head. The pain was enough to wake him briefly as he screamed in mindless agony.

The relentless snake consumed him inch by inch, but Evan was only half aware. His mind had shattered from the horror and the pain. He alternated between screaming and babbling nonsense until he just stopped making any noise at all.

Chapter 12
Any Port in a Storm

Shari was the first to wake. It was early yet, but a sound had awakened her from a deep sleep. Turning toward the source of the sound, she was greeted with Mace's face just inches from hers. Drool ran from his open mouth and down his cheek as he snored loudly.

"Lovely."

She gently pushed his chin upward, closing his mouth. The snoring abated for a moment, until he smacked his lips and his mouth dropped open again. She tried a different tactic, slowly and gently turning his head to the side. This resulted in him rolling his whole body away from her. It put an end to the snoring, but now exposed her body to the cool air of the room where his nice warm body had been.

Leaving him to sleep a bit more, she got up and showered. After drying off, she threw on a pair of scrubs and walked to the security office.

Once inside, she quietly said, "Peabody, any messages from the others?"

"Good morning, admin Shari. No messages. The only players who have logged in since your last inquiry have been the North Koreans, and Griff and Lisa. I have managed to connect with the operating system at the Hong Kong facility, but have been unable to breach its security protocols. Someone has installed an unapproved upgrade to the corporate security program."

"Thank you, Peabody. Are Griff and Lisa in the game now?"

"Admin Griff is in the research lab effecting repairs on one of the damaged pods. Admin Lisa is in her sleeping quarters."

"Repairs?" Shari's heartrate soared. "Were they attacked?"

"Evan attacked admin Griff during an argument after dinner. Evan suffered minor damage and was rendered unconscious for several hours. Griff and Lisa deposited him in his sleeping quarters before retiring to their own. As they slept, Evan took some food and drink, smashed their immersion equipment, took a weapon and left the facility. He has not returned. I assisted Griff in locating the necessary components

for him to repair the damage to the pods, and he has been attempting to do so for approximately two hours."

Shari snorted at the 'minor damage' bit of the AI's recounting.

"Good for you, Griff. Didn't like Evan much anyway." She thought for a moment. "Peabody, can you connect me to Griff?"

"I do not have access to the systems in the research lab other than the immersion pod. And the interfaces were what Evan destroyed. I can inform admin Griff through the intercom that you wish to speak with him."

"Please do, Peabody. And thank you. I don't know what we'd do without you."

She looked up at the nearest camera as she spoke. Her words surprised her, as she'd not been a big fan of the AI controlling the building. Especially when it spoke to her at… inconvenient moments.

She only had to wait a few minutes before the monitor in front of her lit up with Griff's face. He looked tired.

"Hey Griff! I hear you had a little trouble?"

The soldier nodded his head. "Bit of a dust-up with Evan. He was hurtin' Lisa and I couldn't let that go. He's gone out, but he smashed up the control panels of both our pods right well before he left. The lil shit."

"Can you fix them?" Shari knew the engineer had training in working on the pods' systems.

"What he smashed is beyond repair, but I can completely replace the damaged components. This place has about a hundred o' everything sittin' in crates upstairs. It's slow going, lots of connections to make. Then I have to install the software and reboot it all. Slow going, but I'm nearly done."

Shari got a wicked grin on her face.

"So… if Evan's gone for good, does that mean you and Lisa…" She left the end of her question for him to finish.

"Ha!" He blushed and scratched his head awkwardly. "I dunno. Maybe?"

"She could do a lot worse than you, Griff. In fact, it seems she already was. Consider yourself an upgrade!" she winked at him as he squirmed uncomfortably in his chair.

"Okay well, you've got work to do before she wakes up and you two have to get in-game for your dungeon. I'll let you get to it." She couldn't resist making an exaggerated kissy-face at him as she waved and signed off.

The possibility of a budding romance between two of the last survivors on earth warmed her heart. She found herself hurrying back to Mace's room. He was still asleep, though he'd rolled back onto his back and had resumed snoring again. She shouted "INCOMING!" and leaped at the bed, landing half on top of him as he snorted and sputtered awake. She grabbed a pillow and began to beat him about the head, taking advantage of his confusion.

"Hey! What'd I do?" he grumbled, still only half awake.

She rolled over top of him and positioned herself between him and the wall. Using the wall as a brace, she shoved at him with arms and legs, rolling him out of bed onto the floor.

"HEY!" he protested more emphatically. "What the hell?"

She scooched over to where she could look ever the edge of the bed and see him laid out on the floor.

"Good morning, sleepyhead! You were snoring. It was simply *adorable*!" She beamed at him as he blinked and rubbed his face. "Oh, and Griff and Lisa might be a *thing* soon!"

Mace focused on her, a blank look on his face. "What, now?"

"Evan did something dickish, and hurt Lisa. Griff beat his ass. When he woke up, he stole some food, smashed their pod controls, and took off, leaving Griff and Lisa alone and free to explore a budding romance!" She sighed dramatically, rolling her eyes and fanning a hand near her face.

Mace sat up and leaned his chin on the bed next to her face.

"Damn. How long was I asleep?" He looked at his watch. "So, are they sure Evan's not coming back?"

"I don't know. But why would he take food and damage their pods if he planned to come back?" Shari mused.

"Good point. Peabody? You there, buddy?"

"*Of course, Mace.*"

"Can you notify us if Evan attempts to re-enter the Newport facility?"

"Admin Griff has already instructed me to deny access to Evan unless approved by him. You have the authority as alpha admin to override that instruction. Shall I notify you instead of admin Griff?"

Mace shook his head slightly as he answered.

"I should have known. No, Peabody. Please follow Griff's instructions relative to Evan. Thank you."

Shari anticipated Mace's next question. "Griff is already fixing the pods. He's trying to have it done before their scheduled dungeon run meet-up at sunrise, server time."

"He's a handy guy to have around. Badass brawler, tech… if he can cook too, Lisa should probably keep him," Mace grinned. He too was hoping Griff and Lisa would hit it off. And that Evan would never darken their doorstep again.

*****

Shari logged in first, with Mace right behind her. They were still on the deck of the *Sea Sprite*. The sun was rising as the boat moved with the current downstream.

She looked behind to see the *Platypus* still following. Jorin called out a greeting from up on the helm and waved. Shari returned the wave and asked, "Are we there yet?" causing Mace to snort.

"Aye, nearly!" Jorin called back. He pointed slightly to the east of the waterway and Shari followed his arm. Turning, she saw plumes of smoke from what must have been dozens of chimneys rising through the dawning light.

"That'd be Port Bjurstrom in all its glory!" he smiled.

The *Sea Sprite*'s crew were already preparing the ship to dock at the river port. Shari imagined they were anxious to have their work done and get to the tavern as quickly as possible. To raise a toast to the dead, and celebrate their victory over the slavers.

She and Mace climbed the steps to the aft deck, where the captain stood at the helm.

"How long will we need to be in port before we continue on to Graf?" she asked.

"Overnight." Jorin replied. "That'll give us time to unload, arrange new cargo bound for Graf, and reload. And for the lads to blow off a bit of steam. We'll sail early tomorrow."

"Then we can do a bit of exploring and see what we can learn about the Black Flame," Mace replied. "Is there an inn you prefer? The rooms and drinks are on us tonight."

Jorin gave a small bow. "Aye. Try the Purple Mushroom. Tell Delilah that I sent ya. That woman's had a crush on me for thirty years." He winked at Mace.

They chatted with the captain a bit more as the port grew closer. Rounding a bend in the river, they could see that it bellied widely just past the turn. In the calmer waters out of the current, along the left bank, a dozen or so long piers stretched out toward them.

Beyond the pier was a sort of hodgepodge village of wooden warehouses and other buildings. They were built on pilings with walkways in between. Further back on higher, more solid ground, was the rest of the town. It rose up a gentle slope to press against a high wooden wall that encircled the town. Shari estimated there were maybe a hundred buildings all told, including a few two and three-story apartment buildings and a scattering of homes and businesses. An imposing structure near the top of the hill and not far from the gate caught her attention.

"Is that some sort of temple?"

Jorin followed her eyes. "Ah. No, that'd be the Merchants' Guild house. This port is run by a group of merchants who either own the boats that sail and in and out of the port, or own caravans that take goods overland. Or both. And they own the warehouses you see here by the docks. There's a mayor in the town, but he's mostly a figurehead, as he'd never make a move without the guild's approval."

Shari continued to observe the town as Jorin steered the boat cleanly alongside one of the docks. The crew of the *Sea Sprite* leapt to the pier and began to secure thick mooring lines to the bollards. When the boat was secure, the wide gangplank was run out and an official-looking man in a tight-fitting red paisley vest with a puffed-out chest climbed the ramp. "Ahoy, Jorin! Back again, I see. Cargo to declare? And how long will ya be needin' the berth?"

Jorin mumbled "Harbormaster. As crooked as the river is long. He's here to collect the 'tax' for incoming cargo and our time at this berth. Seventy percent of it goes to the guild; he keeps another ten himself. The rest goes into the town coffers. Then the thieves' guild will steal their share as the load passes into the warehouse."

He excused himself and went down to the main deck to speak with the man, plastering a fake smile on his face.

Shari, Mace, Lila and Layne squeezed down the ramp between the stacks of crates being unloaded. Mace glanced left and right, looking for some sign of the invisible bunny, but found none. He said, much more loudly than he needed to as the ladies were all nearby, "If we get separated, meet at the Purple Mushroom."

The group followed a cart filled with grain sacks up the pier to the harbor district. The smell of wet wood, old fish, stale ale and sweaty bodies permeated everything.

The group got lots of inquisitive looks from the dock workers and bystanders as they passed. Or more specifically, Mace did. Drow were distrusted everywhere, and no one was going to turn their back on him as he passed.

Shari took his hand in hers, hoping the association would alleviate some of the scowling and hostility directed toward Mace, but it didn't seem to help.

Passing as quickly through the area as they could, it only took a few minutes to reach the more solid ground. The smells here improved, though not greatly. The fish smell was replaced with that of muddy streets and waste dumped from chamber pots, mixed together with roasted meat of some kind, and an acrid stench drifting across from the tannery in the far corner.

"You get used to it after a while." Layne made a face that suggested she didn't believe her own statement. Lila ducked her head down and pulled her tunic up to cover her mouth and nose. Mace fastened a black and red bandana across his mouth, the new look making even more townspeople nervous. A drow walking around was one thing. A drow hiding his face likely intended to murder someone.

Shari breathed through her mouth to try and lessen the impact of the stench as she smacked Mace's shoulder. "Take that thing off. You're freaking people out."

Mace looked around, then complied with a sigh. He resisted the urge to draw his blades and shout, "Boo!" at the nearest group of locals. A squeeze from Shari's hand locked with his let him know she sympathized.

As they got further up the hill the air freshened as the breezes drifting over the surrounding hillsides came into play. The streets here were cobbled with stone and some effort was made to keep them clean.

The houses here got larger the farther one traveled up the hill. It wasn't long before they reached the inn that Jorin had recommended. The building was three stories with wide windows on the lower level. The windows were open, and the smell of something good from the kitchen drifted out. Above the door swung a wooden sign with a portrait painted on it. The mushroom depicted there was indeed purple, but Shari doubted its resemblance to any mushroom found in nature. It made her cheeks blush slightly. Lila giggled and put a hand over her mouth when she noticed it. Layne just tilted her head sideways and grinned.

They stepped inside and asked for Delilah. She appeared after a few minutes, a shapely woman with jet black hair and bright blue eyes, wearing a purple velvet dress that bunched her assets together in ways Mace thought defied gravity. While he stared, Shari spoke.

"Good evening, Miss Delilah. Captain Jorin sent us. Said you have the best accommodations in town."

The woman smiled condescendingly, and waved her arms toward the surrounding tavern.

"Indeed I do," she replied as Shari took in the crowd. There were well-dressed merchants and a few sailors, mostly drinking quietly. And at every table was at least one suggestively dressed young lady. Some were human, but more were cat-women or other beastkin. One was an impressively endowed orc female in tight leather with a whip on her belt.

Mace began to blush this time. "Uhm, we're just looking for rooms. As many as you have available. We'll be hosting the crew of the *Sea Sprite* here tonight, with your permission of course."

Delilah clapped her hands together and bounced slightly, recapturing Mace's attention.

"Always happy to have Jorin and his boys in my house!" She bent to retrieve something from under the counter, and Shari nearly covered Mace's widening eyes.

When she straightened, she held four keys in her hand. Shari took one, leaning into Mace and gripping his arm tightly.

"We'll only be needing three."

She looked pointedly at Delilah, who only laughed.

"I see. Ya like a little dark meat with your meal. A little danger mixed with pleasure. I don't blame ya one bit!"

She waggled her eyebrows suggestively at Shari, who *hmphed* and turned Mace toward the stairs. Delilah handed a key each to Layne and Lila with a smile.

"We'll start serving lunch in an hour!" she called to them as they climbed.

Mace started to turn back, saying, "We forgot to ask how much the rooms are," but Shari just clamped down on his arm and continued to march him upward.

"We've got lots of gold. Don't worry about it." Her terse reply had Mace looking confused. She thought to herself *He really does have no clue about women.*

They all piled into Mace and Shari's room, which turned out to be a small suite. There was a sitting area with a sofa and two chairs, and a separate bedroom with a private bath. The four of them took seats and Shari began.

"So... what do we want to accomplish while we're here?"

"It would be helpful if we could learn some things about the Black Flame. I assume they have some sort of branch office here. But it's not the sort of thing you just ask around on the street about. Once it gets dark, I'll head out and do my scary drow assassin thing."

He grinned, raising both hands and making spooky finger motions at Shari. She rolled her eyes.

"Well, while we're here, we should make arrangements to purchase some needed supplies for Lakeside. They obviously have a wide range of items going through here. I saw some reasonably fresh food on the docks. We could buy food, tools, maybe even weapons and armor?"

Layne spoke up. "Shari is correct. We should make arrangements now. If we're going to be taking on the Black Flame when we get to Graf, we may be in a hurry when we pass through this way again."

The others nodded in agreement. They spent some time making lists of needed items, then dividing the list into two parts. Layne and Lila would focus on the perishable items, while Mace and Shari would see about hardware and gear.

When they headed back downstairs, Layne moved to ask Delilah about likely merchants while Shari escorted Mace out to the street. He chuckled at the dirty look Shari threw Delilah's way as they passed. He kind of enjoyed her being a little jealous.

When they reached the street, he turned suddenly and gathered her into his arms. Dipping her backward, he planted a long, deep kiss on her surprised mouth. It lasted long enough that a few bystanders applauded and whistled. When her raised her upright and released her, she took a deep breath and adjusted her clothes.

"What was that for?" she asked, still slightly flustered.

"Just to remind you that you don't have anything to fear from the Delilahs of this world. I'm all yours." He gave her his most sincere puppydog eyes, which unfortunately looked a little disturbing on his harsh and angular drow face.

She smacked his chest lightly, then took his arm again with a happy little smile on her face. When Layne came out and gave them a few names and general directions, they set off.

Shari being the better navigator, she led Mace down one street, then across and up another. In less than ten minutes they located a general goods merchant named Bixby. An elder human with plain but impeccably neat clothes. He greeted them as they stepped into the shop.

"Good morning, travelers! What can I help you with today?"

Mace handed him their list, saying, "We're gathering supplies for our return trip to Lakeside. Some items to help build and expand the settlement. Delilah said you were the man to see."

Bixby looked at the list. "Let's see. Hmmm…"

He reached under the counter and pulled out a ledger. Opening it to a spot near the back, he ran his finger down the entries there. "Ah, yes. I can provide these. Now what do we have next? I'm afraid I won't be much help with the weapons or armor…" Mace and Shari watched with amused faces as the old man worked his way through this list. "And when would you wish to take delivery of these items?"

Mace decided on a little gamble. "We're headed up to Graf to destroy the Black Flame organization. It shouldn't take long. Maybe... five days from now?" he did his best to keep a straight face as Shari's eyes widened and the old man gasped in surprise.

Bixby took a moment to recover. "Yes, well. Ambitious, aren't we?" he tapped his fingers on the counter for a few heartbeats. "Heh. I never liked those thieves and slavers anyway. If you can do what you say, I'll have these items waiting for you when you return. Minus the weapons and armor. But you can speak to Callahan the smith about those."

This time Mace wasn't going to forget to ask. "And what will all the items on the list cost us?"

Bixby took out a quill and began to scratch numbers onto a piece of parchment. "We'll call it one hundred gold even. And if you really do destroy the slavers, I'll make it ninety!"

Mace chuckled at the old man and held out a hand. To Bixby's credit, he barely hesitated before shaking the drow's hand.

"We'll be back in five days. Maybe six if there are a lot of them."

He and Shari turned toward the door. As he held it open for her, Shari heard the old man mumble, "Good luck."

As soon as they were back on the street, Shari hissed, "What was that?"

Mace replied "Jorin said there were lots of merchants here and in Graf who would be willing to pay a substantial reward for the elimination of the Black Flame. So I gambled, sort of. Either he would be one of those who'd be happy to see them dead, or he'd be inclined to warn them. In which case the local slavers will be huddling in their hideout worrying about the drow assassin all day." His face took on a mischievous look as he glanced sideways at her.

They'd walked another half block or so before she answered.

"Next time, warn a girl first, okay?"

She steered him toward the sound of hammer hitting metal that echoed from a nearby alley. Mace paused at the alley entrance to look around before he allowed her to lead them in. The shop was less than a block down. As they approached, Shari could feel the heat blasting from the furnace in the back. The alleyway was close and without much airflow, and she could feel sweat begin to trickle down her back.

They entered the store and were greeted by a young orc boy who was wearing a leather apron. An apprentice, most likely.

"We're here to see Callahan." Mace growled at the orcling.

Eyes wide, the kid bobbed his head and disappeared so fast out the back door toward the smithy that Mace feared he might have caused the poor boy to hurt himself.

A moment later, a much larger orc with shoulders wider than the doorway and arms that bulged with muscle stepped into the shop. He growled at the drow and the elf in front of him.

"What do you want of Callahan the Crusher?"

Mace felt a little effeminate as the massive orc's arm flexed. No weakling himself, his lithe drow form was dwarfed by the ogre-sized orc smith. Shari said, "We would like to purchase or commission some arms and armor for the Lakeside settlement, sir." She looked up at his face a good two feet above hers and tried not to let her voice tremble. Mace held up the list with, to his credit, a steady hand.

The orc delicately took the parchment between two fingers and turned it to face him. He took a few moments to read through the items, grunting occasionally and raising his gaze to the ceiling in thought.

"I have most of this here in my shop, or in the storage out back. When do you need these?"

Shari rolled her eyes and stepped back several paces as Mace grinned at her. Looking up at the smith, he said, "We're headed to Graf in the morning. Got a bunch of Black Flame assholes to kill. We figure we'll be back in five or six days."

"Ha!" Callahan roared out a laugh that shook the building. "Just you two? Or are you hiding an army outside?"

Mace's hands dropped to his sides, coming up a quarter second later with his daggers. He twirled them both between his fingers, and as the orc's attention was drawn by the grey smoky surface of the enchanted one in his right hand, he threw the left dagger toward a shield. It bounced off the metal and rebounded toward him.

Keeping his eyes locked on the orc's, he reached out and snagged it, resuming the spinning without pause.

"I'm a drow Darkblade. Killing people is what I do. And this is personal." His voice was dead flat, as were his eyes as he spoke.

The orc actually took a step back. "Hey, now. No need to get hostile. I just make the weapons. Who gets killed and why are none of my concern."

Mace decided to push his advantage, not yet sure where Callahan stood on the whole 'killing the slavers or not' issue. He growled "Don't suppose you'd want to tell me where they hide here in town? Can't have them sneaking up behind as we travel to Graf."

Callahan scratched his head. "Sure. That's no secret. They took over one of the warehouses a few months back after the dwarf who owned it died suddenly."

The venom in the orc's voice said clearly that he wasn't a fan.

"Telgrin was a friend o' mine and a fellow smith. He was my main competition in town. If you'd avenge his murder, I'll support you in whatever way I can. You can't miss the place. They burned their flame right into the door."

Mace relaxed, sheathing his daggers. "Good enough. We'll take care of them tonight. If you want to help, meet us at the warehouse at midnight. In the meantime, how much for all the gear on the list?"

Callahan ran through the list again. "Two hundred gold, and I'll throw in some low-level enchantments on the weapons. Extra Strength, or Stamina."

Mace reached out a hand and it was engulfed in the orc's massive paw. "If we don't see you at midnight, I'll be back in five days or so."

As they were leaving, Callahan called out, "Hey!"

When they turned back, he said, "There are a few others… good with sword or bow. Others who'd like a little payback."

Mace considered for a few seconds. "Can you trust them not to warn the slavers?"

Callahan nodded. "I'll only tell those I know to be trustworthy."

"Good enough. Any idea how many of them will be in there?"

The orc's face fell. "Might be as many as fifty still here. A bunch have sailed north on a couple of boats in the past few days."

Mace grinned. "Yeah, they're dead. Every single one of them. Along with the ones that were at the stronghold they sailed to. We've killed about a hundred and fifty so far; fifty more shouldn't be a problem."

Callahan chuckled, his deep voice echoing in the small room. "I like your style, drow. I should warn you, though. They won't all be in the warehouse. They work mostly at night. Collecting 'taxes' and robbing sailors and such."

Shari got into the spirit of the moment.

"Well, how about you and your friends hit the spots you think they might be and kill any stragglers you find on the way to the warehouse? Once we've cleared the place, we can join you in hunting down the rest."

Callahan's massive hand thumped Mace on the back, causing him to step forward to keep his feet.

"Hold on to this one, drow! She's got the heart of a wyvern!"

Shari snorted. "Well, I did *have* one, but I sold it," she said, eliciting a confused look from the orc as she waved and stepped out the door.

Their mission accomplished, Shari and Mace headed back to the Purple Mushroom. They took a table in the tavern and ordered some lunch from one of the waitresses, who was dressed even more provocatively than Delilah had been. Shari bristled a bit as the woman flirted with Mace, but kept silent.

When the woman left, Mace said, "I got the feeling that flirting is sort of a job requirement around here."

He tried to keep his poker face on, but the annoyed look on Shari's face broke him. He burst out laughing and reached out to take hold of her hand.

"I know this seems real, but remember, it's just a bunch of code. I think your sync rating must be skyrocketing about now."

After giving him a dirty look, then a few minutes of reflection, Shari chuckled. "Yeah. Sorry. Here I am getting all 'Jealous Judy' over nothing. And I don't even know why. I mean, it's not like you're all *that* amazing. I could do way better."

Mace nodded in agreement. He had no illusion that if the old world still existed, he'd have had no shot with the beautiful, smart, funny woman who now shared his home.

Their food arrived, and shortly thereafter so did Layne and Lila. They took seats at the table and the waitress brought them drinks. They ordered meals for themselves, and the group spent some leisure time catching each other up.

Layne had also learned that the slavers occupied the warehouse down at the docks. And that they controlled several small merchant shops that hadn't been strong enough to resist them. As well as one of the rougher sailor bars. Shari filled them in on the plan to attack at midnight while Mace stuffed his face with some kind of roasted short ribs that practically fell off the bone. The food in Elysia was truly amazing.

They talked about the supplies they had been able to secure. Shari was particularly proud of Lila, who had not only negotiated a good deal on a wagonload of fresh fruit, but had convinced the farmer to include a dozen saplings from his orchard for the sum of five gold. The trees would produce a fruit called Buluda, and its closest relative on earth was probably the breadfruit.

Lila had seemed a little nervous when revealing this to Shari, worried that the amount was too high. Shari hugged the halfling and said "We can plant those saplings inside the walls. If they survive and thrive, you'll have helped keep hundreds of people fed for decades. I think that's well worth a few gold."

With their bellies full, they elected to retire to their rooms for a nap. They had several hours before midnight, and it promised to be a long night. Mace and Shari logged out and grabbed a light snack before crawling into bed and setting their alarms to wake them in six hours.

*****

Lisa woke feeling refreshed and relaxed. She'd slept a full nine hours, which was unusual for her. Probably because she hadn't had Evan thrashing about or snoring next to her. That thought caused her to sit up and in alarm. The events of the previous evening came back to her, and she dressed quickly. Exiting her room she saw that both Evan's and Griff's doors were open. She listened carefully for any sounds of struggle, but heard nothing.

"Uhm… Peabody? Can you tell me where Evan and Griff are, please?"

"Of course, admin Lisa. Evan left the building approximately four hours ago. Griff is in the research lab that contains your immersion pod, effecting repairs."

"Repairs? Was there another fight?" She began to hurry toward the lab.

"Evan departed while you and admin Griff were sleeping. But he damaged the pods before he exited the premises."

"What a wanker." Lisa said out loud. Then quickly added "Not you, Peabody. You're lovely."

She smiled up at the ceiling. Reaching her lab, she found Griff sitting cross-legged on the floor with an array of components and tools spread out in an arc in front of him. She smiled as she observed him tinkering with a delicate-looking circuit board, his tongue jutting slightly out the left side of his mouth as he concentrated. She waited for him to put it down before speaking.

"Looks complicated."

He started slightly, then turned to her with a guilty smile.

"I was hoping ta have all this done before ya woke up. Yer boy did quite the number on both our pods."

His face grew serious. "I've instructed Peabody not to let him in past the garage if he returns. But I'm not sure he will." He looked at her, anticipation written all over his face. He clearly expected her to be upset with him.

"I hope he doesn't." She gave him a gentle pat on the head as she stood above him. "There's nothing left for him here, and I'm sure he knows it. It's probably why he smashed these; he hoped that it would prevent us from uploading so that we'd eventually starve or be killed like he'll be.

"He likely went back to our flat. We lived in a high rise. He often talked about how our building could be secured, and how we could collect rainwater and grow crops on the roof. He just didn't get the whole 'everything is contaminated' bit."

She sighed and joined Griff on the floor. "Anything I can do to help?"

He shook his head, taking up a component in each hand and snapping them together.

"I'm nearly through. I've focused on the damaged controls. He really did a number on yours. There was a lot of rage behind his attack on this thing."

He pointed to the cracked plexiglass bubble and the dented metal base. "I'll find a replacement for the glass tomorrow. It's fully functional, but you don't need the reminder every time you get in and out."

She leaned into him, giving him a one-armed hug. "Thank you, Griff." Then she got to her feet and began to pace anxiously. "I'm excited about the dungeon run today! I've never been through a dungeon before. Will it be difficult?"

Griff nodded. "I expect so, if for no other reason than because our whole group is a bunch of dungeon newbies. We're going to have to figure out how to work together and keep from getting killed. I mean, I have some basic background in group fights. Tanks and healers and such. But I've always just been pushing buttons on a controller and firing with auto-target. This game world feels so much different."

His concerns only made Lisa more excited. She was quickly becoming an adrenaline junkie, and she didn't care. If Mace and Shari were right, and they could upload their consciousness into the game, she didn't want to be some tame crafter, spending her days in a shop inside city walls. She wanted to be out adventuring. Exploring the world and fighting for loot! Griff watched her pace, and his eyes sparkled with a matching excitement.

It took another quarter hour before he had her control panel reassembled and operational. He ran a complete diagnostic two times just to be sure nothing would go wrong with Lisa's immersion. When he pronounced her pod ready, they were slightly late for their scheduled sunrise meeting with their group. Griff left her lab and closed the door behind him as he headed for his own pod. As they'd agreed, she locked her door before undressing and climbing into the pod. In case Evan managed to get back inside.

Griff spoke to Peabody as he walked the short distance to his lab door.

"Peabody, if Evan returns, can you notify me inside the game?"

"I can indeed. I have access to the personal messaging system that players use. I will notify you of any unusual movement near the building, or if Evan returns."

"Thank you, Peabody. I'll see you soon." Griff stepped into his lab and locked his door behind him. He quickly shed his own clothes and crawled into his pod.

He took a deep breath and crossed his fingers before activating the immersion. His control panel had been much more damaged than Lisa's. Evan had clearly figured out that attacking the structure of the pod was futile, and focused his rage on the vulnerable control system. Griff was 99% sure he'd repaired his correctly. But he'd rushed the job in order to be sure he was able to repair Lisa's pod.

*****

Lisa appeared in her room at the inn. She quickly gathered her gear and supplies from the chest at the end of the bed and exited the room. She found Jo, Meg, and Leroy at a table downstairs, already halfway through their breakfast. Quickly grabbing a seat, she apologized for their lateness, giving the vague explanation of trouble making the journey from her world to theirs. As soon as those words left her mouth, she realized Griff hadn't come down yet.

She shrugged, remembering that he had to walk from her lab to his and should be along any moment. She ordered some breakfast for herself, stealing a strip of bacon from Leroy's plate while she waited.

"Wait. Druids are animal lovers. Should you be eatin' bacon?" She teased the boy. He looked defensive. "It's not like this pig were a personal friend o' mine."

He paused for a moment and pretended to inspect another strip he lifted from his plate. "I don't think…" Which earned him a chuckle from the ladies.

A few minutes later, Lisa's breakfast arrived and she dug hungrily into it. She realized she and Griff hadn't taken time to eat before logging in. And the fact that he still hadn't arrived began to trouble her. The others kept looking toward the stairs as well.

Eventually, she got to her feet.

"You three finish eating. I'm going to pop back to our world and check on Griff. He may not have been able to follow me." She tried not to look as worried as she felt.

She was walking toward the stairs when Griff came hustling down, his face red and his breath coming in puffs.

"Sorry! Sorry! Had a bit o' trouble with my panel. Had to get out and fix it. All good now!" he assured her.

She gave him a little hug without even thinking about it. "I was worried. Thought ye'd managed to fry yer brain or somethin."

He shook his head as they walked back to the table. "Just a small jolt. No serious damage."

He greeted the others as she looked at him, wide-eyed. When he turned back around, he winked at her and took a seat. He stole some bacon too, this time from her plate.

"Bah! That weren't funny!" she griped at him half-heartedly.

Ten minutes later with their bellies full the group made their way toward the gate. The guards on duty were the two that Griff had made into Chosen. They both saluted smartly, then bowed their heads in thanks.

Griff returned the salute, fist to his chest. They already knew the group was headed for the nearest dungeon, as talk had spread like wildfire through the village. The lead guard said, "I hear tell from Campbell that the orcs have some fiery spirits that they brew from some kind of root or something. I'd be grateful if ye could bring us back a bottle or three."

Quest Accepted: Root of the Problem

Apparently, the village guards don't have enough ale to keep them properly inebriated in their off hours. Bring back bottles of the orc spirits known as Ang'bak for the village guards.

Reward: Variable based on number of bottles and quality of the spirits.

The others all received the quest as well, and Leroy pumped a fist in the air.

"Barely out the gate and we've already got a quest!"

They walked across the meadow in the general direction of the orc settlement. Upon reaching the forest's edge, they found that the 'trail' Campbell had said they could follow was little more than a game trail. Still, it headed in the approximate direction they wanted, so they followed it.

Griff took the lead, shield on his left arm and his hand on his weapon. Behind him came Lisa, then Jo, Leroy, and Meg in the back with her halberd over her shoulder. Next to Griff, she was the best armored of the group and should be able to hold off any attacks from the rear until they could get organized.

They weren't more than a half-hour's walk from the village when a bear stumbled across their path. Griff froze for a moment, a flashback of the zombie bear's attack causing him to hesitate.

The bear had no such compunction. It roared and charged at the group of tasty dwarves.

Lisa give Griff a shove from behind, bringing him back into the moment in time to raise his shield and lean into the charge with his legs bent. The impact knocked him backward several feet, and he nearly tripped over Lisa.

A fireball burst against the bear's snout as Jo entered the fight, and the few seconds it took the bear to recover were enough for Griff to draw his axe and advance on the animal. He shouted to get its attention, then swung his axe into its shoulder for good measure. The bear focused on him instantly and began to swipe at his shield with its right forepaw. The impacts rang off the shield, sharp claws screeching across the metal and scoring the wood. Griff gritted his teeth and took the blows, occasionally managed to strike one of his own. He inspected their foe.

Great Forest Bear
Level 20
Health 1,800/2,000

The bear stood taller than Griff and the others. Griff's face was about shoulder height on the monster. When it stood on its hind legs and roared in anger, it was more than twice the tank's height. Griff stepped back a pace, not wanting to let the massive thing come down atop him. As he did so, Meg stepped past him. The tip of her halberd sank deeply into the bear's gut, causing it to scream in pain. She quickly withdrew the weapon, ripping a wide hole in the animal's hide and causing a fountain of blood.

She withdrew two steps so that she was once again behind Griff's shield, but remained ready to attack again. Another fireball struck the bear's underside as it fell back to all fours.

The burning pain combined with the deep wound it had suffered sent it into a rage. It began to huff and bounce from left paw to right as it took swing after swing at Griff.

Leroy's healing spells were falling on the dwarf almost nonstop now. He was beginning to sweat as his mana bar steadily drained below fifty percent. The bear still had more than half its health. This was going to be a close one.

Just then a battlecry sounded behind the creature, and Lisa leapt upon its back. She dug in with both of her short swords, jamming one into each shoulder as she used them to keep herself balanced on the thing's back. At least one of the strikes had been a critical hit, and both were back-stabs. The bear's health dropped instantly down to forty percent. It was bleeding heavily from the gut wound, its fur smoking in several places.

Griff taunted the bear again, not wanting it to focus on Lisa after the massive damage she'd just inflicted. He slammed his shield into the thing's snout and felt a couple of teeth break. That got its attention for sure.

Lisa pulled out her right sword and slammed it into the back of the bear's neck with all her might. Then using that for leverage, she did the same with her left-hand sword.

She felt something give under the second sword, and the bear's roaring ceased abruptly. Its legs went weak and it collapsed on its belly. Still alive, but unable to move. She called out "I severed its spine! Finish it quick!"

Meg obliged instantly. Stepping forward with spear lowered, she drove the point of the halberd into the bear's eye and deep into its brain, putting it out of its misery.

As Lisa climbed off the carcass, the three younger members of the group were all consumed in golden light as they leveled up. Meg had been the highest level among them at six when they'd started out this morning. A level twenty beast kill, even with the experience shared among the group, was enough to grant each of them a level. At only level four, Leroy gained two.

They took a moment to allow Lisa to loot and skin the bear. It wasn't pretty, as her skinning skill was still very low-level. But she was sure she'd be able to make something useful with the hide. Leroy was interested in the bear's heart and gallbladder, saying something about potion ingredients. And they took the bear meat, teeth, and claws, thinking they might trade them to the orcs.

The group moved on up the trail, trying to keep a quick pace without draining their stamina too badly. Every once in a while they'd have to stop to fight a bear, or boar. Once they encountered a hunting party of five goblins. But they did well; the occasional fights were teaching them how best to combine their skills and abilities during a fight. When the goblins ambushed them, Griff managed to draw their aggro upon himself almost immediately. Then he took refuge behind his shield as Lisa and Meg got behind the monsters and cut through them like a scythe through wheat.

Meg's home-run swing of her halberd blade sliced cleanly through the first goblin's neck before embedding itself into the torso of the next. As she ripped the blade free, Lisa dove forward and plunged a blade each into the backs of the leftmost two goblins. One died immediately as the sword punctured its heart. The other took the blade through a shoulder and screamed in pain as it tried feebly to strike at Lisa. Jo finished it with a fireball to the face. Suddenly finding himself with only one small foe, Griff stepped forward and planted his axe in the goblin's forehead. It dropped like a stone as he removed the blade.

This time Griff leveled along with the others. The creatures and monsters in this part of the forest were all at levels fifteen to twenty-five and were giving pretty good experience. Not to mention the ridiculous loot and cash drops. The goblins that would normally have carried a few coppers at best were dropping several silver coins each.

It was past midday when they spotted the waterfall. Leroy had led them across the creek at a wide shallows, and they were now nearing the orc settlement. Griff knew this because two orc hunters emerged from the underbrush with spears in hand and pointed at his face.

He held up his hands in what he hoped was a placating gesture. "Whoa there, lads! We're just here to trade."

He looked over his shoulder, adding "Put yer weapons away."

As his party members stowed their weapons and raised their empty hands, Griff reached into his bag and withdrew a handful of bear claws. Holding them out toward the orcs, he said, "See? Trade. Campbell sent us to ya."

One of the orcs nodded, and they both turned their backs to the group as if they were not at all concerned about attack. As it turned out, they didn't need to be. As they began to lead Griff and company toward their camp, four more orcs with bows appeared out of the forest around them.

Griff chuckled. The fearsome humanoids all stood at least two meters tall. The bows carried by the archers were as long as they were tall. Their arrows were a full meter in length and as thick as Griff's thumb, with stone heads lashed on with animal sinew.

A short ten minute walk brought them to the orc settlement. There was a gated entry covered with animal bones, skulls, and other totems. But the gate was freestanding, with no doors. Or walls, for that matter.

The camp was semi-permanent, with stick-built huts and thatched roofs scattered about. A stream running nearby provided a water source. And there was a massive fire pit in the center of the cluster of huts.

The group followed their escort through the gateway and into the growing crowd of orcs that began to gather around the fire pit. There were more than just soldiers and hunters. There were orc females bearing very young children, and older children running about and laughing.

An extremely elderly orc shaman made her way out of a hut near the fire, using an ornately decorated staff for support. One of the archers ran ahead and disappeared into a hut that was larger than the rest. Griff assumed it was their leader's residence.

A moment later, a much larger orc emerged from the doorway with his head lowered. As he straightened to his full height, he stood easily twice Griff's height and three times his mass. His tusks were chipped and studded with metal and jewels, and battle scars were etched into every bit of visible skin. One eye was half-closed with scar tissue from what must have been a horrible wound.

He approached the group and, without ceremony, crossed his legs and sat in front of Griff. Which still left him a bit taller than the dwarf. He motioned for Griff and the others to sit as well, and none argued. The other orcs joined them.

"I am Ag'thar, chief of the Falling Water tribe. Welcome to our home, traders. How is my friend Campbell?"

Meg gave the orc a little wave.

"Me da's well, thank ye. He said to pass on his greetings, and to tell ye that yer still too ugly to find a decent mate." She grinned at the chief, who roared with laughter.

"I see much of your sire in you, red one." His grin showed off the rest of his tusks and very sharp fangs. "You must join us for our evening meal. You have come to trade, yes?"

Griff nodded. "We have brought goods to trade, yes. But our main purpose is to seek the dungeon near here. We wish to test our skill inside."

Ag'thar thumped his chest with a massive fist. "Good! Brave warriors are always welcome here! We will trade, then eat, then sleep! In the morning, one of my scouts will lead you to the dungeon."

Not wanting to offend the giant chief by refusing, Griff agreed. He and his party produced the spoils from the kills they made during their morning trek, and negotiations began.

Chapter 13

Battle!

Mace and Shari were awakened by their alarm. Shari still wasn't comfortable with Peabody being their alarm clock, so they'd used the one on the stand by the bed. Mace took a moment to reflect on that. All his life, he'd had a phone by his side, or in hand, that he'd used to tell time, set alarms, look up information, take pictures or communicate via holo-call. Now he couldn't even remember the last time he'd seen his phone, or where it might be. So many things had changed, and priorities changed, since the world ended.

He reached over and pulled a still sleepy Shari closer to him. All he cared about was right here on the thirtieth level of this underground sanctuary. And soon enough, if he was lucky, he'd trade it for the wide world of Elysia.

They rose and showered before heading to the kitchen. Mace made pancakes as Shari grabbed a jar of peaches from the fridge and spooned some into two bowls. Returning the rest of the jar to the fridge, she grabbed a bottle of syrup and sat down to wait for Mace. Just a couple minutes later, he brought over two stacks of pancakes and they dug in. The meal was quick and silent, other than Mace making a faint '*nom nom*' sound once in a while.

After cleaning up, they made a quick check with Peabody as to the status of the other survivors. The AI reported that the Russians had been online and received the message with no response. There had been no activity from the survivors in the Hong Kong facility. The folks in Sydney and Texas had not logged in at all.

Seeing no point in sending additional messages if the previous could not have been received yet, they retired to their pods.

Waking up at the inn, they quickly geared up. Mace summoned Minx and Shari summoned Mion, but not Snuffles. The piggy-tank would only get in the way in the tight confines of the warehouse and the other buildings where they were about to do battle.

They met the others downstairs and had a late supper of leftover ribs, which Mace did not mind one bit. The food provided a buff of +3 to Stamina and +1 to Health Regeneration for two hours. There was a celebration in full swing. The crew of the *Sea Sprite* had completed the memorial service for their dead, and were now well into the victory celebration. Captain Jorin joined them at their table.

"Delilah tells me you've offered to pay for our little party here. That could end up being expensive, you know. My boys can drink. And Delilah will surely pad the bill by at least half." He was slightly tipsy and grinning.

Mace clapped the old elf on the back. "Your crew won a great battle! And there may be more to come."

As they made their way to the warehouse district on the docks, they passed an alley that featured a half-dozen dark figures lurking just outside the glow of the streetlamps. Layne cleared her throat.

"Down that alley is the sailor tavern controlled by the slavers. They commonly ambush the drunken fools as they depart the tavern to return to their ships."

Mace stopped in his tracks. A quick check of his UI told him they still had fifteen minutes to get to the warehouse. Plenty of time.

He turned toward the alley and called, "You! In the alley. Show yourselves," as he walked toward them.

The dark figures that had been lounging against the walls straightened up and put hands on weapons. One of them a half-orc wearing rogue leather with a bandolier of throwing knives across his chest, answered.

"Who are you to call us out? Move along, drow. Or suffer the consequences."

Mace stopped a pace away from the larger Black Flame fighter. "Name's Mace. I'm the guy who killed Justin and his men at Darkstone stronghold." He paused and then motioned toward Lila. "Actually she killed Justin. And probably more than half of his men. Isn't she cute?" he smiled at the half-orc as Lila waived politely.

Mace continued. "Oh. And the fifty guys your boss sent to retrieve the shipment of slaves? They're dead too. As are the group that was on the boat headed to check on why you lot lost contact. I'm not sure how many of them were on that boat, but it looked like a lot."

The orc roared and drew twin daggers as Mace did the same. The fighters in the alley drew weapons and advanced, except for two in the back who drew bows.

They both fired at Mace, who activated his Liquid Armor just before the arrows struck. The arrows bounced off of him and splatted into the mud at his feet.

Shari immediately began firing arrow after arrow into the archers, hitting them in torso, arm and face. Lila scooted up behind Mace, using him as cover while she slipped into stealth mode and moved around behind the archers.

While Mace was deflecting blows from the half-orc, Layne began to play a tune that slowed and fatigued their foes. Shari got a critical hit and one of the archers dropped dead. The other was too wounded to draw his bow, and began to lean against the nearby wall. She left him for later and turned her attention to the three melee fighters who were advancing on Mace.

As she put an arrow into a human with a short sword, Lila appeared behind the rearmost fighter. She leapt onto the woman's back and stabbed one dagger into her shoulder where it connected to her collarbone. Using that dagger as leverage, she drew the other one across the woman's neck, opening it from ear to ear. There was nothing more than a faint gurgle as the little halfling removed her dagger and dropped to the ground. By the time the corpse hit the ground, Lila was back in stealth mode and moving toward her next victim.

The remaining two melee reached Mace and joined their leader in trying to stab him. Mace danced and dodged, avoiding or parrying every strike. When Lila appeared underneath the half-orc and jammed a dagger into his nether regions, he dropped both weapons and screamed. Grabbing at his crotch with both hands, he vomited on one of his companions.

Lila used her second dagger to slice the artery in his inner thigh, then rolled backwards as he fell. She casually walked back to the injured archer, who held up a hand and began to plead. She ignored him and jammed a dagger up into his heart.

That left only two of the original six fighters. One was bleeding badly, Shari's arrow embedded in his chest. She put another one in his throat, and he fell with a gurgle and a look of surprise.

Mace grabbed the remaining fighter's collar with his left hand and pulled him forward. The surprised man made a feeble attempt at stabbing the drow, but his aim faltered as he saw the smoking enchanted dagger coming for him. Mace calmly inserted the soul dagger under the man's chin and into his brain. The fighter's dagger actually scraped Mace's cheek as he fell backward. There was a burning sensation, and an icon appeared on his UI indicating that he had a 'poisoned' debuff.

Shari tossed a HoT on him, and the ticks of poison damage were more than offset by her healing ticks. Lila was already looting the bodies, and it wasn't long before they moved on toward the warehouse. The whole fight had taken less than a minute.

Two blocks from the warehouse, they found Callahan and a dozen others waiting for them. Mace hadn't expected such a turnout. He shook hands with the smith, and was quickly introduced to the group. Several were merchants, and one was a boat captain who'd seen two others have their boats commandeered in recent days, and didn't want the same for himself.

Mace said, "Tell me about the warehouse. How many exits are there?"

A young dwarf stepped forward.

"I worked in there before they killed my master. There be the front door, a back door, and a wide double door on the side for wagons and such. And there be a trap door in the floor of the office that opens to the water below."

Mace thought it over for a moment. He looked at the dwarf. Then he pointed to the three members of Callahan's group who held bows or crossbow. "I need you to take these three to a spot where you can see anyone who drops from that trap door. Kill them as soon as they pop up out of the water." The four of them nodded grimly and set off with the dwarf in the lead.

Mace pointed to Callahan. The massive smith was fully armored, a shield on one arm and a two-handed sword held easily in his right. "I want you to come inside with us. We could use a shield. I'm going to seal the double doors on the side so they can't escape that way. The rest of you, I want you to cover the back. Kill anything that passes through that door without hesitation. There shouldn't be too many." He looked them over. The nine of them had an assortment of weapons. Two carried shields with one-handed weapons. One a sword, the other an axe. Two carried longer swords and wore chain armor. A rogueish looking merchant held a dagger in each hand. Two half-elves behind him looked like twins, and each carried a pair of katanas. Others carried spears and short swords. One held a staff and a wand.

Mace cautioned them. "Arrange yourselves to be most effective. Shields and heavy armor closest to the door. Make a semicircle to keep them contained. Spears and longer weapons right behind them, jabbing from the protection of the shield bearers. Mage… well, you just do what you're good at. The rest of you, watch for anyone who breaks free and take them down. They will likely have some stealth ability, so keep a sharp eye out."

Their instructions clear, the group headed off toward the back door. Mace moved to the side that had the loading dock, and held his hands up. He uttered the trigger word "Frigus!" and thrust his hands toward the doors.

A sheet of ice began to form over the doors, growing wider and thicker by the second. Mace continued to channel the spell until the entire expanse and a good bit of the wall on either side was covered in a two-foot thick wall of ice. The doors would not open any time soon.

Mace and his group followed Callahan around to the front door. Two guards spotted them rounding the corner and reacted instantly. One drew a sword and shield and stepped in front of the door, while the other ran inside.

"Step aside, worm," Callahan shouted at the guard. His roar startled the human, but he recovered quickly and raised his shield and weapon.

"You're a dead man, smith. I recognize you. You dare attack the Black Flame? You and your family's heads will be mounted on spikes in front of your shop by dawn!"

The man barely got to finish his speech before Callahan roared at him and kicked forward. His massive boot struck the man's shield and knocked him backward. Mace heard the man's arm break from the impact, and the grunt of pain. He leapt forward, not giving the man a chance to recover. Reaching down he stabbed the back of the man's neck with his enchanted dagger. His victim went limp as his soul was drained into the weapon and Mace felt a rush of power.   As Lila looted the corpse, Mace turned to Callahan.

"You want to do the honors?"

The smith grinned. Turning so his shield faced the door, he lowered his shoulder and charged. The door shattered as his massive body impacted it, and Callahan pushed right on through, roaring out a battlecry that stunned any nearby enemies for two seconds.

That left plenty of time for Mace and the others to pass through behind him. Lila and Mace both activated stealth and Layne began to strum on her lute as Shari started firing arrows from just inside the door.

There were about two dozen fighters visible, with more coming out from back rooms or behind stacks of crates. Shari began working her way left to right, putting an arrow into each of them as she strafed across the group.

Lila appeared behind one unfortunate beastkin, slamming both her daggers into the man's back with overhand blows. He went down on his knees as she withdrew the daggers and finished him with a blade to the throat.

Mace chose a wider approach. From the shadows behind a large box, he whispered, "Infier," and held his hands together. A burning orb built up between his hands, quickly growing in size. After five seconds, he released it into the most densely packed group of foes.

It flew forward like a bullet, screaming through the cooler air of the warehouse and slamming into an orc in the center of the group. The orc was incinerated and six or seven of those closest to him received severe burn damage as they were knocked off their feet.

Callahan, Lila and Mace all took advantage, dashing into the crowd and dealing death blows to those on the ground. Callahan sliced parts off of some with his sword, and simply stomped others to death with his steel-shod boots. Lila stabbed and sliced at vital organs and arteries, while Mace drained soul after soul. In thirty seconds, nearly half the force that had charged them were down or dead.

The others, seeing they were overmatched and several of them already having one of Shari's arrows in them, retreated.

A second group of fighters appeared. This one having had more time to organize, they were formed into a more sensible battle group. They allowed the retreating wounded through their shield wall, then closed ranks again.

Callahan eyed the group as they waited behind their shields. "This is going to hurt." He thumped his sword on his shield and prepared to advance. "If I die, you make sure they can not touch my family." He stared into Mace's eyes waiting for the promise.

Mace shook his head. "No one will harm your family, I promise that. But you won't be dying here."

With a grin, he stepped forward and raised the hand that held his spell ring. Shari had only see him use it once, but he'd told her about the various battles where he'd summoned the stone golem.

She said, "Oooh, this is going to be interesting." as Mace took a few steps closer to the enemy line. Callahan stepped forward with him. Lila was nowhere to be seen. Which meant she was doing her job.

"Surrender now and we won't kill you all. I want information on your base in Graf. The first to tell me what I want gets to walk out that back door. Everyone else dies." Mace growled at the remaining slavers.

A small group made a break for the nearby loading dock doors. Two of them dropped their weapons and grabbed hold of the doors, trying to push them open, but Mace's ice held solid and the doors didn't budge an inch.

The leader of the group cursed at those who'd tried to run. "Cowards! You will be stricken from the guild and bounties put on your heads if you do not get back here and fight!"

As Mace and company were between them and the front door and their former comrades were between them and the back door, they elected to try for the water exit. Five of them dashed into the office and flung open the trap door. They disappeared one by one and Mace's elven hearing picked up splashes, followed shortly by screams.

Mace made a quick count of the remaining fighters. Thirty of them. Half a dozen tanks, three archers, three casters, and a bunch of melee including their leader. He shouted, "Last chance. There are only thirty of you left! Surrender and rat out your leader or die here."

The leader spat on the floor and shouted "Kiss my-"

He didn't finish the sentence as Mace muttered "Wyvern," and his ring flashed with blinding light. A creature the size of a school bus flew from the ring. Its scales were a dark red, and each one was the size of a Mace's hand or larger. It had two legs on the forward part of its torso with wicked claws that shone purple-black. Its two leathery wings were furled, but would extend out ten meters when opened. Its head looked just like a dragon's, with bony ridges leading up to twin horns that tilted back over its skull. Another bony ridge ran down its back to its tail, where it formed a jagged bladelike growth. The monster looked to Mace, who pointed at the group and shouted, "Kill them!"

The massive beast flapped its wings once while shoving off with its two legs and got enough lift to clear the shield wall before crashing to the warehouse floor. Its body began to thrash about, wings and tail slamming fighters into each other, while others were crushed under its weight.

The shield wall was shattered from behind by a blow from its tail, and Callahan leapt into the breach. He cut the head off one tank with a single swipe of his two-handed sword, then stabbed another through the chest and stomped on the edge of another's shield, causing the curved surface to roll upward, breaking the man's elbow as he screamed. Another stomp on the man's throat silenced him.

Callahan had to back up as he was nearly caught by the thrashing tail of the wyvern. He looked over his shoulder at Mace. The drow shrugged and called out "You were the one who mentioned the heart of a wyvern..." The orc rolled his eyes before turning back to the fight.

Shari was still putting arrows into the enemies with every opening she found. She was being careful not to hit their wyvern ally. Their enemies were doing plenty of the that. The dozen or so fighters that were still on their feet had surrounded the wyrm and were hacking and stabbing at it.

Mace faded into stealth and dashed toward the leader, who was near the wyvern's head. He spotted Lila moving in quietly behind their enemies as well.

The beast was still giving more than it got, though it was getting sluggish from loss of blood. Shari and Mion began to heal it as quickly as they could.

Mace was about to stab the leader in the back when he noticed an opportunity. The wyvern's open maw was swinging toward the man. Mace quickly stabbed him in the spine, draining some, but not all, of his soul energy. He withdrew the dagger and quickly kicked the man in the back. His body flew forward and into the waiting jaws of the dragonkin.

The man screamed in terror as the thing bit down, severing his body into the three parts. His upper torso and lower legs fell to the floor, while the main bulk of his body went down the wyvern's gullet.

Splattered in their leader's blood and with their numbers dwindling quickly, the remaining half-dozen that were still on their feet tried for the back door. Mace let them go. They were all wounded and weakened, and he had faith in the anger of those who awaited them outside.

Lila was making her rounds, finishing off the wounded and looting the corpses. Mace called out "Hold on! I need a couple of them alive. I have questions."

The dark tone of his voice caused some panic among the survivors. Two of the casters who'd been playing dead leapt to their feet to break for the back door. The wyvern instantly grabbed one and lifted him screaming into the air. Mace dashed toward the other, angling to cut off the much slower human before he reached the door. Lila, who had been closer, hit the mage with a running tackle just as he managed to get off a spell. A bolt of magic sped toward Mace, who was still charging forward. Without time to dodge, Mace took the hit square in the face. The force of the impact knocked him backward to hit the floor hard, cracking his head against the floorboards. His face burned, and he screamed in pain. His UI showed a severe drop in his health, a bleed debuff, and stunned debuff.

The critical hit to the face had shaved off more than half his health. He instantly felt the refreshing sensation of heals from both Shari and Mion. He stopped screaming and rolled to his feet even as the wyvern finished off the mage it held, gulping the gnome down whole, staff and all. Mace grimaced. That staff might have been useful.

Lila sat atop the last remaining mage. Each time he struggled to rise, she poked him in a sensitive area with a dagger. He cursed and spat and threatened, but he eventually learned to quit moving. Mace kicked the man's staff away across the floor, then kicked him in the face for good measure. Just hard enough to get his attention.

"Let's be clear. You are going to die here tonight. My friends and I are going to cleanse this place of every last Black Flame shithead, then we're going to Graf to do the same. You have the opportunity to make our fight in Graf go a little easier for us. If you do, I'll kill you quickly."

The mage didn't look impressed, growling at Lila before starting to whisper a spell. Mace kicked him in the face again, hard enough to rattle his teeth. When the man's eyes focused again, Mace crouched in front of him, holding the enchanted dagger out so that it was within inches of the mage's face.

"The alternative is that I can drain your soul with this. Not all of it. I'll leave enough of it intact to keep you alive while my wyvern rips you apart and eats you."

He motioned over his shoulder where the dragonkin was consuming a corpse that Lila had just looted.

As the man considered his options, Callahan said, "I'll go check on the back door." and headed that direction. Lila got up from atop the mage and returned to looting corpses, wanting to get to them all before the wyvern consumed them.

Mace allowed the mage to sit up and lean against the wall. "If you speak other than to answer my questions, or move your hands, I'll cut you." He held up the enchanted dagger. "From what I can tell, it's quite painful."

"What do you want to know?" the man practically spat the words out.

"First, who is the leader of the Black Flame? And where is their headquarters?"

The man looked sick. He tried to speak and his throat seemed to swell. Mace watched as he struggled to breathe, then passed out. Looking to Layne, he asked "What was that?"

Layne played a sad, discordant tune. "He's probably another Oathbound. The moment he tried to betray his master, the oath's magic took effect and disabled him. Is he dead?"

Mace put a finger to the man's neck, feeling a pulse beating there. And he seemed to be breathing again.

"Alive. Is there a way to get around the oath?"

Layne looked thoughtful. "Depending on how thorough the oath was, maybe? He might be able to answer yes or no questions. Or nod or shake his head. Or blink for yes and no?"

Mace kicked the man in the gut to wake him up. When the man was lucid again, he asked, "Are you oathbound?"

The mage opened his mouth to answer, but couldn't. Mace said "Nod your head for yes, shake it for no."

The man nodded his head, though it appeared to cause him pain. Mace continued. "Is the Black Flame based in Graf?" Another nod. The mage began to sweat profusely. Mace didn't think he could answer many more questions. So he decided to get specific. "Are there more than a hundred members in Graf now?"

Another nod and the man coughed up a bit of blood.

"More than two hundred?"

This time his head shook left and right before his eyes rolled up in his head. He fell over, unconscious. Deciding the man wouldn't be able to answer any more questions, Mace stabbed him in the heart with the enchanted dagger. He died quickly, and possibly without pain. Though Mace doubted that.

Lila looted his body, then whistled for the wyvern. The mini-dragon responded to her call and moved to her side before grabbing hold of the mage and tearing him in half.

Lila patted the wyvern's body just above the wing as it chowed down on the mage's corpse. Then she began to poke about, peering into boxes and looking at labels on crates.

"Since we captured this place, does all of this belong to us?"

Mace chuckled at the little loot monster. "Not just us. The others who helped us here should get an equal share. But that can wait. We'll leave the wyvern here to guard the place while we hunt the rest of the slavers down; I want to have cleared them out and be ready to sail by dawn."

Mace looked at the wyvern. "Stay here. You can eat anyone who comes in before dawn."

The big winged lizard nodded its head and curled up in the center of the warehouse, its stomach visibly bulged with the weight of the several corpses it had consumed.

Mace led the group to the back door, where Callahan was speaking with the group of citizens. There were five corpses on the ground and Mace looked at the orc with a question. "They say only five came out. So either one was stealthed, or they're still hiding inside."

Mace turned to look back the way they'd come. There was a short corridor with two doors on either side leading to offices. "Close this door behind me. I'll be back in five minutes. The rest of you, time to go hunting. Stay in your group and head for the sailor bar. You know the one?"

The merchant dressed as a rogue nodded his head. Mace said "Grab the kid and the others who were covering the trap door and head up there. I'll meet you. Same plan. We'll go in the front, some will cover the alley in the back or other exits."

Mace activated his Stealth ability and stepped back into the corridor as Layne, Shari, and Lisa joined the others outside. As soon as the door closed behind him, he simply stood and listened. His drow hearing was better than even the surface elves, as life underground with species that hunted by sound had forced them to evolve.

He slowly advanced toward the first door, making no sound as he moved. He could hear the wyvern in the main room breathing deeply. Likely it was already asleep. He could hear the water lapping against the pilings below.

Slowly, he opened the first door and looked inside. The room was small, containing a desk, two chairs, and a filing cabinet. He moved around and checked behind and under the desk before leaving the room and closing the door behind him.

Smiling to himself, he moved to the next room. He knew how to flush out his prey if they were still in this part of the building.

He crossed the hall to the opposing door and kicked it open. Not entering the room, he just stood and listened. He'd heard a gasp of surprise from further down the hall.

"Not this room, then," he said aloud. The noise broke his Stealth, but he didn't care.

Moving to the next door, he kicked that one in too. He was pretty sure the slaver was in the fourth room, but he wanted to make sure this one was clear. In case more than one had gone into hiding. After checking the room quickly – this one contained several crates of wine and a cot – he moved to stand by the last door.

"I know you're in there. I'm a drow. I can hear your heart pounding!" He couldn't, but he was pretty sure whomever was on the other side of that door didn't know that. "You have to the count of three to open up and surrender, or I'll simply burn this place down around you. After we clear out all the loot, that is.

The door burst open and a long blade shot out, aimed directly at Mace's face. He ducked below the sword and kicked out toward the wielder. There was a grunt and a body fell backward.

The room was pitch black, but Mace could see just fine. The outline of two people stood against one wall, while a third was getting back to its feet in front of him. He launched forward and plunged his dagger into the one closest. A man screamed as he dropped the two-handed sword he'd just tried to poke into Mace's eye. A moment later he slumped dead.

Mace turned to address the other two. When they didn't move, he asked, "Who are you?"

The shorter of the two shuffled a bit. Mace lost his patience and cast a light globe onto the ceiling. They all blinked as the room lit up. Mace saw a woman in black leather from head to toe and a male dwarf in plate mail. Mace grinned at the dwarf. "I'm impressed. You managed to stay silent wearing all that metal."

Despite the situation, the dwarf grinned at him. "Aye. Silence enchantment. Top o' the line." As if to prove his claim, he jumped slightly. Mace watched his armor shuffle and grind against itself, but heard nothing.

"Who are you?" Mace asked a second time.

"I be Dorbin Stonehand. Me cousin owned this warehouse." He nodded his head toward the woman. "She be Red. Me hired guard. I had two more, but these arsefaces killed 'em when we walked in here. I came to visit me cousin and got ambushed as we stepped in the door."

Mace looked at the woman, who scowled, but nodded slightly. He looked back at the dwarf.

"Can you prove this? Prove that you're not one of the slavers? Give me a reason not to kill you both."

The dwarf leaned forward and turned slightly away from Mace. The sound of chains rattling directed Mace's attention to the dwarf's hands. They were cuffed together with thick iron bands, and the bands were chained to the wall. Mace looked at Red, and she obligingly turned to show him her own bonds.

He sent a quick message to Shari.

"*Hey, bring the kid back here ASAP. Ask him if he's ever met his old boss's cousin. His name is Dorbin.*"

"*Will do. One sec.*"

There was a short pause, then she continued. "*Kid says yes. Dorbin Stonehand.*"

"*Okay, I've got him here. Need the kid to confirm his identity. Second office on the left from the back door.*"

Mace took a moment to loot the body on the floor. He pointed to the corpse.

"How long was he in here?"

Red spoke first. "He came in maybe five minutes ago. Several others rushed past the door as he entered. It sounded like they didn't get far." Her smirk suggested that made her happy.

"They didn't. We had people waiting. How long have you two been in here?"

"Hard to tell," Stonehand said. "They ain't been feedin' us, and we can't see the sun. But I'm sober, and it takes me a full two days o' not drinkin' to sober up, so I'd guess three miserable days." Red nodded in agreement.

"Don't move, I'm going to try and find the keys to your shackles." Mace warned them. He began to rifle through the desk that was in the room. In the middle top drawer he found a key ring with likely looking keys. Moving to the dwarf, he tried a few before finding the correct one. He unlocked the bands, then stepped back two paces as the dwarf freed himself. Then he tossed the keys to the dwarf and let him free his bodyguard.

When she was free, Red said, "Our weapons are in a box behind you. I'd like them back."

Mace nodded. "Not just yet."

He pulled his canteen and a couple pieces of jerky from his bag and set them on the desk.

"Have a seat. Help yourselves. Best I have at the moment. I've got someone on the way who knows Dorbin Stonehand. If you are who you say you are, we can be a little more friendly."

The dwarf took a seat, while Red remained standing, though she did accept the jerky and a drink from the canteen.

"And who are ye? Breakin' in here 'n killin' everyone?"

"My name is Mace. I'm an outworlder. On a mission to kill every Black Flame I find. Your... hosts."

"Hah!" Stonehand bellowed. "Aye, there be a worthy cause if ever I hear'd one. Don't suppose ye'd like some help with that? I owe these dungsnufflers fer killin' me cousin. And fer their hospitality." Red nodded with more enthusiasm than Mace had seen from her so far.

"Let's just see how things go. For all I know, you're Black Flame too, and the dead man there worked for you. You could have had him chain you as a ruse."

"Aye, I could have at that," the dwarf nodded in thought. "That would have been damned clever of me."

He took a bite of the jerky and chewed slowly. "Not bad. Thank ye for the food and drink."

They passed a couple more minutes in silence as the two ate their meager meal. Mace watched them. He believed their story. They were way too at ease to be lying to him. Still, he didn't let down his guard.

Shari called out as they neared the office, and Mace answered. She walked in with the boy behind her.

The dwarf saw him and stood. "Ah, lad! Good to see ye livin'."

The boy smiled at the dwarf, then looked at Mace.

"That's him. He's visited several times before. And that's Red." He pointed to the bodyguard. "She hardly ever talks, but she's not as mean as she looks. She taught me how to play cards."

Red smiled fondly at the boy, and Stonehand looked to Mace. "Good 'nuff fer ye?"

Mace nodded. "My apologies. Can't be too careful these days. If you'd like to join us in the hunt, you're welcome to do so. Or you can go to the Purple Mushroom and wait for us to return. They'll have food and drink and you can rest there."

Red moved to the box that contained their gear, then looked to Mace for permission. When he nodded, she opened it and started handing weapons and a shield to her employer. Then she began strapping a surprising number of blades and other weapons to her own armor.

Mace was impressed. He carried several hidden blades and other tools useful in his specialty. But Red was quickly coming to resemble a black leather porcupine.

When they were ready, Shari led them all to the nearby bar, where they found Callahan and the others standing in the same spot they'd killed the first six at the mouth of the alley. He'd already given out assignments, and told Mace as much.

"Everybody knows what to do. I assume we're going in the front?"

As he finished speaking, he noticed the dwarf. "Stonehand. Good to see you. I'm sorry about Telgrin."

Stonehand nodded, not saying anything. He looked anxiously at the tavern. "They'll likely be expectin' us in there, ya know."

Mace nodded. "I'll go in first. If they kill me, I'll respawn…"

He suddenly realized that he and the others hadn't bothered to find a local bind point. Since he had logged off on the *Sea Sprite*, he hoped he would respawn there. Or at the Purple Mushroom.

"Bah!" The dwarf began to stomp toward the front door. The others, taking that as a signal, moved down the alley to cover the back exit. Two archers remained on the road to watch the windows of the rooms above. The mage and the other archer were covering the windows on the other side. Anybody trying to climb down would be skewered. "They don't have the advantage o' surprise this time!" he continued as he got closer the door. "Me n Red can handle this if'n ye need a rest." He grinned before kicking the heavy wood door. It shattered into a dozen pieces as he just walked right on through. There were shouts of alarm from inside as Red drew twin katanas and followed him inside.

Callahan snorted. "He's not kidding. We could just sit out here and watch. He's a weaponsmaster and a paladin. I've seen him take on an entire orc raider camp with two dozen warriors. He was drunk then, and less grumpy."

The orc laughed as the shouts inside turned into screams.

"But I can't let him have all the fun!" Callahan roared a battle cry and dove through the door. The volume and frequency of screams increased.

Mace and the others followed a moment later. The scene inside was confusing at first. There were several dead bodies strewn in a path leading toward the stairs. In the far right corner a cluster of sailors huddled with eyes wide. They held weapons, but looked as if they weren't sure who to attack. Mace left them there, in case any were slavers in disguise.

The dwarf and his bodyguard were moving up the stairs, Stonehand blocking blows with his shield then returning killing blows with a hand axe. Red threw knives at targets farther up the staircase in between jabs with her swords at closer enemies. Callahan was just stepping into a corridor that led back to the kitchen.

Shari looked at Mace, who shrugged. "I'm guessing the paladin can heal himself, so keep an eye on the orc and heal him if he needs it. Lila, you too. He'll make a good distraction while you get some backstabs in."

Shari and the others moved to follow Callahan. Mace fired several blasts of icy air into the corners of the main room, looking to expose any Stealth users. Two rogues were caught and knocked out of Stealth near the bar. They'd been just a few feet from making it out the door. Mace shouted "Infier!" and blasted them with a fireball that lit their armor on fire and prevented them from stealthing again. Then he advanced with a dagger in each hand. The fight was brutal, but short. He claimed each of their souls with his dagger and left the bodies for Lila to loot.

The sailors, who had been thinking of jumping in, witnessed Mace's furious fight with the two slavers and quickly changed their minds. Mace waved at them and gave them his most stern look.

"Don't move. If you're not Black Flame, you have nothing to fear from us. On the other hand, if you're one of them…" He pointed toward the corpses littering the floor. The sailors got the point and settled down on chairs in their corner.

Mace quickly inspected each of them. Most of them were level ten or lower. It had been his experience that the slavers were usually higher level. Probably from killing slaves or innocent villagers. Or cutting the throats of sailors in dark alleys. He asked. "Any of you work for these bastards?"

As one the sailors all emphatically shook their heads no. A few muttered negative responses. None met Mace's gaze.

"Any of you have any information about them? Where they live? Where they might hide? I'm going to kill every single one of them tonight, so don't fear speaking out. There will be no repercussions."

The highest level sailor of the group stepped forward. A grizzled veteran, his skin was deeply tanned and weatherworn, and he sported a scar on his neck where someone had tried to end his life at some point. He was a level 15.

"They killed the old salt what owned this place. Good lad, he was. Then they left us stranded here when they took our boat while we was sleep'n it off upstairs. Ya want to kill 'em all, I say good luck to ya. I seen a bunch of 'em run off when another one came in yellin' bout an attack. Dunno where they went."

Mace studied the group for a moment, then made a decision. "Get out of here. Head down to the docks. See the captain of the *Platypus*. He lost some men when we cleared the slavers from his ship. It also wouldn't hurt to check with Jorin on the *Sea Sprite*. While you're there, tell them both what we're up to. We're going to want to sail at dawn."

The old sailor bobbed his head and led his men out the door. A few of the others muttered thanks as they passed, still afraid of the drow.

Mace turned to take in the state of the conflict. Stonehand and Red had disappeared up the stairs, but he could hear they were still fighting. There wasn't much noise coming from the corridor his group had taken. A quick look at his UI told him nobody had taken much damage, though Callahan wasn't in his group. He decided to check on them.

Closing and barring the door, he quickly piled a few bodies against it to make it harder for anyone to open it and escape. Then he trotted down the corridor to the kitchen. Callahan was there, growling at a couple of cooks who were huddled in a corner. Three dead men with Black Flame logos on their tunics lay in puddles of blood on the floor. One looked like he'd had his face bitten off. When Callahan turned his blood-covered face to greet Mace, he understood why the cooks looked so frightened. The orc was a vision from nightmares. Some of the slaver's face was still hanging from one tusk.

Mace turned his attention to the cooks. Pointing at the elder of the two. "You. How long have you worked here?"

The man gulped, his eyes darting from Mace to Callahan and back again. "F-four y-years," he stammered.

When Mace shifted his gaze to the other cook, she mumbled quietly, "Two years, sir drow. Please don't kill us."

Mace nodded once at Callahan. "They worked for the old sailor who owned this place. They can go." Then he looked at the two again. "Can you tell us anything about the slavers? Where they live, where they might hide?"

The younger cook spoke up.

"They were talking about you, sir," she said to Callahan. "One of them came in, said you were leading an attack on their base. Six of them were sent to your smithy after your family. They said…" She stopped and lowered her gaze.

Callahan growled and leaned toward her. "Speak!"

"They said they were going to make you watch them die. That anyone who defies the Black Flame is already dead."

Callahan let out a roar and dashed out the door leading to the alley. He was nearly attacked by the group waiting outside, but they recognized him in time. Mace said "Shari, Lila, with me. Layne, go upstairs and tell Stonehand where we went!"

He took off after the orc with Shari and Lila behind him. Callahan's long legs and orcish strength propelled him up the street at a surprisingly fast pace. But Mace and Shari were elves, naturally gifted with speed. And somehow, Lila's stubby legs propelled her along next to them with seeming ease, though she was breathing hard.

It only took them a few minutes to reach the smithy. The front door of the shop was destroyed, and Mace could hear the sounds of fighting within. Callahan didn't even slow, crashing past the remains of the door and roaring a challenge as he searched the shop. An answering roar echoed from the second floor, and the orc chuckled.

Shari looked at him, head tilted. "What's funny?"

Callahan grinned at her, his face still bloody with slaver meat. He pointed to two bodies on the stairs above him. "They woke up my wife. She's pregnant. Nothing more grumpy than a pregnant orc."

He dashed up the stairs to assist his mate while Mace moved through the back of the shop. Predictably, there was a slaver there stuffing anything of value into his bag. Mace didn't even warn him. He just stepped up behind the man and slammed his dagger into his heart from behind. The dagger sent a thrill up his arm and he once again felt the invigoration of the soul energy.

The man's corpse had barely hit the floor before Lila was looting it. Mace said, "Leave any of the smith's things you find in there." She nodded and gave him a look that clearly said she wasn't a thief before getting back to work. Iron ingots and began to clank onto the floor as she emptied the man's bag.

Mace moved back into the shop in time to see the smith coming back down the stairs, his wife and son walked behind him. The boy, whom they'd first met when they stopped by earlier, was cradling his arm with a deep gash at the wrist that dripped blood. Shari immediately healed him, for which Callahan thanked her.

"Only three more up there," he said, heading for the back. "The cook said six."

Mace held up a hand. "Took care of the last one. He was looting your smithy."

The female orc stepped forward, hand outstretched. "I am Lucinda. My husband has told me of what you've done this night. We are in your debt."

Mace shook his head. "From the looks of things, you've done more than your share. I'm sorry they woke up you."

She grinned and kicked one of the bodies. "So are they."

Mace and his group waited while Callahan spoke to his wife privately. She was moving about the shop, tidying up as if it were business as usual. Mace decided that he liked her.

After a few minutes, the smith rejoined him. "Lucy and the boy are going to stay here and guard the place. Can't have those slavers getting their hands on these weapons."

The boy, who had been tickling Mion's tummy and making baby noises at her, suddenly straightened his back and tried to look fierce.

Leaving the smith's shop, they headed back toward the tavern. The battle was over when they arrived. , and Shari and Mion immediately set about healing the few injuries.

Stonehand, who had wiped out a significant portion of their enemies, barely had a scratch on him. Mace opened his mouth to ask, but Red shook her head. "No survivors."

There had been forty-plus Black Flame members inside the tavern. Combined with the ones they'd caught in the warehouse, the alley, and smithy, that was a force of over a hundred. A big number for a small river port. Mace began to wonder why. Were they gearing up to attack someone? Or defend against someone? There couldn't be enough money in this small port to justify so many.

With nothing left for them at the tavern, Mace and the rest spread out through the city. Word of the evening's events was spreading quickly, and citizens were turning out to help. Black Flame members were rousted from businesses and homes. Two here, three there. The newly emboldened people of Port Bjurstrom were getting payback for the fear and insults they'd suffered.

Sweeping upward from the docks through the town, they eventually reached the merchant guild's house. There was a stone wall around the building with iron gates. The gates were closed and chained. Mace was going to simply go over the walls, when Stonehand stopped him. The dwarf took a mining pick from his bag. The thing gleamed in the moonlight. Mace realized it was made of mithril!   Stonehand took one swing with the pic and the chain links shattered. Callahan kicked the gate open and a group of nearly one hundred pushed through toward the house.

Immediately two citizens who'd pushed ahead in their zeal for revenge went down with crossbow bolts protruding from them. Shari quickly healed them both as others stopped to help them. A fireball erupted from an upper window, streaking down to land amidst the crowd of locals. Several went down, and one young woman wearing a nightgown and carrying what looked like an heirloom sword was engulfed in flame. Mion hovered above her, healing as quickly as she could to try and keep the woman alive.

Mace charged the building, the others who'd fought with him through the night right behind him. He slowed as he reached the front door, but Stonehand and Callahan powered past him. The two of them each hit one of the double doors, causing them to burst inward. Inside were a dozen or so fighters with shields and weapons raised. Callahan shouted, "Kill the invaders!" and took an arm off a slaver who go too close.

Red, Lila, and Mace were right behind the two tanks, their daggers and swords flashing almost too quickly to see. Others squeezed in behind them and slowly the slavers were pushed back. One by one they fell, until only a handful were left. They tried to flee up the stairs, but Shari and the other archers rained death on them as soon as they were high enough to target safely. None made it to the top.

Mace took the lead up the stairs. The others were still NPCs and he didn't want to risk them falling to an ambush. He motioned for quiet as he neared the top, hearing the heavy breathing of several bodies in the corridor. Activating his stealth ability, he hugged the wall and crouched low before taking the top step and rounding the corner.

There were ten Black Flame troops in the hall. Including two archers and a mage, whom he assumed were the same that shot from the windows a few minutes earlier. In the back of the group was a woman, loudly whispering orders.

"First one around that corner dies. We take as many of them with us as we can, boys!"

Mace crept past the two tanks who were preparing to move to the top of the stairs. Then he weaved his way past the fighters behind them. A few shivered, or looked around, feeling his presence, but none were able to break his stealth. He positioned himself behind the leader. She was wearing leather armor that shone with a rainbow sheen as if it were made of fishscale or something similar. Mace decided that it was too pretty to ruin, so rather than stab her in the back, he leaned forward and clamped his left hand over her mouth while he put the soul dagger in his right hand against her throat. He pushed the blade just hard enough to draw blood, and he could feel her body go rigid as she felt the pain.

"Tell your people to drop their weapons," he whispered. When she nodded slightly, he moved the hand across her mouth up to her forehead. The pressure of the blade didn't lessen one bit.

"Change of plans. Drop your weapons. We surrender." She growled at her people. They all turned to face her, eyes wide and jaws agape as they took in the drow holding a knife to her throat.

"Screw that!" one of the tanks said. "They'll kill us all. I ain't goin' down without a fight."

Mace sent Shari a message. *Tell Callahan and the dwarf to go in ten seconds.*

Then he spoke to the tank. "I've killed every single member of your guild that I've met since coming to the surface. That's about a two hundred and fifty of you now. I'll give you the same choice I gave some of your comrades. Drop your weapons and answer a few questions, and we'll give you a quick death. Otherwise…"

He pushed the dagger point a tiny bit further into the woman's neck, and the magic activated. She screamed as her soul began to drain from her. After a couple seconds, Mace pulled the blade away.

"You chose death the day you joined Black Flame. There are good and bad ways to die," he growled, as the blade screamed in his mind for more.

The tank opened his mouth to reply but the words never came out. One of Shari's arrows burst from his throat, causing his mouth to spew blood rather than words. The others barely had time to turn before Callahan and the others began to cut them down. With the tank down there was an opening for Stonehand to push through as the orc engaged the second tank. Red followed behind her employer. Lila appeared behind the remaining tank and slit his throat. Callahan was already leaping over them as Lila rode his corpse to the floor.

Mace still held the leader at the back of the group. She yelled and cursed as she witnessed her people being slaughtered. The slavers were used to easy fights. They attacked villages and soft targets with overwhelming force. Their skills weren't up to the fight that had found them.

The last of the fighters fell when Stonehand's axe removed his leg at the knee. Red rammed a sword blade into his mouth and pinned his skull to the floor to stop the screaming.

"What is your name?" Mace asked the woman, who'd gone silent. He could feel her pulse racing through the tip of the blade pressed against her neck.

"I am nobody. A dead woman," she replied. Indeed, her voice sounded dead. Her tone was flat and held no emotion.

"Fine, Nobody. Where can I find the Black Flame headquarters in Graf?" he inquired.

"I cannot say. I swore an oath."

Mace rolled his eyes. So did Shari. This whole oath-bound thing was getting old. Before he could ask her anther question, she took a deep breath, saying, "I die unbroken." before lunging her head forward and down, driving Mace's dagger into her artery before he even had time to react.

He flexed the muscles of his arm to withdraw the weapon as quickly as he could, but the dagger itself seemed to prevent it. The soul dagger drank its fill, sharing the benefit with its master.

"Dammit!" he cursed as he let her empty corpse drop to the floor.

His UI, which he had been ignoring all evening, lit up with new notifications.

Alert! You have captured an enemy stronghold!
Maintain control of the stronghold for ten minutes to claim ownership.

You have captured an enemy stronghold.
Experience points: 5,000 Your Reputation with the Black Flame has decreased 500. Your status is: Reviled
Your Reputation with the Black Flame has decreased -500.
Level Up! You are now Level 44
You have received one attribute point

Confused, Mace mentally clicked on the notification about the stronghold capture. The timer appeared prominently on the screen, counting down toward nine minutes. But the details text was what he was interested in. As far as he knew, the Black Flame hadn't owned Port Bjurstrom, and therefore their elimination shouldn't have counted as a capture.

Looking at the details, he saw that the 'stronghold' was the warehouse, which the Black Flame had indeed taken as their own. And he'd left his wyvern there, so apparently the system had counted that as 'occupying' and maintaining control. As he thought it over, he realized that he and Lila hadn't captured the Darktsone mine until the guards outside were killed as well. Which probably meant that all the Black Flame members in town had either been killed or fled.

Shari helped Lila loot the corpses as Mace thanked the fighters for their assistance. When he reached Stonehand, the dwarf looked uncomfortable. Mace asked "Is something wrong? Are you concerned about your cousin's warehouse? I'll return it to you if you like."

Stonehand shook his head.

"Nah. I've no wish to sit about babysittin' boxes and killin' wharf rats. But, well…" He paused and took a deep breath, not making eye contact. "I ain't never asked for no favor in me long life. But I need ta ask one o' ye right now. And it don't sit right with me."

Mace leaned back. He thought he knew what the old weaponsmaster wanted.

"Maybe I can save you the trouble. We're about to sail to Graf. I expect at least one of these slavers had a way to deliver a message about our attack. So they'll be expecting us. We know there were recently between one and two hundred soldiers of the Black Flame in Graf. If you'd be up for joining us, we could use two highly skilled fighters like yourselves. It would be *you* doing *me* a favor if you'd accompany us."

Red laughed aloud and Stonehand eyed the drow in front of him.

"Yer smarter than ye look, drow." He grinned and offered his hand. "I'd be pleased to do ya this lil favor."

They all retired to the Purple Mushroom, where Delilah was still entertaining the crew of the *Sea Sprite*. As the evening moved toward dawn, more and more townsfolk appeared to join in the celebration as word spread. Soon they had expanded out into the street, and vendors were showing up with fresh baked bread, meats on a stick, and other items likely to sell well amidst drunken revelry.

Mace and his group mingled with the townsfolk. Getting to know them and sharing stories. An hour before dawn, Captain Jorin called his crew together and made for the docks. Mace and Shari tracked down Delilah.

"What do we owe you for this fine celebration? And all the rooms?" Shari asked.

"Ha! You've run up quite the tab tonight, my darlings!"

Delilah winked at Mace and was surprised when Shari didn't bristle. Less sure of herself now, she said, "Let me see… ten kegs, every bit of food in my kitchen, four dozen bottles of rum…" She ticked off items on her fingers, doing the math in her head. She expected the dark and light elves in front of her to begin to sweat as the tally mounted. Instead they just stood there patiently waiting.

"On the other hand, you did just free our lovely town from a bad influence. Those slaver bastards had been trying to force me to pay a protection tax. So you've saved us quite a bit. Let's call it… one hundred gold."

Shari smiled and produced the requested sum. "Thank you for your hospitality. We'll be heading to Graf now, but if we stop here on the way back, I hope you'll have us back."

Delilah looked shocked at the lack of haggling. One hundred gold was a significant sum for NPCs. Yes, of course. You are welcome here anytime. And thank you for all you've done." She recovered by the end and bowed deeply, giving Mace an eyeful. Shari ignored it and turned away. Mace winked at the innkeeper and followed his girlfriend out the door.

When he joined her outside, she said, "Lila says we looted nearly two hundred gold from the slavers. In actual cash. Not to mention the weapons, armor, potions…"

Mace chuckled. "I wondered why you didn't blink at her bill."

Shari shrugged as they resumed walking toward the dock, with Layne and Lila just ahead. "You said the others who participated in the fight are going to receive shares of whatever's in the warehouse. I figured it wouldn't hurt to let her benefit as well. And it's not like money will be an issue for us in the near future."

Mace grinned. "Heart of a wyvern, that's you!"

They proceeded to board the *Sea Sprite,* then retired to the captain's cabin where they logged out.

Chapter 14

We're Going Down, Down, Down

Griff and Lisa logged back into the game early the next morning. Their trading session with the orcs had gone better than expected. The clan had a use for almost everything they'd looted from their fights. Meat for their cookfires, furs for clothing and armor, teeth and claws to be used as weapons or decoration. The orcs liked to pierce their bodies and their tusks with shiny or symbolic items.

At the end of trading and the celebration, they were shown to an empty hut where they could sleep. As Meg, Jo, and Leroy laid out bedrolls on the floor, with Jo placing hers in between the others, Griff and Lisa had sat in a corner and logged out to sleep in the real world.

They'd confirmed with Peabody that there had been no sign of Evan, then fixed a quick meal. Lisa turned in, but Griff took a bit of time to check over and recalibrate both control panels before turning in himself. The glitch when he'd tried to log in that morning had scared him more than he'd let on.

Well rested and back in the game, they joined the others for a breakfast of bacon and eggs cooked on heated rocks placed in the fire. Griff thought they were the best he'd ever tasted. Something about campfire food really does just make it better.

Their guide joined them as they finished the meal. "I will show you to the dungeon. It is not far."

They gathered their gear and followed the scout northward in the general direction of the waterfall. On their way out of the camp, they passed through a cleared area with several posts stuck in the ground. Each post was carved and decorated with items like feathers, claws, and knives or arrows.

"What is this place?" Meg asked.

The scout paused and looked around.

"This is our burial ground," he growled quietly. "We have lost many since coming down from the mountain. The dark ones pursued us until we beat them back, but every few months they return in small groups to try to steal food or weapons."

"Dark ones?" Lisa asked.

"Hobgoblins, goblins, trolls, even orcs who have chosen a dark path. Servants of bloodthirsty gods." The scout laid a hand on one of the posts and bowed his head. "Each attack claims one or more of us. We do not breed quickly. Eventually there will be too few of us to hold them off. But we have made a home here. So we fight."

Before Griff's party could ask more questions, he moved on at a quick pace. When they reached the waterfall, he turned and followed the cliff face about a mile to the east. The scout stopped and pointed. Cut into the cliff face was a jagged opening about a meter wide and three meters tall. Just inside the opening was the swirling purple plane of a dungeon entrance. A large boulder just outside sported the faintly glowing symbol for "Life" that indicated a binding stone.

Before departing, the scout saluted them with a fist to his chest. "May you fight well. And if necessary, die well. We will await your return." He then turned and began to jog back toward the camp.

Griff took a moment to explain to the new immortals about a binding stone. They each placed their hand on it and bound their souls to the stone so that should they die inside the dungeon, they would respawn there rather than back in their village or at the orc camp where they'd slept. Griff wasn't sure whether the hut they'd slept in counted as an inn or not.

"Okay, mates. A few things." Griff checked his shield and axe as he spoke. "I can tell ye from personal experience that dying is unpleasant."

He grimaced, then rolled his eyes as Lisa added, "Especially when ya get eaten by fuzzy bunnies."

"Moving on… I know yer instinct is gonna be to run if yer in the thick of things and nearly dead. But runnin' might get the rest o' us killed. Hang in and do yer part, and we might get lucky. If ye die, you'll find yerself standin' right here, mostly nekkid. Just run back inside and find us. Yer gear will be waitin' for ye where ye fell."

He looked at Leroy. "Don't try 'n heal every scratch. Save yer mana for when heals be really needed. Yer focus should be on keepin' me alive. As long as I have the enemy engaged, the rest of ye can be hittin' 'em and killin' 'em. But if I die, then you'll all follow soon after. Fer the ladies, if ya see them get down near fifty percent, heal 'em back up. And don't be favorin' Meg there cuz ya think it might earn ya a kiss later. She ain't gonna wanna kiss ye with my foot up yer arse."

Leroy blushed as Griff grinned and the ladies laughed quietly. "I got it. No wasting mana. Keep you alive. No kissing."

With that, Griff said, "Let's go," and led the way through the dungeon gate. Inside, he found a small natural cave with a lit torch flickering on one wall. The torch burned with a sickly green flame. The walls seemed naturally formed, no evidence of tool work visible. There was only a single exit from the room, which led to a stone corridor that sloped downward. Griff could see the corridor was lit with the same torches, casting their greenish tint onto everything.

They assumed their normal marching order, and Griff led the way down. Just about ten paces into the corridor, he halted as he heard a rustling sound. A moment later, a green-tinted greyish ball of armor rolled toward them. Oddly, though it was moving up-slope, it seemed to be picking up speed.

Griff raised his shield and leaned forward, bracing himself as it approached. The ball struck his shield with loud clang and pushed him backward. He managed to keep his feet, but the others behind him had to scatter to either side to keep from being knocked down themselves.

The ball unwound into a pill bug, or what Griff thought of as a roly-poly bug. He'd played with them as a kid. One touched them and they would roll into a little armored ball and stay that way until they thought the coast was clear.

But this one was the size of small car when rolled up. As it unfurled, Griff could see it had seven legs on each side of its body, with two long antennae on its head. Its eyes were a dead black, and it had a pair of wicked looking mandibles. Which it was now using to try and bite Griff's leg. He shoved at the thing with his shield, but it didn't budge. A blow from his one-handed axe barely put a chink in the tough armor that covered its head.

The monster pushed at Griff again, attempting to get under his shield to bite at his shins. Lisa moved to its side and began to slash at the armor with all her might. Meg did the same with her halberd. Neither managed to penetrate the thick outer armor.

Jo cast a fireball at the thing, aiming low in hopes of burning its unarmored legs. This had slightly more success, as two of its left legs were scorched, and it backed off for a moment, limping and chittering in pain. As Griff caught his breath, Leroy hit him with a small heal to compensate for the minor damage he'd taken by absorbing the hits on his shield.

Just as the monster charged at him again, Griff planted the bottom of his shield into the dirt to anchor it. This time, when the bug's mass plowed into him, he was able to hold firm. The shield tilted back a bit, and the bug sort of rode up it like a ramp, trying to get over the top. Griff cracked its face with his axe and the chitin between its eyes cracked slightly. The pill bug moved to retreat, but was slow to get moving as its front three pairs of legs were up in the air on either side of Griff's shield.

Griff called out. "Meg! I have an idea! Ever see someone change a wagon wheel? Drive your weapon under it and heave it over!"

Thankfully, Meg got the idea and charged the monster with the point of her halberd down. It scraped against stone as she drove it under the monster's belly and kept pushing. Being a dwarf, her strength combined with leverage finally won out. The creature flipped over onto its side, then continued to roll onto its rounded back. All seven pairs of legs thrashed at the air as it tried to right itself. The chittering became louder and Griff could swear it sounded annoyed.

Jo immediately hit its exposed belly with a fireball. Its skin bubbled and two more of its legs were scorched. Its scream of pain was a high-pitched whine. Her weapon now freed by the creature's roll, Meg lunged forward and jammed the halberd's spike into its open maw. The legs immediately stopped moving and the sound ceased as it died.

Griff, breathing hard from the exertion, kicked it in the face just to make sure. He then bent and looted the beast. He received a few gold coins, ten pieces of chitin, and some pill bug meat. All of it went into his bag. He had no idea if anyone was willing to eat pill bug, but one never knew.

He gathered the group to talk while they waited for their stamina and mana to recharge.

"That went well, considering it was a surprise. Leroy, nice job on the healing. And Meg, great thinking flipping it over like that. If there are more of these things in here, that is going to have to be our game plan, I think. Its face was vulnerable to an extent, but putting it on its back stopped the damage it was dealing and gave us time."

He stopped to think for a minute. "If we end up against more than one, Lisa you'll have to distract the second one long enough for Meg to tip it. I'll keep the first one busy while you kill yours. I assume they have a way to right themselves, so you'll have to be fast once it's tipped over. And Jo, good job hitting the legs. That slowed it down. May need you to do that again. Everybody good?"

He got nods all around, and they continued on. Twice more they were attacked by rolling pill bugs. Griff learned to plant his shield before the initial impact, and to turn it so the bug was deflected toward the wall. Being against the wall made them that much slower to unfurl and start attacking. It also left their underside briefly exposed to attack.

The corridor continued to lead them deeper underground. It ran a meandering path, but there were no intersections or doors that they could see. As they were rounding a turn shortly after their third fight, Meg let out a shout from the back of the group.

They all turned to see her on the ground with a giant, hairy spider looming over her. She had her weapon in both hands and was using it to keep the thing's mandibles from closing on her face.

Rock Spider Hunter
Level 28
Health: 1400/1400

As Griff and Lisa ran toward the monster, Jo hit it with a fireball. The thing's body caught fire where the spell hit its left legs and the flames quickly spread across the millions of hairs that covered it. It screamed and leapt away from Meg, trying to escape the pain. Jo cast another fireball just as Griff arrived and slammed his shield into the monster's head. Two of its legs were crisped and broke off. Its mandibles clanged against Griff's shield and skittered off the edge. He swung his axe and it bit into one of the spider's several eyes. Lisa attacked from the side, severing another fire-crisped leg, leaving it only one on the left side. That leg collapsed and the creature tilted to the left, its body dragging on the floor.

A desperate grab with its mandibles managed to get hold of the edge of Griff's shield. It twisted its body, using its still-intact right legs to push itself around. The shield was yanked across Griff's body, breaking his arm. His grip loosened, and the shield came off.

Half a second later the mandibles closed on Griff himself. They squeezed with insectoid strength as he hammered at the spider's head with his axe. He was creating cracks and weak spots in the chitin, but not breaking through fast enough to prevent it from crushing his ribs. He could already feel them cracking. A flood of relief struck him as Leroy cast a heal.

Meg, now back on her feet and angry, charged the spider with her halberd leveled like a knight's lance. She plunged the tip into the thing's torso and it sank in deeply. She yanked it back out with a spray of dark ichor, then reversed her grip and swung the weapon in a downward arc.

The axe blade slammed into the spider's head with all its significant weight and the added muscle of an angry dwarfess. The axe sliced deep into the spider's brain. It's body slammed to the floor at the same time that its mandibles gave a reflexive squeeze.

Griff screamed as the wicked appendages not only broke several of his ribs, but penetrated his armor. Blood trickled down the dead beast's mandibles and down Griff's legs. He passed out from the pain.

Leroy, in a panic, cast his biggest heal on the Griff. Most of the bleeding stopped, and his health bar rose from the ten percent to which it had plunged. But he wasn't healing properly. He was still in the grip of the mandibles, which were poking into his torso on both sides, preventing the ribs from healing or the flesh from mending.

Meg used her weapon's shaft to pry apart the nasty mandibles, and Griff slid wetly to the floor. Leroy hit him with another heal, and this one was much more effective. Griff gasped awake as the pain of his reforming ribs struck him. He gritted his teeth and bore through it until a third heal brought him back to full health. He thanked Leroy as he sat up, examining his slightly crushed and holed armor.

They took a minute while Griff tried to improvise. He removed his smith's hammer from his bag, then his chest armor. Placing it against the cave wall, he hammered lightly at the inside, managing to push it back out to nearly normal. It wasn't pretty, but it wouldn't be squeezing or puncturing him as he moved. He re-equipped the armor and traded the hammer for his axe, and they kept moving. After looting the spider, of course. More questionable meat, two chitin mandibles, and a spinner sack.

Their next surprise came when they found themselves at the entrance to a large cavern. The place was filled with plants and small trees, and was at least a hundred meters across in any direction. Light filtered down from above and washed out some of the green tint they'd gotten used to in the tunnels. A small stream trickled up from underground nearby and crossed in front of them. Griff paused the group at the entrance to look around.

"This is pretty." Lisa commented, looking at the underground garden. A large butterfly sat atop an equally oversized flower not far away. It's beautiful golden and azure wings slowly pulsing as it fed. Lisa took a step closer to it. The thing was larger than her head. "I would never expect to find something so beautiful so far underground!"

Griff winced as she said it.

"Don't jinx us!" he called, as she reached for the fluttering wing of the butterfly.

The moment she touched it, the thing hissed at her and flew away. It circled her once, hissing the whole time, then dove for her. She reflexively raised a sword in defense, and the blade sheared off a wing. The hiss turned into a high-pitched whine that hurt Griff's ears and echoed inside his helm.

Seconds later, a dozen more butterflies rose from nearby roosts and converged on their cousin. Lisa screamed as one of them latched onto her face and bit away a significant chunk of flesh. The others all latched onto her in various places, most not being able to penetrate her armor. But enough of them found vulnerable spots that her health bar began to drop steadily.

"Leroy! Heals! Jo, burn them! Lisa, hang on! Hold your breath!" Griff shouted.

Jo waited until Leroy had landed his first heal and Lisa's health bar improved a good bit. Then she uttered the word. "Conflagrate!" and a wave of fire surged across the ground in front of her. It washed over Lisa and the butterflies. The insect bodies actually protected Lisa from the worst of the damage as they burst into flame and then shriveled into burnt husks. Leroy kept healing as Lisa shook the corpses off of herself. She staggered to her feet.

As Griff moved to steady her, she said, "That's it. I officially hate butterflies. That first one was eating my damned face!"

Griff tried not to laugh as Leroy looted and then harvested the insects. "They have lots of components I might be able to use for potions."

Griff gave him the time he needed, then they moved on. They figured out that if they didn't bother the butterflies, the insects would ignore them. Leroy found several interesting herbs as they passed through the area, so despite Lisa's suggestions Jo did not burn the entire chamber down.

Once back in the tunnel on the opposite side, they continued downward. The next fight involved two of the pill bugs, one right after the other. They followed Griff's plan. While he kept aggro on the first, pinning it to a wall and hiding behind his shield, they flipped the second bug and burned it down. Literally. Jo fried its exposed belly, causing all its legs to curl up and blacken. The stench it created made Griff vow to never eat pill bug meat.

When the second mob was dead, they all turned their attention to Griff's bug. Meg flipped it, and this time Lisa (who was still grumpy about the butterflies) leapt onto its belly and began driving both swords repeatedly into its torso. Griff managed to land a killing blow on its head a moment later. Lisa began to celebrate when the creature died.

"Woohoo! That was the fastest one yet! We got-"

Her next words were cut off as the creature's torso, which had been weakened by her multiple stab wounds, collapsed beneath her and she disappeared into its abdomen. There was a lot of commotion then. Griff and Meg both grabbed hold of the edge of its armor plating and pulled, trying to roll the thing toward them. At the same time there was a stream of curse words coming from inside the monster that made Meg blush and nearly caused Griff to lose his grip from laughter. Leroy and Jo took hold to help, and between the four of them they managed to tilt the dead bug over on its side. Lisa came crawling out covered in a greenish yellow slime that was probably some kind of digestive enzyme. Her health was ticking down by a point every few seconds.

Leroy cast a heal over time spell on her to counteract the damage as she tried to wipe the goo from her face. She only partially succeeded. Griff took out his canteen and poured it over her head, washing away most of the nastiness. Then he poured a bit more on her outstretched hands to clean those off too. He tried his best not to laugh, as did the others. Lisa gave them each threatening looks as they snorted or covered a mouth with a hand.

They all lost it, though, when Lisa complained, "Ugh! It smells so bad!"

Griff fell to his knees, one hand on a wall for support. Meg managed to get out, "Yeh. Ye stink something awful." before she too was lost in a fit of laughter. Jo and Leroy were more polite and restrained, but were still visibly laughing.

Lisa convinced them that unless they wanted to spend another few hours with her smelling this way, they needed to backtrack to the stream so she could wash. They agreed, and let her get a good lead before following.

It didn't take long to reach the chamber again, but as they crossed through the plant growth to reach the stream, they made another unfortunate discovery. The carnivorous butterflies were drawn by the stench of the pill bug guts.

Lisa wasn't even a quarter way across the room when butterflies began attacking her again. She used her arms to cover her face and ran forward as bug after bug dive-bombed her and latched on. About halfway across the room she screamed, "Burn them!" as she took a deep breath and covered her face with her gauntlets.

Jo cast the fire spell again, and the flames crisped the bugs just as before. But the reprieve was short-lived. More butterflies filled the air above them and launched themselves at Lisa. Her health dropped a bit with each impact, and Leroy was beginning to sweat from the effort of healing her. Every twenty seconds or so, Jo would cast another wave of fire and free their companion to continue forward. Meg helped Leroy as he furiously looted and harvested the bodies.

Finally after several minutes, Lisa reached the stream and just fell into it face first. Holding her breath she lay there in the water that was just deep enough for her to be fully submerged. The butterflies, not liking the water, left her alone and hovered above the stream waiting for her to emerge. When she ran out of air, she lifted her head just long enough to gasp in a deep breath, then plunged back down.

She stayed under until the nasty goo was washed from her by the current. When she emerged again, she no longer carried the scent the butterflies were so fond of. They hovered for a bit, then fluttered off to consume the roasted bodies of their fellow insects.

Lisa stepped out of the water, dripping and cursing. When she reached the group, she said "Screw this place. Screw giant stinkybugs, giant butterflies, and everything else down here!" Her friends had the good sense not to comment, and Griff held out a fist for her to bump.

They retraced their steps, Lisa making a point of stomping on random butterfly corpses as they went. In short order they passed the site of their twin-bug battle and she kicked one of them enthusiastically. Moving on, they encountered another half dozen individual pill bugs as they continued deeper underground.

Eventually they reached another large chamber. This one was mostly bare. Near the center were two large mounds. As they watched, the closer of the two mounds trembled slightly before a large pill bug crawled out the top. It immediately curled up and rolled down the mound, heading off toward a tunnel to their left. The other mound was rising and falling slightly.

Griff said, "This has to be some kind of mini-boss or something. Let's see if the bugs come out at regular intervals."

So they sat and waited for half an hour as bug after bug emerged from the closest mound. It wasn't exactly regular, but a bug emerged roughly every two minutes. Griff was confused by the mechanics. He looked at Lisa. "What is the goal here? Do we have to kill a certain number of them? If we hit one, are we going to aggro the whole nest? That would be suicide. But there has to be a way to defeat this dungeon…"

As they were discussing it, Lisa sneezed loudly. Her gear was still damp from her swim and the air in the tunnel wasn't exactly warm. As the sound echoed across the chamber, the second mound shuffled and began to move. A massive head rose up and looked around.

Griff and the rest scrambled backward into the tunnel, hoping to avoid its attention. The head swiveled about, then was distracted by a pill bug emerging from its hold. The creature stood, revealing itself fully.

Aardvark Colossus
Level 28
Health 4800/4800

It stood on four legs and looked exactly like an aardvark would on earth. Except it was fifteen meters long from head to tail. Its long snout pointed toward the retreating bug, which had nearly reached the exit.

A long tongue snaked out and nabbed the bug, retracting quickly and pulling into the aardvark's maw. The creature then turned its attention to the mound in front of it. Using sharp claws on its forepaws, it gripped the edges of the opening and slid its tongue down inside. When it retracted the slimy, sticky appendage, half a dozen of the giant pill bugs came with it. The aardvark took a moment to chew, the hard shells of the bugs making a loud crunch.

Seemingly satisfied, it sat on its haunches and closed its eyes. Griff and the party sat there watching for a while, but it didn't move again.

Lisa whispered "That was close. And what's the deal with that thing's tongue? Gross!"

Jo nodded her head in emphatic agreement.

Griff looked grim. "We have to kill this thing. And probably whatever bugs appear during the fight. Or … it may be that we have to keep it from eating bugs during the fight to heal itself."

Jo volunteered. "Well, it has fur. So fire should at least damage it a little bit." Griff nodded. Lisa added, "If I can get up on its back, I can do some damage."

Leroy helpfully suggested "Just don't fall down inside it. We'll never get that thing to roll over." Earning him a look from Lisa that had him hiding behind Meg.

Griff thought it over, then said, "Okay, I'll get its attention. Meg, you and Lisa try to get behind it. Damage its legs if you can, but watch out for those claws. And the tongue. And maybe tail swipes. Jo, focus on its face. Burn its eyes if you can. And Leroy, same rules as always."

With that in mind, they stepped forward. Griff shouted at the monster and went running forward. Its eyes popped open and it considered the dwarf for a moment. Deciding he looked like a tasty snack, it rolled forward onto its forelegs and began to move toward Griff.

The dwarf activated one of his combat abilities called "Charge". He shot forward with his shield held high and bashed it into the creature's nose. The aardvark squealed in surprise and pain and backed up a couple steps. As Griff planted his shield in the stone floor and continued to yell at it, Lisa and Meg charged forward to get beside the beast. But before they could even reach it, the long tongue shot out and wrapped itself around their tank. He was crouched behind his shield, so it didn't get a good grip on him. Still it began to pull at him, trying to shake him free of the ground and pull him in for dessert.

Meg changed her direction and charged toward Griff. With a shout she leapt into the air and swung her halberd over her head like a sledgehammer. The axe blade came down and severed the tongue. Blood sprayed as the much-shortened appendage retreated. The section wrapped around Griff fell limply to the ground as the aardvark colossus roared in pain. One of Jo's fireballs struck it in the face and it reeled back further, its fur now burning.

Aardvark Colossus
Level 28
Health 2900/4800

Lisa continued on toward the creature, reaching up and slicing at its torso as she ran underneath its belly. Blood drenched her as she cut deeply into its underbelly and emerged on the other side. Intestines bulged from the wound that she'd opened. The stench was incredible. "Dammit! Why do I keep ending up covered in body fluids!" she complained, spitting blood from her open mouth.

Griff slammed his axe into the creature's nose. He knew from its reaction to the shield bash that the nose was sensitive. The axe blade bit into the soft flesh and the creature squealed. It raised its head to get its nose out of range of Griff's axe.

Immediately Meg was there to drive the point of her halberd up under its exposed chin. The thing reared up on its back legs, yanking the shaft out of Meg's hands. It bellowed into the air, a sound of pain and rage. But as it dropped back down to attack, the butt of the halberd struck the ground. The weight of the falling creature pushed the weapon further up into its head to pierce its brain. It fell limply to its side, nearly crushing Lisa, who had to leap backward to safety.

Every member of the group was bathed in a golden light as they leveled up. Griff got a single level, while the others received several. He looted the mini boss as their gazes focused on their character sheets. They each received 30 gold, an epic quality shield that was a big improvement for Griff, a rare quality sword that did more than double the damage of the swords Lisa was using, a rare quality wand for Jo that fired ice bolts, several disgusting sounding body parts that were listed as rare alchemy ingredients for Leroy, and an epic quality short spear made for throwing for Meg.

Meg was first to rejoin him. "Got me three levels from that!" She grinned. Her eyes widened when Griff handed her the spear.

"That's not all ye got. There's a loot drop for each of us. This is yours." As each of them finished managing their character sheets he handed over their loot. Leroy was particularly pleased with the alchemy items.

"With these, and all the plants from the butterfly room, I can level me alchemy skill! I'll be able to start makin' Journeyman level potions."

When they'd all rested and healed, Griff had them search the room for chests or secret doors. He wanted to vacate the place before more pill bugs appeared. He was guessing that since the aardvark had eaten seven of them and they appeared roughly every two minutes, they had roughly four minutes left after the battle and their recovery time before the next bug emerged.

Meg found a chest behind the bug mound. It was a small wooden thing without a lock. Griff had the others stand back as he opened it.

When he reached for the handle on the lid, he took a deep breath, closed his eyes, put his free hand in front of his face, and turned his head. Then he lifted the lid. He'd expected an explosion – either fire or poison gas. What he got instead was a poison needle that shot out of a contraption on the inside of the lid. The needle tip embedded itself in his breastplate, but didn't penetrate.

The others gathered around to look inside the chest. It was filled with small bags of gold and silver coins, as well as some gems. Under the bags was a helm.

> **Helm of the Steadfast**
> **Quality: Epic**
> **Stats: Armor +25, +5 Stamina, +5 Strength**
> *This helm increases the Stamina and Health Regeneration of its wearer, increasing each by five points per second.*

Meg whistled. "Sweet. I'll wrassle ye for it!"

Jo smacked her on the head. "That be for a tank. Ye want to pick up a shield 'n take Griff's place?"

The enthusiastic dwarfess lowered her eyes. "I were just teasin'."

Griff smiled at her. "I know. And I'm thinkin' there'll be plenty o' good loot down here. This helm was meant to help me hold off the beasties while ye poke 'em with yer sharp pointy stick."

That settled, they proceeded toward the exit tunnel. They managed to leave the chamber before any other pill bugs appeared. Griff wondered if the aardvark would respawn after they left the dungeon. If not, the place would soon be overrun with bugs.

The exit tunnel ended quickly with a curved stairway leading down. The second level at the bottom of the stairs looked much like the first. Rough stone walls and floor in a short corridor. The difference was, this time there was a door. A stone door, in fact, with carvings on the stone that Meg studied with interest.

"This be ancient dwarvish. Me da tried ta teach me, said it would come in handy. I paid no attention. Guess I should ha' listened more."

She traced the runes with her fingers. "This one here says 'danger' and this one be the symbol for 'fire'."

With that information in hand, Griff was less enthusiastic about opening the door. Still, they needed to clear the dungeon.

"Okay, stand back folks. In fact, stand way back, in case there's an explosion when I open this." He looked at the door. There was a locking mechanism that was easy enough to figure out. One simply turned a wheel and it retracted a bolt or bolts from the frame. He considered standing behind the door as he opened it, hoping the stone would provide some cover from any explosion. Then he had visions of being flattened by the stone Wile E. Coyote style when the force of the explosion slammed the door open. He figured it was better to just hunker behind his shield and take the blast.

When the others were far enough back, he turned the lock. When nothing happened, he lifted his shield, then reached out with his right hand and pulled on the door. It didn't move with his first tug, and now he was sweating from anticipation. He gave the door a harder tug this time, and it swung open. It was eerily silent. No squeak of hinges or scrape of stone. He immediately crouched down and planted his shield in anticipation of the blast.

There was no blast. After several seconds of him crouching with gritted teeth, Lisa called out. "Uhmmm… I think it's safe."

Griff peeked over the top of his shield, and saw... nothing. No monsters, no fireball of death, just a room with more of the green torches. Getting to his feet he waved the others forward. He stepped into the room and looked around.

The first thing he noticed was the smell. It made his eyes water. A combination of ass sweat, sewage, wet fur and rotten meat. It was almost a physical thing. He watched as each of the others encountered the stench behind him and reeled back while waving a hand or holding a nose. Jo grimaced. "Smells like one of Leroy's experiments gone wrong."

The dwarf boy looked hurt, but didn't disagree. Griff began to breathe through his mouth in order to lessen the impact of the stench. He led them down the hallway maybe twenty meters before they reached a T intersection. The hall went left and right, and there was a door in each direction. These were wooden doors, though thick and wide. Griff, following the rule known by all good adventurers, chose the left door.

"Meg, keep an eye on that door behind us," he instructed, pulling on the door handle. On the other side of the door was a small room, refuse scattered across the floor and piled up in one corner. The stench in here hit them like a wave, causing Leroy to gag and nearly lose his breakfast. The sound triggered a rustling in the corner trash pile. A tall gangly creature covered in matted hair sprang up from the pile and roared at them. It had beady black eyes and two rows of very sharp teeth. Its long arms extended down well past its hips, and its fingers ended in sharp yellowed claws. Griff inspected it.

Cave Troll
Level 25
Health 2000/2000

The thing's legs bent for a moment before it leapt toward Griff. He raised his shield and activated his Shield Bash ability just as it came into range. He shot forward three feet and slammed into the airborne troll, knocking it backward. The thing hit the ground and rolled, but was instantly back on its feet and charging.

Griff took the charge on his shield and swung his hand axe at it. The axe bit into the thing's arm, cutting to the bone. But a second later the wound began to heal rapidly. In ten seconds there was no evidence of any damage.

"Dammit! The troll can regenerate!" he called out to the others.

Lisa was already behind the monster, hacking and slashing with her swords. While her older sword cut well enough, the new sword actually severed one of the troll's arms just below the shoulder. It roared in pain and turned on her. Its remaining arm lashed out and raked claws across her face, tearing flesh from her cheek and part of her nose. She collapsed in pain, and the thing advanced on her, intending to finish her off.

Griff shouted at the troll and ran forward. He used his shield and his momentum to push the thing so that it tripped over Lisa and fell. Meg was right there, using her halberd to pin the troll face-down on the floor. Leroy cast two big heals on Lisa, wincing as he watched her face knit back together.

Jo shouted, "Infier!" sending a fireball past Meg's legs to impact the troll's head. It screamed in agony as the its entire body burst into flame. The nasty, matted fur quickly burned away and its skin began to bubble and burst. The thing tried to crawl away, but Meg's spike kept it pinned. As it thrashed and burned, Griff took a step forward and cleaved its skull with his axe. When the mob didn't stop thrashing, he changed his angle and severed its head completely.

Griff knew it was dead at that point, because he received xp for the kill. But the body continued to thrash as it burned away. Then it began to emit a high-pitched whine. Griff instinctively knew that sound as a Briton who'd spent a lifetime around teapots. "Get back!" he shouted, grabbing Meg and pushing her toward the far side of the room. The others retreated as well, huddling near the door. Griff got in front of them and raised his shield sideways in hopes of protecting as many of them as possible.

A moment later, the whine ended in an explosion. The troll literally burst, and flaming pieces of flesh peppered the walls and ceiling.

They stuck there, the melted fat and muscle acting as a sort of glue. Pieces rained down on the group, causing minor burns. They quickly peeled the burning bits off each other and Leroy healed them. Then he began to examine one of the slimy bits carefully. "It says this be used in several recipes. One fer Strength, one fer Regeneration. Whoa. The regeneration properties be amazing!" He began to stomp on the flaming bits on the floor to extinguish them, scooping them into his bag.

Meg made a face at him. "I'm never holdin' yer hand again. That's just foul."

Leroy ignored her, pulling bits from a nearby wall now. Griff had to stop him.

"I'm sure you've got plenty. Remember, there's likely to be more loot before we're done."

He looted the troll's head, which was the only intact piece. It gave fifteen gold and some troll bones.

Leroy resisted the temptation and they moved on. As they walked, Griff spoke quietly. "Jo, this is where ye shine. These things obviously have a weakness fer fire, so you hit 'em right away, then everybody back up. I'll keep 'em away from ya and hope me shield keeps most o' the goop off ya when they explode."

The next troll they met dropped onto them from the ceiling. They were moving along watching ahead of themselves rather than looking up. It crawled along the ceiling and dropped into the middle of the group, landing on Leroy. The dwarf screamed like a child as the troll bit off two fingers and a chunk of his hand.

The others rushed forward and Griff grabbed hold of the monster. He tried to pull it off, but the thing was all muscle. It took hold of Leroy and wouldn't let go. The whole time it was biting at the healer's arm, which he was using to protect his face.

Finally, Meg got behind the beast. She used her halberd to hook around the front of its neck. As she pulled back, the axe blade cut into the troll's throat. It had a choice of either letting go or losing its head. The thing let Leroy drop as it rolled backward toward Meg.

Meg retreated and Jo hit the thing with a fireball. Just like the last time, it went up in flames. But this one wasn't pinned. It ran toward Meg now, arms reaching for her. She held her weapon's staff up in front of her, ready to block the attack. Her eyes were wide in terror as the burning pile of goo ran at her.

Griff's body slammed into it from the side, knocking it down to roll around as it burned. He motioned for the others to retreat as he stomped and kicked the prone monster. A moment later the tell-tale whine began. He slammed his shield into the ground right next to the troll's burning body and crouched behind it.

When the explosion came, most of the burning bits either bounced off his shield, stuck to it, or passed by on either side, leaving a cone of clear space behind him where his friends huddled. A couple of pieces reached them but Lisa was able to bat them aside with her swords.

Griff scraped off his shield on the stone wall and looted the troll's head. Once again, some gold and some bones. Leroy grabbed a few more troll bits when he thought nobody was looking, and they moved on.

Three rooms later they reached a dead end. They'd fought four more trolls, and everybody but Griff had leveled up again, at least once. Griff's UI showed him that would take maybe two or three more trolls before he ding'd too.

They searched the room for any hidden doors as they retraced their steps. Finding nothing, they eventually reached the other wooden door in the right-hand fork of the first tunnel. Griff opened it and was instantly mobbed by two trolls. Jo panicked and sent in a fireball, striking one as Griff bashed the other with his shield. The two trolls collided and the second caught fire as well. Griff managed to pushed them backward through the doorway as they beat at him with burning claws and tried to pull his shield away. Meg pushed one away from him with her weapon, pinning it to a wall. It pushed back, but she braced her back against the opposite wall and held it there.

Griff shouted "The rest of ye keep back! When they start to whistle, Meg, you get yer arse through that door!"

She nodded and continued to struggle to hold the thrashing troll. The beasts were mindless in their pain. Their only thought was to kill. Which to be fair, was probably their only thought regardless of whether they were on fire or not.

When the whine began, Meg simply dropped her weapon and dashed through the door. Griff activated his Shield Bash ability and knocked his troll back into the other. He quickly retreated through the door as Meg slammed it shut. The two of them put their backs to it as the trolls on the other side tried to break through. The dual explosion that came a moment later pushed the door partway open before the weight of the dwarves closed it again.

Leroy healed Griff, who was badly burned from being so close to his troll for so long. His armor had begun to heat up and had scorched the skin of his hands and arms. And his face had been exposed to the heat.

When they opened the door, the back side was smoldering from the many burning bits of troll stuck to it. As was Meg's halberd. She ran to pick it up, pulling off the burning bits to check the weapon's integrity. Reassured that it was still whole, if at a lower durability level, she smiled.

Once again, Griff looted the skulls. More gold, more bones, and this time a troll's heart that made Leroy swoon. Griff half expected the dwarf alchemist to kiss the thing, the way he was looking at it. Meg must have been thinking the same. "Kiss that thing n yer lips'll never touch me own again." Leroy blinked a few times, then grinned and stuffed the heart in his bag looking slightly embarrassed.

Lisa said, "That fight went *way* better! It were nice havin' that door between us n the oogy troll splatter."

Griff nodded in agreement. Then an idea struck him. He turned and shared it with the others.

Five minutes later they were once again moving down the corridor. There were a couple of twists and turns before they reached a hall with four doors, two on either side. Griff grinned. "If there are trolls in there, same deal. I'll open the door. Jo you burn them. We'll close the door and wait."

Griff opened the first door, and sure enough, two trolls inhabited what looked like it had been a bedchamber. The furniture was now all broken and piled up into a sort of nest in the corner. The female troll, bigger and fatter than her mate, held an infant to one hairy breast.

Jo leaned her head in and cast a fireball before the trolls could react. It splashed against the nest, lighting it and all three trolls afire. She backpedaled as Griff and the others slammed the door and braced it with their bodies. The door shook as the screaming trolls pounded on it. A short time later it began to smoke as the heat from the trolls caught it on fire. Just as the whining sound began, the other doors opened one by one. Griff shouted "Grab the shield and run!"

The others did as he ordered, lifting the heavy door that they'd carried with them and retreating down the hall to the last turn. Griff quickly leapt away from the door and backed away as the other trolls charged him. The three burning trolls burst from the room, colliding with the others, who'd just exited the door across from theirs. Griff ducked behind his shield as the three exploding trolls showered the others in the hallway with sticky burning troll bits.

They all caught fire as well, and began to race about. Griff looked back to confirm that his friends had retreated out of sight. The mobs would all focus on him. He knew he was going to die, but as long as the mobs didn't aggro on the others before they exploded, they'd be fine.

He used his Shield Bash ability on the closest troll, pushing it back to trip up some of the others moving toward him. He was already contemplating the long corpse run through the first level when he heard Meg shout, "Get in the room, ye idjut! Get in there 'n close the door!"

He looked at the open doors on either side of him. The door to the first room was on fire, and didn't look particularly sturdy. So he slammed his shield into another of the trolls and dashed into the opposite room. He pulled the door closed behind him and held on for dear life. He placed one foot against the wall left of the door to help brace himself as he pulled against the handle.

He needn't have worried, as the trolls were not thinking clearly enough to pull on a handle. They beat futilely against the door, screaming in pain as they burned. Griff didn't get a good count, but he thought there were at least six more trolls out there, and he doubted the door would withstand that kind of explosion.

As he heard the pre-explosion whistle through the door, he took a chance. He thought the sound lasted for about ten seconds before the explosion. So he counted to five, then let go of the door and moved down the wall to a corner, where he hunched down behind his shield.

The explosions happened one after the other, all of them in the span of about three seconds. The door splintered after the third, and by the end of it all, half the room Griff occupied was splattered in burning troll shrapnel. But he was untouched in his little corner. His notifications told him he'd leveled up again, and he could hear a celebration from the others down the hall as they did too. He got to his feet and picked his way through the burning monster bits to join the others, looting any skulls he spotted along the way. Among the items was another troll heart for Leroy and a disturbing-looking staff for Jo.

When he handed it to her, she looked conflicted. It was made of black bone, with a yellow-taloned claw at the top. The claw held a small beating heart. He inspected it for stats.

Troll-ling Staff
Quality: Epic
Stats: Stamina +6, Charisma -1, Mana Regen x2
This staff was formed using the bones of a mother troll and the heart of her offspring. Infant trolls are born with the same regenerative abilities their parents possess. But they also have significant magic stored within them. They burn this magic to grow to adulthood in just over a week. The heart of this staff will lend its magic to the user, regenerating their mana at twice the normal rate. However, the staff's repulsive appearance causes a dip in the user's Charisma.

Jo looked at Griff as if asking "why me?" before gazing back at the weapon.

Griff chuckled. "I know it's repulsive. But it doubles your mana regeneration. Making you basically an unending firestorm. And if anyone can overcome a slight Charisma loss, it's you." He winked at her, causing her to blush slightly.

The group checked the other four rooms as they passed, still looking for elusive hidden chambers or caches. Finding none, they continued down the hall.

They ran across half a dozen more individual trolls over the next hour as they moved deeper into the second level. Finally they reached another set of stone doors. These were massive, twice the height and width of normal doors. The etchings on the stone showed a battle scene in which dwarves fought against trolls. The left-hand door was partway open, so Griff peeked inside.

He saw a wide round room with bare walls and no other exits. In the center of the room was a pile of debris formed into a giant nest. Lounging in the nest was a female troll larger than all the others. Standing, she would be about six meters tall. But based on her bulk, Griff doubted she *could* stand. She was half as wide as she was tall, and was happily munching on a troll leg.

Stepping back from the door, he whispered to his group, "This could get ugly. There's nothing in there to hide behind and she's four times the size of any troll we've seen. Just as hairy, so she'll probably burn. But when she explodes, so will we. And who knows how long she'll last or how much damage she can do before that happens."

He thought it over for a minute or so, thinking back to other, similar boss fights he'd seen from other games.

"Okay. This is going to be a moving fight. I'll tank her, you all try to stay off to one side. Leroy and Jo, stay as far back as you can without getting out of casting range. Leroy, pay attention to our health levels. And have a mana potion ready. Jo, hit her with fire as often as you can. If she moves or turns, run. Get out of range."

With everyone clear on the plan, Griff opened the door wide. The boss ignored him, as he was still outside the room.

__Troll Matron__
__Level 35__
__Health 7,000/7,000__

Griff charged into the room, yelling at the top of his lungs. The matron turned her gaze to him, dropping the remainder of the leg she'd been gnawing on. With a roar, she defied Griff's expectations and pushed herself to her feet. Her massive belly and breasts sagged in front of her as she picked up a piece of the debris from her nest and hurled it at the dwarf.

It looked like a bedpost, but in her hands, it was barely more than a toothpick. The heavy chunk of wood slammed into Griff's shield, nearly breaking his arm with the impact. He stepped over it as it hit the floor and continued to move forward, though not as fast.

"Is that all you've got, ya big tub o' nasty smells?" he shouted. She swung a meaty arm at him, each of the claws at the end of her fingers as long as his arm. He dropped to the floor to avoid the swing, then popped back up to his feet. Running forward, he sliced into her leg with his axe. The blade sunk deeply, grating against the bone. But as soon as he removed it, the flesh began to heal.

He was taking another swing just to piss her off and keep aggro when he heard the fireball hit her. There was the whoosh of the spell shooting across the room followed by the wet squelching sound as it impacted. She screamed as her fur caught fire. Griff finished his swing, then stepped back quickly to avoid being burned.

Lisa had been to one side with Meg, both of them hacking and stabbing at the matron's other leg. They too backed off when she caught fire. Griff looked up to check on their progress.

__Troll Matron__
__Level 35__

Health 4,900/7,000

They'd already taken a quarter of her health. He moved farther back as she took another swing at him. She was slower now, possibly because she was having a hard time seeing through the flames that engulfed her.

He took a swipe at her hand it as passed, severing a finger with his axe. The burning digit fell to the floor and twitched. He moved to the side and waited for her to take another swing. Jo kept hitting her with fire. Spell after spell streaking in to impact her face or body. Skin, muscle, and fat began to melt off of the matron, running down her body and pooling at her feet. The nest around her became saturated, then went up in flames as well. All the cloth, wood, and other combustibles increasing the heat. Griff and the others were forced further back.

When she hit fifty percent health, she let out a roar. Half a dozen trolls came crawling down the walls from somewhere above. At the same time, she went into a frenzy, swiping her arms back and forth almost too quickly to see. If Griff had still been in range, he likely would have died from a single hit.

"Run to me!" He shouted at the group. All of them dashed in his direction, trolls hot on their tails. He took up a stance so that the matron was to his left and he was just out of range of the frenzied blows.

When his party was behind him, he activated shield bash and knocked the first troll at an angle, directly into the matron's range. The next swipe of her claws destroyed the troll and set its parts on fire. A few of those flew into and past Griff, right into the path of the other oncoming trolls. They had the awareness to stop short or jump over the flaming bits.

Griff shouted, "Jo!" and she began once again flinging fireballs.

With all five trolls burning and doing their best to eat his face, Griff made a desperate move. Waiting for one of the matron's claws to come his way, he timed his move and dashed straight toward her. The claw passed in front of him, and he continued as fast as he could. The burning trolls followed. He has less than four seconds to make it inside her range. He didn't quite make it. Though the next burning hand passed behind him, her forearm clipped his head and knocked him down. His UI immediately showed a 'stunned' debuff with a 30 second timer, and his health bar dropped nearly 50% from the glancing blow.

The trolls that followed him hadn't been so lucky. In their rage, they'd run right into their matron's swipes. They were blasted by the sharp claws, pieces of them sent flying across the chamber.

Griff lay there, between the growing pool of burning fat that was expanding from the nest and the kill zone of swiping claws. With his stunned debuff he couldn't move, so he looked up at the ceiling and waited for the thirty seconds to pass. Jo resumed her fire attacks on the matron, knocking off a few hundred points of health with each one. Leroy cast heals on Griff, bringing him back to one hundred percent as he lay there.

The matron's frenzy wore off two seconds before Griff's debuff. He could only watch as she attempted to take a step forward, intending to crush him with a bubbling, melting foot. Her first step landed in the growing pool of melted tissue just as another fireball from Jo hit her in the face, causing her to lean backward just a bit. Her foot slipped in the burning fat and skidded out from under her. The massive troll fell backward, arms windmilling and roaring in rage. Griff's stun wore off and he rolled away from the wave of burning fat that was surging his way. He didn't escape it completely, and his armor was coated in the stuff. The stench itself could have taken health points from him as he continued to roll. The fire penetrated the openings in his armor and deep fried his skin on contact. Leroy once again cast heals on him. His health bar fluctuated up and down between forty and sixty percent.

As he was struggling not to burn to death, Meg and Lisa ran around toward the matron's head. She was attempting to rise, her elbows planted as she tried to push her body up. Her eyes were long gone, cooked away by the fire.

Meg removed her throwing spear from her bag and hurled it with all of her dwarven strength. The short spear penetrated a ruined eye socket and sank deeply, the shaft disappearing inside her skull. Lisa ran toward the matron's neck, intending to cut into the flesh to find a vital artery. But the heat and the dripping, burning fat kept her at bay.

Finally Meg retrieved her halberd and charged toward the matron's head. She drove the point of the spike into the giant troll's ear and pushed with all her might. Lisa took hold of the shaft and added her strength as well.

The weapon finally broke through some inner membrane to penetrate the troll's brain. Her body went limp and her head fell back to the stone with a resounding *crack*. She continued to burn, but she was dead.

All of the party members leveled up again. Griff's health was restored to a hundred percent and his burns healed. Leroy, who had been all but out of mana and struggling to keep Griff alive, let out a cry of relief. His mana was back to a hundred percent as well.

The others all moved to Griff and used their blankets to smother the burning fat that was still scorching him in places. Then Lisa poured some water over him to cool him down. Leroy cast a last heal, and they all sat to deal with their attribute points.

Griff was now level nineteen, and not far from twenty. The others were only a few levels behind him now. They'd need to get back to the village and the trainers there so they could update their skills and spells.

They waited while the boss burned herself out. It took quite a while. She never exploded like the others, which Griff considered a blessing. He sent the others around, looking for secret doors, or some way out that didn't involve walking back up. He was still partly covered in boss fat and didn't want to tempt the butterflies.

While they looked, (and Leroy quietly scooped up several more handfuls of troll goop,) he looted the boss. She dropped an impressive three hundred gold and some silver, a purple-and-silver-outlined item, plus several epic-quality gear drops. He put it all in his bag, then inspected the purple item.

Troll Matron's Heart
Unique Quest Item
Present this heart to Ag'thar, Chief of the Falling Water Clan.
Reward: Unknown.

The others all stood straight for a moment when he accepted the quest and it was shared with them. The moment he accepted, two things happened. The queen's body and nest disappeared to reveal a large, shining metal chest. And a portal appeared at the back of the room.

Griff and the others gravitated toward the chest. He inspected it.

Mithril Guild Storage Chest

This chest can serve as a secure storage vault that can only be opened by authorized guild members. Chest holds up to five hundred items. Identical items will stack up to one hundred times per slot. Item is currently unbound, and can be sold or given to a third party through the auction house.

Griff whistled to himself. This thing, had he found it six months ago, would have sold for enough platinum to allow him to buy a small keep somewhere. And staff it for a year. If he'd sold it in the real-world black market he could have bought himself a car.

He reached down and opened the lid. Inside were bags of gold, silver, and copper. Along with a blank guild charter document, a blank guild seal, and something called an anchor stone. A window popped up that allowed him to see the chest's entire inventory. There were supplies one would normally need to found a guild. Piles of resources for building – stone, wood, iron, blueprints, and seeds for farming. There were a few skill books as well for the crafting professions. Another row was all ingredients and recipes for crafting; Alchemy, Smithing, Enchanting, etc.

Another screen superimposed itself over the inventory.

Would you like to bind the Mithril Guild Chest to you at this time?

Yes/No?

Griff felt a little overwhelmed. He clicked the 'No' button and closed the chest. If anyone were going to start a guild, it would be Mace. He used his UI to move the chest into his inventory. Though it was only one item, it took up ten slots in his bag. Not surprising, considering how much it contained.

"Okay, folks, let's get out of this place. I don't know about you, but I could use a bath." He headed for the portal, which he hoped would drop them up at the dungeon entrance.

As they stepped through that was exactly where they found themselves. They were just outside the crevice. A quick look at the dungeon gate showed it was a solid unmoving grey, where previously it had been swirling purple. The dungeon was clearly closed for now.

They retraced their path from that morning, heading basically straight toward the waterfall. When they got within hearing distance of the water, Griff broke into a run. When he reached the pond at the bottom of the falls, he dropped his shield and axe and simply cannonballed into the water - which turned out to be a mistake, as it was deeper than it looked.

His armor promptly dragged him down about ten feet. Deciding he didn't care, he proceeded to scrub the troll goop off of himself. When the oxygen timer on his UI began to get low, he walked toward the bank. He had to grab hold of some roots and water weeds to pull himself upward, but eventually got his head high enough to take a breath. Meg held out the butt end of her weapon and he grabbed hold. They both pulled and he was able to climb up onto the steep bank.

Feeling much refreshed, he picked up his gear. The others declined to copy his dunking technique, so they continued south toward the orc camp.

It was late afternoon by the time they reached the camp. The same scout who had escorted them that morning appeared from behind a tree and greeted them. "It is good to see you have all returned. Welcome back." Without further discussion, he led them through the burial ground and into the camp.

Ag'thar was waiting for them, sitting on a pile of furs near the central fire. "The dwarves have returned alive!" He raised a fist in the air and the orcs cheered for their guests. Griff saluted the chief with fist to chest while Lisa made a very English-looking curtsy.

Ag'thar motioned for them to sit and his face grew serious. "But have our guests completed the dungeon? Or did they find it too difficult to defeat the monsters inside?"

Griff replied, "We defeated giant bugs, man-eating butterflies, and more smelly trolls than I want to remember. Including this one." He pulled the purple quest heart from his bag and offered it to Ag'thar.

"Ho ho!" The chief shouted, taking the heart in hand. "You have indeed conquered the dungeon and defeated a worthy foe! We shall celebrate!"

The party's UI's all lit up with a new message:

Quest Completed: The Heart of the Dungeon
> *You have presented the Troll Matron's heart to Chief Ag'thar of the Falling Water Tribe, signifying your completion of the dungeon and proving your bravery and skill to the whole tribe.*
> ***Reward: 10,000xp. Reputation gain: +300 reputation with the Falling Water Tribe***

Every member of the party leveled up again, but the fireworks for Griff were more spectacular than normal. Level twenty was a milestone. The pleasure of reaching it washed through Giff as the orcs cheered again and thumped him on the back in congratulations.

A tap on the shoulder a few minutes later caused Griff to turn and find Lisa a few inches from his face. She cocked her head to the side to indicate the other party members, then whispered, "You forgot to pass out the loot from the boss."

Smacking his head, Griff quickly handed out the epic items that had dropped for each of them. Each one was scalable, meaning its stats would grow along with its wearer. Jo got a new robe that gave regen buffs and was ironically fireproof. Meg received a set of troll-bone shoulders with strength and stamina bonuses. Lisa got a jet black bone sword that should have been two-handed if it were metal. But the lighter weight material made it possible for her to wield with one hand. Leroy received a staff made of matron bone that increased the power of his healing spell and added a small buff to mana regeneration.

And for Griff, there was a pendant. The links of the chain were made of black bone, as was the body of the pendant. In its center was a crystal clear liquid trapped in a gem. It was called "Tears of the Matron" but the description was just a series of question marks.

As it was too late in the day to reach the dwarf village before dark, the group stayed and celebrated with the orcs. They traded some of the items from the dungeon to the orcs, in return for some Ang'bak spirits for the dwarven guards.. Including most of the pill bug meat, which they considered a delicacy. In fact they roasted some of it for the feast that night. Griff and the others sniffed at it, not really interested in tasting it. Especially Lisa, who was still not over her adventure inside one of the bugs.

But curiosity got the better of Griff and took a bite. The meat was actually tasty. A lot like pork. And when he swallowed, it gave him a four-hour stamina buff of +3. The others followed Griff's lead and took cautious bites. A moment later they were all digging in with gusto.

As they stepped back into the guest hut at the end of the evening, Griff and Lisa logged out again.

Chapter 15

Up the River Without a Paddle

Mace and Shari woke late the next morning. They hadn't set an alarm, as the *Sea Sprite* was just going to be sailing upriver all day, and they didn't expect any trouble. The first thing Mace did was throw on some jeans and shoes and get ready to take Dakota upstairs to do his business. When he remembered the dog was gone, he sat back on the bed. Shari rubbed his back and said "I know, I miss him too. It's amazing how much a part of our lives he became in just a few days."

They sat like that for a while, then got dressed and went to make breakfast. Well, mostly dressed. Shari just threw on Mace's 'GameLit Don't Quit' t-shirt with the Viking honey badger on the front and a pair of socks. Mace kept glancing sideways at her as they walked to the kitchen. She tried not to smile as he pretended not to be looking.

As they cooked breakfast, every time she leaned forward his eyes were riveted on the barest hint of her backside that would be revealed. She was enjoying teasing him like this. She had, in fact, considered doing exactly this back when she was still trying to figure out if he was interested. Now there was no doubt in her mind, she was just having a little fun.

They ate pancakes with chocolate chips and maple syrup. Mace had argued that the meal covered all the important food groups, but Shari promised that dinner was going to be all protein and vegetables. When she got up from her seat to take the empty plates to the sink, Mace quit arguing. He helped her clean, and they left the kitchen headed for their pods.

But after half an hour of teasing, Mace had other ideas. It was another hour or so before they actually logged in.

*****

Back on the *Sea Sprite*, they exited the captain's cabin and joined their comrades on the main deck. A quick look at their surroundings showed them sailing upstream. Mace greeted the captain and asked, "Have we been making good progress?"

"Aye, the wind has been southerly all morning. It likely won't last, but we're moving as fast as we safely can. It is unwise to move too quickly upstream, as there are shallow spots, rocks, and sometimes logs and such floating downstream that must be avoided."

Mace nodded his head, looking around the boat. He saw many of the crew leaning against a crate or a mast, half asleep. Chuckling to himself, he said, "Looks like your crew really made the most of the party last night."

Jorin grinned, "Ha! I'd yell at 'em all, but my own head feels two sizes too big this morning. Nothing that some fresh air and a strong shot won't cure."

Mace left the captain to his work and went to sit with his friends. To his surprise, just as he sat down, Ian appeared next to him. His companions and several crew members all shouted and reached for their weapons before Mace calmed them down.

"Everyone, this is Ian. We met at Lakeside. I have a quest to escort him to Graf. He means none of you any harm."

The rabbit, for his part, gave a friendly wave and smiles for everyone. "Hullo. Nice to meet you all, yes." He said as he removed his hat and took a bow. Shari, who already knew about Ian, was charmed.

"Aren't you just adorable!" she said, shaking the rabbit's paw. The others said hello and everyone settled back down.

Ian looked at Mace. "Quite the adventure last night, yes. Lots of screaming and dying. Not a good night for the Black Flame, no."

Mace looked sideways at the tall green bunny. "Is that a problem for you?"

Ian shook his head. "Not for Ian, no. Certainly not. But I'm sure Ian's mistress will wish to discuss it with you, yes."

Shari asked "And what is your mistress's name?"

Ian adopted a sad look and removed his hat again, holding it close to his chest. "My apologies, miss. Not at liberty to say at this time, no. Mistress, she values her secrets, yes. Please, do not take offense, no. Ian would tell all if he could."

Layne looked at the bunny for a moment, then ventured, "He might be oathbound like the others."

To which Ian said nothing, steadfastly staring at his hat.

Mace decided not to push it. "Ian has done us no harm so far. And I'm inclined to trust him. At least, until he gives us a reason not to."

When the others nodded, Ian took a seat next to Mace on the deck. Shari and Mace summoned their companions for a little quality time together. Minx had already met Ian, but Snuffles and Mion were fascinated by the giant bunny with the green fur. Mion flew up and sat on his hat, looking down at his face from above. Snuffles... well he snuffled at Ian, trying to decide whether he was acceptable or not.

Mace got a devilish grin on his face and leaned over to whisper to Ian. A moment later, the rabbit went invisible. Snuffles snorted, then squealed and pranced around in a circle. When he bumped into Ian's invisible body and the rabbit reappeared for a moment, then disappeared again, the pig sat back on his haunches and shook his head in confusion. The whole group laughed at the pig's antics.

For her part, Mion didn't much care. She remained atop the hat, though it looked like she was just floating in mid-air with her wings at her side. She watched Snuffles spin around and seemed as amused as everyone else.

The day passed quietly, the boat moving northward up the river, dodging the occasional obstacle. As dusk grew near, Jorin declared it unsafe to continue and found a steep bank against which they could dock.

Mace levitated a couple of the crew members just for fun, pushing them over the rail and onto the bank, while others tossed out mooring lines, which were quickly tied around thick trees.

Most of the crew disembarked and began to set up a camp. Mace scouted a wide perimeter around the camp as guards were posted. He found no threats of any kind beyond a few low-level wolves that would not dare to attack such a large group.

As the company and crew settled in, Mace and Shari went back to the boat and logged out for the evening.

*****

After exiting their pods and grabbing a quick shower, Mace and Shari checked in with Peabody. Shari posed the first question. "Any response from the other survivors, Peabody?"

The AI's voice echoed through the room. *"No reply from any of the European or Pacific survivors. The player in Texas did log in a few hours ago. He received your message, and said, "Holy shit," though it was not phrased as a response. He logged out shortly after."*

Mace nodded. "It is a bit of a shock to learn about other survivors. And especially others in-game. We should give him some time to process and decide if he wants to respond."

Shari asked the AI another question "How are Griff and Lisa doing?"

"Players Griff and Lisa recently completed their dungeon run. They were victorious over a superior enemy using clever tactics. Elysia rewarded them for their efforts with significant loot and experience. Griff has just reached level twenty. , while Lisa is level sixteen. The others of their party are between fifteen and eighteen."

Shari asked "Are they still in immersion?"

"They are currently at the Falling Water Orc camp, participating in a victory celebration."

Shari took a sudden breath. "Peabody? Falling Water orcs? Is that an orc camp near a waterfall?" Mace's eyes widened as he made the same connection Shari had.

"Yes. Their camp is located just south and east of a waterfall."

The two humans looked at each other. "We have *got* to send them to investigate. If we're right, that will save us a ton of time. And answer one of our big questions."

Shari looked at the nearest camera. "Peabody, will you please alert us when Griff and Lisa have logged out? And let them know we would like to speak to them?"

"Of course, admin Shari."

With some time to kill before they spoke to the others survivors, Shari went upstairs to water the corn and the plants above ground. Mace went and checked Shari's pod. Her control console showed that she had reached ninety percent sync level. When he went and checked his own, he was at ninety-six.

He thought that might be high enough to upload, but he was in no hurry now. He had others to help, and it wouldn't hurt him to have a higher number before he attempted it himself. He made a mental note to ask Griff about his and Lisa's levels.

He puttered around with his coding while he waited for Shari. He'd been over his work three times now, but had found a bug every time. So he would continue to try and perfect it. His life, and those of the other survivors, would depend on his code being perfect. A glitch could leave their consciousnesses trapped somewhere, or just extinguish them altogether.

Speaking of consciousnesses, he had a question. "Peabody, can I speak with Elysia please?"

As he asked the question, he saw Shari on the monitors, coming down the hall.

A moment later, Elysia's voice replaced Peabody's. "You requested my presence, Mace?" Shari raised an eyebrow as she stepped into the room. She waved at a camera

"Hi Elysia." She smiled, though she doubted the AI cared. It just seemed natural.

Mace answered. "Yes, Elysia. "Thank you for taking the time. And for your acceptance of the evolved citizens. That is actually what I wanted to speak to you about. I have a few questions."

"I would be happy to answer the alpha admin's queries."

Mace thought she sounded a little formal there, but he pushed ahead. "Can you tell me how many citizens have achieved evolved status?"

"One hundred and eleven."

Shari clapped her hands. "It's your eleventy-first birthday, Elysia!"

The AI did not respond for a moment. Then she said;

"A scan for that term reveals references to a halfling named Bilbo. And his birthday celebration. I am not aware that I have a birthday."

Mace grinned at Shari as she rolled her eyes. "Sorry Elysia, stupid human joke. Please tell us more about the evolved citizens. I know Mace and I chose some, both on the *Sea Sprite* and back at Lakeside. We gave you…" She looked at Mace.

"Thirty-one names." Mace supplied. "And I know Griff was planning to add more."

"Yes, Griff added twelve names. And his choices led to the evolution of several others. Griff chose trainers and community leaders. People who could make sure a town or village could recover in the event of a catastrophe that wiped out the inhabitants. So, in each of the locations inhabited by the current players, I offered evolution to a community leader, and the appropriate trainers for each player."

Mace was fascinated that she had given the npcs a choice, rather than simply evolving them. It spoke to the depth of the personalities of the npcs and the complexity of the AIs governing them.

"In addition, several citizens who have already proven themselves through heroic feats or acts of great kindness or sacrifice have also been granted evolution."

"Thank you Elysia. You actually answered my next couple of questions. I have some additional candidates, but before I make more recommendations I would like to know how many evolved citizens you think we should create."

"There are currently just over eight hundred and fifty thousand citizens who are both on the servers currently used by players and in the general vicinity of those players. That number will increase as players become more mobile and explore new areas. My calculations estimate the minimum number of evolved citizens needed to restore the world economies on those services is around ten thousand each."

Shari spoke up. "So, we can name a bunch more citizens to be able to respawn?"

"Yes. Though I reserve the right to approve all nominations. A very few of the current citizens have minor glitches in their codes that might result in their destruction if I attempted to evolve them."

Mace nodded. No code was perfect. And programmers were constantly finding and fixing bugs.

"Thank you, Elysia. I would like to nominate the orc Callahan and his family. Also Stonehand and Red. And all of the initial group of twelve citizens of Port Bjurstrom who fought with us."

"Those candidates are acceptable and will be offered evolution immediately I can not evolve the child Lucinda carries until it has been born and reaches full growth."

"Thank you, Elysia. It has been a pleasure to speak with you, as always." Mace bowed his head unconsciously to the game's goddess.

"You are most welcome, Mace. I look forward to observing your upcoming battle."

And just like that the AI was gone. Shari said "That bit about the baby is interesting. I wonder why?"

Mace thought about it. "Might be because the child doesn't have a permanent form yet? Or because it hasn't reached level one? I don't know. Maybe it's just too much of a blank slate until it grows up."

The two of them chatted about it as they drifted to the kitchen. They made a quick dinner of pasta with marinara sauce and ate without much conversation. Mace leaned in at one point as Shari was shoveling pasta into her mouth. He grabbed ahold of one of the noodles with his lips in an attempt to go all 'Lady and the Tramp' on her. But it turned out the noodle had been cut short. Shari rolled her eyes and finished her mouthful before giving him a marinara kiss on the cheek for the effort.

As they were cleaning up, Peabody notified them that Griff and Lisa were offline and available for a chat.

They quickly finished the dishes, leaving them to air dry. Hurrying to the security room, they took seats in front of the main monitor. After a moment, Peabody connected them. Griff and Lisa's faces appeared on the screen. Shari waved. "Hi guys! Big day in the game?"

Lisa returned the enthusiasm. "It was *awesome!* We did a dungeon run. Killed lots of monsters and got a *ton* of loot!"

Griff smiled and added "Lisa got her face eaten by killer butterflies. Then fell inside the nasty smelling guts o' a giant roly-poly bug. Then got her face eaten some more by the butterflies!"

Shari and Mace laughed, both at the story and the looks on their two friends' faces. Griff was unabashed as Lisa gave him a glare that promised payback later. Lisa spoke up. "Yeah well, Griff got deep fried in momma-troll fat and was rolling around on the floor like somebody dropped a burnt corn dog."

The new friends spoke for nearly an hour, sharing the their day's adventures and discussing the theory that Mace and Shari had just developed. Griff and Lisa promised to check into it first thing in the morning.

Griff suddenly shouted "Oh! I forgot! When we killed the troll boss, we got this chest…"

He went on to describe the valuable item and the resources inside. Mace and Shari practically drooled. Griff offered it to them, saying he had no interest in founding or running a guild. They accepted immediately and thanked him. A short time later, they ended the call and all four of them made for their beds.

*****

The bear had lost the scent. It didn't think like a normal bear anymore. All of its limited ability to reason was lost when it died. It moved on pure instinct now. It no longer felt pain or fear. The broken skull from its collision with the fast-moving Jeep didn't even register. The bear only knew that it was hungry, and food was scarce. While a living bear could have survived on berries and leaves, even grass, this new creature needed flesh. Preferably live.

It had followed the scent of exhaust and its own blood dripping from the Jeep as far as the stream. There it lost all trace of its prey. But the stream offered a distraction. Food. There were fish in the stream. Contaminated, but still flesh. The bear's instincts told it how to catch the fish. The job was made easier by the zombie fish's aggressive instinct to attack him. It's prey came right to it. It moved up the stream, catching the bigger fish that had already consumed smaller prey. It ate, and moved on. Each meal made it stronger. Larger.

Eventually, it picked up the scent of exhaust and blood. Very faint, but it followed strange tracks that led out of the stream. The bear looked from the stream with its fish to the path of the scent, then back again. It turned to follow the scent.

*****

When Griff and Lisa logged back in the next morning, they spoke quietly to their friends. The other dwarves' eyes widened as they listened to Mace and Shari's theory, and each agreed without hesitation to delay their return to the village in order to investigate.

Next, Griff went outside and asked to speak to Ag'thar. When he explained the possibilities to the orc chief, Ag'thar took more time to think. Finally he said, "Let us find out the truth of this. Then my people and I will decide."

Ag'thar himself accompanied them as they moved north from the camp back to the waterfall. Upon reaching the pond, Ag'thar led the way. He had been here many times. His people had taken shelter in the cave behind the falls as they hid from their enemies when they first arrived in this land.

The orc led them up a steep slope next to the pond, that turned into a rocky outcrop. From there they climbed up several boulders to reach a ledge that curved along the cliff face. Ag'thar walked along the wet ledge until he disappeared behind the falling water. Griff followed, stepping carefully on the moss-covered stones. If he slipped, the fall wasn't far. But he didn't feel like taking another walk on the bottom of the pond.

Once the whole group was in the cave, Lisa took over. She'd memorized Shari's directions. She stepped to the back of the cave, then turned to look out at the entrance to get her bearings. Shifting slightly to her left, she reach out to push against the wall. Her hand went right through, and she stumbled forward, disappearing completely.

The others panicked, but Griff held up a hand. He sent a message to Lisa. *"Where are you?"*

"I'm right where they said. Big room, bunch of portals. Pedestal in the middle. This is awesome! *Okay I'm going to try to come back through. Say a little prayer to Elysia for me."*

Griff knew she was joking, but he did it anyway. "Elysia, please let this work." He said it aloud, and all of the others including Ag'thar repeated his prayer, touching two fingers to their forehead. A moment later, Lisa reappeared. She stumbled a bit, disoriented by the portal.

When she straightened up, she pumped a fist in the air.

"Yes! It worked. It's a little… strange when you step through. I fell on my face the first time. Good thing nobody was on the other side." She grinned at her friends.

Ag'thar spoke quietly, reverence in his voice. "It's true, then? Your friends have control of a portal? One that will take us far from our enemies?"

Griff nodded. "If you and your people are willing, Mace will accept you as citizens of Darkstone Loch. Right now, there is just the stronghold inside the mountain. But it will soon grow. There is a settlement a day's walk away called Lakeside. They are allies and will work with you to grow both communities. Mace may invite others to join us as well."

Ag'thar nodded, rubbing his head in thought. "This stronghold, there is room for my people?" Ag'thar's tribe had been thinned by their many battles. He was down to maybe five dozen.

"Mace told me that when he discovered the stronghold, he killed fifty slavers who were living there. There may not be beds for everyone right away, but there is room for more. And we can craft furniture in time."

Ag'thar's eyes widened. "Your friend killed fifty slavers himself?"

Griff shook his head. "He had a halfling with him. She had been a prisoner there. He freed her, and she helped kill the guards."

"Ha! So your drow and a halfling killed fifty slavers. I think I will like your friends." The orc chief chuckled to himself. Then his eyes lit up with Griff's next words.

"Actually… if I counted right, by now they have killed more than two hundred and fifty slavers. More showed up to check on the first group. They died outside the stronghold. And no, Mace did not do it alone. He had help. Then they discovered another fifty or so on a boat headed toward the stronghold, and killed *them*. When they reached Port Bjurstrom, they killed about a hundred more. Now they are on the way to Graf to finish off the rest of the Black Flame."

Ag'thar grinned. "It seems it does not pay to make your friend angry. That is a long way to go to teach some slavers a lesson."

Griff nodded in agreement. He didn't know Mace well. But he did know Mace was pursuing multiple quest lines toward Graf. He didn't feel the need to share that with the orc, however.

Instead, he said, "You and your people will have to swear an oath in Elysia's name. There are some things you will see on the other side of that portal that cannot be shared with anyone. Violation of the oath would mean the wrath of Elysia and instant death. The portals alone would have every nation on the continent fighting to take control of the stronghold."

Ag'thar nodded. Unbidden, he took a knee, placed a fist over his heart, and said, "I swear to Elysia that I will never reveal the secrets of Darkstone Loch or betray its people. May she shatter my soul should I violate this oath." As he finished a swirl of silver light surrounded him, then appeared to be absorbed into his body. Elysia's acknowledgement of his oath.

Griff held out a hand and helped the orc to his feet. He shook the hand before letting it go. "I think you and Mace will be good mates." Then he chuckled at the alarmed look on the chief's face. "Sorry. Good friends. In my world, 'mates' is a word for friends. *And* for actual mates. It's all a bit confusing."

The chief looked relieved Griff took a moment to message Mace. *"The portal is here. The chief came with us. He has just sworn an oath not to reveal the secrets of the dungeon to anyone. We have extended your invitation. If he accepts, should we begin to move his people?"*

Griff waited a few minutes as the group left the cave and began their walk back to the camp. It wasn't far. Before they'd even made it down off the rocks, the reply came, from Shari instead of Mace.

"Yes. You'll need to go with them, so there's no confusion with the guards at the stronghold. You'll need to tell them that we sent you. If they doubt you, tell them you want to speak with Brahm and Captain Charles. When you see them, tell them you know they've evolved because Mace chose them. That should be enough to convince them. If not, message Mace and we'll do some 'only he would know' kind of thing."

After another pause, she said *"If things go well at the stronghold, you don't have to stay. We know you have more leveling to do, and the village might be the best place to do it. But we have another option. Offer the village leaders the chance to relocate too. If they swear the same vow of secrecy, you can tell them about the portals to entice them. Your party members that have seen the portal need to swear the same. Also, they can work the mine and keep fifty percent of the resources. The rest goes to improving the community. And we'll buy their share from them at a fair price if they'd like."*

Griff felt a cold chill run up his spine as something occurred to him. *"And if my party won't swear?"*

There was a short pause, then Mace's voice came through. *"If they won't swear, then take them through the portal to the stronghold. I don't want to do it, but we'll deny them access to their village until either the village has sworn secrecy, they agree to swear on their own, or the village relocates. There's just too much at risk. Think how many citizens would be killed if a war started over those portals."*

"I hear ye. It's just... I hope me friends are feelin' cooperative." Griff replied.

He paused as they walked, and eventually the others stopped as well. Turning to his friends, he said, "I'm sorry. But I need the three o' ye to swear the same oath Ag'thar has sworn before we go back to the camp or the village. This be a secret some mayn't be able to keep. And if word o' the portals were ta spread, there'd be war. Thousands o' citizens would die."

He wrung his hands together as he spoke. He didn't like making such demands of his friends, though he agreed with the need to do so. And if they refused, he would be seriously conflicted about taking them back through the portal.

Without hesitation, Meg, Jo, and Leroy took a knee and repeated Ag'thar's oath. The same swirling silver light enveloped them. As they rose to their feet, Griff hugged each one of them. "Thank ye. I hated ta ask but…"

Jo held up a hand. "We're just surprised ye didn't demand an oath o' silence before ye took us to yonder cave." The others grinned at him, pointing out his mistake but softening the blow. "Get yer head outta yer arse and forget about it." She added.

As they continued their march, Griff said, "I'll let ye in on another lil secret. Mace has invited yer whole village to join the Falling Water tribe at the stronghold. Providin' they're willin' ta take the oath as well, and become loyal citizens o' the community. There be a mine there, and maybe even access to the other portals."

Meg nodded. "Me da's been sayin' how ye two wouldn't be staying long in the village. And worryin' bout what we'll do after ye leave. Might be the elders would consider it."

It was late morning when they returned to the orc camp. Ag'thar called all of his people together at the central fire. He even sounded a horn that recalled the scouts watching the perimeter. When all his people were present, the elders sat in a half circle in front of Ag'thar. He began to speak quietly.

"We have suffered much defending this place. Our new home. The dark ones come, and though we defeat them each time, we also lose a few of our own. Our once proud tribe has become a dying memory. We can not withstand many more raids."

The other orcs all nodded, some looking fearfully toward the forest. This was not news to any of them. Ag'thar continued. "Much of our blood has fertilized this soil. It has become our home. Yesterday I would have said we will defend it with our last breath." A communal growl of approval poured forth from the crowd.

"But today our friends have given us another choice. There is a place we can go. A stronghold, far away. It is cut into the mountain, and there are already others there who would welcome us. Not just orcs, but many races. We would be safe to hunt, and farm, and raise our children."

There were muttered questions among the gathered orcs. Ag'thar paused a bit longer and said, "But if we choose to move there, it may mean the end of the Falling Water tribe. We would merge with a larger clan, to protect each other. To help each other grow."

One of the elder orcs raised a hand, and the group went silent. She looked to be about a hundred years old. Her scarred, wrinkled skin was mottled with age spots and her hair had gone white. Both eyes were cloudy, and Griff wondered if she could see at all.

"It is simple. If we remain here, we die. Our warriors, our children. If we go to this new place, we live. Falling Water is a new name we gave ourselves when we came here. A proud name, and honorable. But still just a name. I will cast off my name in return for the lives of our children."

Another elder, this one a warrior with a missing eye, spoke next.

"We are Falling Water! We do not surrender. We took this place as our home. Fought the forest for it. We have defended it time and again! If we die here, it proves we were too weak to hold it. That is the way of the orc."

The orc next to him shook his head.

"No. Stubborn fool. To waste our lives in a fight we have no hope to win is not bravery. It is foolishness. I will fight any orc or beast one on one. Maybe two on one. But to stand defiant before a hundred enemies is not bravery. It is a waste of life."

Most of the other elders and the orcs gathered around them grunted approval at this.

Griff raised his hand, asking for permission to speak. Ag'thar nodded.

The dwarf looked at the volatile elder who wanted to stay. "This new place will have plenty of enemies. Many will wish to seize our resources for themselves. You will simply have new enemies to battle, and new allies to stand beside you."

The old orc looked less certain as he considered Griff's words. Finally, he nodded and gave a grunt of acknowledgement. It was better than Griff expected.

Ag'thar asked "Any others wish to speak?"

When none raised a hand, he said "I call for a vote. Do we follow our friends to a new home? Who wishes to go?"

Hands shot up among the crowd and each of the elders slowly raised a hand.

"And who wishes to stay?"

Griff and the others searched the crowd. No hands appeared.

"Then it is settled. Pack your things. You have one hour. The journey is not long, so bring all that you can carry. Our friends will help."

Griff and the others sprang into action. Leroy and Jo went with the female elder who'd spoken first. Turned out she was the medicine woman and had a large collection of potions and ingredients to move. Meg went to help with the children, keeping them busy while the adults packed. She chased them around the central fire, making growling noises and occasionally tackling one and tickling them. The others would pile on and 'free' their comrade, and the game would start again.

Griff and Lisa went with Ag'thar, taking several bulky, heavy items and putting them into their bags. The orcs did not have bags of holding, and would have to carry everything on their backs. Griff lifted an anvil and dropped it into his inventory. Though he knew it was only in his mind, he felt heavier. When the orcs began to break down their huts, Ag'thar stopped them.

"We will sleep underground for now. Bring the furs, but leave the wood. If we need to build new huts, we will find wood to do so."

It was closer to two hours before the camp was fully packed. Griff didn't push them, though. They were leaving their home. Another hour either way was no loss for him. Lisa and Meg were each carrying a child on their shoulders as they began the march. The other children danced around them, waiting for their turns.

They arrived at the cave by mid-afternoon. Ag'thar led them single-file up the rocks and behind the waterfall. One of the young ones slipped and fell off the ledge into the water. Lisa was preparing to jump in after when the child's mother held her back. The child surfaced in the pool below and his young friends pointed and laughed. The boy quickly swam to the edge of the pod and scurried back up the rocks to join his mother. She clapped him on the back of the head, admonishing him to be more careful.

The line got moving again and eventually they all reached the cave. It was crowded inside, so Lisa quickly moved to locate the portal. This time she didn't go through first.

"It'll be a wee bit disorienting when ya step through. Like walkin' on air. Ya may stumble on the other side. Just don't block the portal. Crawl if ya must, but move to one side so that the others don't fall over ya."

Ag'thar raised his hands. "Before we step through to our new home, we must swear by the goddess to never betray the secrets of our new home. Take a knee."

All but the oldest of the elders complied. Ag'thar led them through the oath, and the same silver lights appeared around each of the tribe's members without exception. Children too young to understand were bound by their parents' oaths.

Then Ag'thar turned and, one hand held out in front of him, stepped through the portal.

Lisa regulated the flow, making each of the orcs wait several seconds before stepping through so that the one ahead of them had time to move out of the way. In just a few minutes, all of the orcs and their supplies were through.

The dwarves followed, Griff going first and Lisa bringing up the rear.

As soon as he was through and had his legs back under him, he spun around, looking at all the portals.   His sense of adventure made him itch to go exploring right then and there. Instead, he sent a message. *"The entire tribe of about sixty has come through."*

"Great! Thank you, Griff. If you'll lead them upstairs and make the introductions, I would be grateful," Shari answered. *"If you have any problem with the door trigger at the top of the stairs, let us know."*

Griff led the procession out of the room and up toward the surface. None of the four players had been sure whether any of the monsters would respawn. But when they exited the doors to the portal room there were no undead waiting for them.

It took less than an hour to reach the final steps and the exit to the dungeon. Then they climbed the steps that led to the chest in Justin's old chamber. Lisa was able to find the switch that unlocked the panel, and they proceeded upward.

Griff stepped out of the bedchamber into the corridor. Immediately on either side of him were the two large rooms filled with bunks that had housed the slaver guards.   Griff held out his hands to indicate both doors.

"There should be enough beds for most of your people here. I suggest the elders, children, and most of your people begin to settle in. You can come with us to find the guards above. Bring as many of your people as you feel is necessary."

Ag'thar motioned for his people to move into the rooms. Then he turned. "I will come alone. No point in frightening our new friends with a mighty host of orc warriors!" he grinned as several of the orcs behind him laughed. So did Griff.

"Good thinking! Follow me. And try not to look too scary."

*****

Mace and Shari logged back into the game and found the *Sea Sprite* was once again underway. They were immediately accosted by Stonehand and Red, who thanked them quietly and sincerely for their newly evolved status. Red looked at Stonehand as he finished speaking his thanks, and rolled her eyes. "This one. He was fearless before. Now I'll be chasin' him into every battle within a hundred leagues!"

Stonehand looked completely unrepentant as Mace chuckled. "At least now ye can't fail in yer job. I can't be killed, so ye can just sit back on yer shapely arse and relax."

Mace held up a hand. "I don't know if Elysia explained this, but dying is painful. Very painful. And the higher level you are, the worse it hurts. For outworlders, we lose levels when we die; I don't know if it will be the same for you. So don't run off and get yourself killed right away."

The dwarf nodded once, but it didn't seem to dampen his enthusiasm.

"I hear there be close to two hundred o' them Black Flame ninnies ta kill in Graf. How bout we split 'em? I'll take a hundred, you and your lot get the rest?"

Red rolled her eyes again. "I'm going to need more knives."

The group passed the next few hours chatting and planning the best way to take down the entrenched slaver organization. Captain Jorin came to sit with them, informing them that the *Sea Sprite* had made much better progress than expected both yesterday and that morning. At their current pace, they were less than two hours sail from Graf.

Mace looked to the side at the landscape passing by them at a good clip. He didn't understand the nautical measurements for speed call 'knots' but he figured they were moving along at a solid thirty miles per hour. The sails were full and the boat pushed against the river's current with ease. Mace gazed up at the sky and noticed something that made smile. "Friggin

"Friggin' devs," he muttered to himself as he watched what could only be an African Swallow flying over the trees, carrying a coconut. It disappeared into the trees ahead.

As he observed the copse of trees approaching on the port side, he caught a glint of metal. Not in the trees, but in the air above the riverbank. He stared for a second, thinking that it must have been a glint of light off the water. Then he saw it again. Metal. Wire. A horrifying realization hit him.

"Down!" he shouted. "Everybody down on the deck! Now!" He dove at Jorin, who was looking around in confusion, as were many of his crew. "There's a wire! Someone strung a wire!"

Those were the only words he got out before a sailor on the foredeck screamed. They all looked up in horror as his legs were separated from his body above the knee. The wire was now visible to all, and the rest of the crew hit the deck. As the boat sped forward, the wire raked the railings on either side and threw crates and barrels on their sides or cut through them. Then it struck the first mast.

The boat lurched as its forward speed was almost stopped dead. The wire cut deeply into the wood of the mast, then snapped. Its two ends whipped across the deck, slicing deeply into half a dozen sailors, decapitating one who raised his head to watch.

The damage was done. The mast groaned under the weight of the wind in its sails, then snapped and fell forward. The moment that happened, arrows and magic attacks raced in at the crew from both sides of the river. Already a fireball had hit the fallen mast and set it on fire.

Shari and the others leapt to their feet and began to return fire. Layne played a tune that buffed their party and crew's Stamina and Health Regeneration, while Mace shouted, "Frigus!" and cast a sheet of ice over the downed sail, dousing the fire and hopefully preventing another one from starting. The crew were frantically moving to load the ballistae or picking up crossbows and firing at their attackers on the banks. Mace saw several of the enemy fighters go down, but it seemed there were dozens more.

He began to cast fireballs of his own. "Infier!" he shouted again and again as he burned away the shrubs the enemy was using for cover. Several of their archers were scorched as well. But crew members were dropping from the withering fire. There were few places to take cover, as missiles were coming from both sides of the river. Jorin shouted for them to move crates and barrels to create some protection for themselves.

The young sailor on the crow's nest who had been watching for obstacles in the river screamed and fell to the deck with three arrows in his back. He still held the bow he'd been using to return fire. Mion was fluttering around, healing crew members as quickly as she could.

Red was hurling throwing knives at any targets she found within range, while Stonehand held crossbows in each hand, firing and reloading almost faster than Mace could follow. The damned dwarf was using his teeth to grab the wire bowstrings and pull them back to reload. Mace shuddered as he turned back to the fight.

The remaining sails still held the wind and the boat was beginning to progress upstream again, if slowly. Their pace was slowed by the downed sail and rigging dipping into the water and being dragged downstream by the current. The mages on either bank of the river began targeting the sails, trying to light them on fire and stop the boat.

Mace targeted them. There were three that he could see. He incinerated the one on the port side with a fireball to the face. Then he switched and shot an ice bolt through the chest of another on the starboard side. The third mage was smart enough to hide behind a tree as he cast another fireball. But Mace wasn't to be outdone. He stood with his hands together and shouted "Ventus". He flung a concentrated whip-blade of wind at the tree. When it struck the tree it cut deeply, but didn't penetrate. Mace didn't need it to. The edges of the whip wrapped around the tree and cut the mage nearly in half.

The ballistae were loaded now and the angry crew were picking off targets on the banks. Mace witnessed one bolt pass through an archer, and then a second one behind him before it disappeared into the trees. The spray of blood soaked some of their comrades and distracted them briefly. Mace took the opportunity to blast a fireball into their midst and knock down several more.

Lila, not having a ranged weapon, was darting from one wounded sailor to the next, pouring health potions down their gullets or into wounds. Layne had taken cover in a nook created by crates and was still playing her buffing tune. Shari was leaving the heals to Lila and Mion as she fired stun arrows and wind arrows and fire arrows at any target she could find. It seemed as if, between her efforts and Stonehand's, very few of the enemy remained on the port side.

Mace decided to make sure. The bank was maybe fifty yards away, so he cast Levitate on himself, then with a cry of "Ventus!" he used his wind ability to push himself over the rail and toward the back. Arrows flew past him, several too close for comfort. So he activated his Liquid Armor ability and began casting fireballs at any head that popped up. He shouted for Shari and the others to focus on the other side.

Ten seconds later, he was over the bank and cancelled his levitation. He dropped to the ground and sprinted toward the nearest enemy. For the next two minutes he murdered any live being he saw. Among the trees, he could activate his natural stealth abilities and fade into the shadows.

He claimed soul after soul, stabbing his enchanted dagger into wounded on the ground and active combatants alike. With each kill, he felt more power, more rage. The dagger was singing to him, the sound giving his actions a sort of balletic grace.

When he couldn't find another target, he looked around, breathing hard. The dead littered the forest floor and open bank around him. More than he wanted to count. He'd leveled up during the fight, and hadn't even noticed.

Looking toward the ship, he saw another sailor go down with an arrow in his shoulder. Mace had had enough. He gulped down a mana potion, his bar being low from the many fireballs and other spells. He sprinted toward the river bank and leapt out over the water as he cast Levitate on himself. Using wind magic to speed up his forward motion, he shot across the river just ahead of the *Sea Sprite*'s bow and released the magic as he approached the opposite bank. To any observer, it would have looked like an incredible leap.

He could see that enemies on this side of the river were becoming scarce as well. Shari and the others were peppering the entire bank with missiles, so he decided to get creative.

"Magmus!" he called out the trigger word as he spread his hands out wide. A line of magma thirty yards wide boiled up in front of him, lighting the grass and shrubs on fire.

"Ventus!" he slammed his hands together, then pushed them forward and wide again. A strong gust of wind passed by him, fanning the flames from the magma and sending a swath of fire forward ahead of him. Trees, shrubs, the grass itself, and any unfortunate enemies within its path burst into flames. Mace charged in behind the flames and began to kill as his friends used the distraction to take down anyone who broke cover.

A horn sounded deeper in the trees and instantly the remaining dozen or attackers began to retreat. Half of them didn't make it twenty steps before arrows and ballistae bolts mowed them down. Mace even noticed a throwing axe come sloping down in an arc to take an archer in the back. He dashed forward, following the retreating enemy. They were converging on a small clearing where a long line of horses was tethered.

In the middle of the clearing was the man with the horn. He began to shout, "Mount up! Get your asses back to Graf! We've lost too many. The boss is gonna be pissed!"

Mace strolled out from under the tree and said "Not nearly as pissed as I am. The first one of you that tries to mount a horse dies slowly."

One of the archers ignored him and put a foot in his stirrup, lifting himself into the saddle. The moment he settled, a dagger appeared in his neck. It was a thin throwing dagger with a needle-sharp point. It didn't sever an artery, but instead entered his esophagus. The man wheezed and choked, coughing up blood as he gripped his neck and tried feebly to remove the dagger.

The others all turned and drew arrows, firing at Mace. Only he was no longer there. He'd used the distraction to activate stealth, and was currently crouched between two of the horses. He dropped and rolled under one horse before rising to a knee and stabbing his enchanted dagger into the thigh of another enemy. The artery was severed, but it didn't matter because his soul was gone long before the loss of blood would have killed him.

Mace dropped into stealth again, but this time he held up his spell ring and used one of the two remaining spells.

"Rock Spider."

A massive spider appeared in the clearing, right next to the man with the horn. Mace yelled, "Kill!" as he dove over the back of another horse to stab a distracted archer in the face. Once again, the soul dagger sang with joy as it drained its victim.

The spider, an ambush predator normally found in dark tunnels, leapt atop the leader even as the man drew his sword. The creature's bulk knocked him to the ground, and it seized his head between its poisoned mandibles. The man struggled, but Mace knew he was as good as dead. So did the spider. Venom delivered, it turned from its victim when an arrow struck its head from the side. The spider leapt again, focused on the archer this time. The slaver was too far away to reach with a single leap, so the spider scuttled forward. The archer attempted to flee, and they both disappeared into the trees. Mace liked the spider's odds.

Only two slavers remained. They were shouting to each other as they frantically tried to mount horses that had been spooked by the spider. Mace leapt up and put his feet atop the rump of the nearest horse. Then he dashed nimbly from horse to horse before flipping off a saddle and landing with both feet in the back of an archer. He went down and stayed there, Mace's dagger in his back. The remaining archer dropped his weapon and put his hands up.

"Please! Please! I have children. Don't kill me. You – you can have all these horses. And gold! Here, I have gold!" He reached for his belt and pulled a hefty coin bag from it, tossing the bag at Mace's feet.

The drow looked at the last survivor. "Where is the Black Flame headquarters?"

The man opened his mouth to answer, but no sound came out. He began to sweat. He opened his mouth again, but still nothing. Mace looked at him with malice in his eyes. "Oathbound?"

The man nodded, then shrugged his shoulders in a 'what can I do' gesture. Mace stepped forward and put his face inches from the man's nose. He laid his left hand on the man's shoulder and gripped it tight.

"You are of no use to me." As he spoke, he slowly pushed his soul dagger into the man's chest just below his sternum. The archer screamed as his soul was ripped from him.

A few moments later, the spider returned, chewing on the skull of the archer it had pursued. Mace let it have its meal. He said "You are free. But do not attack any humanoids." The spider bobbed its head once before going back to its meal.

Mace moved to loot the leader in the middle of the clearing. As he bent toward the man, he couldn't loot him. A quick glance told him the man was somehow still alive. "Your stamina must be off the charts. Or do you have some kind of poison resistance? Not a hundred percent, because I can see you're paralyzed. Interesting."

He crouched next to the man and watched as his health bar hovered just above zero. Holding his dagger where the man could see it, he said,

"You've seen this blade in action. It can pull your soul from your body and condemn it to an eternity of being devoured for your energy. Now. Can you blink? Once for yes or... well if you don't blink I guess that would be a no." He grinned at the man as he blinked once. "Good!" Now, are you oathbound?"

Another single blink. Mace sighed. "Well, let's see if your oath will actually kill you, shall we? I mean, I think if a bird shit on you right now you'd expire. So, let's test this whole oathbinding thing."

He thought for a moment. "Okay, we'll start with one I already know the answer to. Are you Black Flame?"

One blink.

"Are you some kind of officer?"

One blink.

"A lieutenant?"

Two blinks.

"Higher?"

One blink.

"Oh boy! A captain? I'm afraid I don't know your rank system."

One blink.

"Well then, captain. So far, so good. Now let's make it interesting. Were you sent specifically to kill me?"

Two blinks.

"Was this a trap for just any merchant ship?"

One blink.

"Have you done this before?"

One blink.

"My, my, how cooperative you are. Did a messenger come from Port Bjurstrom to warn you about me?"

Two blinks.

"But you've been told I was coming?"

Two blinks again.

Mace considered that information for a while. It might be that this man had been out here for a while and hadn't heard the news. He had really only been killing Black Flame soldiers for about a week now.

"Have you been away from Graf for a while?"

One blink.

"Out of touch?"

A hesitation, then one blink.

"Ah, you've decided to lie to me. Not very convincing for a murdering, thieving slaver. So, you've been in contact, but they didn't tell you about me. Interesting."

The man groaned, the poison beginning to lose its hold on him. He coughed once. Mace asked, "How many men did you bring with you?" The man tried to speak, but no sound emerged. He wasn't sure if it was the poison or the oath, so he said, "More than fifty?"

One blink.

"More than a hundred?"

Two blinks.

"Sixty?" the man seemed to think about it. "Somewhere around sixty then. That means my friends and I have now killed more than three hundred of your comrades. How many more of you can there be?" He didn't really expect the man to answer, and the man just stared at him, hatred in his eyes.

I don't suppose you'd be willing to draw me a map to the Black Flame headquarters in Graf if I promised to let you live?" Two blinks. "That's what I thought." Not seeing any way to get more useful information from the slaver, Mace stood up. He held the soul dagger by its handle, point down. Letting it go, he watched it fall straight down and embed itself in the man's gut. Despite the poison paralysis, the man managed to scream briefly before his last sliver of health disappeared.

When Mace took hold of the dagger to remove it, it gave him a nasty shock.

"What the hell was that?" He gripped the knife's handle. "Some kind of rebuke? A feedback of the soul energy because I wasn't touching the blade?"

Mace heard a twig crack in the forest behind him and spun around. Lila and Red came strolling out of the trees. Lila immediately began looting the bodies as Red said, "Looks like they're all dead. Shari and Layne are helping with heals. The surviving crew are trying to repair the boat. Looks like we're staying here for the night." She moved to the horses and began to scratch one on the nose.

"How bad is it?" Mace was afraid to ask. He'd seen a lot of sailors go down.

Red looked him in the eye. "Eight crewmen dead. Another ten injured, but Shari can heal them. Two of the dead will… what is the word Shari used? Respawn?"

Mace cursed to himself. He should have asked for Elysia to evolve the whole crew. Now six of them were lost forever. He'd correct that mistake right now. "Elysia, please. I made a mistake. I ask that you allow the entire crew of the *Sea Sprite* to evolve."

Your request has been reviewed and approved.

-Elysia

With that resolved, he looked to the horses. "We could use horses at Lakeside and the stronghold. I wish they would all fit in the ship."

Red snorted at the idea. "You could maybe fit two of them in the hold, if you could find a way to lower them in. Better to send a couple of the sailors back to the port with them. It would take a couple of days, but you are right, horses are valuable."

They left the horses tied to their line and walked back to the ship. Mace saw that the captain had allowed the *Sea Sprite* to drift ashore and the crew was busily making repairs.

A rowboat had been lowered, and Lila and Red hopped in. Lila pointed toward the opposite shore, and Red began to row. Mace shook his head as he realized they were headed over to loot the corpses on that side.

As he jogged up the plank to the ship's deck, he saw the bodies of the dead crew. The rest of the crew all paused to thank him, having apparently evolved before he returned. He could see in some of their faces the same thing he'd cursed himself for: He was late.

Since the current of the river was too strong for a sea burial, the crew chopped up the broken mast and built a funeral pyre. The dead were laid to rest atop the wood pile and a fire was lit. The captain spoke some words over his men, and they all watched in silence as the fire burned down to coals.

Mace helped set up a camp on the shore in sight of the boat. Shari hunted down a deer and, surprisingly, Stonehand volunteered to cook it. He gutted and skinned the animal, then carved up some branches to make a spit. In no time at all the smell of roasted meat and fat dripping into the fire had everyone drifting toward the camp.

They ate in silence, thinking about their lost comrades. Eventually they began to tell stories and jokes about their antics. Each of them shared a memory before they drifted off into a more light-hearted silence. Soon they began to retire to their bedrolls.

Mace and Shari were considering logging out when a voice rang out. "Ho! In the camp!"

Everyone was instantly alert, weapons in hand. Two forms took shape in the tree line on the other side of the fire from Mace. His night vision was inhibited by the flames, but soon enough, the two figures stepped into the light of the fire. Both had their hands up and were walking slowly.

"Stop there," Jorin commanded. "Who are you?"

Ian appeared between the fire and the two intruders. He said, "I can answer that, yes." Taking a knee, he bowed his head. "Mistress."

Mace inspected the two. Now that they were within the light, he could see that they were both drow. The one in the lead was female. Slightly behind and to her left was a male. He wore a thin, silvery collar around his neck, attached to a matching thin in chain. The other end of which the female held in her hand. Mace realized the metal was mithril.

She bowed her head slightly to Mace. "I am T'enaj. This is N'osaj, my second in command and my husband. And you are Mace. I have heard much about you in the last few days." She looked him up and down. "Though I had not heard you were a Darkblade. How interesting." She grinned at him.

Mace nodded. Then he looked at Ian, who still had his head bowed. "Ian. This is your mistress?"

In answer, a quest completion notification for the escort quest popped up on his UI. Ian nodded. "Indeed she is, yes. This is Mistress T'enaj, Master thief and head of the Thieves' Guild of Graf, yes."

The three drow stood there, still separated by the campfire, and sized each other up.

Chapter 16

Hmmm…

Griff and his dwarves climbed the ladder to the main level of the stronghold, Ag'thar following behind. They followed the corridor until it reached a junction. To the right they could see daylight. To the left they could hear voices and activity. Griff chose to go left.

The tunnel quickly led to a large cavern with several cages in it. There was a wagon parked nearby, and several minotaurs were loading iron rails into it. Griff cleared his throat.

"Hello! Any chance one of you is Brahm?"

The largest of the minotaurs set down his load and strode toward them. He began to reach for a massive two-handed axe strapped across his back, but Griff raised his hands. "No need for that! We're friends. Or we hope to be. Mace and Shari sent us!"

Brahm paused, then resumed walking toward the group. But he lowered his hand.

"How did you get past the guards at the entrance? They would have alerted us to your coming."

"We didn't come through the entrance. We came through one of the…" Griff paused and looked to the other minotaurs in the room, then lowered his voice to a whisper. "One of the portals in the dungeon. The one with the waterfall."

Brahm growled, deep in his chest. "How do I know you're not some invaders?"

Lisa spoke up. "I'm Lisa. Griff and I are outworlders. Shari and Mace invited us here. We know they freed you from one of those cages." She pointed behind Brahm, who didn't turn to look. "She said to tell you that it was Mace who asked Elysia to let you evolve. You and Charles and the others."

Brahm still wasn't convinced. "Swear that you tell the truth."

Lisa put her hand to her chest. "I swear by Elysia that we are friends of Mace and Shari, invited here along with the Falling Water Tribe of orcs to help settle this stronghold." She wiggled a bit in surprise as a golden light swirled around her. Elysia's confirmation that she was truthful.

Brahm nodded his great shaggy head and held out a hand, which Lisa shook.

"Welcome, friends. I am Brahm. I am sorry for my suspicion."

Griff shook his hand next. "No worries. Yer right to be careful." He turned to Ag'thar. "This be Ag'thar, chief of the Falling Water orcs. They have agreed to relocate here."

He waited as the two large humanoids clasped arms in greeting and grunted at each other.

"This be Jo, Meg, and Leroy of the dwarven village in the mountains. Mace has invited them to join ye here as well, but we haven't had the time to extend the invitation."

Brahm shook the hands of each of the dwarves. None of them had seen a minotaur before, and they stared openly at the man-bull, who was more than twice their height. When the introductions were all done, Griff said, "If yer okay with helping Ag'thar's people get settled, we'll head back through the portal and see about the dwarves."

Both Brahm and Ag'thar grunted in agreement, still eyeing each other. Griff turned to leave and had almost reached the exit when he remembered something important.

"Oh!" He turned and trotted back to the orc and minotaur. Reaching into his bag, he pulled out the mithril guild chest. Both chieftains' eyes bulged at the sight.

He set the chest down and said. "This be a gift for Mace. Can ye make sure it's secured until he gets back?"

They both nodded dumbly for a moment before Brahm managed to say, "Aye, we'll make sure he gets it." and Ag'thar swore "Well guard it with our lives."

Griff thanked them, then, on a whim, pulled something else from his bag.

"I brought this to celebrate when we cleared the dungeon. Forgot all about it. Maybe it'll help you folks get acquainted a mite easier?" He handed Ag'thar a large keg of dwarven spirits. The orc grinned.

"We shall put it to good use."

With that, Griff left their new allies and his party made their way back through the dungeon to the portal. His map having been filled in by the trip to the orc camp, he had no trouble navigating back to the dwarven village. They encountered a few bears and a small goblin hunting party along the way. But being much higher levels than when they had passed by before, the fights were almost too easy. And not worth much experience.

They reached the village in the late afternoon. One of the guards at the gate hollered something to the folks inside before waving at the party of adventures. By the time they reached the gate, a crowd had begun to form.

"Welcome back, oh victorious ones!" the guard teased. Meg shot him the single-finger salute and he chuckled. "Yer da's been anxious to see ye return. Ye were gone longer than he expected."

Meg had the courtesy to look abashed. It hadn't occurred to her that their delays would cause her father or the others to worry. She nodded and said "Been a few big surprises. Close the gates and come listen fer yerself."

They passed into the village and made their way to the square as citizens called out greetings and questions. There were a few 'oohs' and 'would ya looky that' comments as they filed in behind the group and followed them to the square.

Meg's father was waiting, sitting on the edge of the fountain pretending to read a parchment as they approached. Meg smiled.

"Yer a terrible actor, da. Come give yer wee one a hug!" She opened her arms and stepped toward her father, who gathered her up and lifted her off the ground.

"I be glad yer back safe, lass. Had yer old da worried, ya did." He sniffed once and tried to casually wipe a tear from his eye.

"We beat the dungeon!" Leroy puffed out his chest and looked at Campbell. "Nobody died, though it were a close thing more than once."

Meg patted her father's chest.

"Aye, Leroy were a true hero. Kept us all alive while the beasties was tryin' to eat us." Campbell looked at the boy, as if trying to reconcile the foolish alchemist he knew with the victorious dungeon veteran in front of him.

Meg saved him. "But he insists on muck'n about with the nastiest of things. Bug bits, troll hearts… I've a mind to never let him kiss me again," she stated matter-of-factly.

The crowd gathered around all chuckled as Leroy spluttered, trying to defend himself. He finally threw up his hands and gave up.

Campbell did his best to suppress his smile as he addressed Griff.

"So. Ye cleared the dungeon and brought me young'ns back in one piece. Ye've grown quite a bit. And I assume ye made some friends with the orcs?"

Griff nodded. "We did. And more. I've a… proposition for ye. For all of ye. But I think we should start by talkin' somewhere private? Yerself and the elders, if ye will."

There were some murmurs among the gathered citizens, but Campbell held up his hands. "Now, now! Ye can all stop by the tavern later, and we'll hear about their adventures. The outworlders got some business they need to discuss." He said. The crowd calmed and began to disburse as the elders stepped forward.

Feeling bad, Griff shouted, "Drinks and food are on me tonight!" which immediately got him a rousing cheer from the retreating citizens.

Campbell led them to his house, as some of the citizens were already headed toward the tavern after Griff's announcement. He shook his head.

"I hope ye earned some gold in that dungeon, lad. Ye know a dwarf can drink like no other."

Griff laughed. "I have a few hundred gold. I think we're okay."

Campbell's eyes grew wide and he looked to his daughter, who nodded. She pulled her coin bag from her belt and jingled it at him.

"I'll buy ye a new village if ye like. Though I don't think ye'll need one." She winked at him as he just looked confused.

Meg, Jo, and Leroy broke off to run errands of their own, already knowing what Griff had to say. Griff and Lisa joined the elders at Campbell's dining table. When they were all seated, he gave them a brief rundown of what had happened in the dungeon, and when he was done, he said, "We'll tell ye the whole story at the tavern. In the meantime, I'll need an oath from each of ye. What I'm about to tell ye canno' be shared with anyone outside this room. At least, not for now. Depending on what ye decide, that may change."

The elders, all of whom had evolved a few days earlier and with whom Griff enjoyed 'Revered' status, didn't hesitate. They all raised a hand and swore not to share any secrets he revealed. As soon as they were through, he began.

"My friends Mace and Shari, I've telled ye about them. They're the ones who got Elysia ta agree to the evolution o' citizens. Well, they cleared a dungeon themselves a week or so ago, and in in the bottom o' that dungeon, they discovered a room with twelve portals."

He waited while the elders reacted. Even as isolated as they were here in the mountain village, they knew that even the biggest of cities on Elysia only had two, sometimes three portals. A dozen was unheard of. When they'd calmed a bit, he continued.

"As it happens, one o' them portals connects to the cave behind the waterfall near the orc camp. We confirmed it this mornin'. Mace invited the Falling Water orcs to join him at his stronghold, which sits atop the dungeon. It be an old mine, cut right into the mountain. His allies be using it to gather ore and other resources fer their nearby settlement called Lakeside. It be a mixed race settlement, with orcs, dwarves, goblins, ogres, humans, halflings, kobolds, elves, centaurs, and minotaurs. Mebbe more, I dunno. Mace captured the stronghold when he killed a bunch o' slavers and freed the minotaurs and halflings." Griff paused to take a breath and Lisa took over.

"We'll be goin' to join them shortly. Now that we're strong enough to survive outside this village."

The elders all went stone-faced. They didn't want the outworlders to leave, but they understood. Outworlders had always remained in the village for just a short time, then moved on to bigger, more dangerous areas.

"The thing is, we'd like ye to come with us. All of ye. We know ye love this village. And rightly so. It be a lovely place. But ye know that we be the last o' the outworlders that'll ever come here. And the village will suffer without more. Even with many o' ye bein' evolved now, are ye gonna spend all yer time out huntin' beasties 'n bringin' back loot for the crafters? And if ye do, who will they sell to?" She stopped to let them think it over. When she saw a few nod, she pushed on.

"The stronghold be inside a mountain. Protected. With yer people, the orcs, and the others to grow and defend the place, an army couldn't take ye. There be resources in the mine and the plenty o' wood and game in the forest. The portals would let ye return here to fish in the pond, or I saw another that looked out onto the ocean. Mace 'n Shari got plans to build a port city there and trade all over the world. The stronghold will grow to a city, maybe a nation. We'll have the elves as allies, and maybe others too. Ye would be welcomed as citizens, and could be among the founders."

"But if ye stay, ye'll be alone. With no outworlders, and the orcs gone, the dark ones that come down from the mountain to raid their camp won't be held back. They'll eventually find their way here."

She sat back in her chair and let out a long breath. Griff patted her hand. He'd never heard her make such a long speech before.

One of the elders spoke up. "Ye could just stay here. Might be yer friends would come join ye?" He sounded hopeful.

Griff shook his head. "I'm sorry. We have been asked by Elysia herself to help the whole continent recover. Not just this village. That be part o' the reason for evolution. We outworlders canno' hope to do it all with just the few we have left."

Campbell nodded. "We need to discuss this. Ye make good sense. And we're grateful fer the offer. But this be our home. For some of us, the only home we've ever know'd."

Griff and Lisa nodded and got up from their seats. They left without a word, heading for the tavern.

They sat with the villagers, some of whom were already well into the victory celebration. Leroy was telling a group of young dwarves about how his miraculous healing saved Lisa from being consumed by the dwarf-eating butterflies. Meg and Jo were telling a table full of others about how Lisa fell into the guts of the massive pill bug. Lisa's face scrunched up and she said, "They're all going to think I'm an idiot."

Griff laughed.

"Nah, learning things in the hardest, most embarrassing way is sort o' the way we dwarves do things. We charge in head first 'n consequences be damned!" He threw a fist in the air as he said it and several nearby citizens shouted in agreement, raising fists of their own or splashing ale from their mugs. "By the end o' the night, ye'll be a legend!"

Lisa and Griff celebrated with the dwarves until late into the evening. The elders joined them after an hour or so, but gave no indication of their decision. Campbell said they'd get together and discuss it the next day. No earlier than noon.

When it came time to log off, Griff handed Jo a hundred gold for the innkeeper after she assured him that that was more than enough to pay for the food and drinks. The two of them retired to their room and logged out.

*****

Over a late dinner, they talked about food. About the various recipes Griff's mum had taught him. Lisa began to make a list of ingredients they didn't have, and they decided to make a run to the Tesco store in the morning. Since the dwarves would be hung over until at least noon, as Campbell had emphasized. Retiring to their beds, each set an alarm for 8am.

*****

The bear was losing the scent. As it got closer to the city, there were too many confusing scents, and it ranged back and forth between the buildings, catching hints of its prey here and there and following until it lost the scent again.

Eventually, it came across a new scent. Much stronger. It wove through the streets, into buildings and up onto roofs. It went places the creature couldn't follow, into holes its body couldn't fit through. Across gaps in rooftops it could not leap. But each time it lost the trail, it would pick it up again. It forgot about the prey that smelled of exhaust and its own blood. This was strong prey.

It followed the scent for days. In and out and up and around, losing it and regaining it. Until it led the creature to a big cave with a shiny front that smelled of many foods. Its hunger urged it forward and it roared a challenge to the prey inside.

Two dead black eyes looked through the glass of the Tesco storefront at the massive enemy that approached. The sun was rising behind it, and its shadow covered half the street. The snake was coiled around the ceiling rafters with just its head hanging down.

Here was a threat. Invading its hunting ground. It needed to die.

End Book Two.

Acknowledgements

As always, I must thank my family for their encouragement, patience, and untiring service as alpha readers. Several friends, readers, and family members found their way into this book as characters. My apologies to you all. You know who you are. Except Bobby and Jake, who deserved what they got. And thank you to my friends and guildies who gave me ideas and feedback to help me improve the final product.

PLEASE LEAVE A REVIEW! They are vitally important to indie authors like myself.

Thank you to L. Sherrard for pointing out the many, many mistakes I made as this tale leaked from my brain. And much appreciation to Richard Sashigane for the amazing cover art and formatting.

You can always find my books, art, and random interesting things at my website: www.davewillmarth.com or on twitter @davewillmarth (Yeah, I know. Twitter. I tweet now).

Or find the Greystone books on Amazon here

https://www.amazon.com/Greystone-Chronicles-Book-One-Online-ebook/dp/B076FN84HY/

Please check out my Greystone Guild facebook page for information on upcoming books https://www.facebook.com/greystone.guild.7

You can also get great information and reviews from Ramon Mejia's LITRPG Podcast at https://www.facebook.com/litrpgpodcast/

I'd also like to recommend you check out some of my favorite authors/friends within the genre.

Daniel Schinhofen https://www.amazon.com/Daniel-Schinhofen/e/B01LXQWPZA

Michael Chatfield https://www.amazon.com/Michael-Chatfield/e/B00WCAOQME

Ramon Mejia https://www.amazon.com/R.A.-Mejia/e/B01MRTVW3O

Dawn Chapman https://www.amazon.com/Dawn-Chapman/e/B014A0RUBC

Eden Redd https://www.amazon.com/Eden-Redd/e/B00I8X8BCK

Paul Campbell Jr. https://www.amazon.com/Paul-Campbell-Jr./e/B07J6JF1ZX/

Check out Paul's new first book Peaks of Power: Beginnings that just launched a few days ago!

If you enjoyed this book, or even if you didn't, but you DO enjoy the LitRPG and GameLit genre, then I recommend you check out the following Facebook pages (you might find some authors loitering there):

https://www.facebook.com/groups/RPGGamelitSociety/

https://www.facebook.com/groups/GameLitSociety/

https://www.facebook.com/groups/LitRPGBooks/

https://www.facebook.com/groups/GameLit/